Purgatory Academy
Class of 666

By Draco Amethystus

Storm Dragon Publishing

Purgatory Academy: Class of 666
By Draco Amethystus

Published by Storm Dragon Publishing, LLC.

Copyright © 2025 by Draco Amethystus.

Cover design by Draco Amethystus.

Printed in the United States.

Cataloging-in-Publication Date on file with the
Library of Congress.

www.dracoamethystus.com

To my "teacup." Thank you for putting up with me.

Divine Governments

Heavenly Hierarchy and Hosts

Houses of Heaven – There are three types of angels, namely the archangels, seraphim, and cherubim. Each house is governed by one of the seven archangels: Michael, Gabriel, Raphael, Azriel, Uriel, Sariel, and Ariel. The seraphim and cherubim serve within these houses.

Ascended Nephilim – The children and legacies of angels. Their families serve in the house from which they are descended. Depending on what type of angel they are descended from they fall under the designations of archim, serachim, and cherachim.

Hellish Hierarchy and Hosts

Houses of Hell – Demons are more varied in powers and their hierarchies more flexible in shape. However, there are six governing houses including Lucifer, Lillith, Cain, Beelzebub, Asmodeus, and Mammon.

Descended Nephilim – The demonic Nephilim are called Descended as they are the children and legacies of demons. Likewise, their families serve in the house from which they are descended. Also depending on what demons they are descended from they may be vampires, succubi or incubi, or dragons. Dragons are by far the rarest of the three kinds and are only born as direct children of Lucifer.

Purgatory Hierarchy and Hosts

Death and the Four Horsemen – There are no houses governing Purgatory. However, there is a ruler, Death, and their Four Horsemen of the Apocalypse serving as lieutenants.

Creatures of Purgatory – There are a number of creatures originating from Purgatory. Some of them include gargoyles, ghouls, and wraiths.

Chapter One
Torture Time
Post Purgatory Academy – Hell

No one does torture like a demon. I know first-hand. I've experienced my fair share of pain, but never anything quite like this. It's like swallowing razor blades whole and chasing them down with vodka. Balor is a true professional. I have to give him that. He understands the importance of mixing it up, of variety. It isn't just torture all the time. Not that there's a sense of time in Hell anyway, but be that as it may, he doesn't bring the pain constantly. Oh no, he stops and gives me a break here and there. Well, I should clarify. He has already broken and magically healed more of my bones than I can count, but he also stops every once and a while. We even chat on occasion.

Other times he runs his claws along the curves of my body. He plays with the tresses of my long, fire red hair. I've always thought it was my best feature, and I love the color of it. I used to be too shy to admit that even to myself, but not anymore. I digress though. I was talking about Balor and his methods. He really understands that providing an inkling of hope makes it all the worse for me and all the sweeter for him.

"Closing your eyes won't make me think you've lost consciousness," Balor's baritone voice carries an Oxford English accent I would have previously associated with a haughty professor on a BBC television show. If I survive this, I don't think I'll ever be able to hear that accent again without having nightmares.

"I was meditating. I thought you might appreciate that. It keeps me present. You know? Right here and now…with you…and all this wonderful fun." It isn't easy to sound sarcastic while completely naked, drenched in sweat, and hanging suspended by my arms from invisible bonds. I think I pull it off nicely though.

Balor chuckles. It's just wrong that demons can chuckle. "I'm happy to hear my efforts haven't gone unnoticed." We're standing in a spotlight surrounded by the deepest darkness. Seriously, I can't see anything beyond Baylor and myself. I'm not even sure there's an actual floor or if we're floating through some sort of hellish magic.

"Oh, they haven't. I know how hard you try. No doubt it's to make up for other areas of your life that are, shall we say, lacking." I glance down to emphasize my penis insult.

The demon chuckles again. Stepping forward on goat hooves, he presses up against me. It isn't the first time the shaggy black fur that covers him from torso to hooves caresses my bare skin. His manliness…no, demonliness? Meh. Whatever. It pushes hard against my stomach. Fucking disgusting whatever you call it.

"Don't pretend you don't like it now. You didn't complain before." Balor is huge, probably eight feet in height given that we're face to face and I'm dangling in space from bonds I can't see. His skin is blood red and meets his furry torso right below the belly button. Demons have belly buttons. Huh. Who knew?

"I wanted to say something, but my mouth was full." I put as much venom into my words as I can. Balor takes the opportunity to run his claws along my sides again. Shivers of hate run up and down my body anew.

Leaning in, he whispers through a mouth of shark teeth and the stench of rotten flesh, "It was full, wasn't it?" The black, swirling horns on top of his head rise slightly as he raises his eyebrows.

I give him an eyeroll as response. Balor's leathery black, bat wings shift as he smirks at my poor attempt to wordlessly mock him. "Since we're talking about my…girth, I think now is a good moment to share the surprise I have for you."

"Is it a magnifying glass? One like Sherlock Holmes has. Oh, is this a mystery? Like the Strange Case of the Demon's Missing Dick?"

"How droll," Balor says. "No, this is more of a challenge." The demon grabs the back of my head with his left hand. His paws are so big the claws dig into the edges of my face. "It's time that you answered a few questions."

I don't bother trying to escape his grip. I know I can't win. "Great. You haven't asked me a fucking thing yet."

"And I won't," Balor answers. "We're going to go through your memories. My lord is in need of information that you may have. It shouldn't take too long though. I just need the last year or so of your life."

My blood runs cold. "What? Why?"

"Something has occurred that could upset the precarious balance existing between Heaven and Hell. It could lead to war."

My mind reels. "Heaven and Hell are already at war."

Balor huffs. "Not like this. My lord believes the key lays with your memories, within your year at Purgatory Academy."

"You know I didn't even want to fucking be there."

"All twenty-year-old Nephilim train there to become influence peddlers over humanity in the divine war between Heaven and Hell. You know that. Don't play dumb. It isn't your style."

Fear rises like a blade of ice in my stomach. This couldn't possibly be a painless process. "Where does the challenge come in?" I try for sarcasm, but it's more like a mouse's squeak masquerading as my voice, my innards still frozen.

A shark's smirk smears Balor's face. "We're going to find out how wide you can open your mouth."

I don't have a chance for a snarky retort. The hand in front of my face splits open at the palm and out of it slither two thick appendages, snaking toward me. Instinctively, I try to jerk away, but Balor's other hand holds my head in place. My eyes crisscross and I'm seeing double as the appendages poke hard at my mouth. They're like giant earthworms, one the same blood red as the demon's skin, the other black as his horns and wings. That fear has frosted my stomach into an ice cave.

Balor makes a small tsk tsk sound before slamming his palm against my face. My eyes widen in fear. I clench my teeth, but my lungs are about to explode from lack of air as his hand smashes my nose. I'm not going to last much longer. "Just remember, my Little Fox, don't bother trying to swallow."

Hatred born of helplessness burns through my body, evaporating the ice but it doesn't matter. My mouth opens of its own volition. The headless snakes move like lightning. Before I entirely understand what's happening, they're in the back of my throat. They slither up, not down. I literally feel them in my skull and attaching to my brain. There's even a sharp suction cup sound as they do. Holy Hell.

I bite down hard, my teeth pressing into the demonic worms, but I can't dig very deep. Their hide is thick. Spots float in front of my eyes. Darkness gathers at the corners of my vision.

"That's a good Little Fox. Now, Lilly Foxflame, let's see what we learn." At his words, I'm slammed into a darkness even deeper than the one surrounding us. Then memories begin to rise and take form like shades from the Underworld.

Chapter Two
The Reaping
January – Purgatory Academy

HELL

They're not actually memories, strictly speaking. I see myself third person. Wondering how that's possible, a response comes directly into my mind.

"Magic, of course." Balor's voice rumbles in my head. *"I believe humans would use terms like 'modification' or 'software,' but the effect is the same. Now, let us proceed,"* his Oxford accent commands. Shock doesn't allow me to consider it further.

It isn't the soft glow of fairy lights that wakes me up, lined up like vines along my ceiling and the built-in bookshelves. Oh no. It's the motherfucking dark figure at the foot of my bed. Someone in my RV equals brass knuckles out from under my pillow and me on my feet. It's January 2nd and the new year's already off to a fucking bad start.

The windows are closed to the southern Louisiana winter air, but I still hear the normal sounds of camp. Cirque de la Lune's animals make plenty of noise during the night, let alone the almost vampiric nature of many of my circus friends. I would have heard someone unlocking my door and stepping in. But I don't.

A bad history with creepy men combined with the odd visage of the stranger stop me from attacking. I hate myself for the hesitation. The being wears the black robes of the Grim Reaper one sees in the movies. The only thing missing is a two-handed scythe. The depths of the raised hood are filled with shadows, no hint of a face.

I'm about to speak, when one robed arm reaches out toward me. From the darkness of the sleeve a fire sparks to life. It glows violet. Sharp forks of lavender jump as rich royal purples dance. It's so mesmerizing I don't even realize the robed figure is standing right in front of me until it's too late.

I attempt to hop back, but the other robed arm strikes out, grabbing my forearm. I register a cold right before the flame slaps down on my open palm. And the pain begins.

My brain fights to compute the agony. It burns, yes. But it's so much more than that. The flames remain on my palm, but they're not burning the skin. Even so, a fiery agony runs like a raging river through my veins, beginning in the hand that holds the flame and traveling to every other part of my body. Not only does it burn, but it invigorates me. It's as if my entire body had been asleep all my life and now it's waking up to realize it missed so much.

My mouth opens to let loose a scream, but the burning pain flares up and it's all I can do to grind my teeth. Thankfully, I'm still next to my bed because it rises to meet me, and all goes black.

When I wake up, I'm somehow standing again. That alone is surreal. And it's only the beginning of the bizarreness. I'm not in my room anymore. Not even close. I have no fucking clue where I am, but I'm definitely not in Louisiana anymore, Toto. Fog floats around me, grasping at my pink unicorn pajamas and the curls of my hair. Don't say a word about my PJ's. They're off limits. My feet touch something soft. Squinting down, I find moss.

Raising my head, I spot the same robed figure standing in front of me. Crouching a bit, I ready to pounce on the fucker. No more hesitation, but my planned attack is interrupted by a cacophony of sounds. It's only a voice here, a cry there at first. Soon enough though, it morphs into an orchestra of pain and fear. There's an eerie sense of something dangerous and unseen as if I were playing around with a Ouija board.

In that moment, a wind sweeps through, and the mist almost

magically dissipates. I gasp. Rising above me on a green hill is a Gothic monstrosity of a building. Soaring towers of black stone dot it. Gargoyles of various shapes and sizes stand sentinel on the parapets, armed with wings, claws, and fangs.

An ornate iron-wrought gate surrounds the grounds, the entrance before me. To my left is a cemetery of gray slab tombstones complimenting the slate skies. To the right is a forest unlike any I've ever seen. The trees are bone white. I'm seeing them clearly, but I squint in disbelief anyway. They aren't only bleached white in color, they're literally made of bone. The creepiest part is the low dangling fruit. They're human skeletons in differing states of growth. From what I gather they grow down starting at the skull and finishing with the toes.

"It's amazing and terrifying all wrapped up in one, right?"

Over my right shoulder a young man with caramel skin stands there grinning. His teeth are bright white even in the watery light glowing sickly in the overcast sky. He wears a white tank top and a pair of black pajama pants.

He steps up next to me and we continue to stare. "Yes and yes," I whisper but my voice carries in the wind. I take in the others around us. There are more than I can count, scattered all over the mossy hill before the gates. Behind me are even more. Guessing, I'd say they're all about my age, around twenty years old. Many are dressed like me, pajamas or t-shirts and boxers. The chill in the air makes me grateful I have long pants on at least. Others wear normal clothing as if they'd been up and about when, whatever this is, happened.

My mind begins to spin. There's too much going on to take it all in. "Hey, you okay?" the handsome young man asks.

I attempt and fail a smile. "It's all a little overwhelming, isn't it?" he says. I can't tell if he's intuitive about emotions or if he feels the same way. My smile is a bit more authentic though.

"I'm Rodrigo." The more he speaks, the more I hear his accent.

"Texas twang?" I ask.

Rodrigo leans back in surprise. "Yes ma'am. How did you know?"

"I've spent some time there." Growing up in a circus, I've spent time in most places in the US. "Lilly," I return. Rodrigo holds out a hand and we shake.

"Nice to meet you, Lilly."

"Likewise."

Another voice reaches out through the dissipated mists. "Hello, Nephilim. Welcome to Purgatory Academy." The voice is a tenor steeped in the deepest, flattest monotone I've ever heard in my life. My eyes are drawn to a small, mossy overlook just below the front gates. Standing there is a man.

Even with the fog settling back in, I make out his pasty skin. A round face is framed behind horn-rimmed glasses, a scraggly beard, and thinning brown hair combed to the side. He wears a brown sweater of geometric designs and khakis.

"I shouldn't assume you all know what that is, what you are. Nephilim are the children and legacies of both angels and demons. For those of you from angelic lineages, you are more specifically referred to as Ascended Nephilim while those from the demonic lineages are referred to as Descended Nephilim."

My brain is prepared to explode. I'm a what? The man doesn't give me time to consider the rollercoaster my head has become. "My name is Gressil. I will be your dean of students this year. Please move forward and climb up here to the front gate."

I'm reminded of the Grimm Brothers' story of the witch in the candy house. Feet begin shuffling forward, but how do I know I'm not about to be eaten? Rodrigo has the answer again, "Don't worry. He can't hurt you." His bright smile flashes in the gloom, warm and friendly. Tension releases its death grip on my shoulders a bit.

"How do you know?"

"It's one of the rules here. No violence outside of the Tribulations is allowed."

"Tribu-what? I feel like I've been sent to Hell."

Rodrigo laughs. It's a handsome laugh, full of mirth. "Actually, we're in Purgatory. That's why the school is called Purgatory Academy."

"What is Purgatory?" I ask as we shuffle up the hill and gather with the other Nephilim.

"It's an overlapping plane of existence that coincides with Heaven, Hell, and Earth." I stop in my tracks to stare at Rodrigo.

"How the fuck do you know all of that? Sorry for the language. I'm just shocked."

Rodrigo chuckles. "No te preocupes. I get it. Mi familia is Descended on both sides." He starts walking again as he speaks.

"Meaning?" I roll my hand in a please continue to explain sort of manner.

"Meaning that mi papá y mi mamá are both Descended Nephilim. Our family belongs to the House of Asmodeus. We haven't been around that long, compared to other families but we do okay for ourselves." There's no small trace of pride in his voice.

"I still don't get it, but whatever. As long as he isn't going to eat us."

We arrive at the gate. Looking around, the fog is rolling back in, but the gathered multitude is still visible. There are so many of them, some more shell shocked than others. A few look perfectly at ease as if this were all normal, like a Sunday stroll in the park.

Gressil stands before the front gate, the towers towering behind him. "Now that we're all congregated comfy and cozy, allow me to congratulate you, one and all. This year's class of Purgatory Academy consists of each and every twenty-year old Nephilim around the world. The total number of Ascended was 1543 while the total number of Descended was 1722." I don't care for the emphasis Gressil places on the word "was."

"There are thirteen Tribulations you will face during your full year here at Purgatory Academy. You should be pleased to know that each of you has already passed the first one. The Reaping was the moment your Malak placed the fire in your hand. For our Descended students, this was Hell Fire. For the Ascended, it was Celestial Fire. These both respectively function as catalysts to wake up the divine blood flowing in your veins. If there wasn't enough, the would-be student was quite literally burned to a greasy spot where they stood." Gressil stops to let the fact sink in, that some of those who were forced to take that stupid fucking fire in their hand are now dead.

"I'm happy to report that of the original 1543 Ascended, there still remains a hearty 1307. Of the 1722 Descended Nephilim, we still have 1598. Statistically, this is quite agreeable." What an asshole. Apart from his professed position here at Purgatory Academy, I don't know who or what Gressil is, but I know I don't like him.

"The exciting news is that you have yet one more today. After that it will be only one per month. I must warn you though." The smug smile suggests he's enjoying this immensely. "Many of them are quite deadly. As the name of the first Tribulation, the Reaping, suggests, they are intended to weed out the weak and strengthen the strong. Your second Tribulation is no less harrowing and is intended to test your concentration as well as your magical ability."

Red anger flashes as hot and wild as my fire red hair. I've only been here for a little while, but I'm already getting sick of all this bullshit. A reckless idea washes through me, a burning desire to rage at the stupid little man. I've taken a step forward but just then there's a scream in front of me.

"No! No, I can't do this. I don't belong here." A blonde-haired woman shoves at a couple of the others near her who are trying unsuccessfully to calm her. One of them, a dark-haired woman, runs after her, calling. I look up at Gressil who wears a smaller, quieter version of the smug smile he'd had on a moment ago.

The woman runs right for Rodrigo and me. We're both able to shift out of her way, but I catch the scent of mint from the blonde locks that flow by as the panicked student flees down the hill. She's all but disappeared when a robed figure just like the one that collected me appears out of the mist.

The blonde stops dead. I regret my mental choice of words a moment later. With a speed that I barely comprehend, the figure draws out a sword hidden within the robes and slices through the air. The woman doesn't make a sound. She stands stock still for a moment before a slight breeze wafts by and her head topples from her shoulders, rolling down the hill and vanishing into the mist.

Chapter Three
Mistporting
January – Purgatory Academy

HELL

"*Sometimes you gotta shoot a hostage,*" Balor growls in my mind.

Bitter experience tells me he's right. I don't have to admit that to the demon though. He's already in my head.

"*Yes, yes I am,*" he confirms.

The dark-haired young woman catches up but having seen the Malak execute her friend right in front of her, she comes to a sudden stop. Falling to her knees, she lets out a keening scream, calling her friend's name over and over again. "Annebelle! Annebelle!" She pulls at her hair and claws her own face.

Anger and disgust at the murder wash through me like a tidal wave, but I move forward to help the young woman. No one should be alone in a moment like that. Of course, a moment like that should have never happened in the first place. Wherever and whatever this is, I fucking hate it.

I sense more than see Rodrigo try to grab for me as I move toward the crying woman. I kneel next to her, not certain what to say. Before I can, someone rips me away, sending me tumbling backwards, my knees scraping over stone and moss. I spring right back up, fists clenched and in a fighting position. I may be shy and introverted, but I refuse to be bullied.

Three Nephilim stand guard over the sobbing woman. It's the first and tallest that grabs my attention. Golden hair and a tan that glows even in this feeble light are accompanied by ocean blue eyes matched by the silk pajamas he sports. He isn't just handsome. He's beautiful, a blonde Superman. His expression is wary.

On his shoulder to my right is a woman. Caramel skin and shoulder length curly black hair frame a scowl that rivals storms for intensity. Her words are biting and nasty. "Fuck off Descended. Don't touch Lenore and don't ever deign to come near another Ascended again."

Shock and fury war to win my attention. Rodrigo said violence wouldn't be tolerated here. And while I don't appreciate being thrown like that, I figure further physical altercations won't make the situation better. "I only wanted to help her."

A second Nephil male crouches next to the woman named Lenore. She grasps his hand and shoulder as they stand up together; he's nearly as tall as the golden one. Black hair flows to his shoulders, his complexion pale. His face is screwed up as if in pain, but his movements are both strong and gentle as he supports Lenore.

The golden-haired one holds out a hand of warning toward the pissy woman as if to suggest she needs to calm down. He speaks quietly, "That's enough, Trist. Eli has her. We'll get her up the hill to the academy." His blue eyes inspect me as Rodrigo comes up from behind to stand near my left shoulder, just out of my periphery.

"You know what their kind is like, Gabe," Trist says. The disdain in her voice is thick. Instead of responding, Gabe simply leads the four of them up the hill.

"What the fuck," I whisper.

"They're Ascended. We're Descended. We don't mix. We belong to Hell. They belong to Heaven. Opposite sides of the great divine war among the immortals." I shake my head, not bothering to tell Rodrigo that I don't belong to anyone.

Gressil has gathered everyone closer to the gates of the academy. "Now that the dramatic disturbance is over, we can get back to the business at hand." Cold, heartless bastard. That's what he is. "As I was saying before I was so rudely interrupted, your second Tribulation is right now. You are to mistport."

Mistport. What the actual fuck. They could at least have come up with a better name than that, whatever this is. Seriously.

The dean of students raises his hands, and mist rises from the ground around him, till it's covering and finally engulfing him. A moment later it dissipates, and he's gone. A call from beyond the gates draws the crowd's attention. Gressil is inside the academy grounds. It's teleportation. Stupid name for it but fucking cool trick.

Moments later mist flows around him once more and he's right back where he started just outside of the gates. That must be the way I arrived with my Malak or whatever the fuck they're called.

"Mistporting is an essential aspect of what it is to be Nephil. It is how you travel and move among the planes of existence, among the worlds. If you're not able to do it, you won't survive long beyond graduation…assuming you survive to graduation. So, much of the magic that flows in your veins is enacted through will and imagination. You will yourself from one place to the next and you use your imagination to create the reality."

I sure as Hell…or Heaven? Purgatory? Whatever. I sure as shit don't believe it's as simple as that. "If you are thinking that seems simple, wait till your turn." Gressil really is an asshole.

The dean of students grins as he takes in the gathered Nephilim. "Are there any volunteers?" It's so silent in the wake of that question, I think I hear the fog moving.

Gabe, the blonde god, raises his hand. Trist and Eli hover behind him. I glimpse Lenore farther back, her face stricken with grief but watching along with the rest of the Nephilim.

Gressil motions him forward. Gabe doesn't hesitate. I gather he's a man of action, confident and prepared to do what must be done. The mist covers his feet and then his legs and finally his body. Just as that golden hair is all but gone from view, Gressil leans in and whispers something to the Nephil. Gabe's shoulders twitch, but then he's gone.

Beyond the gates where Gressil appeared, Gabe misports into existence, whole and perfect. There's some scattered cheering, the loudest coming from Trist and Eli. Gabe only has eyes for Gressil; a scowl scars his handsome face.

Gressil ignores him, asking for more volunteers. Trist and Eli go next. The dean whispers something to them just as they're about to mistport. Each time there's some twitch or physical show of shock by the Nephilim. They arrive on the other side of the gates though.

Unfortunately, Gabe and his two friends are the only ones to volunteer and Gressil has the rest of us line up. I'm stupid enough to have moved forward with Rodrigo and there are only a few other students in front of us. Butterflies don't float in my belly; they kamikaze their way through it.

A pale young man with a pair of dark boxers on, shakes intermittently right in front of me. I can't tell if it's because of a lack of clothes or because of the mistporting. Most likely, it's a combination of the two.

It's too soon that the pale young man has his turn. Rodrigo is right behind me. Those pasty shoulders shake even more as the mist rises and Gressil whispers to him. I'm not close enough to hear what the dean is saying to the students. Nevertheless, the pale young man appears on the school grounds. He shakes even more than before, so badly that he falls to his knees and looks as if he might vomit, but then slowly pulls himself together and stands. He hugs himself till the quivering lessens.

Gressil waves me forward. I'm overwhelmed by his stench, something akin to a skunk who washed in a river of trash. I hold my breath and concentrate on the task at hand, on this mistporting. Closing my eyes, I imagine the mist rising around my legs, a tingling touch of its caress as it prepares me to move from one spot to another across space. I'm all but certain I feel it and for a moment open my eyes…to find the mist doing its job. I close them again and focus on imagining myself in that spot within the grounds and just as everything grows darker and still, I hear Gressil whisper. His words rip through the veil with me as I move onto the academy grounds and open furious eyes to stare at the back of his head through the iron bars of the front gate.

"I know what happened to your mother," he whispered. I don't know what that means, but I have every intention of finding out. I shut my eyes again, meaning to mistport right back to Gressil and demand he tell me what he knows about my mother. As far as I know, my mom died young from cancer. But with all the shit I'm experiencing right now, the truth could be something else completely.

I'm distracted from my anger for a moment because Rodrigo is up next. We make eye contact as the mist blankets him, Gressil whispering in his ear. Rodrigo's eyes grow wide with surprise, but then he's gone.

I wait for the mist to appear near me, but when it does, it doesn't reach very high. Within moments I understand why. Rodrigo is nothing more than a pile of blood, bones, and broken flesh, a mound of gory clothes and the innards of what had been a young man from Texas. I'm so shocked I forget to scream.

Chapter Four
The Rings
January – Purgatory Academy

HELL

"Sometimes you gotta shoot a hostage."

I wonder if Balor can sense my mental eye roll. *"You already said that."*

"Hmmm. Well, sometimes you gotta shoot two hostages."

I really hope he can at least sense my mental sigh.

I don't really know Rodrigo but tell that to the full on fury in my chest. Forget mistporting. I'm about to climb right over the gate and beat Gressil with my bare hands.

"Good riddance. One Descended down." Trist stands nearby scowling at what had been Rodrigo.

"What did you say?" There's a storm of anger and hurt swirling in me.

Trist glowers. "I said-"

"That's enough, Trist," Gabe interrupts. Eli and he move in front of their female friend, blocking the two of us from direct sight of one another.

Nevertheless, I step forward. Gabe continues, putting a hand up to stop me. "Trist knows the rules. There's no fighting outside of classes unless deemed necessary or in the Tribulations. Don't let her get under your skin."

His voice is calm, warm and kind. My angry heat morphs into something more sensual, more alluring. And that is what Gabe is. I thought him handsome but being this close I realize he's glorious. I don't understand how his golden hair glows so much in the faded light of this world, but it does. Unlike Gressil, his scent is appealing, a mixture of pine trees and coastal sunlight. He has the tan for it too. I haven't been this close in proximity to men besides my dad for a long time. It's…confusing. Gabe smiles gently and I realize I'm staring.

"He's right, you know." A quiet voice accompanied by a cold hand on my arm pulls my attention away from Gabe. I shift away from the hand but glance over to see the pale young man who mistported right before me.

"We should really get out of the way while other students mistport. Please." He beckons me to follow him away from Rodrigo and the trio.

The desire to be far from Rodrigo's melted remains shames me. Reluctantly, I go with him. Gabe holds my gaze for a moment before turning back to Trist to say something that has her scowling even more than she already was. "I apologize for, uh, getting in the way there. I just…" The pale man's words trail off and he looks down.

I shake my head. "No, I appreciate it. You're right. I doubt I could have taken Trist in a fight anyway. And certainly not Gressil."

The young man has to look up at me as he responds, "No, probably not. Gressil is a well-known demon in Hell. It's been a long time since such a powerful one was given the job of dean of students here. Not that it isn't a prestigious position. And Trist. Well, the Triumvirate are all archim."

My eyebrow rises in question. "Archim?"

"Yeah, you know Ascended Nephilim descended from archangels."

"I, um, I didn't know that." I hate admitting it, but I'm not about to lie just to save face. I have a lot to learn here, and I know I won't be able to bullshit my way out of it.

"Oh, I see. You're not a legacy," he says gently.

"I don't know what that is either." Anger tinges my words. I might not know much about this world, but that doesn't mean I want it thrown in my face every five seconds.

He rushes to explain apologetically. "Oh no worries. There are plenty of Nephilim, both Ascended and Descended, who don't come from legacy families. That just means it's a family that has been around for multiple generations among the ranks of Hell or Heaven."

"Rodrigo mentioned something about that, that his family was Descended from Asmodeus."

"Rodrigo?" Clearly, he doesn't know everyone.

"The one that, um…"

"Oh, right. I'm so sorry. Did you know him?" His compassion mildly surprises me.

"No, but…" My words trail off because I don't really know what else to add to that.

"I get it," he says. "No one wants to be alone here. You won't make it long like that."

"Is that why you reached out to me?"

"Well, I'd be lying if I said that wasn't true, but you just looked like you needed help." He hesitates. "Is that okay?"

I don't answer immediately. "Yes, it is. Thank you."

He shrugs and sticks out his hand, "Marius."

I hesitate again. I just did this minutes before with Rodrigo and now he's a pile of blood and clothes. I shake my head, knowing that sort of thinking won't help. I reach out my own hand and grasp his cold one. "Lilly."

His smile is filled with genuine happiness and no small mix of relief.

"I'm going to expect you to teach me a lot about all of this though," I joke but only partially.

His smile widens. "Happily."

"Okay, explain to me what the archim are then."

"There are three classes of angels in Heaven – the archangels, the seraphim, and the cherubim. Each class is more powerful than the next. The archangels are fewer in number than the other two kinds and they have very few children. Most of the archim are legacies instead of direct children of any one archangel. They're quite powerful and it's unheard of that three of them are here together."

"You mean all three of them are archim, not just the bitchy one?"

Marius laughs. He's tentative even with this small show of humor, shifting as if to make certain no one besides me hears him. "Yeah, all three of the Triumvirate are archim."

"Triumvirate?"

Marius' laugh is louder this time, a bit more natural. "Yeah, they have a collective nickname already. They have been upcoming since they were born. Heaven expects big things from them."

I let that sink in as we quietly watch other students attempt to mistport into the academy grounds. Most of them make it, but not all. There's quite the mess when it's all over and we both find other places to look.

My thoughts drift back to my mother and what Gressil said. She passed away when I was thirteen. That was a tough time to say the least. She wasn't the only thing I lost that year. The dean of students returns through his misty teleportation, interrupting my rumination. "Congratulations to you all for successfully mistporting onto the grounds of Purgatory Academy. Please follow me."

Marching past the entire gathered Nephilim, he leads us up the rocky, mossy hill, fog still drifting by in small spurts of clouds. I crane my neck to take in the grotesque size of the school. It's just, well, overwhelming.

Gressil steps in front of what must be the main entrance of the academy, two large oak doors with half circle tops. It's what is above the doors that stands out the most though.

There's a rectangular slab of dark stone; etched into it are Gothic letters and numbers. At the top and left it reads "Ascended" while the top and right reads "Descended." Below each of them is a number. It dawns on me what they are. When we arrived, Gressil mentioned how many of the Nephilim there were and how many survived the flames of either Heaven or Hell. Below the Ascended it now reads 1284 while under the Descended it shows 1517. For fuck's sake…so many died just from the mistporting Tribulation.

It's perverse. They're keeping a count of how many of us die, of how many yet live. I've felt a lot of anger today and this is another bout of it.

Gressil's voice rises over the tide of my ire. "That will be all for the day. Again, I want to congratulate each and every one of you for successfully completing your first two Tribulations. You only have eleven more to complete."

I really don't like this guy. "Please report back here tomorrow at the same time for your first day of classes. Your Malak will be there to make certain you don't lose your way." Gressil smiles nastily. And with that, the pompous asshole walks into the school, the oak doors shutting tight behind him.

For a moment the Nephilim mill about without direction. However, the Triumvirate, led by Gabe, make their way back down the hill toward the front gate. Many of the Nephilim, presumably the Ascended, follow them. The rest aren't far behind.

I walk next to Marius without speaking. What is there to say at this point? The Triumvirate mistport successfully outside of the gates, but as they move to leave this plane of existence, Malakim appear before each of them. Many of the Nephilim stop to watch, but the robed guards look to be giving each of the students something before they mistport away, nothing more. I don't really want another "gift" from my cowled creep.

The rest of the Nephilim see it's safe and they mistport out, each being met by their Malak. Marius and I both make the jump and are met immediately as well.

My Malak glides up. A robed arm stretches out. The last time this happened, which seems like an eternity ago, the bastard put a flame in my hand that could have burned me to a crisp. Taking a deep breath, I hold out my hand. A gold ring drops into it and reflexively I close a fist around it.

Looking back up at my Malak, I peer into the depths of that hood, but spy nothing. Mist rises and the reaper wannabe is gone. Marius heads my way.

"I'll show you mine if you show me yours," he tries to tease.

I smile at the attempt. "What are these?"

"They show you what house you belong to."

"Don't you already know which house you belong to?" I ask.

"Yes, but it's a sort of rite of passage," he answers.

"Alright, let's see it."

Marius passes over his ring. It's gold like mine and there's a ruby set in it. In the gem is the face of a man I don't recognize. It's like those one-dimensional images on coins. Above the face it reads "House of Cain."

"House of Cain? As in Cain and Abel from the Bible?" I ask, handing the ring back.

"Yeah. Cain is the third Lord of Hell, and the final member of the trio referred to as the Unholy Trinity along with Lillith and Lucifer himself."

Nothing intelligent comes to mind. Instead, I open my fist and pick up the ring, holding it between thumb and pointer finger. A ruby, red as blood and bright as a star, holds the countenance of a woman who even in one dimension is beautiful. Above her face are the words "House of Lillith."

"I'm not surprised at all," Marius says.

"What does that mean?"

He shakes his head, embarrassment evident with the slight red tinge to his cheeks. "I just mean, well, look at you."

Anger blossoms anew. "What does THAT mean?"

Marius huffs a nervous laugh. "It's a compliment. You're, well, I mean, you're gorgeous…objectively speaking."

My face almost matches the color of my hair. "Oh. Um. Thank you."

Marius really leans into his awkward shrugs. "Don't worry about it. Listen, how would you feel about walking to classes together? Meet here same time tomorrow morning?"

The idea of trying to make friends here scares me especially if they're going to die as easily as Rodrigo did. Then again, so does the idea of walking in alone. "Okay. Sure."

Worry creases on his forehead smooth out with his relief. "Great. I'll see you in the morning."

"Okay."

Marius walks off a few feet. Right before he mistports away, he calls out. "Welcome to PA!"

"PA?"

"Purgatory Academy!" And then he's gone.

Taking a deep breath, I prepare to do the same. My eyes close and I try not to think of becoming a pile of meat and bones with unicorn pajamas soaked in blood. Instead, I concentrate on a mental image of the inside of my RV, focus on the details of my room. The bed and twinkling fairy lights. The mist wraps around my legs and snakes up my arms. There's a moment of sheer, otherworldly cold and then it's warmer.

Opening my eyes slowly, I let out the breath I only now realize I'd been holding in. I'm back in my room, my home. I'm safe. At least for the moment. The knowledge of that fact takes all the strength out of me and my knees buckle. Thankfully, I'm standing right next to my bed and effectively sit down on it. I let myself fall back on the soft comforter and put my hands in my hair, trying to comprehend everything that just happened. It doesn't work very well. Instead, I opt for curling up and staring into space. It's strange how effective that can be. I might need to do it more often. I just drift away.

Time floats off. I'm surprised, perhaps even a little startled after the day I've had, when a soft knock comes at the door. My first thought is that the Malak is here to collect me and it's morning already. But then I remember that the robed fucker just appeared in my RV. There was no knocking, no politeness. No, only flames that could have burned me to ash if I hadn't had enough demon blood in me. Fucking spectacular.

Blowing a raspberry, I slide out of bed, shuffling over to the door. I unlock and open it to find my dad there, his hands full with two plates of steaming spaghetti and garlic toast on the side. One of my favorites. My stomach rumbles at the sight of it, loud enough that my dad hears.

"Oh good, you didn't eat yet." The warmth in his voice is so soothing.

I move out of the way for him to step up into the RV, going straight for the booth style seats, sliding one plate across the table to me. I take a big whiff of it before grabbing the fork and digging in. A moan of happiness escapes while I chew. I twirl more spaghetti on my fork.

My dad laughs. "I can't remember the last time you ate like that, as if tomorrow might not come."

I almost choke on my spaghetti and find myself staring at my father. He's a handsome man, or at least I think so. Standing 5' 10" he's neither tall nor short, just above average, about three inches taller than my long body. He isn't stocky or skinny either, but rather wiry and toned. His red beard is streaked with white now but it's still a beautiful red. It's just as bright as my own. His hair is the same color and almost as long as mine, but whereas I have curly hair, his is straight and glossy.

He gives off major outdoorsman vibes. He's rarely seen without a flannel shirt, jeans, and hiking boots. He lives up to the stereotype too. He and I spend a lot of our time out in nature whenever we aren't doing something for the circus.

The smile and laugh wrinkles around his eyes disappear as he senses I'm upset. My dad is always able to do that, discern when I'm not happy. "What's up, Little Fox?" He's called me that for as long as I can remember, and I love it.

I keep chewing, not certain how to begin. The biggest question is whether my dad even knows about any of this. If he doesn't, I don't necessarily want to burden him with the fact that I might not come home some day in the next year and he's never going to know what happened to me. On the other hand, that would be cruel. One thing I don't doubt is that if I tell him all this is real, he will believe me. He always does.

Still, if my dad did know, then I have questions. So many questions, some angrier than others. I decide to finish my food first. He doesn't push, but rather goes back to his own and we eat in companionable silence for a while. That's something else I love about my dad. He always gives me the time and space I need to figure things out in my own way.

We both let out a sigh of contentment as we finish and sit there sharing the moment. "Thank you," I say. He mumbles, "You're welcome."

"Dad, can I ask you a question?"

"Of course. You just did. I bet you can do it again."

"Haha." I do appreciate my dad's dad jokes. It's part of his charm. "Did Mom ever talk to you about her time in college?"

My question is something he wasn't expecting and my father cringes, "Yes, some."

It's enough to let me know what I suspected. There is no way my father is part demon. He is a wonderful man, but he is just so, well, normal. My mom, on the other hand, had been…otherworldly.

"Did she ever give you any details?"

His lips purse in hesitation as he searches for the right words. "Not really, no. Your mother was a very private person and didn't like to talk about her family or life before us. Still, she did share tidbits here and there."

"And you were okay with that?"

"I loved your mother for the person she was, not for who she might have been before I met her."

Yeah, I love the man that my father is. "So, did she give you any details about her college days?"

"She only mentioned it a couple of times, but it was clear that it hurt to talk about it, so I didn't push. But, when she did talk about it, she said that it was very difficult and that she didn't miss it."

"Did she happen to tell you the name of the school she attended?"

"Um, yeah, it wasn't one that I knew though and I'm pretty sure it was an acronym."

The fear of certainty shrouds me. "Was it PA?"

My dad's brown eyes grow. "Yes." I inherited my mother's green ones, but his have a warm glow.

"Dad, I need to tell you something. I'm not going to be able to help with the circus much this next year because I'm going to be attending PA as well. I need to leave early in the mornings and I'm not sure what time I'll be home. I should have the weekends off to help more though, I think."

My dad sits quietly for a moment but finally responds, "Lilly. You are my Little Fox. You do what you need to do. I will support you whatever. I love you."

Tears blur my sight, but I rush into my father's arms, nonetheless, barely giving him time to stand before I'm there. His warmth envelops me, and I hold on tight. No words are spoken, and none are necessary.

Chapter Five
First Day of School
January – Purgatory Academy

HELL

"Yuck," Balor rumbles. It's the first thing I hear after the demon detaches his snaking appendages from my brain. Sagging under the weight of the memories, I can't hold my head up without his demonic assistance. I'd be pissed off about that if I weren't so fucking exhausted.

My mouth is a desert, which is strange given how slick and slimy those overgrown worms are that just burrowed through my skull. I can't conjure words beyond the fatigue anyway.

Given my silence, Balor continues. "Your relationship with your father seems quite healthy. It makes me sick. And I'm not learning anything new or necessary from your memories."

I find my ire through his words. "Piss off," It sounds more like "hiss off."

Balor gets the gist though, chortling. "I know you're tired, but we need to keep going."

"Don't stop on my account" sounds more like "Hon't op on my count."

Balor doesn't and the snakes suction back on.

It isn't with fear that I wake up to the alarm and the Malak at the foot of my bed. It's annoyance. I didn't sleep well and I sure as hell don't like waking up early to find that creep doing who the fuck knows what under that robe.

The messenger could easily kill me, but that doesn't stop me. "Good morning, shithead. You look like death. Rough night?"

The Malak doesn't make a sound, just holds out two handfuls of folded clothing. A disgusted sound rises from my throat as I get out of bed. Coming around I take each pile from the robed douche. The first set is workout clothes including black leggings, a black tank top, ankle socks, and tennis shoes. None of them are mine so I assume they come from the school.

The second pile is much more disconcerting. It's a fucking school uniform, something right out of a Catholic girls school porno. "You have to be fucking kidding me."

I glare at the Malak, but it's no more effective than my snark has been. Holding each piece up, I huff in deeper annoyance. There's a white button-up blouse with a black blazer. The skirt is pleated with plaid, checkered in black and white. Knee high socks are white and the shoes black.

The blazer has the school emblem on the left breast, the name at the top and a gargoyle in the middle. Flanking it on the left and right are a winged demon and angel respectively. Below the gargoyle are words that must be Latin, "Niger et albus, diei ac noctis, inter est grieso."

I arch an inquisitive eyebrow at the Malak, but no response comes. Figures. "You can't translate the Latin for me, but you do a great impersonation of a statue."

Still no response. Fuck it. "I'm getting in the shower." Taking the school uniform with me, I close the door and lock it, to make certain the Malak doesn't get any ideas. Of course, the messenger could just mistport into the bathroom with me, but at least I would have caused some minor inconvenience for the bastard. That makes me feel a tiny bit better.

I take my time in the shower, again mostly only to annoy the Malak. I shave and shampoo before getting out, brushing my teeth and hair, and dressing. When I have the uniform on, I storm out.

"This is so demeaning and sexist. I seriously doubt any of the guys will be wearing something as skimpy as this." Unsurprisingly, the Malak says nothing, but I get some satisfaction at making the fucker listen to my useless rant. I'm petty like that.

Walking over to the full-length mirror in the corner of my bedroom, I don't want to admit how much I enjoy what I see. I'm tall for a woman and my long legs often scared away boys when I was a teenager, especially since I was typically able to express myself better too. It's one of the many reasons I appreciated being homeschooled by my parents as we traveled the country with the circus. They introduced me to all kinds of academic fields growing up and as I got older, they gave me freedom to choose what I wanted to focus on. Reading and writing were at the forefront, and I attribute much of my smarts to that. Both of my parents read a lot too. Books make people smarter or at least less dumb than they would be otherwise. Boys didn't like a girl who was both taller and smarter than them.

I don't have my mother's hourglass shape; I'm too tall for that. The skirt does accentuate my long legs. My red hair blazes against the contrasting black and white uniform; I'm a pale flame. My freckles gleam alongside my green eyes. Overall, I look pretty damn good, perhaps even sexy if I wanted to be kind to myself. The thought of being noticed sexually scares me though and that familiar old anxiety rises in my chest and throat, making it difficult to breathe.

I refuse to allow the Malak to know any of this. "This uniform is completely inappropriate for the climate in Purgatory. One day was enough to know it's going to be chilly there." Again no response. Shocker.

I consider where to put my other set of clothing and spot something on my booth table. It's a black backpack with a notebook, a package of pens, a package of mechanical pencils, and a note. Opening the last it reads:

Little Fox,

You were in the shower, and I needed to get to work. I bought this last night for your first day of school. I hope it helps.

Love,
Dad

Tears threaten, but I take a deep breath and fight them off. I need to have my wits about me returning to Purgatory, my head on straight. Still, it's a comfort to know my dad is thinking of me. I pile the school supplies and the spare change of clothes into the bag.

I don't know where to put my keys. The skirt doesn't have pockets. That is quite possibly the greatest bane of women's clothing…no fucking pockets. As if women didn't need to put things in them. My keys with my plush elephant would just have to go in my backpack, but at the last moment I decide to take the elephant off my key chain and put it on my backpack zipper. It feels good to have the elephant there, a gift from my parents.

I have to leave soon but am procrastinating. I spot a banana. Eating sounds terrible, but maybe it's a good idea. I'm not sure. Turning back to the Malak, I ask, "I know you're not much of a talker, but could you at least tell me if I should eat something before I go? I feel nauseous already, but I don't know if food will make the mistporting worse or better."

At first the Malak doesn't respond, but then a robed hand points at the banana, accompanied by a subtle nod of the head. I breathe a sigh of relief. "Thank you." Sitting down, I peel the banana and force myself to eat it, following it up with a half a glass of tap water.

Slinging the backpack onto my shoulders, I look at the messenger. "Okay, I'm ready. Let's do this."

Closing my eyes, I concentrate and soon enough mist tickles my legs and arms, the strange coldness following for a moment. Opening my eyes, I'm in Purgatory again. It feels wrong to be relieved to be back, but it's more because I didn't rip myself apart than that I'm at the academy.

The Malak appears next to me a moment later. Out come the robed arms again and this time two pieces of paper are there, one in each unseen hand. I take them both. One is a map of Purgatory Academy, both inside and outside. The other is my class schedule. It's a block schedule over two days. "Thank you." The robed head nods once before mistporting away.

Blowing a raspberry, I march up the hill through the mist and moss, stone and grass. I stop in front of the giant iron wrought gates. I can do this, I tell myself.

"There you are." Marius approaches out of the fog. "You look…Wow. You look great."

I roll my eyes. "Don't start. You clean up pretty good too though."

Marius bows. "Why thank you my lovely lady."

I was right. Marius isn't objectified with a skirt. He wears a white button up shirt with a black tie. The blazer with the school emblem is the same. Instead of the skirt, he wears black suit pants.

"Ready to go?" I ask. Marius' smile slips away. He glances nervously at the front gates. "Hey, you made it this morning and yesterday. You got this," I say. I am probably just as nervous, but there's something comforting about comforting someone else.

Marius girds up his will and nods slightly. I hold out my arm and he smiles again, looping his own through mine. We take a few steps closer to the gate and stop. Without a word, we both mistport and are standing together on school grounds.

Exchanging relieved glances, we walk up the hill to the front doors. Others are headed up as well. The Triumvirate are almost there. I grasp at anything solid to think about, talk about, just to keep my nerves at bay. I mistported safely, but that was only the beginning.

"Hey, do you know what the words are on our blazers?" I ask.

"You mean on the school emblem?"

"Yeah."

"It's Latin. It means, 'Between black and white, day and night, there is gray.'"

I think about it for a moment as we walk. "Does it refer to Purgatory with this lovely weather?"

Marius chuckles. "Yeah, but also that Purgatory doesn't take sides in the war. That's why the academy is housed here. The faculty may be from both Heaven and Hell, but the school itself and its denizens belong strictly to this realm. Gray is neutral."

We reach the front doors. I pull my phone from a pocket on the strap of my bag to check the time. No signal.

"Phones don't work in Purgatory," Marius says.

"Why?"

He shrugs. "One of the many perks of being a student here."

Sighing, I put it back in its pocket. "Alright, let's do this."

A nervous agreement from Marius and in we go.

Chapter Six
Angelology and Demonology
January – Purgatory Academy

I don't love the hallways in Purgatory Academy. True to the gothic architecture outside, it feels like a castle on the inside too. They're made of stone and tunnel through the innards of the school, the only light, torches in sconces on the walls every few feet. Modern me doesn't feel like I fit in at all. I should have been wearing some long dress and spoken with thees and thys. Marius laughs when I mention it.

We follow his map because the school is new to him as well. He explains, "Even families that have been in the business for a long time aren't allowed to bring their children here. It's considered an unfair advantage. And the old families have enough of that already."

"Because they actually know this world exists?" My tone is snarkier than I intend. It isn't Marius' fault he was born into the family he was.

He grimaces, "Basically, yeah."

We walk in silence for several more minutes before finally arriving at the door of our first classroom. Like the front doors, this one is large and oaken with a rounded top and a brass door handle. The number of the classroom is etched into the stone above it.

We hover there together for a moment. Despite my reservations, I like Marius. He attempts to appear confident, but it's obvious he's more introverted and shy like me. He lacks my fiery anger though. I'm honestly grateful to be here with him. It's certainly better than being alone.

I give him a small smile which he returns. I reach for the door handle and we walk into a totally normal classroom. Whatever I expected, this wasn't it. It's a lecture hall seen in any university. It has those folding cushioned chairs with the seats that pop down when someone sits in them and the little tray that comes up from the arm to put things on like a laptop or a notebook. They're formed in a half circle elevated at the top with steps leading down and pointed toward a desk at the bottom with a whiteboard where I assume the professor will be. It's empty at the moment.

Torches blaze on stone walls at the top and somehow, they light the room much more than those in the hallways. We make to the right, around the top of the half circle of seats. More students arrive in a steady stream. Most of them come in twos and threes like we did. It's unsurprising that others are making loose alliances or even friendships already. Imminent death bonds people together in strange ways like nothing else quite can.

I run into a wall as I turn to ask Marius where he wants to sit. Or at least that's my first thought, but when I stumble back a bit, two strong hands grasp me by the arms and keep me upright. I get a whiff of a strange mix of campfire smoke and cinnamon. It has a unique allure.

Getting my bearings, I'm confronted with the chest of another student and have to crane my neck to see the face. I stare into eyes so blue they're violet. They're set in a face fierce with a scowl, brutal with lowered brows, all framed in a strong jawline and black hair that's tied up in a manbun.

He's handsome but not in the way that Gabe is. Whereas the golden god is runway model gorgeous, this man is warlord harsh. It works though. I try to apologize but the words don't come out right. "Apologize I."

One of those dark eyebrows swoops up, but the scowl remains. "Mean I, pologize…" Oh shit. Smooth, Lilly, very smooth.

Marius saves me. "Excuse us, Drake. We were just on our way to our seats." Gently putting an arm around my shoulder, he leads me away and we find two seats in the top row to the right. I'm so shellshocked I don't even feel uncomfortable with the closeness and touch of Marius. Tall, dark, and brutal walks past us and takes the last seat in the same row. Taking a paperback book in hand he begins to read. He doesn't look back at us.

My face burns red. I hate that about my skin. It's milky white but when I get embarrassed, I turn into a ripe tomato. When I finally have the courage to look at Marius, there's sympathy written all over his face. Great. Pity. Just what I need.

"Don't worry about it. Drake has that effect on almost everyone."

"How do you know so many here already?"

"Like I said, many of the older families know each other. It's basically a realm all its own. Like the Triumvirate, Drake's family has been around for centuries."

I hate knowing so little about this world. It really does give others an unfair advantage and I wonder how many here are like me.

I spot the Triumvirate taking seats at the bottom in the middle of the front row. Figures. A low chatter arises among the students as they continue to pour in. The lecture hall is huge and somehow able to hold thousands of Nephilim.

I take in Drake again. He's still reading, and no one sits by him. It's almost as if he has a big sign on him that reads "Fuck off."

"If Drake comes from one of the old families, why is he sitting alone like that? Shouldn't he have at least a couple of others around him?"

Marius grimaces again. "Yeah, he has a bit of a reputation." He hesitates and doesn't seem to know how to continue.

A thought occurs to me. Why is Marius here with me? If he was also from an ancient family, why isn't he sitting with some of them as well?

I'm trying to think about how to broach the topic when three bells chime and the chatter dies down. There are two doors, one on each side of the table at the bottom of the lecture hall. The left one opens and out walks our professor.

She wears the same school uniform as the students, but her curves are those of a more mature woman. She has long, glossy black hair that flows free and she appears to be of Asian descent except for the black ram's horns that curve around her skull and hair. Clicking heels stop to mark her arrival at the table. Silence falls among the students.

When she speaks, her voice is somehow magnified. "Hello class. My name is Corinthia. I will be your Demonology professor." Her voice has a melodious cadence that's soothing.

"As I am sure you are all aware, the name of this course is Angelology and Demonology. However, it will be split up between myself and my…counterpart. You will have each of us every other period when this class is offered. The horns alone should give me away as a demon so naturally, I will teach you all things demonic. The other professor will educate you on all matters angelic."

I can't help but notice that Corinthia doesn't bother to mention the other professor's name. There's a war between Heaven and Hell, but this just seems sort of petty.

"We will begin with your books." Corinthia extends her hand toward the door from which she entered. The knob turns and the door opens on its own. Well, by whatever power the demon uses. Heavy, hardback books float out one at a time. They drift over to the front row first and then come around the sides and move along the rows to land gently in the arms or laps of each of the students.

Since we're in the back top of the lecture hall, we're a couple of the last students to receive ours, but most of the students are so impressed by the demonic magic that they're too busy to be impatient. When my copy floats over, I grab it with my hands. The first thing I notice about the book is the sheer size and weight of it. It's one of those ancient tombs which make it bizarre that there are so many of them. It's covered in black leather. On the cover is a blood red figure in the shape of an angel, but with leathery wings instead of the feathery ones I would have expected. The pages are gilded in gold but are beaten up a bit. At the top it reads "Demonology." Running my fingers over it, I turn it over and, on the back, and upside down is another cover. This one is blue and reads "Angelology" and on it is a blue angel with the feathery wings that I expected the first time around. That would make the red one a demon.

With all of the books passed out, Corinthia begins with her lesson. "One of the most important things to know about Heaven and Hell is that they aren't as different as you might think. After all, the original demons were all angels first. Nevertheless, Heaven is far more hierarchical in nature. That is not to say that Hell isn't, but it is less so than Heaven.

"Time and evolution have changed those angels into myriad demons. For reasons yet unknown, many of the Fallen have experienced changes both in shape and power as have their prodigy both hellish and earthly."

There are a few coughed murmurs of them being evil. Some scattered chuckles follow. Corinthia is clearly experienced in what she does because she only gives us a condescending smile and continues on with her lecture.

"There are six Houses of Hell. Each is led by one of the Lords of Hell. Your families, some more ancient and glorious in history, all fall under the direct jurisdiction of one of these Hellish Houses. The first is, of course, the House of Lucifer. The second is that of his consort, Lillith. The third house is that of Cain. These three make up what is referred to as the Unholy Trinity. Consequently, their houses have held a higher sense of pride and prestige through the millennia.

"Having said that, the other three houses are vital to the success of Hell in the war against Heaven. The fourth House of Hell is that of Beelzebub. He serves as Lucifer's lieutenant and is basically in charge of the whole of Hell as a domain. The fifth House of Hell is that of Asmodeus. He serves as Lillith's lieutenant. The sixth and final House of Hell is that of Mammon. He serves as the lieutenant to Cain.

"In practice, the secondary trio are the true lords of Hell – Beelzebub, Asmodeus, and Mammon. The Unholy Trinity concern themselves with loftier goals and leave the administration of the realm to their lieutenants.

"Now, I want to take an aside for a moment and consider you Descended Nephilim in general terms. We will discuss you and your history and abilities in more detail as the year continues, but for the moment I want to explain your connections to the six Lords of Hell. I'll begin with the lower ranked pairings and move up from there."

I cringe at the professor's continued use of hierarchical terminology. It's terrible that some Descended are considered better than others simply because of their heritage. Nothing good can come from that, but then again what did I expect; it is Hell.

"Mammon is a vampire. As the lieutenant to Cain, he was one of the first Cain turned. Despite what the fairy tales of the Bible tell, Cain was no mere human being. He was one of Lord Lucifer's most trusted generals in the War in Heaven, he and his brother Abel both. After the Fall, it was discovered that Abel had betrayed our cause. When Cain learned of his brother's betrayal, he slew him in single combat and out of sheer anger with Divinity, he drank the blood of his brother. This was one of the earliest accounts of the changes that the Fallen began to undergo."

I have to rush with my writing just to keep up with the amount of information Corinthia shares. I'm not religious. My parents never attended church, and we don't have any other religious connections I'm aware of. Carnies don't tend to participate in institutions much, simply because they're always on the move and don't have the time or the ability to participate in any rooted organizations.

Corinthia continues with her lecture. "Most vampires are descended from one of these two lords and belong to their houses. It is important to note that even among Nephilim there are two subsets beyond the two main strains of Descended and Ascended. In each case, there are also legacies and children. Legacies are born from the families of these great houses of both Hell and Heaven, but they are not the direct children of demonic or angelic beings. Most Nephilim are legacies. However, there are occasionally those born directly to these divine creatures."

It's strange to listen to our demonic professor refer to herself as a creature and put it in such detached terms. I glance over at Marius to see if he has any kind of response, but he's writing even more furiously than I am. He notices me and gives a passing smile before continuing to write. I wonder again why he's bothering to connect himself to me when he knows all these old families in the Houses of Hell. Why befriend someone like me who knows nothing of the politics or hierarchy of Hell?

Shaking my head, I focus on the lesson again. "Next, we come to the House of Asmodeus. He is the brother to Lillith and her lieutenant. He and his sister served as spy master and mistress as well as assassins to Lord Lucifer in the War in Heaven. Asmodeus is the first incubus as his sister is the first succubus. While Mammon and Cain live off the blood, these siblings live off sexual energy."

I keep writing, but my mind is racing. This is from whom I'm descended? A succubus? I'm supposed to live off sex? My face reddens at the thought. I try to ignore this connection to Lillith and keep writing, pretending this is about someone else, not me. Perhaps I can learn a thing or two from Corinthia about being disconnected from the truth.

"When each of you took the Hell Fire in your hand, it began to activate your powers as well as your needs. Over the next year you will begin to see them both manifest."

Well, fuck. That doesn't sound like something I can ignore.

"Next, we come to Beelzebub. Like Cain and Mammon, he is also a vampire, the very first whom Cain turned. Given that three of the six lords are vampires, the vast majority of Descended Nephilim fall under this category, followed by the incubi and succubi of Asmodeus and Lillith. The relationships among the Lords of Hell are a complex web. When beings live for as long as the Lords do, that is to be expected."

It sounds incestuous to me, but I tear myself from that vein of thought because it's about sex and having learned I am supposedly a succubus makes me not want to think about that whatsoever at all.

"Finally, a few words on Lord Lucifer himself. The families tied to the Lightbringer are few in number but are among the most ancient and powerful. There are a couple of anomalies among them that we still do not understand. Although Lord Lucifer is neither vampire nor incubus, those Nephilim of his house almost all manifest as one of these, albeit generally more powerful than those of other houses. The strangest anomaly though is those few who are his actual children. Lord Lucifer has occasionally blessed a member of his own house with a mating ritual. He grants this only to those of his house and in even rarer instances a child has been born from this mating. These children have always been extremely powerful, more so than any other Descended Nephilim in history. They are called dragons."

That catches my attention. I love books, especially fantasy fiction and dragons have always been one of my very favorite mythical creatures. Now I'm learning that they are real in some way.

"Dragons are so powerful that they have been known to rival even demons and angels in strength. They are also almost always quite famous, or infamous, depending on your perspective. No doubt many of you have heard of them. Some of the more well-known ones have included Alexander the Great, Napolean, and of course, Adolf Hitler."

At that I almost drop my pen. I'd heard of Alexander the Great and knew that Napolean was a French military genius. Hitler though. They were all warlords, conquerors. Butcherers.

A hand rises at the front of the room. No one has dared ask a question, probably because they're too busy trying to keep up with the rapid-fire information the professor is throwing at us.

Corinthia stops and calls on the student. I recognize the dark curls of Trist, the nasty archim. In a sickly-sweet voice, she trumpets for all the class to hear. "I heard a rumor that there is a dragon alive today and that he's allegedly supposed to bring about the Apocalypse."

The professor's eyes dart to the back of the class. It's a quick movement, but the students follow it. Many of them turn to look back and I realize they're staring at Drake.

I understand what Trist has done. She put a target on the Descended's back. But perhaps it's deserved if that was what the dragons are, monsters and mass murderers.

Drake stares stoically back at the class, but his head shifts my way, and those violet eyes catch mine. I shrink from that gaze, my heart racing.

Corinthia clears her throat and continues with the lesson, but class ends soon thereafter, and my mind is filled with more questions than answers.

Chapter Seven
Temptations and Fortitude
January – Purgatory Academy

Marius agrees with me that walking in silence is best right now. My head's saturated with so many different avenues of thought it's like a city with far too many streets, many of them running unceremoniously into each other.

It doesn't take us nearly as long to arrive at our next class. The general flow of students rids us of the need for a map at the moment; we just follow the crowd.

While the door is comparable to the one we entered for our first class, that's where the similarities end. If our first classroom is basically a university lecture hall, this one is more like a meditation retreat room. The ceiling is high and adorned with wooden beams and dark corners. The floor is a strange contrast of white marble lined with cracks of black. They're so disorganized they have to be intentional.

The weirdest part about the room is that there are no chairs. Instead, there are pillow cushions. At the middle of the room is the smallest circle of them and each new circle beyond is just slightly larger. With thousands of Nephilim, there are a lot of pillowy circles, like the layers of an onion.

We're able to snag cushions on the outermost ring. It's a real pain in the ass not showing my ass while I attempt to sit down in my skirt. Mission accomplished, I find Drake is to our right again. I'm all but certain that we left the last classroom before him, but he's seated already, reading his paperback, not a care in the world.

I figure now is as good a time as any to ask. "So, Drake is a dragon? Drake the dragon? That's a bit on the nose, isn't it?"

Marius chokes on his laugh. "I mean, it's basically like what Professor Corinthia stated. The dragons are only born to Lucifer directly, are extremely dangerous, and tend to have short but very destructive lives."

I glance Drake's way but turn back to Marius quickly, remembering how Drake seemed to sense my interest in the last class. "Has he done something to suggest that he is a…a dragon?" It feels mildly silly thinking of someone as a mythical creature, but then again I'm a succubus.

"Nothing really, but he does come from the oldest surviving Descended family in the world. They have had more dragons in their lineage than all the other lines combined. They don't associate with the other houses much. They keep their secrets close to the chest and that's saying something among the Descended and powers of Hell."

I'm tempted to inspect Drake again. I've almost given in to the temptation when the class bells chime. And then a whole other kind of temptation clicks into the middle of the room on the tallest high heels I've ever seen in my life.

She melts from the shadows. While the high heels might have been the first thing I hear, the woman's body gobbles up the rest of my attention. And that of practically every student in the room.

She's not nude but it feels like she is by the way that she moves. Her platinum blonde hair with wavy curls pastes her shoulders like a Hollywood stereotype. It works. I always considered myself straight as I've never been with a woman. But this female gives me thoughts of running my hands through that blonde hair, caressing her.

It's confusing because while the woman comes to a stop in the middle of the circle, she's wearing the same school uniform as the students. Corinthia wore it too, but definitely not like this. It makes it difficult to think of her as an authority figure.

I don't consider my skirt long. It's above my knees, but the skirt the blonde wears is way shorter. In fact, I don't understand how there's no glimpse of panties yet, but then I realize why…the woman isn't wearing any. My cheeks warm with heat at the thought.

She pops her hip out so far, I'm concerned it will slide out of place. The blonde smiles. And that smile. It's filled was promises of such pleasure. I'm in the farthest, largest circle from the woman but I still get a whiff of her scent. I don't know how to describe it, but it reminds me of roses and dripping caramel.

The white blouse the woman wears is so tight with cleavage, I'm certain the buttons are about to pop right off. She's definitely not wearing a bra either because the coldness of the room clearly defines the pointed, hard nipples trying to stab their way out. Even the shadow of her areolas seeps through like two dark suns.

Her slow turn to take in the students shows off her assets, emphasis definitely on her ass. My breathing stops for a moment, a strange mix of arousal and envy filling my body instead. I want the woman, want to experiment with her, touch her, be touched by her. But I also want to be her. That mental admission alone fuels an insecurity about my own body, even more than I had as a teenager. I learned to love my body, but it isn't an easy thing to maintain. This certainly isn't helping.

"Hello." There are several moans throughout the room and from the range I know they aren't all from the men. That isn't a voice. That's oral sex, pun intended. Whoever she is, this woman isn't an angel or a demon, but a goddess. A sex goddess.

"My name is Emilie. I am from the House of Lillith." The words pour like honey from her mouth. "Welcome to Temptations and Fortitude. You will not have a textbook for this class as it is more of a, shall we say, experiential course. To demonstrate this, may I have a volunteer please?"

A wind of whipping hands shifts my hair. Marius and I are among a very few who don't put our hands up. Drake doesn't either. Neither do the Triumvirate.

"My, what gusto. I like that in a class." Emilie's words are like a purring cat. Her smile is equal parts sweet and sensual as she raises a long, slender finger and points. She speaks in a sing song voice, "Eenie meenie, minee mow."

I can't tell who Emilie points at, but I do see how the professor, because this definitely is our professor, crooks a finger in invitation. The movement is absolutely tantalizing.

A dark-haired man steps forward. Weaving through the pillows as quickly as he can, he trips and almost falls into the lap of another male student. A few guffaws and snorts follow his chagrined face till he reaches the middle of the circle and stands twitching before Emilie.

She isn't bothered in the slightest. "What's your name, darling?"

"Ad-Adam," he stutters out after a moment.

"Adam." She says his name like a prayer. I wouldn't be surprised if he just jizzed in his pants. He's definitely drooling.

"Adam, thank you so much for volunteering. Tell me, do you like games?"

The Nephil nods with a dazed sort of look on his face. I'm pretty sure Emilie could have asked if he enjoyed chewing on gravel and he would have nodded in the same way.

Still smiling in that mix of seduction and sweetness, Emilie shifts closer. "I am going to lean in farther to kiss you. In order to win, all you have to do is tell me no. That's it. Got it?"

Adam nods with glazed eyes. That dude is done for.

Emilie leans in even farther like she said she would, getting slowly but surely closer to Adam. He leans in too. Wetting her lips, Emilie halts right before their lips touch. Adam sways back and forth slightly before she speaks again. "Do you want me to kiss you?"

Adam nods again. "I need verbal confirmation, sweetie. Do you want me to kiss you?"

His voice is barely above a whisper, but it's saturated with so much desire and desperation, my cheeks redden even more. It's more of a growl than a word. "Yes."

Emilie knows what she's doing because she waits a moment longer. The hesitation is almost too much for Adam. His entire body strains forward. The professor reaches her hands out, cupping his face, and kisses him long and deep. Apparently like everything else about Emilie, the kiss is both sweet and sensual.

When she finally pulls away, Adam does growl. It's a sound no human could make. That's what lies below the skin of each of us in this room, something more, something dangerous.

The professor wags a finger at him as he tries to reach over for more. The movement wakes the Nephil from his daze. He shakes his head as he shifts back, away from the seductress. Confusion creases his face still as Emilie tells him firmly but kindly that he should return to his seat. Adam staggers his way back, tripping multiple times as opposed to just that once on his way over.

There are multiple gasps as he walks, accompanied by more than a few snickers too. The reason is apparent. The erection Adam carries back to his pillow must hurt it's so hard. Emilie claps her hands once though and brings our collective attention back to her.

"Now then class. It is often assumed that men are more susceptible to seduction. However, I personally believe this to be inaccurate as well as unkind. Seduction is about power, yes. But there is power in both giving it and receiving it. And women enjoy that just as much as men. Allow me to demonstrate if I may."

The nervous, heightened energy in the room increases several degrees. The students understand what is about to happen and although some want to think that it isn't different, they just don't believe it. For many of them, and much of the world, what Emilie is about to demonstrate is even more taboo. And because of that, much fucking hotter. That's my two horny cents anyway.

"Do I have any female volunteers who'd like to attempt the same experiment with me?"

A number of hands shoot up unabashedly. Any shame some might have felt otherwise is not present. Taboo or no, most in this room want to experience Emilie's lips. I don't labor under the illusion that any of them are going to put up a good fight. It's all just an opportunity to make out with their wickedly hot professor, even if it's in front of everyone else. Then again, that might make the taboo even more enticing.

Emilie's pearly white teeth gleam as she scans the crowd of willing victims. That might be a better and more accurate term than volunteers. The professor twists in a delicate and graceful circle till she stops before the Triumvirate.

Trist has her hand up in the air, a look of determination on her face. I'm wrong. There's one woman in here dead set on proving she can resist Emilie's demonic charms.

Her friends seem to harbor some concerns about it though. Eli's face is furrowed with worry. Gabe is stoic, but he leans in to whisper something to Trist that I can't pick up from across the room. Trist doesn't acknowledge it but remains staring at Emilie with the same resolve.

The Ascended wants to prove she can handle the temptation. She wants to show how tough she is. Emilie realizes the same and her smile grows at the challenge. She crooks her finger in that come hither manner.

Trist stands and walks through the pillows with an intentional, slow gait; she's already doing better than Adam did. Emilie waits patiently, hands resting on her hips which somehow are both popped out at the same time. I don't even know how that's possible.

The Nephil absolutely refuses to smile. "What's your name, darling?" Emilie asks, unfazed by Trist's attempt to be unimpressed.

"Trist." The answer is cold, quick, and cutting.

"Trist." Emilie says it as if she's testing a delicious champaign. "You understand the rules of the game, yes?"

Trist doesn't bother with words, but rather nods curtly.

Emilie's smile never falters. She raises one hand slowly as if she's about to approach a wild animal. Trist looks like one, shrinking back a bit at first, but then realizing she doesn't want to be phased by this at all, so she stops and lets the professor touch her. Emilie takes a small curl of Trist's hair between her fingers and plays with it for a moment, rolling it back and forth.

The demon reaches for more of Trist's hair. It isn't sensual; it's sisterly. And it works. Trist's shoulders relax and she leans into the touch. Emilie brings up her other hand and caresses the Ascended's hair with both hands.

Most of my classmates are leaning forward too, many of them forgetting to breathe. It's as if they're all under the demon's spell. I'm not certain that isn't true, to be honest.

"You are so beautiful. I love these curls. They are so lovely. And you are so strong, so driven to be the best. I admire that so much."

I don't really know Trist, but the couple of nasty interactions I've had with the Ascended certainly point toward what Emilie is saying. It's as if the demon knew intuitively what to say and how to approach the Nephil.

Emilie caresses Trist's face now. The student leans farther in just as Adam did, their foreheads so close their breath must mingle.

The demon whispers loud enough to be heard. "Do you want me to stop?"

Trist groans a mix of desire and frustration. Emilie opens her mouth to ask again, but Trist lunges forward and kisses the professor deep and hard, urgent. Emilie matches her vigor.

It's several long, hot moments before Trist finally pulls away. She looks out at the students, comprehending what just happened. Trist's beautiful face scrunches up in consternation. Emilie's voice pulls us all back to her though. "Trist, thank you so much." Her words heave with huskiness, pure porn star.

Trist slinks away to her seat. Eli's face is lined with concern. Gabe reaches out a hand to touch her shoulder, but then thinks better of it and puts it back down. "This has been absolutely wonderful so far," Emilie says. "I'd like to have one more volunteer before the end of class please."

Hands shoot up again, even quicker than before. I know now that I will never raise my hand. When I glance at Marius, I see the same resolve on his face.

Emilie's fuck me heels click loudly as she turns with that same serpent's smile, looking for her next snack. She appears to be looking for someone in particular, her gaze skipping over raised hands left and right.

For one horrible moment, I'm afraid the demoness might be looking to "voluntell" someone. I'm about to raise my hand just to avoid the possibility and am turning to Marius to suggest he do the same, when Emilie speaks again. "You, young man, why don't you come up please?"

I whip around to look at the professor, scared that Emilie is calling on Marius. She's not looking at us though. She's staring at Drake. And he definitely doesn't have his hand up. Most of the other students also look his way.

I realize that Emilie knows exactly who and what Drake is supposed to be. He has that same stoicism I'm beginning to believe he wears all of the time. He doesn't respond to Emilie. He simply stares her down.

Emilie's smile refuses to be defeated. It survived both Adam and Trist and clearly has no intention of losing to an uninterested Descended. "Yes, you, young man. What's your name please?" Now I know for certain Emilie knows who Drake it. It's evident in her voice. That question isn't a question, but rather a way to confirm he is what she believes him to be, a dragon.

Drake appears resigned to the fact that he isn't going to get out of this one. He doesn't go without a fight though. He stands up and walks to the middle of the pillow circles, but he doesn't say a word, doesn't provide his name.

He towers over Emilie. He really is huge. The demon isn't bothered. In fact, I think she might be enjoying it, all kinds of dirty ideas floating in her lust filled eyes.

"You are a handsome one, aren't you?"

Drake still doesn't bother to answer. Emilie makes a circle around him, surveying his every inch. She even rubs against him in small, casual ways that are obviously intentional. His facial expression doesn't change one bit.

She halts in front of him and reaches up on her tip toes and asks if he would like a kiss from her. In a very clear, curt, and concise voice, Drake gives his answer. "No."

There are gasps of surprise and shock throughout the room. Emilie isn't deterred or hurt. She continues to smile. "Are you certain?"

Drake takes his shot, "Professor Emilie, you should know better than anyone….no means no."

I'm certain the demoness will be furious at Drake's snark and denial. I'm wrong. Emilie bursts out in laughter. Even her laugh is sexy, for fuck's sake. She addresses the class, "I think that is enough for your first day. We've had two great examples of the power of temptation. And one excellent example of fortitude. Please know this though that we will have plenty more opportunities together this year, assuming you all survive long enough."

Emilie isn't kidding even if she's still smiling.

Chapter Eight
The Cafeteria
January – Purgatory Academy

HELL

"*Your faculty are a bunch of bitches. Of course, that doesn't include Emilie.*"

I have to wonder if I heard the demon correctly. "*Are you in love?*" I ask mentally.

Balor gives me the equivalent of a mental scowl. "*Love. Ugh. No, Little Fox. Emilie is so much more than that. She's my mistress.*"

I'd choke on the thought if I weren't already choking on his nasty appendages. "*Do you mean as in a dominatrix?*"

"*Of course. She taught me everything I know.*"

"*You're nothing more than a romantic in demonic skin and fur.*"

"*True,*" the demon agrees. And I can't tell if he's being sarcastic or not.

Drake leaves immediately after the dismissal. Most of the students aren't departing as quickly. Many mill about and cast sidelong glances at the professor. A few are brave enough to approach her, but soon drift off when they realize she isn't going to be making out with anyone else today. Within a few minutes she clicks off into the shadows and disappears. The student exodus begins in earnest after that.

Marius and I arrive at the cafeteria within a few minutes. Drake's already seated with a tray of food near a wall on the far side of the room, nose in the same paperback.

The cafeteria is large enough to easily fit all the Nephilim. It's stacked full with long, wooden tables and benches among stone walls and candelabras ensconced in high ceilings. The food is self-serve, but there's quite the variety which I appreciate. Given that the Nephilim come from all around the world, it makes sense.

We get into line with our classmates, choose what we want, and find a corner at an end table one over from where Drake is eating and reading alone. A large pack of the Ascended Nephilim, led by the Triumvirate sit together in the middle of the cafeteria. Gabe and his lieutenants are like gravity to the other Ascended.

I can hear their eclectic collection of conversations despite the level of noise all around us. More than a few of the Ascended gang, led by Adam's two best friends, rib him about his encounter with Emilie.

"I'm surprised you were able to walk in here without running into anything with that hard on she left you with," one of them teases.

The pack roars with laughter, but Adam scowls. "Please…did you see Trist? She was way worse. I thought she was going to drop her pa-" His words cut off when he sees the much more impressive scowl Trist throws at him. There's more laughter at his expense. His eyes wonder about for some sort of distraction from the unwanted focus on him, and they land on Drake.

He begins whispering to his two friends and soon others lean in as well. Many of them look up to stare at Drake. Adam, realizing he has redirected the negative attention he was getting, decides to take it to another level. He stands up with a big grin on his face and winks at his buddies. Walking over with swag, I'm not the only one watching him anymore.

There are other students, mostly loners it seems, at the same table as Drake, but there is a certain distance between him and them. It's as if he has an invisible bubble around him. Adam uses the space to sit down right next to the Descended and pops the bubble.

Turning toward his friends, Adam smiles and winks again. Drake doesn't bother to acknowledge the dark-haired Ascended. He simply continues to read and eat. Most of the cafeteria is watching now.

Marius has his fork halfway to his mouth, but it lowers slowly back down of its own will.

Adam speaks as loudly and annoyingly as he can. "You must think you are real special, huh? Dragon, End of Days, the 666. And you don't even fall to the temptation of a piece of tail like that demonic professor of ours. What's wrong, can't get it up, limp dick? Or do you even have one?"

There are a lot of oohs and aahs at Drake's expense, lots of laughing too, mostly from the large gaggle of Ascended. Trist laughs along with them, but Gabe and Eli don't. I'm impressed by that. They seem decent even if Trist is a total psycho bitch. Obviously, I'm not biased against her.

Most of the Descended, as far as I can tell, because I still don't know how to identify them beyond association like the Triumvirate's pack, are scowling. None of them speak up though. It's interesting that so many of them are not in large groups the way that the Ascended are with Gabe, their de facto leader.

Drake continues to ignore Adam. He keeps right on eating and reading. The paperback is a copy of JRR Tolkien's Fellowship of the Ring. He has good taste; I have to give him that.

Apparently, Adam doesn't agree. When his taunts don't work to get a rise out of Drake, he takes the Descended's tray and begins eating the food. Drake reads on, but Adam finally just smacks the book right out of his hand. The paperback slides across the floor and comes to stop near my feet.

That's when something strange happens, even by the standards of what I've experienced in the last two days. The wall behind where we sit begins to move in ripples. It's as if someone threw a pebble into a still pond.

Two giant gargoyles step out of it. They're both easily eight feet tall and built completely from stone, yet somehow malleable. I wouldn't have believed it if I hadn't seen it in that very moment. They have bald pates except for a pair of horns jutting out of their high foreheads. They have what would have been leathery wings if they weren't made of stone. Their mouths are larger than a human's and take up most of their faces. Their feet and brawny arms are decked out with claws. The chests are huge and all that they wear is a strange stoney loincloth that somehow moves like fabric. The two gargoyles are basically twins. The only thing that's a bit different between them is that one has ram's horns while the other's spiral upwards like thicker versions of a unicorn horn.

They step up to the bench and the clickety clack of their clawed feet echoes throughout an otherwise entirely silent cafeteria. Peering down at Adam and Drake, the one with the ram's horns speaks. "Is there a problem here?" The voice is deep but rumbles as if someone were gargling pebbles.

Adam's voice on the other hand is filled with a nervous squeak. "No…uh, no."

The gargoyle smiles, revealing a mouth full of shark teeth, rows of them. "That's funny because if that were true, we wouldn't be here. There is no unsanctioned violence allowed on the grounds of Purgatory Academy. That goes for the faculty as well as the students."

Adam mumbles, "There's no problem."

The ram's horns gargoyle shifts slightly and asks Drake. "Is that so?"

Drake holds up the hand Adam hit when he knocked away the paperback. His middle finger is crooked, popped out of place. It gives me an inkling of how strong the Nephilim are, what happens next. Drake grasps the finger with his other hand and pulls hard. There's a pop and the finger is back in place. He doesn't even grimace as he does it. Others certainly do, including Marius.

Drake shows the middle finger to the gargoyles. The ram's horns gargoyle grins again before they melt back into the rippling stone wall. I have to admit I'm impressed. Drake embarrassed Adam by protecting him after the Ascended popped his finger out of place. Adam scowls at Drake as he stands and walks away, but he doesn't touch the Descended again.

Chapter Nine
War and Weapons
January – Purgatory Academy

Marius and I head to our third and final class of the day and I ask him, "Am I crazy or were those gargoyles that just stepped out of a stone wall?"

"Yeah, gargoyles are beings from here, from Purgatory. Here is where their loyalty lies as well. They are basically a sort of police force for the school. They make certain that we keep the rules. Well, rule. No violence unless sanctioned in class or the Tribulations."

"I guess that makes sense."

"If they didn't, many of us would already be killing each other." That's a happy thought.

Like our first two classrooms, the last one is nothing like the others. There's a sign on the door that informs us we have ten minutes to change in the locker rooms. If we aren't ready in that time, we'll be dragged out naked. Marius and I take one look at each other and rush to the door.

It opens up into a hallway that stretches to the left and right. On the left is a wooden sign that hangs from the ceiling and reads "Females." To the right is the same but the sign reads "Males." We glance at each other and speed walk to our respective locker rooms.

Seven minutes and thirteen seconds later, I'm dressed and ready. There's a note on the door out as well informing me that I need to line up along the farthest wall. When I enter, it's into a gymnasium. It's huge, easily the largest room I've seen today, not that any of them were small. The vast walls are decorated with weapons. They're as diverse as they are scary with everything from katana swords to rocket launchers. The floor is matted like for wrestling or in a dojo to practice martial arts.

Marius waits for me by the door of the men's locker room. We walk over to the wall where some of our classmates are already lined up. We agree without words to go as far back in the line as we can. However, by the time all the students are there, we wind around almost three of the four walls.

The Triumvirate is closer to the beginning of the line while Drake is the very last. Being the End of Days does have its perks. Across from the locker rooms on the opposite side of the gymnasium is another door. Two figures walk out of it and the students crowded nearby squish back to give them space. They walk in sync to the middle of the room.

They stop and make a slow circle, taking all the students in as if they were a pair of hawks looking for their next meal. It also gives us the opportunity to assess them. Both are tall, well built, and wear gis for martial arts. One of them is the color of onyx with a bald head and a neatly trimmed goatee. He has small horns that point slightly inward from his forehead. The other is sun kissed with long, blonde hair and beard. The hair is up in a manbun topknot.

The horned professor calls in a deep bass. "My name is The'slin. As you may have noticed because of the horns, I am a demon, from the House of Beelzebub. This ugly mug here is Khal'ith, an angel from the House of Azriel. He's a seraph. We will be your tandem professors this year. Welcome to War and Weapons!"

The angel grunts at the backward compliment and almost smiles. I didn't expect that. The'slin continues, "As the name suggests, you will learn about weapons and war in this class. We will begin with hand to hand and move onto weapons. We will also cover military history, tactics, and strategy. Finally, you will learn to use your shifted forms."

There are ripples of questions and confusion at those last words. The'slin holds up a hand and continues. "Yes, now that you've all been activated, your shifted forms will come out soon enough. We never know when or how exactly it will occur, but if you survive long enough, you will all show your claws and more within the next year."

I have a million questions about what "shifted forms" means, but The'slin keeps talking so I don't have the chance to worry about it. I'm starting to think that is part of the collective plan here at Purgatory Academy. "First things first though. We need to know what you're all capable of already. So, who wants to volunteer?"

Unlike Emilie's class, there aren't any volunteers immediately. But after a few moments Gabe raises his hand right before Trist holds up hers. I wonder if Gabe is trying to spare his friend some more embarrassment after what happened in our Temptations and Fortitude class.

The'slin says, "Let's start with the blonde." He smirks at the angel as if sharing an insight joke. Khal'ith just grunts agreement.

Gabe steps forward and I have to harness my lusty thoughts. He seems…decent. And he is definitely gorgeous. He didn't laugh at Adam's cruel jokes or try to bully Drake. He tried to help Trist when she was obviously near self-destructive just to prove herself. And he is definitely gorgeous.

The'slin motions for the Ascended to stand across from him as they face each other. Khal'ith gives them instructions. The'slin and Gabe bow to each other and take up their fighting positions. "Fight!" Khal'ith calls.

Gabe wastes no time in coming at The'slin. Apparently, Trist isn't the only one who has something they want to prove. His movements are fast and fluid. He is obviously well trained. The'slin puts on that same smile from earlier and lets the Ascended come on in his fury. The professor blocks each attack with equal fluidity. These two are dangerous, and their fight is a dance. It's beautiful in its own right. Finally, The'slin holds up a hand and Gabe stops almost without missing a beat. The Ascended isn't able to land a hit, but it's impressive, nonetheless.

Most of the students clap as Gabe and The'slin come back and bow to each other once more. Gabe doesn't smile as he returns to his spot along the wall, but he stands tall and proud.

"Who's next?" Khal'ith calls out. When there are no hands, a few others are voluntold to dual, but none of them do as well as Gabe did. Most of them are punched, kicked, or head butted into submissions or knock outs. Marius is right about that archim thing. Gabe is tougher.

I allow myself to think I've made it through the class period when The'slin's gaze stops on me and waves me over. Dammit. Khal'ith takes up a position across from me. Fighting the angel is the better option of the two from what I've seen in the earlier bouts. It isn't that he is a weaker fighter. In fact, it's difficult to tell which one of them is better. All I know is that they are both very good and most likely are holding back against the students. That's scary enough, but it's more that The'slin fights dirty. He's also willing to take chances while the angel plays it safe.

I take up my position across from Khal'ith and the demon calls for us to bow, take up our stances, and fight. Khal'ith doesn't move to strike right away. He's definitely more cautious, feeling out his opponents. The'slin mostly bulls right in and figures out his opponents by their responses to his attack. Both are effective in their own way.

We dance around each other for a few more moments before the angel takes a couple of exploratory jabs at me. I either block them or dodge out of the way. A small smile finds its way onto Khal'ith's face as he realizes that I might just know what I'm doing. Coming on harder and faster, the angel throws multiple combos of punches and kicks but I'm able to dance away or block each one even at this speed. I don't go on the offensive though.

Khal'ith's eyes gleam with excitement, and perhaps curiosity. I know he's coming on stronger. And he does. His movements are so fast I struggle to keep away and realize what he wants. He's forcing me to move to attack. My own strikes come from a place of flow, from muscle memory. This isn't my first fight and if I'm going to survive Purgatory Academy, it can't be my last.

The angel is able to block each of my attacks, but he seems pleased and finally steps back to call a halt. He rewards me with a small nod. We go back to our starting positions and bow.

As I walk back to my place, I feel more than see eyes on me. Marius stares, slack jawed, questions in his eyes as I return to the wall. Clapping breaks out among the students for my showing. They only clapped louder for Gabe. We're the only two not to end up on our backsides on the mats.

Marius opens his mouth to ask the million questions milling about in his mind. The'slin saves me from the barrage. "We'd like one more volunteer." I don't know why they keep using that term when no one bothers to raise a hand anymore. "Let's have you come up."

The demon is pointing at Drake. The Descended doesn't blink but walks over without making a sound even on the mats. He comes to stand across from The'slin as Khal'ith takes up his position to begin the bout.

The'slin bows, but Drake doesn't bother. Irritation flashes across the demon's face. As the angel calls for their fighting positions, Drake still doesn't bother. He just stands there. The'slin bobs about a bit after the angel calls them to fight. But Drake doesn't move. The demon, anger simmering in his eyes, throws an easily blocked haymaker. Drake still doesn't bother. The hit knocks him to the floor. He shakes his head and stands back up but doesn't take a fighting stance. The'slin only stops and smirks at the student and waves him off. Drake stalks back to his place at the end of the snake's tail of a line.

Grumbling and whispers sprout among the students. I don't know what I expect from a student who is supposed to bring about the end of the world, but that certainly wasn't it.

Chapter Ten
New Friends
January – Purgatory Academy

I shower and change. The school might be Gothic in architecture, but the plumbing has plenty of hot water. I'm just fine with that. I meet Marius outside the main class door. We're about to walk out when Drake emerges. We're standing off to the side, so he doesn't look our way as he heads down the hallway. My insides can't decide if they're happy or upset by his lack of attention for me.

He has his paperback in hand and opens it to read while he walks. "Wow. He can read and walk at the same time. Doesn't he worry about running into anything? And how the hell does he know where he's going already?" I whisper to Marius.

The pale young man shrugs. "Honestly, I don't know, but I'm not surprised. I have more important questions to ask you anyway."

Marius is practically bouncing with curiosity. Oh crap. "Where in the worlds did you learn to fight like that?"

I start walking just to make certain that Marius does the same. He hurries to catch up. "Seriously though, where did you learn to fight like that?" He hovers at one shoulder and then switches to the other, flittering back and forth like a hummingbird.

I don't know if I want to giggle at his energy or be annoyed at his questions. "I wasn't that good. You saw Gabe. He was clearly the best fighter in there, at least from what we've seen so far."

"That's my point," Marius crows. "The only one who did better than you was the Golden One, an archim. That's amazing. How did you do it?"

I quicken my pace, but Marius sticks right with me. I sigh, "My dad taught me."

"He did? Cool. Is your dad Nephil?"

I giggle at that. "No way. He's just, my dad. We work for a traveling circus. He was taught by his dad. He taught me. And what he didn't know others in the circus taught me."

We slow as we get closer to the front doors and more of our classmates are bottlenecked on their way out. "That is so cool. Very badass."

I work hard not to let my face light up bright red in embarrassment at the compliment. I hate when that happens, but I can't control it. We get out the front doors and make our way down the hill toward the gates. Marius looks like he wants to say something, but he keeps it contained. I center myself and mistport outside of the academy grounds.

As soon as I have, Marius doesn't wait any longer. His fingers are cold on my hand. "Lilly, train me."

I blink, not certain I understood what he said. He raises his hands in a way that says he's going to explain more. "Look, I am not what you would call a warrior. I come from an ancient family, but I…" He shifts his weight hesitantly from one foot to the other. "I can't fight. And I am going to die here if I don't learn. So, please, I am begging you. Teach me."

It could be some mist in his eyes, but I think he might be on the verge of tears. I can't stand it. But I'm still so shook up from the last two days. Ricardo was funny and charming and before I had the chance to get to know him, he was dead. Reduced to a pile of meat and bones. Now this fragile, pale shadow of man wants my help to avoid the same fate. Who am I to do that?

We stare at each other for a moment longer. The pleading on his face is so plain, so evident. Yeah, I can't stand it. "Alright."

His face glows with a gentle light that reminds me of the moon. "Yeah?"

I smile. "Yes. Yes. I'll train you."

Marius literally jumps up and down and hugs me in his excitement. It's awkward; I don't return it but I don't stop him either. It's the best I can do. He senses my hesitation and steps back. "Sorry. I'm just excited. Thank you. When can we start?"

I roll my eyes. "We can start next week. We'll train after school on the days we don't have War and Weapons. Deal?"

"Yes. Absolutely. Whatever you say. Thank you. Thank you so much. If I survive it will be because of you."

All I can think is to ask myself if he doesn't, would it be my fault. The thought haunts me all the way back to my RV as I mistport home. It remains with me when I find a warm plate of food and sweet note from my dad. I even dream of it as I sleep.

Chapter Eleven
Sinners and Saints
January – Purgatory Academy

HELL

"Your kindness is so pathetic." Balor's mental voice mocks me. *"I wish I could argue your point."* But I can't.

Marius is there waiting for me outside the gates the next morning. His smile is more relief than happiness. It's unclear if it's because I'm alive or that he won't be alone.

Our first class today is called Sinners and Saints. The room is a lecture hall like the first class yesterday. Drake has what I'm already considering his normal seat, in the back on the right. I have to laugh about how quickly people, be they Nephilim or human, create and hold to their habits. Most of our classmates are looking for the seats they had yesterday. But in a crazy environment like this one, it's good to hold onto something.

The bells chime and our professor steps out of a side door at the bottom of the room just as Corinthia did. My first thought is that it's a Malak. Once my brain is done playing tricks on me, I realize the robes are a dark brown, not black. There's a golden tassel tied off at the waist like a belt. Toes peek out below the hem of the robe and arms folded in front like a Medieval friar.

Our professor draws back the hood to reveal a medium height man with lightly brown skin, tanned from a sun that does not exist here in Purgatory from the little I have seen. The weird thing about him is that he isn't from the CW. Almost everyone up to this point who I've met here in Purgatory is beautiful, even beyond it. It's like watching a show on the CW. Unrealistic. But here it is. Reality at last.

That's not to say that the Sinners and Saints professor is the first one here that isn't handsome. And it isn't that he is ugly either. He is just unremarkable. Forgettable. Gressil is slimy looking. Marius is handsome, but more in an awkward teenage boy way even though he's twenty years old like the rest of us. No, it isn't everyone, but it is definitely most.

"Hello all. My name is Manciel and this is Sinners and Saints." His voice is more of the same. Average, common, normal. It isn't monotone though, but rather warm. It's weird because I want to focus on his words, but once they're spoken it's difficult to remember what he said. I notice it and make certain to take notes.

It's fascinating that he doesn't share if he's an angel or demon. Most of our professors seem quite keen to share their lineage. "We'll start with your class books." He motions to several rolling library carts behind him. "You will all need to come up and get them. So, please line up." He's also the first one to not give out the books in some sort of magical manner. And consequently, it takes a while to hand them out. There's a lot of chatter because of the timeline.

Sitting back down with my textbook, I take a look at it. It's just as dense as the others. Like Manciel it's more common looking though. It looks like what I expected from a textbook. The front cover is a bit cheesy. It has people with halos of either golden light or bright red. The title is the same as the class, Sinners and Saints. Once everyone has a book, Manciel clears his throat and we all quiet down.

"It's relatively easy to explain this class. I know that you've all been to Emilie's Temptations and Fortitude course. This is basically the opposite of it but I promise I won't attempt to kiss any of you."

The laughter is surprised and genuine. "This class is about history, but it's more academic in nature than experiential. The good news is that many of you should get plenty of sleep that you're probably missing out on otherwise while attending school here." More laughter, even louder this time, follows.

"If you do happen to stay awake, you will have the immense joy of learning about the lives of the greatest sinners and saints in human history. The caveat is that, while some of them may be known among other humans, many are only known among angels and demons. They are the pride and joy of one side or the other. Humans, and perhaps a few of you, will not have heard of them because they were good enough to keep hidden their evils or their righteous actions. Think of this class as a mix of hagiography and a true crime podcast." More laughter, filled with interest and even a smidgen of excitement.

"We will examine and discuss the choices each of these figures made throughout their lives that brought them to be known for whatever it was they were known for. We will see how what appear to be small decisions can make big differences, one way or another."

I'm curious to learn more. Manciel begins with an alternative history that I've never heard before, "Angels were the first to populate Earth. Humans were created much later. They were part of the peace agreement between the Divine and Heaven with the Fallen. The pact stated that they would no longer have all-out war, but rather a cold war of sorts, operating off influence over humanity to see who would win more souls to their side in the end.

"Adam and Eve are a human cosmogony myth. They did not literally exist but are important as a story for the beginning of humanity. It demonstrates the struggle between Heaven and Hell to control humanity. Much of the truth of the history and even its chronology has been lost to the sands of time, at least among humans.

"The history of humanity is much more complex than the Divine creating one man and then using a rib to create a woman. In fact, many humans throughout their history would consider the truth to be blasphemy, namely evolution."

How would religious people feel if they knew that particular tidbit of truth? Evolution is the tool of the Divine. It's mind boggling. I'm not especially religious and don't think about theological things often. However, the last couple of days with Purgatory and everything else, my perspective has definitely shifted.

Chapter Twelve
Evocation
January – Purgatory Academy

A certain amount of anxiety courses through me when our next classroom resembles that of Temptations and Fortitude, all dark corners and beams in the ceiling. Thankfully, there are desks instead of pillows. They're still arranged in a circle expanding outwards. In the middle of the room and circle is a white nine-pointed star on the floor.

I scan for a certain blonde Ascended and a particular dark Descended. Dammit. It's time to have a heart to heart with my libido. They're both exquisite, but I just need to focus on my own survival.

Before class officially begins, our teacher walks out of a dark corner and comes to stand in the middle of the star. Student chatter dies down and there's an awkward, pregnant silence until the bells chime.

Our professor has dark skin with long purple braids down her back almost to her waist. She's curvier and looks like someone's librarian mother. She begins to speak even as the last bell is echoing. "Hello all. My name is Ren'el. I am a seraph from the House of Raphael. And this is Evocation. You should be relieved to hear that you will not have another hefty textbook to worry about."

There's a smattering of polite laughter but more sighs of relief in agreement. Ren'el continues. "I know. Like about half of your classes here, Evocation is experiential in nature. Can anyone share with us what that is?"

Trist's hand shoots up among a few others. Ren'el motions for her to respond. "Evocation is the ability to call up either angels or demons to another plane of existence or location."

Ren'el remarks, "Very good. Thank you. Yes, evocation is the power to call into person angels or demons. And you have all participated in this innate ability already. Can anyone tell me how?"

Only Trist's hand rises this time. Stupid teacher's pet. Ren'el looks around for a moment before calling on the Ascended again. "Misporting. Because we have divine blood, we're able to move through the planes just like any angel or demon can."

"Very good. Well done again. Now the question is if angels and demons can be evoked, is the same true with Nephilim?"

Trist's hand is up again and there's some snickering. Even Gabe is looking at her with concern. Ren'el's smile is crooked with amusement. Another hand rises though and Ren'el calls on the blonde-haired woman who answers in an Australian accent, "It's not, because of their human blood." Trist's irritation is evident in her frown, pissed she didn't get to show off more. Her misery brings me smug happiness.

"Correct. Thank you. Nephilim can evoke and mistport because of their divine blood, but they cannot be summoned because of their human blood. It is one of the few advantages Nephilim have over angels and demons." There is a bit of snark in that last comment. Obviously, Ren'el considers herself better than the Nephilim, but given what I've seen so far that seems accurate.

"Evocation is one of the forms of divine magic with which humans are actually familiar. It's where the history of seances, Ouija boards, and other forms of so-called conjurings come from. It's also why they never work. No divine blood and there's no evocation. It only works for the Nephilim.

"Now, there are a few things to know about the process of evocation, but we will get to that momentarily. First and foremost, you need to understand the following. Evocation is a contest of wills. It pits your own against that of the divine being you are attempting to evoke. And it is not only a question of whether you can call up the being, but also if you can contain them. There is no shortage of stories about Nephilim who have attempted to evoke a being more powerful than themselves. In each of these accounts, things almost never end well for the Nephilim. This is also the reason why angels and demons rarely evoke one another. The hierarchical nature of Heaven and Hell makes certain of this. Trying to evoke a being more powerful than you will end just as poorly for angels and demons.

"For this reason, we will begin with calling imps from Hell. They are powerful and cunning in their own way as are all denizens of both Heaven and Hell. Comparatively speaking though, they are among the weakest ranks of the demons. This class isn't about Demonology, but a short background about imps is appropriate here.

"After the Fall, the angels who rebelled began to undergo a number of changes. We still don't understand why or how this occurred, but it did. A direct byproduct of this was that several new hellish species were born or evolved into being. One of them were the imps. Each is an abomination in the eyes of Heaven." The condescension in her voice makes it clear that Ren'el agrees with this assessment.

Pausing a moment she switches gears. "Alright, let's discuss the process now. The first thing that you will need is a drop of your blood. It creates a connection between you and the being you are calling upon. The blood also contains your will and is utilized to create a prison for the being. Beyond that, some evocators find it useful to use words to concentrate and realize their intentions. However, the only words absolutely necessary are the name of the being you call up. You call their name three times to complete the evocation. It doesn't have to be said aloud, but again using thoughts is more dangerous because it takes higher concentration.

Ren'el wears a long black robe over her school uniform and from them she pulls out a ceremonial knife, an athame. Holding up a finger, she pricks the very tip of it and lets a drop of blood drip onto the floor, right in the middle of the nine-pointed star.

Replacing the athame in her robes, Ren'el wiggles her hands in a creepy manner that reminds me of Saruman hovering over his crystal ball in the Lord of the Rings. The professor whispers something that I can't discern.

A small bloom of mist rises up where the blood fell. It seems to have boundaries in the shape of a tiny dome because the mist stops and stays, outlining the invisible half bubble. There's a loud pop and a minute creature that can't be more than six inches in height appears in the middle of the misty prison.

The imp is black in color with a shining hide reminiscent of a rhino. Its limbs are long and stick-like. Its bald head is round and two horns jut out, the shape of rose thorns. Its arms and legs are clawed and bat wings, leathery and smooth, are folded on its back. The creature is completely nude, but where I would have expected genitalia, there's nothing. It's just more shiny rhino hide.

It screeches and jumps straight at the angel. It hits the dome though, hard. Staggering back, its little snake slit nose bleeds black blood. That's the moment I realize I shouldn't be able to see that from my seat across the room with a creature that small. Thinking quickly, I look around. Nope. Not a one of my classmates wears glasses. Apparently, my hellish blood is active and working. I have to admit that's kind of cool.

More screeching brings me back to the present. The imp slams against the dome with fists and howls what have to be insults in a guttural language I don't understand in the slightest. The body language is clear though. The imp's pissed.

Ren'el has her hands folded together in front of her and waits patiently for the imp to run out of verbal abuses. All the scratching and swiping against the dome does absolutely nothing.

"Grez'ek." The angel says the word with such authority. The imp stills. "That's enough." I realize that is the imp's name. The imp knows it too. There's power in that word and in the way that Ren'el says it. The angel stares down the imp and the creature lifts a shark's mouth with multiple layers of dagger sharp teeth, growling silently.

Ren'el turns back to the students. "Class, I'd like to introduce you to Grez'ek." A shudder runs through the little creature at the sound of its name again. "As you can see, I have complete control over him." Him? Huh?

"For example…" She turns back to stare at the imp. She doesn't utter a word, but the tiny black beast howls in pain, clutching claws to his skull. The screeching was terrible, but this is so much worse. Pity swells in my stomach.

Ren'el says nothing, but the pain must have dissipated because the howling stops. Grez'ek is breathing on the dome. The hot breath leaves moisture behind as if it were a window. Hatred seethes in those black eyes.

I'm not the only one grateful the torture is over. Others are relieved. That isn't the only emotions some of my classmates are displaying though. There is also disgust and a healthy helping of anger.

Ren'el is an angel and here she is torturing a creature weaker than herself...and enjoying it. There's a smug smile on her face even now.

She continues to smile as she says the imp's name three more times. The mist ascends once more as she does, covering the black body from view. The same loud popping sound rings out as the mist fades along with the dome and the imp is gone.

"Now then, who would like to try it first?" Ren'el's voice is pleasant, motherly. No hands come up. Across the way I notice Gabe with Eli and Trist. For once, they all wear the same look on their faces. Horror. Perhaps mixed in with a bit of anger.

A wave of appreciation for the trio, even grudgingly for Trist, washes through me. They might be on the opposite side of this cosmic war, but none of them condones torture, and certainly don't get any pleasure from it. That much is clear from their expressions and my opinion of them goes up. Trist might be self-righteous, but she isn't a sadist.

Ren'el has a slight frown on her face now, seeing that no one wants to attempt an evocation. Tsking with disappointment, the angel continues to scan the students. Her eyes stick on someone to my right. Whatever Drake might be, I don't think he deserves such scrutiny from all our professors.

"What's your name please?" Students seated near Drake shrink out of the way, hoping she isn't speaking to them. The angel moves forward a couple of steps and points. There's still some confusion, but I know from the way Ren'el speaks that she knows the Descended's name already. This is all just a game to her.

"Drake. Yes, of course." She says his name in the same authoritative manner she spoke the imp's name. It isn't even my name, but I feel the pull that the angel uses on it. Feel the energy and command. Demanding.

"The End of Days. The 666. The dragon of Lucifer." The silence that was already pregnant with awkwardness is so intense now, I'm nearly suffocating on it. Ren'el's voice is quiet venom, a sneer painted across her face.

Drake doesn't say a word. He simply stands up and walks over. It's like a glitch in the Matrix, watching him do the same thing all over again. I admire how fluid his movements are. He moves like a big cat, feline grace in human form. Well, Nephilim form. Nephilic? Ugh. Whatever.

He towers over the professor as he had with Emilie, unafraid of proximity and uncaring of the situation. Without a word, he holds out his hand. I don't understand at first, but Ren'el does. She smiles with smarm and produces the athame from the hidden location in her robes. Point first, she deftly flips it in the air so that it's handle first and reaches out to give it to Drake. The Descended doesn't so much as flinch as he takes the knife from her, his stoic mask still in place.

Holding his pointer finger just as Ren'el did, he pricks it and sprinkles his blood on the same spot in the middle of the nine-pointed star. He still doesn't say a word, but the mist comes anyway. The dome appears. The pop sounds. He has called up the demon without speaking its name out loud. Impressive.

The mist falls away and there is another angry imp. Well, it might be another imp, but it looks exactly alike so I can't be sure. It could be the same one. If it is, I'm certain Grez'ek will be even more pissed off than he was on his first visit.

Either way, the imp shrieks and claws at the dome. But then Drake finally speaks. However, it isn't English or anything else that I even remotely recognize. No. That isn't quite right. I have heard sounds like that before. From the last imp. He's speaking the same language as the imp.

The effect on the tiny demon is immediate. It quiets and turns toward Drake. Then it does something that I really don't expect. It bows. Drake returns the motion and continues to speak with the imp. The Descended says something that has the imp smiling. It's a scary sight even if the imp is no more than half a foot in height.

The brooding Descended moves to the side so that the imp and Ren'el are in one another's sight. Shark teeth smile at a scowling but bewildered angel who clearly doesn't understand. Whatever is happening is not something our professor expected.

The imp steps closer to the dome and thrusts out its pelvis toward the angel. The hard shell where genitalia would have been splits open and out snakes what is undeniably a penis. It is disproportionately larger in size to the rest of the imp. He doesn't seem to have a problem with it. In fact, as he licks both of his palms with that same shark's smile, he demonstrates that he is quite practiced.

The smile never leaves his face as he strokes right then and there. Ren'el doesn't look away, but her lips are pursed together in a very pissed off manner. The imp's smile grows wider and takes up most of his round face. He strokes faster and faster. It's only a few more moments and strokes before the imp cries out in screeching ecstasy, thrusting forward in repeated convulsions as he orgasms. A phosphorescent violet gel, his cum, shoots out and splatters on the side of the dome, leaking slowly down and smearing the wall with a glowing purple.

He trembles for a few more moments and then shakes off the remainder from his tip till it falls on the floor. His penis retracts inside and he steps back, a contented smile without teeth on his wicked face.

The professor is steaming with hatred. Everyone else is, well, just shocked, mixed with plenty of disgust. I'm trying not to laugh out loud.

Drake breaks the silence, ignoring Ren'el completely and addressing the imp again. The imp responds and then bows. Drake bows in return once more. The mists rise but before the imp disappears and pops back down to Hell, he flips off the angel.

The silence is a bit more stunned now. The dome fades away, but the glowing violet cum remains, splattering on the floor. The stunned silence branches out in two directions. It's on the faces of my classmates. The Ascended simmer with rage at the insult of an angel even though minutes before they'd been disgusted by the same angel for her torturous ways. The Descended harbor a heated satisfaction. Considering what Ren'el did to the imp, I get it.

Drake returns to the angel, the athame suddenly in his hand again. He's holding the blade and offering her the handle. Her hand reaches out to take it, a glare marring her face. Almost quicker than I can follow, Drake deftly flips the knife around before Ren'el can take it and the point is facing her, only inches away.

There are several gasps at the audacity. No gargoyles appear though. Apparently, the threat doesn't count as actual violence. Ren'el's eyes grow large with anger and then fear; I swear I can taste it in the air.

Ever so carefully the professor takes the knife from Drake and for one small moment she holds the dagger there, outstretched, a struggle in her eyes. Drake waits stoic as always to see if the angel lunges to stab him then and there. But then the knife is gone again, hidden in Ren'el's robes. Drake walks back to his seat and the angel dismisses class. So, it's like that.

Chapter Thirteen
Intervention
January – Purgatory Academy

We eat at the same spot at lunch. Collective snickering brings my attention to the table next to ours where Drake sat yesterday. It isn't him there now though. It's Adam, the Ascended who started shit with Drake. He's hunched over his lunch trying not to laugh out loud, his face all red and his shoulders heaving from the effort.

Most of the laughter comes from that big gaggle of Ascended diagonal from us near the middle of the cafeteria. Trist is laughing. I'm back to disliking her. Apparently, she isn't okay with torture, but bullying is fine. Alright then. At least I know where the Ascended stand metaphorically on the moral gauge. Gabe and Eli aren't laughing though. Gabe has a look of disapproval on his face. Eli just looks pained. He wears that face about as often as Drake does his stoic one. My estimation of the two goes up even more. I have to wonder what they find to be redeemable in Trist beyond the fact that the three of them are archim.

When Drake appears with his food tray, he sees Adam sitting there. His face doesn't show a thing. For the first time I smile at his stoicism. I understand how he uses it as a weapon as much as a protection.

Drake walks right by and sits down next to me with Marius across from us. His face goes slack jawed, but when Drake raises a quizzical eyebrow at him, Marius quickly puts his head down and nervously shoves food in his mouth.

I'm still staring at him when he turns to meet my gaze. I get lost in those eyes, two pools of liquid lilac. His eyebrow rises in question even more which is impressive given how high it already is. I respond with a silly smile and try to introduce myself. "Mellow, I'm me." Shit. Not again.

I decide to take a page from Marius' book, putting my head down and shoving food into my mouth. My face burns hotter than I can ever remember; I try to focus on chewing and not choking on the larger than normal amount of food I just pushed into my mouth.

I'm chewing so loudly that I don't hear Adam approach at first. When he sits down between the two of us, I have to slide down a bit, so we aren't touching. Adam ignores me completely, his body facing Drake. He's so close he could touch the Descended, but a small bubble of space between the two still remains.

Drake opens his paperback of the Lord of the Rings and continues eating his food. He doesn't look up once. Adam leans over and takes the sandwich that Drake had on his tray.

A different sort of heat blooms on my face, a hot flash of anger. Before I know what I'm doing I speak up. "Leave him alone."

I can't see Marius' face, but I hear his flinch of surprise and concern at me involving myself unnecessarily. Adam acknowledges me with a sneer. "Mind your own business, you hell bitch."

That only fans the flames of my anger, coaxing it toward fury. Drake dumps cold water on it. "He's right. Stay out of this." His voice is calm, cold even. He doesn't need my help. Fine. Fuck him. I return to my food.

Adam leans back to take us both in. "Oh. Trouble in Paradise? Or should I say Purgatory?" He chuckles at his own lame joke. There are bursts of laughter from his friends too.

Drake keeps on eating. Adam keeps on stealing it from him. I keep my eyes on my own food. Marius does the same. Awkward does not even begin to explain the atmosphere. Finally, when Drake and Adam finish off the food, the Descended puts a bookmark with a dragon on it back in his book and stands up to take his tray.

Adam scoffs and stands up to follow Drake. Anger burns in his eyes. He isn't getting the rise out of the Descended he hoped for.

Rushing forward, he grabs Drake's shoulder and punches him in the face. The Descended's tray lands against the wall and his book slides across the floor to land near my feet. Déjà vu.

Drake staggers back up from the impact of the punch. I have to tell my feet not to get up. He made it clear he didn't want help. Of course, I don't need to bother anyway.

I think it's the same gargoyle as before who melts out of the wall behind us. I can't see a difference in the ram's horns or face anyway. Adam has his hands up almost immediately. "I didn't do anything. He slipped and I was just helping him up."

The gargoyle's stoney poker face gives nothing away. Adam only has time for his eyes to grow wide with surprise before the boulder like fist smacks him, sending the Ascended sliding across the floor behind Drake. When he comes to a stop, he doesn't move.

Looking out at the still sea of Nephilim, the gargoyle speaks in that same gravelly voice from yesterday. "You all know the rules. There is no physical violence allowed here and all acts of such will be met with the same in response." With that, he melts back into the wall, leaving us to our stunned silence.

I sit with one thought. I figure Adam will need to drink his food through a straw for a while after a hit like that.

Chapter Fourteen
Magic Weaving
January – Purgatory Academy

For our last class of the day, and the only one we haven't had yet in our block schedule, we're in another climbing lecture hall. Drake, seated once again to our right at the top, looks as unfazed as ever. He's as ruggedly handsome as he is cold.

When the bells chime, there is no sign of our professor. We wait for a couple of minutes and some of my classmates get a bit twitchy. Whispers have just broken out when something catches my eye from above. Our professor is floating down from the rafters into the middle of the room. He lands gently and I have two immediate thoughts. First, he looks like a mix of an evil Dr. Strange and Jafar from Aladdin with slicked back sides of iron gray and a curl of blackest, greasy hair over his forehead. His clean, close-cut goatee is accompanied by a waxed curlicue mustache. He wears black robes with blood red trim over his school uniform. Second, there's an oiliness to him. In the last two days, I've met several demons and angels. They're haughty, arrogant, cocky, mean, and even cruel. But none of them has felt the way that this professor does. Evil.

When he smiles, it's so insincere I want to take a shower to wash it away. In a voice just as oily he speaks, "Welcome to Magic Weaving.

I am your professor, Nekleth, from the House of Lucifer." He waits a moment to allow that idea to sink in, the fear.

Nekleth's greasy grin remains as he pulls up his robe sleeves. Twined around both of his forearms are a pair of emerald tree boas, their tongues tasting the air. Holding his arms out toward the students, they slither slowly to his open palms. Quick as a, well, as a serpent, his hands close on the pair and there are twin pops left echoing lightly in the air. He broke the snakes' necks.

He doesn't release them as they continue to convulse for a few moments longer before finally going limp, and he lets them thud to the floor. Disgusted silence at his unnecessary brutality permeates the air, from Ascended and Descended alike.

A slick, sick smile rises on one side of his face as he crouches down to pick up the snakes, their bodies no longer moving. Closing his eyes, he mumbles something indecipherable. I half expect a demon to pop up right there in class. The truth is scarier. The snakes begin to writhe in his hands again. There's a difference though. Their eyes are a smoky white film.

Nekleth stares out at the students. "There are two kinds of zombies. But there is only one kind of being that can raise them. Necromancers."

Holy shit. He can raise and control the dead. It's like something out of a horror movie. A creepy feeling of dread on the back of my neck has me on high alert as if someone unseen is watching me. Definitely horror movie material.

"The white eyes demonstrate what we call 'the walking dead.'" A snarky thought slides through my head that the snakes are more like 'the slithering dead,' but whatever. "The walking dead do not have souls. They are controlled solely from will. In this case, my will. The more powerful the necromancer, the more easily and more fluidly the dead are controlled. The more powerful the necromancer, the more walking dead they can possess."

My hand hurts from writing so fast to keep up with the information. Nekleth continues, "The second kind of zombies are called 'the living dead.' They are reanimated corpses with actual spirits recalled and forced to do the bidding of the necromancer. Just as mistporting and evocation are related, cousin powers really, so too is necromancy. However, it only flows in the blood of a select few and then only among demons and Descended."

Closing his eyes and mumbling once more, the snakes grow still and their eyes glow green. "Where once there was nothing, now there is something." Goosebumps pimple my arms. Our professor just recalled the souls of the snakes.

"Necromancy is only one form of magic among the Nephilim as well as demons and angels." His voice makes it clear what he means. Necromancy is the most powerful and dangerous divine magic. I can't think of an argument against it.

"As I'm sure you've already learned, the Hell Fire or Celestial Fire acts as a catalyst for your powers. Over the next months, they will develop, and you will change. Become stronger. More powerful. More dangerous. Angels and Ascended generally have elemental gifts. Demons and Descended have much more diverse powers, often dark in nature. However, before we continue, we should hand out your textbooks."

With a wave of his hand a side door opens and out float the books up to the students one at a time. It's a neat trick, but not the first time I've seen it in the last two days. The zombie snakes are definitely more impressive.

The books are easily the most disturbing though. The cover is bound in skin, not leather, and I don't want to know what kind. My gross-o-meter has already just about had it for the day. It reads "Magic Weaving: An Introduction." The words are spelled out with bones. Again, I have zero interest in knowing what kind they are. At the bottom of the book is Nekleth's name. I don't need to open the book to know that while it might discuss magic weaving generally, there will be a focus on some of the darker shades of it.

"Your magic will be weak at first, but as you grow and age, so too will it, not unlike a fine wine. You will become stronger, more powerful. Assuming you live that long. However, it is vital that you learn your own limits. If you use it too fast, too inefficiently, you could drain it as well as yourself. It could kill you. You should not hold onto it too long because that would also result in your death."

Nekleth holds up the snakes again, their eyes still green. He retains their souls captive the entire class period while lecturing. We all watch as the green glow fades finally and they fall to the floor once more, limp ropes of scales.

Chapter Fifteen
Family Time
January – Purgatory Academy

HELL

> *"Nekleth is such a poser."*
> *"Balor, for once you and I agree completely."*

I head straight for the shower when I mistport home. Dead snakes slither through my mind as I wash off the oily feeling of the day. Standing under the hot water, a deep exhaustion settles. Two days into my enforced year as a student at Purgatory Academy and I'm bone deep tired.

When I get out of the bathroom, there's a plate of food from my dad on the booth table. Lasagna with corn. It smells delicious. It's only been a couple of days since I last saw him, but it feels much longer. I need his strength, his comforting presence. Tears well up at the corners of my eyes. Finishing my meal, I head out to find him.

The circus doesn't have a show until the weekend, but the carnival runs all week. I know where to find him. Dressing in comfortable sweatpants and a pink hoodie with a unicorn riding on a rainbow, I head out. As I get closer, the smell of straw fills my nose. There's my dad with my surrogate siblings, the elephants. My father raised them, all four. Before that he worked with their mother who worked with my grandfather.

There are four of them, two males and two females. I got my love of books and reading from my dad. My mom enjoyed reading too. While I share my mother's love of romantasy, that sexy subgenre blended of fantasy and romance, my dad prefers Gothic horror. It shows in what he named the elephants – Mina, Lucy, Johnny, and Abe.

My dad's cleaning up while the four play around. As soon as they see me, they trumpet and rush over. Abe is the oldest and pushes his way forward to have his trunk scratched. He holds it out and I use my nails to scratch at the bottom.

Lucy and Johnny grow impatient and crowd Abe, one on each side. I love on all three of them the best I can. Mina doesn't bother with any of that. Instead, she comes around from behind and sniffs at my hair with her trunk. She does it every time. While the other three prefer to be loved on, Mina is fascinated with my hair. I don't know if it's the texture or the color or what, but she vacuums it up with her trunk and plays with it till I finally stop her. I'm going to have to wash it again after having it teased so much by Mina.

After a few minutes of this, my dad intervenes, gently pushing them away. Mina is the most reluctant, but they finally go off to play with each other some more. Dad remains behind. He's wearing his normal sort of outfit for work, boots with jeans and a flannel shirt. His graying red hair is up in a man bun on the top of his head.

"I've missed you," he says. I rush into his arms. My dad is one of those amazing huggers. He doesn't just hug you; he holds you. You feel both loved and protected. It's exactly what I need at the moment.

"How are you, Little Fox?"

The words won't come. He doesn't push but hugs me again. When we step back, he returns to work. My thoughts make their way toward Gressil, our dean, and the words he whispered to me that first day, that he knew my mom.

I gather my thoughts. "Dad, I know it's tough for you to talk about mom."

He stills at my words. "But you have questions."

"Did Mom ever talk about her family or her life before she met you?"

He sighs. It's with so much pain and longing, it hurts to see him like that. It always happens when I ask about Mom. The light dims in his eyes, and he looks older. Most of the time he doesn't elaborate, and I feel guilty about asking. "Not much. In the early years I would ask occasionally but she almost always gave the same answer, that her old life wasn't worth mentioning and her family wasn't something she wanted to remember. I saw how much it pained her so after a few years I stopped asking." It must have been just like the pain in his voice and face now.

He pauses for a moment. "You asked me the other day about her university experience, and I shared what she explained to me. But her family…her life before…the way she talked about it. It was like…it was like she didn't want to tell me because she wanted to protect me."

My mom tried to protect my dad, and he is trying to protect me. Perhaps my mom was right. Maybe the best thing I can do for Dad is put him before my curiosity. I should stop asking questions and keep him as far away as possible from Purgatory Academy and this whole shit show.

"Lilly, my dear Little Fox, you are my daughter. You will always be my daughter. I'm here if you need to talk. I can listen. Whatever you choose though, know that I love you."

Tears well up in my eyes. My dad always knows what to say. I nod, wordless. We hug one last time before I head back to my RV. "Lilly, just don't forget to use what I've taught you."

A smile finally graces my face. I know exactly what he means. He wants me to kick ass. That's exactly what I intend to do.

Chapter Sixteen
The Houses of Heaven
January – Purgatory Academy

Marius meets me the next morning outside the gates. It's already beginning to feel like a routine. We head to our second class of Angelology and Demonology. When the bells chime, Corinthia isn't there. As she mentioned, it's an angelology lesson day. Our angelic professor is present instead.

He's a tall, dark-skinned man with a goatee. When he speaks, it's in a deep baritone. "Hello, Nephilim. Welcome to the first session of Angelology. I'm your professor, Bas'el. I am a seraph from the House of Sariel. I believe you have your books already so we're going to jump right into it.

"We'll begin with the Divine." Students poised to write stop and look up. He's going to speak about God, the being about which the least is known but who is quite possibly the most widely discussed throughout the history of humanity. "There is little to be said as even less is known. Nearly every piece of conjecture about the Divine is precisely that – conjecture." Fucker. I like the angel less already. Stupid tease.

"Now, let's discuss the Houses which make up the main structure of Heaven. We know much more about them. Each of the seven houses is led by one of the seven archangels. At one time there were nine archangels and nine houses, but a couple Fell in the Fall."

There are a mumbles and rumbles at his words, mostly among the Descended. Obviously, one of the two who Fell was Lucifer, aka the Lord of Hell. Clearly, some of my classmates don't like the mention of the failed rebellion.

"Heaven is extremely hierarchical in nature and each of the houses is ranked according to the power of the archangels themselves. In order of most to least powerful the archangels include Michael, Gabriel, Raphael, Azriel, Uriel, Sariel, and Ariel.

"There are three types of angels, and they too are hierarchical in structure and power. As stated, the archangels are at the top and the other two kinds serve within individual houses. The second type of angel are the seraphim and the third the cherubim. In appearance most angels look the same, humanoid form with feathery wings. Their magic too is similar, most of it elemental in power. It is the depth of their magic that sets them apart from one another."

My hand cramps with everything Bas'el is sharing. Marius and pretty much most of my classmates are doing the same. Drake isn't taking any notes at all though. I'm beginning to wonder if he knows it all or if he just doesn't care to learn it.

"Let's move on to the Ascended Nephilim." There are a few yips of excitement from my Ascended classmates. Bas'el smiles. "The children or legacies of cherubim are referred to as cherachim and those of the seraphim are called serachim. The final kind, and easily the most powerful, are the archim." The yips turn into yells of excitement and hoots and hollers at the Triumvirate. Gabe is gracious with his smile. Eli looks even more uncomfortable than usual. Trist eats it up, a big grin on her face. One of the Descended boos and others snicker. Trist glares daggers, looking for who booed.

Bas'el holds up a hand for attention. "Archim, the children or legacies of archangels, are relatively rare. This is the first time in the history of Purgatory Academy that we have not only one or two but three archim in one class. They are some of the most powerful of Nephilim."

One of the Descended shouts this time. "We have one more powerful than them all. We have a dragon." There are muttered agreements. Bas'el stares at where Drake sits. Captain Stoic remains exactly that way.

Trist is pissed. "We can take him, any of us." There are scattered oohs and ahhs, but Bas'el hushes them. Drake remains immune and it isn't long after that Bas'el dismisses the class.

Chapter Seventeen
Sway

January – Purgatory Academy

No one seems to really like Drake, but then the Descended cheered for him in some weird sense of solidarity. I figure it has less to do with him and more with wanting to piss off their rivals, especially the archim. When he isn't the scape goat for others, he is the banner for the cause. Either way he's a thing, an inanimate object. He's a reason and an excuse.

The bells chime and Emilie waltzes out. Today she isn't wearing the school uniform. She has on far less, a string bikini of shining gold. My jaw isn't the only one that drops. The gilded color of her bikini draws the eye to all the right curves, deep and sensual. Her top only just covers her nipples and even then, it's obvious where they are because they practically cut through, they're so hard and big.

I shake my head to try to focus on something else, but most of my classmates are either staring in lust or envy or a mix of both. Even the Triumvirate are focused on her, gazing. I can't tell if Trist's look is one of desire or something else. Whatever it is, it's intense. Eli, on the other hand, is an open book. He's embarrassed or ashamed. He looks down at his lap as if trying to unsee what is seared into his mind. Gabe is staring too, but there's a sternness to his gaze and tightness to his jaw, like he is judging the professor. I don't know what to think of that. On one hand, it's impressive that he can combat what she's doing. On the other hand, sex shaming is not cool in my book. Sure, this is wild, but sex is a natural and normal part of life, even with my history.

My own emotions are a blend of desire and envy with a sprinkling of shame. For whatever reason, it makes me think of Drake. He is as stoic and unfazed as ever. Annoyance vibrates in my body. It bothers me that nothing seems to affect him. Marius at least has the good graces to be embarrassed. Like Eli, he keeps glancing up and down, uncertain where to look or just to close his eyes.

And then the scent hits me. It's like an essence permeating the room. I can't see it, but I feel it. It must be because of my growing Nephilic senses. It's like a perfume, arousing the body. There are several sharp intakes and I'm pretty sure more than a few dilated pupils. Anyone who wasn't looking at Emilie before definitely is now.

The professor grins. "That is just a small taste to show you all what Sway is capable of accomplishing. Sway." Her voice lingers on the word, like something rich in her mouth that she wants to let melt so that it will last longer.

"Today we will be playing a little game. I like to call it 'Secrets, secrets, are so much fun.' I could explain it more, but it's easier to show you. Volunteers please."

Despite the fact that our professor has just used some sort of magic on us, plenty of students raise their hands to volunteer. I want to think of them as pathetic but looking at Emilie again I know that just isn't true.

The demoness chooses a dark-haired woman. "What's your name, darling?"

"Hazel." She has a German accent. Hazel gazes at Emilie's chest. She is either under a spell or doesn't feel any shame about her staring.

Emilie doesn't mind either. She does her little leaning routine and whispers to Hazel loud enough that the entire class can hear. "I will make you a little deal, Hazel. I will give you a kiss if you tell me a secret about you, something that no one else knows. Yes?"

Hazel has a glazed look on her face. It's what I'm beginning to expect when I see students interact with Emilie. The Nephil nods. Emilie grins.

"Perfect. I'm listening."

Hazel struggles with herself for a moment, but finally words come out. "About a year ago, I wrecked a friend's car and fled from the scene. Even my friend didn't know what happened. I told her someone stole it. Which wasn't a lie, except that I was the one who took it."

"Ooooh. That's a good little tidbit. Thank you, my dear, for sharing." Hazel swallows hard and leans in, waiting impatiently for Emilie to come closer. The professor acquiesces and their lips meet. The kiss deepens with passion and a moan escapes Hazel before Emilie pulls away gently. Hazel licks her lips before coming back to her pillow.

"Sway is an innate magical ability that all Nephilim possess. It is their quintessential magic, in fact. Your job as influencer pushers on humanity is highly dependent on your ability to use Sway. It is not the power to possess but rather the capacity to influence. You use it to push humans toward specific choices. It can't force, only influence. It doesn't create desire but enflames or cools it.

"A major part of learning to use your Sway well is to glean information from the subject and then use it appropriately to persuade them. In other words, you find out what their pressure points are. You do that by discovering what their goals and desires are. Then you will know how to push the correct buttons.

"As with all forms of divine magic, your imagination is key to enacting your abilities. You imagine it and it will come into being. Visualize your Sway falling over them, and you will feel it actually come alive. But nothing can replace good old-fashioned practice. So, I have chosen a partner for each and every one of you. I put a lot of thought into each of these so please be aware of that. Once I've called all the pairings, you will find a spot in the room together. Your objectives are simple. Each of you will take a turn attempting to use Sway on the other for a minute. Once that minute is up, you switch. That's it. Any questions?"

The room is quiet but saturated with a humming nervousness. Using Sway on each other, who knows what will come to light? I certainly don't want to share everything about my life with a complete stranger.

The professor begins calling out names. I'm announced with Trist. Shit fuck. You have to be kidding.

Trist spots me, a grim determination written all over her face. Gabe leans in toward her. Trist doesn't bother looking at him as he whispers. Eli says something too, but she turns and snaps at him. Gabe looks furious with her for speaking to Eli like that. Trist stands up and stomps over to me. I'm already on my feet, so now here we are, staring at each other. Trist's hands close in fists, pumping lightly, an angry gleam in her eyes.

I'm determined not to let her bully me on top of using Sway on me. Trist seems to think she is gaining some kind of upper hand by not speaking first. I roll my eyes. "So, should we find a spot to sit and do this?"

Trist nods curtly. We sit near my original seat. "Would you like to go first, or should I?"

The snark in Trist's voice is impressive. "I'm not scared of you. You can go first." When I roll my eyes this time, I make certain she sees it. I'm pretty sure the Ascended is going to attack any moment. That gives me an idea.

"You know," I say. "I really do believe that you are quite brave. You volunteered with Emilie before and that was impressive." I imagine pushing influence into my words.

Trist's face scrunches up as if she is trying to resist. I pour more Sway into my words. "It's okay. You can admit it. I'm not here to judge you."

The Ascended's shoulders sink. "I just wanted to prove that I can withstand her."

"Why? Where does that need to prove yourself come from?"

"My family." She almost stumbles over the words.

"It must be a lot of pressure." I don't even know where the words are coming from. They pour out and I let the Sway flow with it. "I mean, you are one of three archim in a class, the only female."

"So what?!" Trist bursts out. "You think I'm not up to it, you lying Descended bitch?!" She stands up, hovering over me, her hands clenched in fists.

Others are distracted by the outburst. I stand up slowly, afraid Trist might attack while I'm seated. It isn't a good position from which to start a fight. "All I meant was that it must be tough having all those expectations about being an archim, but also a female one. It's a lot of pressure." My pulse rises, fight or flight battling inside me. I try to push soothing Sway into my words, but they sound scared, apologetic in my own ears.

Trist doesn't speak for a moment. She just stares at me. Her hands finally unclench, and she speaks again. "There is a lot of pressure. No one in my family has earned a flaming sword in generations. And I desperately want to be worthy of one."

The comment takes me by surprise because I have no idea what she's talking about. I want to ask another question, but then the bells chime. The round is over.

"Thank you for sharing with me." Trist's face contorts with rage. Her hands clench into fists again, but then comes Emilie's sing song voice telling us it's time to switch roles. Trist splays her hands out as if to stretch them. A small, devious smile spreads across her closed lips.

"It must be difficult to be from a family that doesn't know jack shit about our world." Trist's words aren't only biting and cruel, but there is a weight to them. They push down on me. "You have to wonder if your family even cares about you. Our world is so brutal and vicious. For those of us who grew up in it and were aware of Purgatory Academy and everything awaiting us, it was still difficult. But for you, having no idea at all. That's a level of cruelty only Hell could appreciate."

My knees wobble as if the words, the truth of them, is going to crush me physically. Trist has expressed some of my worst, deepest fears about this place, about being a Descended Nephil. How could my mother never tell me what she was? Why did she leave me so unprepared for it? This place is deadly and I'm pretty sure I still don't know the half of it. A cringing frown ruins my game face.

Trist grins at my discomfort. She is winning and she knows it. She's about to continue with her venom, but the bells chime, and Emilie calls out that we're finished. I turn toward the professor, but I know that I'm hiding from the nasty truths Trist shoved at me.

"It looks like this has gone quite well," Emilie says with a bright smile only porn stars can pull off. Glancing around, there are a whole lot of unhappy faces. Apparently, that is the demon's goal. "To finish class, we're going to switch partners and do the practice one more time." A stone drops in my stomach. I don't know if I can take more of this.

Emilie reads off the pairings and I'm shocked to hear my name with Gabe's. Shit. The only thing that could have been worse than Trist is Gabe. Well, perhaps Drake.

Gabe spots me and for a small moment I think there's a smile tugging at the corner of his mouth. As he walks over, I stay seated. I forgot how big he is. I'm tall for a woman, but he dwarfs me. I try to smile, but he's taking a page from Drake's proverbial book, all stoicism now. My smile wilts before it can bloom.

He has a swimmer's build with those broad shoulders, but the black slacks show off his soccer legs. An awkward silence settles between us.

I take the moment to look around. Marius is paired off with Eli this time. They look even more pained than I feel. I shouldn't laugh about it, but a small giggle escapes my lips.

Gabe's eyebrows lower sternly. "Sorry," I whisper.

"What's so funny?" There's a brusqueness to his voice.

I decide to take a chance. "I was just thinking that poor Marius and Eli look even more uncomfortable than I feel."

Gabe glances their way and when he looks back the crease in his lips has curved upwards just a little bit, a smile trying to emerge. Our eyes meet and we both burst out laughing.

Pairs around the room give us strange looks. "Sorry," I say again.

"Why are you sorry this time?" Gabe asks.

"We probably shouldn't be seen laughing together. You're the Golden Boy, archim, Ascended…whatever. I'm…Descended."

Gabe looks like he wants to laugh again. "Golden Boy?"

"Wrong title?"

"It's…something like that. I certainly didn't choose it though."

Now a smile tugs at my mouth. "You'd give yourself a different title? How about Triumvirate?"

Gabe rolls his eyes and sighs. "I wouldn't give myself any titles. Gabe is good enough for me."

I allow myself to really look at Gabe. Those blue eyes practically glow, they're so bright. His golden tan. Even his blonde hair shines metallic. If it's that gold looking in a gray place like Purgatory, I can only imagine what it looks like on Earth. On Earth. What a weird fucking thing to think. But it's true.

"Are you okay?" he asks.

I shake the cobwebs from my brain with the same physical movement. "Yeah, just thinking. Sorry."

Gabe huffs. "You said that already. Three times now." He smiles.

"Would you prefer to go first, or should I?"

"I'll go first if that's alright." I swallow the knot in my throat and nod.

The Ascended closes his eyes and takes a deep breath. A calm falls over him. When he opens his eyes, his smile is warm and inviting; its influence spreads through the air and settles on me.

The same occurred when Emilie demonstrated for us. Where the demon's Sway is all seductiveness, Gabe's feels more like a golden coziness like when you stand facing a summer sun, basking in it, letting it soak into your bones. It's the sort of warmth that puts you to sleep.

Leaning forward Gabe asks what my name is. I'm pretty sure he knows already, but I tell him anyway. "Lilly." A smile spreads across my lips as if it were someone else doing it.

"I think you know my name is Gabe, but we haven't yet been introduced to one another officially." That smile is a ray of sunshine. "Where are you from?"

The question bothers me. I want to consider it but can't focus enough. Leaning back, I ask, "Why do you want to know?" I throw as much Sway into it as I can. I figure the best way to fight Sway might be with Sway. Fire with fire and all that.

"I just enjoy getting to know new people."

I smirk. "Oh really? Even the diabolical kind?" I laugh with a heat to it I've never had before. Where did that come from? Was it his Sway? My Sway?

Gabe shifts closer. "Depends on the person."

My laugh this time is straight up throaty, the sort you hear from the villainess in a movie who seduces the hero right before attempting to kill him. "Is that all the more convincing you can be?"

"I can be much more convincing. I'd be happy to show you if you like."

I'm about to respond, but then the bells chime. I blink and sit back, realizing I inched forward again. It's like waking from a daze.

I take a deep breath, trying to figure out what my angle should be on Gabe. It was much easier with Trist. She was an open book. A really angry, bitchy book, but open, nonetheless. I don't think it likely, but I figure why the hell not. I have a plan.

I put on what I hope is a dazzling smile. "You know, we could just pick up with our conversation before we were interrupted."

"Oh really? Where were we?"

"I believe you were about to tell me where you are from."

Gabe laughs. It's a rich, deep sound. I like it quite a bit. "I was, huh?"

I shift closer, trying to imagine my Sway all around him. He smells delicious, like cedar wood and coastal winds from a sparkling sea. We stare at each other for a moment before Gabe laughs again. "Alright then. I grew up in the San Francisco area."

"I love it there. The redwoods are amazing."

"You've been?" Gabe's smile grows more…sincere?

I imagine running my hands through his hair. What the fuck is that? I am the one who is using the Sway. But then again, I fought his with my own. Perhaps he is doing the same thing now. And yet, we continue to stare at each other.

I pour my will into that look. Gabe mirrors me. I feel it for certain now. "Where at exactly in the Bay area?" My words feel heavy.

"Berkeley." His whisper is filled with sensual promise.

"Thank you," I say, only inches from his lips. The bells chime and I thank whoever I'm supposed to worship for small mercies.

Chapter Eighteen
Caring and Sharing
January – Purgatory Academy

Marius catches up with me on our way to lunch. I'm still caught up in what happened with Gabe. I don't know what to think. I'm feeling all kinds of things though. Confusion is at the forefront, wondering whether it was all Sway or hormones or demonic and angelic powers. Maybe a shit bomb of all the above? Fuck.

Gabe is hot, yes, but having any kind of actual relationship with him has to be frowned on at the very least. More likely, I'd be beheaded for it.

"How did yours go?" Marius asks. I open my mouth, but nothing comes out. He nods at my fish out of water face. "I don't really want to talk about mine either."

I give him a grateful look and we keep on walking in silence. A few moments later though he blurts out. "It was so embarrassing."

"I'm happy to listen and I promise not to judge."

Marius huffs a small laugh. "Oh, you'll want to judge me. And rightfully so." I want to reassure him that I won't, but there is a small smile on his lips. "It's okay," he says. "I do want to share."

"I'm listening."

Marius explains as we walk. "My second one was with the archim, Eli. I went first. I couldn't think of anything to say so I tried to use Sway on him to tell me his favorite color."

I cough to hide the laugh I choke on. Trying to be more serious, I ask, "Did he tell you?"

Marius shakes his head. "He just stared at me. No blinking. No nothing. Super awkward."

I'm about to agree, but then figure that might not help.

"We both fled as soon as the bells chimed."

I'm curious to know what Eli tried to glean from Marius but think better of asking. "At least it's over now."

Marius nods in a sort of dejected way. I wonder for the millionth time how he is going to survive the year. He's so…delicate. I would never say that to him, but it's obvious. There is a frailty to almost all his movements and words. He really needs my help. And surprisingly, I find that I want to help. It was surreal to watch Rodrigo die the way he did. He conveyed such confidence, so much ability. Marius is the opposite, but he's alive and Rodrigo is dead. I know it's probably unwise to get close to anyone here, but then I see how many of the Ascended band together. It has to help. Safety in numbers.

Beyond that, I actually like Marius. We share a lot in common. We're both private and introverted. That suits me just fine. Besides all that, I know what my dad would say. Helping Marius is the right thing to do. I might be Descended from a demon, but I have my free agency.

We arrive in the cafeteria a couple of minutes later and sit in our regular seat. Marius takes out a notebook and begins writing in it while he eats. Gabe is with his giant posse. We make eye contact for a moment, but he doesn't smile or acknowledge me in any way. Right, things need to stay divided. The idea hurts my heart more than I want to admit, even to myself.

I look back at Marius. "What are you writing?" It's a harmless question, but his face turns red, a shade even my cheeks would be proud of.

"I'm just doodling," he mumbles.

Clearly, it's more than that, but I figure I should leave it alone. Instead, I turn to my food and push it around a bit, occasionally taking a bite. I'm not as hungry as I should be. Finally, I start playing with the elephant keychain on my backpack.

"What's up with the plush elephant?" I find Marius watching me curiously.

Feeling snarky I respond, "I'll tell you about the elephant when you tell me about the notebook."

"Touche. Marius smiles. He looks like he's about to share, but just then our attention is pulled away by something far more surprising.

Drake sits down next to us. Marius' mouth drops open. I'm not much better. Wondering about this development, I look past Drake to find Adam and several of his friends have taken Drake's old seat again. Their heads are down, snorting and choking on their food as they laugh. Two days in a row. Assholes.

I experience some perverse pleasure to see Adam sipping all his food through a straw. I have to admit he's devoted to his demented cause. Being decked and having your jaw broken would have deterred most people from continuing along the same path of conduct. Here he is though. I shake my head at the absurdity of it all. I never attended high school, but I have seen plenty of shows and movies with high school students. They might be a bit older, and they might be partially divine in nature, but right now the Nephilim don't appear to be much better than high school students, in my eyes.

Drake doesn't say anything. He goes straight to his food and book. He's almost finished with the Fellowship of the Ring. While I appreciate his taste in books, I'm pissed at him for being so rude to me yesterday. I tried to help him, and he was nothing but bad-mannered. Before I can think better of it, I'm speaking. "Are you going to be gracing us with your presence from now on?" Venom spits from my voice. It's easy to do. I just pretend to be Trist.

He chews as he puts his finger in the paperback. The small movement is enough that his masculine musk drifts toward me. It's delicious. That strange blend of campfire and cinnamon. I hate that I find it attractive. It's toxic to find him anything but rude. At least Gabe has a good sense of humor even if he's ignoring me right now. Fuck. I'm comparing them. I shouldn't even be thinking about them. I have way bigger problems, like surviving, for example.

I'm suspended in the moment by his eyes. I have green eyes, and they nearly glow; people tell me frequently. However, Drake's eyes are violet. With Gabe's sky-blue eyes, I could get lost the way I would floating along on a soft sea. Those lavender eyes will never reveal a thing though. They're a shield and a weapon, as stoic as the rest of his face.

But then something unexpected happens. He finishes chewing, blows a breath out, and speaks. "I apologize for yesterday." His voice is a deeper baritone than I realized, being this close. "I was rude, and it was most unbecoming. You were attempting to help. I am sorry and appreciate what you were trying to do."

My mouth is definitely hanging open and slack now. Marius starts coughing, choking on his food again. I am just about to hop over the table to give him the Heimlich when he finally swallows whatever piece of food was trying to kill him. He waves a hand to tell me he's okay and takes a long drink to clear his throat.

When I look back at Drake, he's wearing a smirk as he watches the two of us. "I apologize again. I would really appreciate it if moving forward you would both allow me to sit with you during lunch."

"Blily."

Drake blinks.

Marius coughs.

My face turns red.

Drake blinks again. "I'm sorry. What was that?"

I glare at Marius who is coughing harder now. "Lilly. I'm, uh, I'm Lilly."

"I know, but it's nice to meet you officially…Lilly." It's pretty clear he's about to say "Blily" just to be funny. He's wiser than that though.

I glare at Marius harder. He speaks up. "I'm Marius."

Drake nods as if he knows this too. Which he probably does since he knows who I am. Which I can't believe.

"You know who I am already? How?"

Drake looks at me and gives a small smile. Okay then. "I'm Drake."

Marius and I exchange a look and smile in return. At the same time, we speak. "We know." We laugh, but Drake just nods as if this were totally normal. He turns back to his food and his paperback.

Chapter Nineteen
Bait
January – Purgatory Academy

Although Drake eats with us, we don't speak the rest of lunch. He doesn't accompany us to War and Weapons either. The'slin and Khal'ith start us off with stretches and exercises before beginning with a series of martial arts techniques. There are thousands of Nephilim, but the two professors do their best to move among us and help with our forms.

Next, they have us all pair off to spar. It's nothing but practice and we go through the motions slowly. Marius and I work together. I'm helping him as much as I can. He's clumsy and uncoordinated, but eager to learn and takes direction readily.

Once the lesson is over, The'slin makes an announcement, "A few of you will be chosen to spar with the professors again." There's more than a little bit of grumbling about it. They're right to grumble. Through four bouts, each of the victims, and they really are victims, get their asses handed to them by either the demon or the angel.

I'm just beginning to think that we got lucky and aren't going to be called on, when The'slin calls Marius' name. Shit. My friend's face grows paler than usual. "It'll be okay," I whisper. We both know it might not be okay. His face goes even whiter; much more of that and he'll be Casper the Friendly Ghost.

Marius shuffles toward the middle of the gymnasium, The'slin waiting for the Descended. My friend takes up his position opposite the demon. However, Khal'ith says nothing about beginning the bout. Instead, The'slin speaks again. "Drake! Step forward."

Whispers break out all over the gymnasium. He's striding forward from across the room. The'slin motions for him to take up a place next to the demon. "I will not be fighting Marius. No. Drake, you will be."

This isn't good. And the timing is terrible. Marius and I finally make some kind of headway with Drake, if not friendship and now that's about to be shattered when he beats the shit out of poor Marius.

Khal'ith calls out for them to bow and take up their fighting stances. Marius looks like he might pass out. They bow though and prepare their stances. The angel calls, "Fight!"

And Drake puts down his fists. Marius hesitates at first, but he inches his way closer and with some reluctance throws a weak punch that connects with Drake's jaw. He barely moves from the gentle impact, but suddenly he's falling to the mats.

Laughing breaks out among the Nephilim all over the room, echoing everywhere. Marius looks embarrassed, but Drake holds up his hands in defeat. Meeting the demon's gaze, he says, "I surrender." The'slin's eyes burn with anger, but he doesn't say anything. He just smiles. To me, it's much scarier than anything he might have said.

Chapter Twenty
Sinning and Sainting
January – Purgatory Academy

The next day in our first class, Sinners and Saints, Manciel leads us in a philosophical debate about what it means to be a sinner or saint. "It's important to define both before we can discuss them at length. So, I will ask again, what does it mean to be a sinner or saint? You're welcome to answer about one or the other or both. I'd like you all to find a partner and discuss together for a few minutes and then we'll come back and share what we learned."

Marius and I laugh because neither of us really knows where to begin. That's about as far as our conversation gets. Manciel brings us all back together and shares some points on what makes a human being a sinner or a saint. It's all kind of ephemeral and nebulous in my mind, but then again perhaps that's how it's supposed to be.

The one thing that does stand out to me is Manciel's words about how neither means you are perfect either in sin or good deeds. "It's important to know that sinners can make good choices and saints can sin. It isn't the lack of one or the other that makes them what they are. Rather, it is a culmination of their deeds, their actions along with their intent. Indeed, actions alone do not define a person. Instead, it is the intent behind them that matters perhaps even more."

I don't know if I agree, but I find the conversation interesting, at least when I've finally grasped it. I have to think of that old adage about the road to Hell being paved with good intentions. Maybe it isn't though. Manciel explains, "Intention is a difficult thing to discern. Humans, as well as Nephilim, demons, and angels can be very adept at lying to themselves and others. However, true intentions are transparent and honest."

It has me considering if nothing else. It makes me wonder about the nature of the Nephilim. We're descended from either angels or demons which suggests we may be inherently good or evil. If I am being honest though, I don't consider myself evil. Of course, I don't think of myself as good either. I'm just…who I am. Imperfect but trying. Beyond that, I know my dad is a good person. I also know my mom was a wonderful mother if nothing else.

Still, the fact is demons were originally angels. If they were inherently evil, how had they been angels before? My head is starting to hurt a little bit on account of all these damn questions.

Manciel continues to explain, "There is a complexity to all sentient beings. While each would like to argue that they are either light or dark, the reality, the truth, is that most of us are much grayer in our actions and thoughts. Each of us is capable of both good and evil, both small and great. But you as Nephilim are children of multiple worlds and as such you are perfect for peddling influence. As the school's motto states, 'Niger et albus, diei ac noctis, inter est grieso.'"

Chapter Twenty-One
Pushing Limits
January – Purgatory Academy

I'm still contemplating the philosophical mindfuck I received when Marius and I arrive to our Evocation class. Ren'el wastes no time beginning. As soon as the bells chime, she asks for volunteers. Several students try out their skills with varying levels of success. More hands come up, but Ren'el holds up her own.

"Let's see how our archim do with their first attempt. Gabe, please come on down." The professors are as curious and cautious about the archim as they are about Drake. They want to know how powerful they are. It appears to be out of a mix of hope and fear, depending on which of the professors is making the request.

Gabe walks up, golden glow as present as ever. I swear I even glimpse a halo. His evocation is textbook perfect; Ren'el says so. He walks back to his seat with a satisfied smile on his face.

"Trist, you're next," Ren'el calls. I hate how Trist struts up to the nine-point star to evocate an imp. Dark thoughts of grabbing the Ascended by the back of her curly hair and slamming her face into the floor invade my mind. My imagination is so intense that I nearly miss Trist calling up an imp easily enough. I've never been violent by nature or vicious in general, but there it is now. I thought puberty was bad enough, but these urges I'm having as my powers wake up and expand scare me.

The imp does its typical angry dance, slamming its tiny fists and feet on the invisible barrier that is Trist's will. "Nicely done," Ren'el applauds her. "Now send it back please."

It bothers me that Ren'el calls the imp an "it." From the display with Drake, it's obvious they have gender. Ren'el doesn't seem to care though.

Trist closes her eyes and whispers. A nasty idea occurs to me, and I cough loudly.It's enough to break Trist's concentration. Her eyes fly open and just like that, her tiny dome is gone. The imp realizes almost immediately that freedom is at hand and zips into the air. Watching the tiny creature fly is like watching a pixie on a Peter Pan movie. That's how quickly the wings beat and how fast the imp flitters back and forth.

The movement has a pattern. I figure it out just before the dive bomb comes. The imp spirits straight for Trist's face. The movement is so fast, the Ascended doesn't have time to react. Her face moves to the left as if she's been slapped and the imp zips away just as fast, hovering and waiting for another opening.

Trist has three long, bloody lines on her cheek where the imp clawed her with those nasty talons. The wound heals quickly. All that's left over is a very pissed off Trist.

Ren'el holds her hands ready at her sides in case the imp decides to change targets, but other than that, she seems to be waiting to see if Trist will be able to capture the imp on her own. This is the first time one has escaped. Plenty of students have been unable to call up one or even send it back without help from the professor. No one has let an imp out though. It gives me a surprisingly large amount of satisfaction to know that honor goes to Trist.

The archim extends her arm toward the imp repeatedly, trying to shoot out her will to catch the demon. At least that's what I think the Ascended is trying to do. The diminutive creature is so quick, she keeps missing. With each miss, Trist grows angrier and her shots wilder. Finally, Ren'el throws out her arm and I can see the difference. While Trist was shooting long, spider web-like points of her power to capture the imp, Ren'el sends out something more akin to a catcher's mitt in baseball and scoops the imp up. She brings the tiny demon back down to the nine-point star and banishes it.

Trist's humiliation is evident from her refusal to stop staring at the floor. And I don't give a shit. The Ascended is not only unkind but mean on purpose. A little more embarrassment might be good for her.

After Trist takes her seat, Ren'el calls Eli up for his turn. He has his head down as he walks over, nervousness etched in every movement of his body. He takes a deep breath as he conjures the tiny dome and calls up an imp. It snarls at him, and a thundercloud gathers on Eli's face. His countenance is filled with a dark hunger, an anger that runs deep.

"Go ahead and send it back now, Eli." Ren'el's voice is softer than usual as if she too senses the angry energy wafting off the Ascended.

He doesn't acknowledge her but holds out a hand as if to focus himself. The imp snarls and slams against the prison even more, little flecks of spit appearing on the dome to mark its otherwise invisible presence.

A vein throbs in Eli's head, and he sweeps his hand up in a fist. The imp explodes and all that remains are splatter and stunned silence.

Chapter Twenty-Two
Clumsy Bridge Building
January – Purgatory Academy

The stunned silence quickly melts away into utter chaos. Thousands of voices try to speak at the same time. More than one argument breaks out between Ascended and Descended about what Eli did. Ren'el's magnified voice restores order, "Class is dismissed. I will take care of the mess."

Gabe and Trist rush over to comfort Eli and usher him out. His head hangs even lower than usual. His accidental execution of the imp plays on repeat in my head. Splat. Splat. Splat. The explosion follows me all the way to lunch.

The group of Ascended at Drake's former seat laughs and snorts, but not nearly as much. The joke must be losing its humor. That, or the shock of Eli's actions is still fresh.

Drake sits with us again. He doesn't bother with pleasantries today, but rather goes back to his stoic, silent self. He started The Two Towers and reads it while he eats. Marius is still starstruck by his presence, but I don't want to go back to the quiet awkwardness. It bothers me. Usually, I like the quiet, but my entire body buzzes when Drake is around. I don't like it.

I decide I'm going to say something to him, but then I get a big whiff of that campfire and cinnamon scent of his and stumble over my words once again. "Blehol."

Drake turns to look at me, unblinking. Marius drops a piece of chewed food out of his mouth and onto his plate he's so surprised. My face burns and I hide behind a mouthful of my own food, but it's too late. Drake speaks, "Are you okay?"

Still chewing, it's safer to mumble. "Mmmhhmm."

"Are you sure? Because it sounded like you just had a stroke."

This time Marius chokes on his food. Good. Fucker.

Drake understands more is going on. He puts a bookmark in his page. "If I had to guess, I imagine that our shared silence is more awkward for the two of you than it would be if we were speaking. At least, that's what you think right now. Yes?"

Marius blurts a "no" at the same time I screech a "yes." I fling ocular daggers at Marius who blanches and mumbles a "yes" now.

Drake smirks. It's not a smile but it is handsome. "Would it be easier for you both if I sat somewhere else?" Drake asks.

This time Marius says yes while I say no at the same time. Drake's face doesn't move, but I swear his eyes shine a bit. With trembling voice, Marius speaks. "I'm, um, I'm just concerned with being associated with the Apocalypse." He huffs and I realize it's supposed to have been a joke.

Drake's face is deadly calm. It's different from his typical stoicism because I sense every muscle in his body has tensed. Marius blanches an even deeper milky white and pulls back from the table like he might actually make a run for it.

I take in a deep breath and say what I hope Marius intended to say. "We want you to stay. Please. Stay."

Drake peers between the two of us. "Okay, but I'm not going to speak and don't expect you to do so either. Please feel free to chat among yourselves though."

Marius mumbles, "Thank you."

I glare swords at him this time, but when I look over at Drake, he's smirking again. At least he isn't easily insulted. That has to count for something.

Chapter Twenty-Three
Magic Weaving
January – Purgatory Academy

Nekleth wastes no time jumping into our magic weaving lesson. I'm developing a sense of urgency that permeates from the professors. I wonder if it's because we have so much to cover or if we need what they are teaching just to survive. It's probably both given what I've seen so far in Purgatory.

"As with so many of the forms of magic that Nephilim possess, it is often best to begin using words and body language. Both will help you to control and direct your magic. With time and practice, you will need these less and less. Consider them training wheels.

"Also, like other forms of divine magic, it all begins with focus and imagination. You will learn to visualize and direct the flow of your magical energy. However, unlike most other forms of magic you possess, your weaving will be dependent mostly on the kind of Nephilim you are and the house from which you hail. For the Ascended, you will typically have some form of elemental magic. For the Descended, forms differ more broadly because your nature is more chaotic and less hierarchical, at least in comparison with Heaven. So, I want each of you to find a standing position somewhere in the room and we will begin."

Marius and I remain near our original seats. I try to focus, but I'm distracted by Marius' look of constipation. I have to swallow the laugh that threatens to burst out and I look away quickly to refocus myself.

Most of my classmates are doing as poorly as I am. Drake isn't doing anything. He just stands there. I wonder how Nekleth will take that. The Triumvirate is having more success though. Gabe conjures a small ball of light the size of a marble. He's rolling it playfully on his palm. Trist has a tiny flame about the same size. It's jumping from one outstretched finger to the next. Small but beautiful displays of magic.

Eli's face is scrunched up in concentration like so many other faces around the room, but nothing is happening. I already feel the hint of a headache from my own attempts but looking at him I feel it getting worse out of sheer pity. Misery loves company after all.

Chapter Twenty-Four
Getting to Know You
January – Purgatory Academy

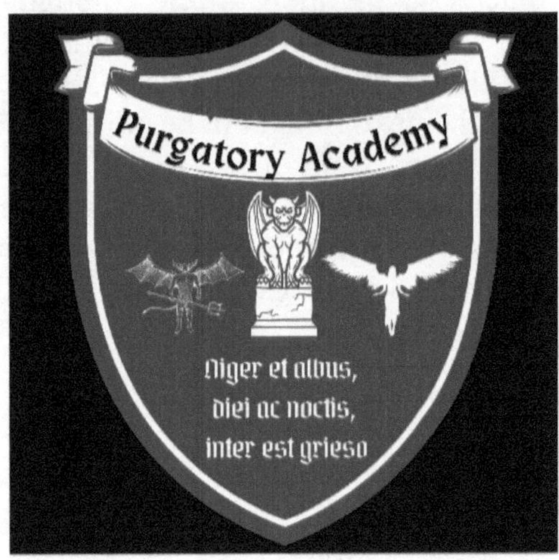

I walk out with Marius, my head still aching lightly. It could be worse. We mistport outside the gates. It's the first evening we're supposed to practice together.

"I didn't even think about it. How in the world are we supposed to get you there when you've never been before?"

"You'll have to help me the first time," Marius states.

"How do I do that?"

"Compared to so much of what we do here, it's relatively simple. I just hold your hand and let you do all the work. I will be taken with to wherever we're going. Once we're there and I've seen it, next time I can go it alone."

I hold out my hand with a smile. Marius' hand is cool. I picture the big top tent where our RVs are parked. For a moment I consider going straight into my RV like I usually do, but I don't care for the idea of anyone mistporting straight into my personal space. My Malak already does that plenty.

I still haven't opened my eyes during mistporting and I'm not certain I ever will. I feel that foreign, strange coldness of in-between or wherever that is and then the cool humidity of southern Louisiana hits me.

I open my eyes and we're in front of my RV just as I pictured it. Thankfully, no one is around to see us appear out of a mist that shouldn't have been there. It does make me wonder if anyone ever sees angels and demons and Nephilim just misting about. Misting about. I'm funny.

Marius takes a couple of steps toward my RV and then turns around to take in his surroundings. "You know, I've never been to a circus before. What do you and your dad do?"

I flash him the plush elephant on the keychain attached to my backpack.

"You work with elephants?" His voice rises with excitement.

I smile and nod. "Would you like to meet them before we practice?"

"Yes please." He shifts back and forth with eager anticipation.

I'm relieved to not have to show him my RV. We head over to the elephants and find my dad there. When he sees us, his facial expression shows nothing of surprise, only a warm smile as always.

"Hi Little Fox. Who's this?"

Marius looks to me for an explanation about the nickname.

I shake my head to suggest later. "This is Marius. We go to school together."

"Ah," my dad says. Reaching out his hand, he speaks again. "I'm Sam, Lilly's dad. It's nice to meet you, Marius."

My friend shakes his hand. "You too."

"So, would you like to meet our elephants? I'm sure that's why you're here. It can't be to only meet me."

Marius opens his mouth to refute the words, but then he recognizes the joke for what it is. "I'm teasing," my dad assures him anyway, waving him over.

The enclosure is a makeshift corral. The elephants could break through easily if they wanted to, but they don't. Their trust in my dad is complete.

They push and jostle each other on their way over to see the newcomer. Marius looks a bit nervous at first, but he laughs brightly as Mina redoes his hair for him. I've never heard him laugh so heartily. It warms my heart. He looks younger now even though I know we're the same age.

We remain there for a few minutes, Marius scratching the elephants' trunks and having his hair turned into a really bad faux hawk by Mina. Dad watches and grins, standing next to me. While we don't speak, it is comforting to be near him.

When Marius finishes up, his new hairdo complete, I turn to my dad. "Marius asked me to train him."

Dad knows exactly what I mean. "He's lucky to have you."

"It'd be better if you taught him as you taught me," I suggest.

My father shakes his head. "No, it's only right that you teach him. Besides, you're better than me now anyway." I laugh in response.

"How about I start on dinner for the three of us while you teach him?"

I grin. "That'd be great."

Marius joins us and my dad tells him the same. He smiles at the news as well, genuine happiness shining on his face.

The two of us walk over to the small ring the circus members use for their sparring. Although I've grown up all over the country, this wrestling mat has traveled with us through the years. It's a new place we're in, but the mat remains the same.

I start Marius off with the same process we use in class, stretches and warm up exercises. Then we begin on some different forms. I guide him through, slowly, making certain he's getting the techniques down properly. We do this for about an hour before we stop.

"You'll get better," I reassure him afterwards. Doubt remains on his face. "We do need to do other things to help you along though, build up your endurance and strength. Running and weights."

"You'd think it would be enough that we're Nephilim. I can feel it though, can't you?"

"Feel what?"

"Our divine blood waking up. I have no doubt I'll get stronger and faster, but will it be enough against others? That's my fear."

I can only nod in return. I don't want to share about the urges I'm noticing more and more. The sexual drive building without release. That part of my being is still a sensitive subject. "Come on, let's get some dinner."

We walk over to my dad's RV. He has spaghetti and garlic toast waiting for us. We have a great time, chatting about elephants and nothing at all. The warmth spreading in my chest confirms that it was exactly what I needed.

Chapter Twenty-Five
Familiars
February – Purgatory Academy

It's early February and the third Tribulation has arrived. It's the end of the week and there aren't any classes. My Malak waits for me, as always. Making certain I go where I'm supposed to go, as always.

Fluttering butterflies of endless nerves bounce around my stomach as I shower. The nausea remains as I dress. No school uniform today, only workout clothes. I have no idea what we'll face, but the clothing suggests I will need to be able to move around well. That comes as no surprise, but at least it's something.

My Malak surprises me when I step out of the bathroom. In one robed hand is a coffee cup and in the other is a small paper bag. Both are from a famous indie coffee shop in Manhattan. I love the place. A couple of summers ago the circus was there and I went with Dad. After that, we went at least once a week.

And now the Malak is offering me that same coffee. Inside the bag is a chocolate croissant, just like I remember. Words fail me for a moment.

I intend to thank the creepy bastard, but instead the only word that slips out is, "Why?"

Naturally, the Malak doesn't answer. I do better on the second try. "Thank you."

I turn my attention to the coffee and the croissant. The chocolate melts in my mouth just how I remember it. I wash it down with a sip of the warm coffee. A tiny "mmm" escapes my lips at the deliciousness of both.

My nervousness doesn't fade, but the nausea does, leaving me wondering about my Malak. A month into classes and all I've seen is that the Malakim one and all are heartless, cold creatures. They could be paranormal robots for all I know since I've never seen underneath those robes.

I try a third time. "Seriously, thank you." To my utter surprise, the Malak inclines its head ever so slightly. I blink, wondering if it actually happened.

I throw away the bag and the empty cup when I'm finished. Turning to the Malak I nod that I'm ready. Neither of us speaks a word as we arrive. It waits, but I hesitate. I feel like I should say "thank you" again, but I figure three times in a row is too much for our budding friendship. Snorting out loud at my internal joke, I mistport inside the grounds where Marius is waiting for me already.

He mumbles "Morning." I respond with the same anxious tone. The nervousness is definitely on the rise. More students are streaming in all around us as we collectively make our way up the hill to the front doors of the school.

The numbers in red above the doors are the same. None of us died since the last Tribulation. No one tried to escape either. That's a lesson learned on the first day.

The doors open only moments after we gather with the others. The dean, Gressil, walks out. He doesn't bother to wait as more of our classmates come up the hill. "Welcome all. Please follow me."

Marius and I stick close together as we wind our way through the halls. I have no idea where we're going, but time stretches on, and with it my nerves grow. The rhythm of my steps helps some.

Finally, we arrive at a pair of oaken doors. More doors. Shocker. Marius and I are close enough to the front that we can still see Gressil who opens them without preamble. The students follow him. I think of the term "lambs to slaughter" as we do.

Strangely enough, the doors lead outside. We enter a huge outdoor courtyard. Evenly spaced columns with an overhanging roof line it. The inside of it is rectangular in shape and opened to the ever gray, cloudy skies of Purgatory.

The ground is all cobble stone with plenty of options to trip and fall. It's a sucky combo. The middle of the courtyard draws everyone's attention though.

In a large pile there are thousands of what appear to be eggs. They're about a foot in height and width. They exude this strange silvery gray coloration, shining serenely in the gloom of Purgatory. They're beautiful in their own peculiar manner.

Gressil gathers us around the eggs. As we approach, rustling from above catches my eye. The Malakim are collected above, around the edges of the columned roof. Even from this perspective I see nothing but robes. I feel their eyes on us though and I shiver. Scattered among the black are our professors, their faces grim. That can't bode well for us.

"This is your third Tribulation, and its focus will be on your ability to use your Sway." There is a lot of nervous shifting of feet on cobble stone in response. "These eggs are unborn Familiars. They are creatures original to Purgatory. As with Hell, new species have developed and grown here too. In a moment, your Malak will bring you an egg. Once they have all been handed out, your task will be simple. Convince the Familiar to hatch and bond to you."

Whispers of fear slither about at his announcement. Gressil holds up a hand and it goes silent again. "When the Familiar hatches, it is important that you choose the form it takes. If you are not able to use your Sway to convince it of this, the consequences could be quite hazardous." His smile at his own pronouncement is mild, but that is what makes it scary.

Mist rises around the eggs and soon Malakim are gliding all about, delivering their chosen egg to the Nephilim. Gressil mistports to the roof and joins the faculty who are all bunched together now, watching intently. The Malakim seem to know exactly which egg they want as if they were pre-chosen and as if they can tell the eggs apart from each other.

My Malak floats over, egg in robed hands. Now that it's so close, I can see the differences. There are individual imperfections that give it personality. The longer I investigate the more I realize they aren't imperfections. No, that's the wrong word. They are unique aspects, peculiarities. Little flecks of black here and there, but the glow is warm and lovely as my Malak hands it over.

It's so smooth, it's slick. The fear of dropping it actually overrides any nervousness I was feeling. I hold it from the bottom, cupping it in my hands. It really is warm.

And then I notice something else. There's a subtle humming coming from it. I realize what it is. It isn't humming although it's rhythmic. It's a heartbeat. A smile pulls at my lips.

I close my eyes and reach out with my mind toward the egg. I imagine making contact with another mind and sure enough, it happens. There it is. The Familiar's mind is anything but familiar. No, it's alien. But there is something emanating from it to which I can relate…a sleepiness like it's just waking up. And after that, a gentle curiosity about this being holding it and reaching out to it with its own foreign mind.

There's a connection there, dangling in the mental space between us, and instinctively I reach out with unspoken words. It's the same gentle, soothing voice I use with the elephants. *"Hello there. My name is Lilly. It's such a pleasure to meet you."*

The gentle curiosity wakes up some and reaches out as well, gathering closer through the telepathic bond. The creature's mind is difficult to explain. It's like a river of running silver, beautiful yet foreign.

I wait but so does the Familiar. The egg continues to hum that lovely heartbeat. Finally, I speak again. *"You know, I always wanted a cat. I was too busy though."*

The Familiar sends me what can only be described as more curiosity, a question. I conjure a mental picture of a sleek black cat and show it to the Familiar through the mental bridge we built, and both stand on now.

The curiosity from the Familiar grows and it sends something to me. It's a warm, fuzzy feeling. I smile again. The egg is trying to make me happy.

I give it a mental image of a cat purring and how happy that sound makes people. The humming from the egg subdues and the sound of a cat's purr takes its place. It becomes so loud that the egg actually vibrates slightly. I hold it closer just in case, but the purring continues.

"How would you feel about coming out of the egg and meeting me officially? I would like that very much."

The purring increases and with it, the vibration. I grasp it as hard and close as I can out of fear but also with mounting excitement. Long cracks begin to draw themselves along the sides of the egg and then curve upward and downward and all around. The bottom curve of the egg remains intact, thankfully, but the rest of it is spider webbing into thousands of tiny cracks. Suddenly, the vibrating purr stops, and the egg sits silent.

I hold my breath. An uneven section of the egg at the top pops off, leaving a lopsided circle and something stirring once more inside the remainder of the shell. I bring it to my chest and peer down into it. Two giant, glowing blue eyes framed in darkness stare back at me.

A squeal of happiness escapes me at the sight of the adorable monster. The eyes blink slowly at me, just once. Then a sticky, wet black paw pushes out of the side of the shell facing me, another batting away much of the remaining top of the egg. Little by little the matted furry creature emerges from the broken egg. A tiny tip of a tail hangs over the edge of the shell at the bottom, the only large piece left and then only because it rests in my palms.

We stare at each other for a moment longer and then I'm hit with the full brunt of the Familiar's mind entering mine. It flies over the bridge connecting us. I'm shocked by the force of it. Still, I get the sense that it isn't trying to be unkind or attempting to hurt or threaten me. It's just curious, super curious. His mind flows just like the silvery river I understood it to be. Moments later it withdraws, but small droplets, creeks, and streams remain behind. I don't know how I understand this, but I know that our bonding is complete.

He purrs so loud and intensely, it rips through the remaining shards of the egg which fall in pieces to the cobblestones. The Familiar turned kitten shifts and sits up on his hunches. And my belief is confirmed, seeing for the briefest moment that my Familiar is definitely a he.

He cleans the rest of the egg off my hands and his little butt is warm on my palms. He's so adorable, even with all of that egg goo left over, matting his fur down. I decide to speak out loud to him. "It's so lovely to meet you. I was wondering if you have a name."

Those azure eyes don't blink, but he does begin to clean all the goo off his body in an extremely effective manner. The purr continues as he does. "Hmmm. What do you think about me giving you a name?" I ask.

The cleaning and purring continue unabated, but he does blink at me once as if to say yes please. Slow blinking is a good sign in cats, I know that much. And my Familiar chose the form of a cat so I figure it must be positive. He cleans his back side while I contemplate.

I consider some of my favorite books. "I've always wanted a black cat named Salem after Stephen King's book, 'Salem's Lot.'" The cat Familiar keeps right on cleaning himself. There is a vague sense through our bond that he doesn't love it. "Alright then. Let me think." I consider a bit longer, but I keep coming back to "Salem's Lot." Another name from the book comes to me. "What about Barlowe?"

The cat stops cleaning himself and purrs even louder, blinking once again. This time there's a faint sense of satisfaction. "Barlowe it is then."

And that's when the screaming begins. Barlowe hisses and spits, jumping up onto my shoulder, his claws digging in to find perch. I've been so focused on hatching my Familiar egg and bonding with Barlowe, that I didn't pay attention to my surroundings.

What I see is difficult to compute because it's utter chaos. Egg shells lay broken all over the courtyard and many a nightmare is born from the eggs. Now I understand what Gressil was saying. If the students aren't able to Sway their Familiars into hatching and taking the shape they want, the Familiars will take a form the Nephilim not only don't want, but which scares the hell out of them. They're nightmares and fear born into flesh.

There are a number of snakes, spiders, and rats among other rarer creatures and terrors. They're biting and gnawing and constricting students all around me. It isn't all my classmates, but it is a lot of them.

A voice calls my name, and I find Marius has a nightmare of his own. It's on his shoulder, attacking him. I rush forward to help, prepared to knock the feathered monster to the cobblestones, but Marius sees the look on my face and puts his hands out to stop me.

"This is Blackbeard," he says as if it were the most normal thing in the world. "He's a Pesquet's Parrot, but they're usually just called Dracula Parrots." The bird's head is more like a miniature version of a vulture than what I associate with most parrots. He's all black except for a blood red color on the lower half of his chest and both of his wings. I can definitely see why they are called Dracula Parrots. I'm about to ask why in the world Marius would choose to have his Familiar take this shape, but more screaming reaches us, and we turn to find that the many nightmares hatched from eggs not under proper Sway are finishing off their own Nephilim and are moving on to attack others.

"We have to get out of here fast," I say. There are four entrances of double doors around the rectangular courtyard. We move as quickly as we can toward the closest one. We're not able to run outright though because neither of us wants to uproot our Familiars from their perches. As it is, Barlowe digs his claws deep into my shoulder. I'm certain that Blackbeard is doing the same to Marius.

We're the first to get to the doors. Most of our classmates are spread out near the other three sets. When Marius reaches for the knobs, they don't budge. We're trapped here. We turn back to face the oncoming onslaught behind us. There is more and more blood all over the place, puddles of it in the cracks of the cobble stones, more splashed on the columns. Bodies lay unmoving to our left and right.

"We have to mistport out of here. I'll hold off any rogue Familiars that come this way. You go first." Marius looks like he's about to argue, but I stop him. "Now isn't the time for false chivalry." He only nods and closes his eyes to concentrate and probably to block out the horror happening all around us.

I keep watch. A group of Nephilim have gathered by a pair of double doors along one of the two longer walls of the courtyard. There's Gabe along with his sidekicks, Eli and Trist, gathering Ascended to them. I blink twice, but I'm pretty sure that is a Golden Retriever puppy next to Gabe's ankle, yapping loudly at any nightmare Familiars that get too close. I have to admire him for that even if it's only for Ascended, not the Descended. Eli has a weasel draped around his neck while Trist has some sort of snake wrapped around her arm.

Our Familiars are already trying to protect us. Barlowe growls deep in his throat but he's just a kitten, or rather, a Familiar in the shape of a kitten. My hand-to-hand combat and martial arts skills aren't going to help much against claws and fangs, poison and venom. And I can't conjure shit yet. It doesn't even look like Gabe or Trist are able to with this much chaos going on.

"Lilly." Marius is still there, no mist to be found. We lock eyes and I know. We're not mistporting out of here either. The faculty have blocked it somehow. We're stuck in this shit. There's no way out.

I consider calling others to gather more here just as Gabe has. We're so far from everyone else though, except for a few who are unmoving or missing limbs. Some of the nightmare Familiars are slithering and scraping their way toward us now. I push Marius into a corner behind me. Barlowe doesn't speak into my mind, but there's a fierceness roiling in his own. He's ready to fight if it comes to it and that gives me courage and comfort.

Then a new sound fills the air. At first, I don't recognize it. But then I see what it is. It's the combined noise of what has to be every nasty Familiar in the courtyard. En masse, they are crawling and climbing, flapping and soaring right toward us. Oh fuck.

I tense as the few that have already come this way, turn to face the others and then join them. They don't swerve toward our corner though. Instead, they come to a halt all together in front of the doors where we'd just been.

Then something even more bizarre comes our way. A kitten, just like Barlowe, but completely white in color, trots up, herding the other Familiars next to the doors. When any of them gets an idea of inching around the kitten, it hisses and spits and the Familiars, docile now, rejoin the group.

And then the weirdest part steps up. Drake. Standing directly behind the white kitten who begins to purr like a tank when the brooding Descended gets close. Drake is controlling the rogue Familiars with only his newly hatched Familiar and his own sheer will. Holy fuck.

Chapter Twenty-Six
Aftermath
February – Purgatory Academy

The collected nightmare Familiars wait at the doors. One here or there attempts again to skirt around Drake's white kitten Familiar, but he swipes at them with his miniature paw, and they back up into the group.

Gressil and the rest of the faculty mistport down. Apparently, this is sufficient for the Tribulation to be over. Some Malakim come down as well, those who have lost their Nephilim. They collect the bodies, or the pieces as it is. I assume that they take the deceased to the cemetery on the academy grounds to be buried along the numberless others who have died trying to survive their year at Purgatory.

The doors next to us open from the inside and out walks a gargoyle. He growls at the rogue Familiars and after taking one last look at the white kitten and Drake, they turn and follow the stone giant out of the courtyard.

Gressil speaks out to the survivors. "You are all dismissed for the day. We will see you here bright and early on Monday." With that, he misports away. The faculty members follow suit.

The Nephilim trickle out the doors the gargoyle opened. Most of them have shocked looks on their faces. Some have tear-stained cheeks.

Nearly all of them have their Familiars with them though. There are a few who don't and while their wounds are healing, they are clearly worse off. These must be the few who survived being attacked by their own rogue Familiars they weren't able to convince or control.

Marius and I wait in our corner while most of our surviving classmates shuffle out. I don't see Drake and there's no glimpse of his white kitten either. I do see the group of Ascended go out with the Triumvirate after them. Sure enough, Eli has a weasel-like creature wrapped around his neck. On closer inspection, I realize it's a ferret. The funny thing is that Eli looks happy with his Familiar. He isn't quite smiling, but he looks pleased. The ferret Familiar and Marius' parrot Familiar stare at each other as they pass. Trist's snake is moving up and down her arm and the female Ascended looks less than happy about it. I fight not to laugh out loud, but I have to wonder if Trist's Sway didn't work as well as she wanted. She doesn't seem to like the snake all that much.

Gabe comes last with his Golden Retriever puppy right on his heels. The little guy's paws are too big for him, and he keeps slipping and tripping on the cobblestones. Gabe stops and looks down at him. I'm pretty sure they're having a telepathic conversation, but the puppy keeps right on trotting along with the Ascended. Gabe takes in Marius' parrot, trying to keep a straight face from the look of it. He turns to me then, the puppy creeping up behind him. Barlowe eyes the dog but doesn't puff up or make a sound.

"You should have joined us," he tells me. My mouth works, but no words come out. Gabe smiles. "I know what you're thinking. It was a gathering of Ascended, but I…I'm just glad that you made it."

I still don't know what to say. "Me too," is what I settle on. I smile back. Gabe moves with his puppy but gives me one last lopsided grin before they walk out of the courtyard.

Marius and I share a glance and head out together, winding our way through the halls till we make it to the front door and out and down the hill toward the gates. I try to block out the things I've seen, but it isn't working.

"It will get better with time." They are the first words Barlowe has spoken to me since his hatching.

"How do you know?" I ask.

"I may have just been born, but Familiars can wait a long time to hatch. In the meantime, we listen, and we learn."

I consider this. *"Well, I could always use a bit more wisdom in my life."*

"Don't worry. I may be young, but I'm filled with that." I huff a laugh at the teasing in his voice. I'm glad that I have Barlowe. *"Me too,"* he replies to my thoughts. That's weird and it's going to take some getting used to. *"You'll figure it out,"* he jokes.

"Can you mistport?"

"Of course. I will just hitch a ride with you though as you go." I nod and we mistport as do Marius and Blackbeard.

Marius and I hug, making certain to have our Familiars on opposite shoulders so they don't run into each other. The hug lasts longer than I think it should, but I need it, and I can tell that Marius does too; it's strange I feel that way given my history. When we finally step back, Marius echoes what Gabe told me earlier. "I'm glad you survived."

"I'm glad you did too. Three down, right?"

"Three down."

With that, we mistport home. I let out a sigh of relief and sit down on the edge of my bed as soon as we're back. Barlowe jumps down from my shoulder and begins the cat-like behavior of inspecting the entire RV inch by inch.

While Barlowe investigates everything, I head into the bathroom and take a long, hot shower. I still feel soiled afterwards though. I curl up on the bed under the covers and Barlowe soon joins me. My thoughts are dark and filled with blood and dismembered limbs, but Barlowe's purring soon puts me to sleep, a sweet oblivion.

Chapter Twenty-Seven
Resting Up
February – Purgatory Academy

The next morning my dad knocks on my RV door. I pull myself out of sleep. Fuzziness remains, but I'm pretty sure it's Saturday. No Malak greets me anyway. Barlowe is curled in a ball next to me. His little body rises and falls in a steady rhythm. The sight is both soothing and disconcerting. It's soothing because Barlowe is warm and comforting. It's disconcerting because if Barlowe is here, that means that yesterday really happened. Dozens of my classmates are dead. My brain struggles to compute. My emotions fight each other for my attention. I swallow it all down though, force myself to focus on Barlowe's soothing presence.

I slide out of bed and unlock the door. Swinging it open, I see my dad there with a heaping pile of pancakes on a couple of stacked plates and a bottle of maple syrup. My stomach grumbles at the sight.

He steps up and in, setting the pancakes and syrup down on the table. I close and lock the door. Typically, I wouldn't lock it with my dad here, but my short time at Purgatory Academy already has me feeling paranoid. A lock isn't much, but it's something.

Dad takes my appearance in but then notices the cat sleeping on the bed. "You got a kitten. You always wanted one." He steps passed me to the foot of the bed and watches Barlowe sleep.

"He or she?" Dad asks.

"He."

"He's so sleek and beautiful."

"He is."

"Did you give him a name yet?"

"Barlowe."

"As in the vampire from Stephen King's Salem's Lot?"

I point a finger gun at him. "That's the one."

He smiles and shrugs. "The pancakes are going to get cold." I don't need to be told twice. I sit down and my dad takes one of the plates out from under the other. He produces two forks from a pocket in his flannel shirt. I grab three pancakes and drown them in maple syrup. "Would you like some pancakes with your maple syrup?" Dad jokes.

I smile in between bites. "Nope." And keep right on chowing down. I don't bother with a drink. I inhale the food.

Five minutes and seven pancakes later, I sit back and let out a very satisfied sigh. "That was delicious. Thanks, Dad."

He nods. We're quiet for a moment. "You know, your mother had a fox at your age."

Somewhere in the back of my mind, I think I knew that, but I'm not certain. "What happened to it?"

"She was hit by a semitruck. I remember when your mother told me. She was so upset. It was several days that she lay in bed, despondent and depressed. I was scared she wouldn't come out of it. I held her and loved her the best I could, but it was a while before she was anything like herself again. When I asked her about it, she said a piece of her had died." I understand what Mom really meant. Even now with Barlowe asleep, I feel his mind at the edges of my own, our two consciousnesses connected, combined into one.

My dad watches Barlowe for a moment, lost in thought. The cat Familiar opens his slit eyes slightly, feeling attention on him. Dad holds out his hand, just in reach, an offering for Barlowe to sniff or ignore as he sees fit. The Familiar cranes his head forward a little and licks my dad's hand. Apparently, he likes what he tastes because he stands up, yawns, and stretches in that U-shape way that only cats do. He purrs like a tank as my dad pets him. Barlowe rubs his face and body against his hand as much as possible, twirling in a little kitten circle.

"Wow, you're nothing more than a little purr pet," I tease Barlowe mentally.

He doesn't bother to respond verbally or mentally, but rather just flicks his tail at me in annoyance and goes right back to being loved. They remain that way for a few more minutes before Dad speaks again. "I should go. We are headed out early on Monday morning after the shows are over."

We hug and I hold on longer than usual; it's turning into a pattern. I spend the rest of the weekend helping pack up. Normally I would assist with the shows, but I'm not up to it. As the weekend comes to a close, I have to wonder if I shouldn't give myself to more physical labor. It might help fight off more of the images that float in my mind from the massacre that was the third Tribulation. The moments where I do lose to the memories, my body fills with a nervous energy. If it weren't for Barlowe and my dad, I probably wouldn't be able to handle it at all. Shoveling elephant shit helps too.

Chapter Twenty-Eight
Dwindling Numbers
February – Purgatory Academy

On Monday morning I wake up to a horrible realization. The circus will be leaving soon. We'll be at the next town before I'm finished with the school day. How in the world will I know where to mistport? I can't believe how stupid I am, that I forgot to prepare better. It could literally get me killed.

"*Have you been to the town before?*" Barlowe asks.

"*Yeah, but it's been a couple of years.*"

"*Does anything about it stand out to you?*"

I consider it. "*Well, there was a wooded park nearby. I had a...rendezvous there once.*"

"*Rendezvous? Really? For fuck's sake.*"

"*Hey, aren't you a little young to be using such bad language?*"

"*Fuck no! I told you, I was in that egg for a long time. Now look, if you remember the woods from your make out session with some random local, I'm sure you can mistport there just fine. Plus, if you show me, I can help guide you.*"

I want to argue about the random local comment, but there isn't much to be argued if I'm being honest. "*Good. Then we can skip that.*"

"*Stop that!*" I retort.

"If you want me to stop reading your thoughts, stop leaving your mind open to me."

"How do I keep you out?"

"I'll help you with it, but right now we need to leave. Show me the park and then we can go."

"I don't have a picture of it," I say.

Barlowe gives me the mental equivalent of an eye roll. *"In your mind, silly. Show me the park in your mind."*

I imagine the park and try desperately to leave out the twenty-two-year-old who drunkenly clawed at me in one of the clumsier sexual interactions I've had. Barlowe's silvery river mind runs gently over the memories.

If Barlowe does see him in my mind, he's gracious enough not to say anything about it. *"I've got it. We'll be fine. I'm not dying during mistporting. I'm not letting you either. When we go out, it will be glorious."*

"Gee. That's comforting," I grumble out loud.

I sling my bag on my back. Barlowe comes over to sit next to me. "Ready?" I ask.

"Ready," he responds.

We mistport into Purgatory. *"Ugh. It's wet,"* Barlowe complains about the moss and the grass.

"Are you seriously complaining about Purgatory? Aren't you technically from here?"

"And? What's your point? It's cold and wet on my paws. Have you seen kitten paws?"

"I have. They're adorable. Would you like me to carry you?"

Barlowe doesn't answer right away. I figure he's trying to decide which is worse, wet cat beans or being carried like a sack of flour. *"I'll ride on your shoulder again."*

I crouch down and up Barlowe jumps, claws catching perch in my school jacket. We walk up to the gates and mistport in. As usual, Marius is there already.

"Morning," Blackbeard calls in a parrot voice.

I blink but reply. "Good morning."

Marius shakes his head. "Don't encourage him. He thinks it's funny to pretend to be one of those dumb parrots that only mimics your words."

"Knock knock." I hear the voice in my head, but it isn't Barlowe.

"Who's there?" I ask hesitantly.

"Old lady."

"Old lady who?"

"Oh, I didn't realize you could yodel! Ha.Ha.Ha!"

Blackbeard's laugh resonates in my head exactly like the high-pitched sound of a regular parrot.

"What do you get when you put a cat and parrot together?"

Barlowe tenses with annoyance on my shoulder, his claws digging in deep. I go along with the joke though, more concerned that Barlowe is about to pounce at Blackbeard. *"I don't know. What?"*

"A carrot! Ha.ha.ha!"

I have to work really hard not to roll my eyes. The parrot's consciousness comes closer to my own. Barlowe growls deep in his little throat and goosebumps rise on my arms at the sound of it. Blackbeard stops right across from the mental bridge. His mind doesn't feel anything like Barlowe's silver river. It's more like a tiny silvery sun shining on me. I feel myself smiling mentally. But then Blackbeard ruins it with another joke.

"A priest, a rabbi, and a devil worshiper walk into a bar..."

"That's enough, Blackbeard. They get it. You're hilarious." Marius speaks in a tone of exasperation, but kindly. Turning to me, he says, "Sorry about that. He loves jokes."

"That's alright. Barlowe thinks he's funny too."

"Unlike bird brain here, I am," the cat Familiar rebuts.

Marius laughs, but so too does Blackbeard. Out loud this time...Ha.Ha.Ha!

The two Familiars stare at each other from their perches for a moment. If they have a conversation, they don't share it. Finally, I clear my throat. "Perhaps we should head up."

Marius waves us on. "I couldn't agree more."

As we walk, I pay special attention to our classmates with their newborn Familiars; there are all kinds. As we get closer, I become keenly aware of the red, glowing numbers. They fell considerably on both sides of the divine divide. From what I can remember, the Ascended numbers were 1307 and are now at 908. For the Descended, their numbers dipped from 1598 to 1012. Hundreds of my classmates died in the third Tribulation. More of them are Descended than Ascended. I hate that my own kind, for that is what they are, I'm realizing, died because they didn't band together the way the Ascended did...and continue to do. Something has to be done about that, but I don't know what. Yet.

When we enter the lecture hall for Angelology and Demonology, I immediately sense there's something different. I stop and look around, but I can't put my finger on it. As Marius and I find seats, I realize what it is. The room is smaller.

Marius develops the same puzzled look I'm pretty sure I just wiped off my face with my dawning comprehension. "The room shrank. I think it's because so many of us died in the Tribulation," I whisper.

"It's almost as if the school is alive," Marius whispers back.

I hadn't considered that. "Have you ever heard rumors of that?" I ask.

"No, but that doesn't mean much. PA is shrouded in mystery as much as Purgatory is in mist."

The bells chime before we can continue our conversation. Bas'el steps forward. "We have a strange situation in class today. We will be discussing the strengths and weaknesses of Nephilim, both Ascended and Descended. I will discuss with you those of the Ascended for the first half of the class. Afterwards, my counterpart will go over the powers and weaknesses of the Descended."

The two professors still refuse to use the other's name. It goes to show how great the divide is between the denizens of Heaven and Hell. I don't get it, but it is what it is.

"I will admit up front that there is plenty of overlap to your powers and weaknesses. However, there are differences too. When you underwent your first Tribulation, the Reaping, Celestial Fire was used as a catalyst for the Ascended and Hell Fire for the Descended. You've heard this before, but you should also know that the two fires are rare and extremely powerful, having many more properties not yet understood fully by either angel or demon. In fact, the Malakim are only granted use of them for the Reaping. Great spells of powerful magic are used by the Divine and Lord Lucifer to do this.

"Now, let's shift to the topic of your age briefly. Throughout the history of Purgatory Academy, we have attempted to have Nephilim enter at earlier ages. The results were mixed at best and disastrous at worst. We have found that the age of twenty is most appropriate. From what we have been able to gather, it is more effective at this age because you are old enough to survive as you are much closer to maturation. Furthermore, the children, and even the teenagers, who survived the Reaping, could not be trusted with their newfound abilities. More times than not, they had to be put down by our own soldiers."

I'm willing to bet the majority of those who survived came from these ancient families who taught their children from birth who and what they were. No doubt the highest mortality rates were among those like me, who had no clue what the fuck they were.

Bas'el continues his lesson discussing the various powers Ascended have. They are almost exclusively elemental in nature. Their weaknesses are the same as the Descended. Decapitation, burning, and intense forms of magic are the most likely ways to kill them. When he finishes, he leaves. Only after he's gone from the room does Corinthia enter from another door. Her lecture is more of the same except to state that the magics of the Descended vary in form much more. It's awful how their petty squabbles get in the way. The ones who pay for it are the students. Especially those not from these snooty ancient families. Images of my torn-up classmates during the last Tribulation impose themselves on my mind's eye. The more I think about it, the more it bothers me. The lessons fall to the background as I continue to consider how I'm going to survive the year with so little going for me.

Chapter Twenty-Nine
Visions Swimming in My Head

February – Purgatory Academy

The circle of pillows is considerably smaller too with so many of our classmates killed in the latest Tribulation. Blackbeard remains perched on Marius' shoulder. Barlowe climbs down into my lap, his tail whipping as he stares at the Dracula Parrot.

"You do know that you're not actually a cat, right?" I remind him.

"On the contrary," Barlowe responds. *"When we take on a permanent form, we also inherit their natures. Their abilities, their weaknesses, their proclivities. They all become part of what we are once we hatch from the egg."*

"So, in other words, you have a drive to kill Blackbeard."

"Yes and no."

"What do you mean, yes and no? I thought you said you basically do become a cat."

"I'm still way smarter than any cat. I can control myself."

"You call this controlling yourself?"

"Absolutely. I haven't attacked. Besides, I don't want to eat him. I just want to smack him. He's irritating."

I don't have anything to say to that. I look around, pretending for a moment that I'm not looking for Gabe…or Drake. But then when I find Drake, who still only sits with us during lunch, and doesn't speak much even then, a small gasp escapes my lips. It's a gasp of adorableness.

The white kitten Familiar Drake has is climbing all over him. And Drake is playing with him. Barlowe notices where I'm looking, and he peers over my leg at the other feline Familiar. His body tenses at the sight. His butt starts to wiggle. I recognize the signs.

"You can't go over there and pounce on them."

"Why not?"

I shake my head. I'm about to explain, but thankfully the bells chime. I have to admit that Drake has good taste, hatching a feline Familiar. I do wonder about the kitten being white what with Drake's reputation as a dark lord to be and everything. It's difficult to reconcile the two ideas. I glance his way one last time. The kitten is curled up in Drake's lap who is absently stroking its little head with two fingers. I just can't see him as the End of Days or the 666 when a pure white kitten is curled up almost sleeping on his lap like that. I'm pretty sure I can even hear it purring.

Barlowe breaks in, *"Now that I've taken on this form, I can't but agree. It is a very pleasant form. My only regret is that I don't have wings."*

I like the idea of that, a winged cat Familiar. Badass.

"Indeed."

All thoughts of Purgatory-born beings flee from my mind when our professor, Emilie, makes her grand entrance, clicking on long black high heels accompanied by her audacious outfit. She has a propensity for wild attire that both flaunts her assets and makes the students uncomfortable in multiple ways. Today's costume is a catsuit. For fuck's sake. Sure, it's one of the tamer outfits she's worn, but there's still something about it. It's made of black leather and is right out of the DC Universe. Yes, it covers everything, but it also hugs everything. It's one piece and zips up in the back all the way down to the curve of her ass where a cat tail hangs. I can't imagine not using soap to get in and out of it. There's a head piece that shapes her face with cat ears on the top. Emilie has the tail in her hand as she clickety clicks in, swinging it in a slow sensual circle.

"All that's hellish and holy, who is that?" If Familiars can mentally drool, I'm pretty sure that is what Barlowe is doing.

"Aren't you a little young for her?"

"I told you. I was in that egg for a very long time. Far too long. Consider me less of a kitten and more of a long-term prisoner. One who is ready for his first conjugal visit."

"I don't think that makes much sense since you're out of your egg now."

"Whatever. Just introduce me."

"You're not even the same species."

"Potato. Potato."

"That's not how the saying goes."

"Whatever. Just introduce me."

I roll my eyes instead.

"Hello all, it's so lovely to see you again. I'm so happy that you all survived the latest Tribulation. I see that you have your Familiars as well. I'd like to welcome you, one and all. You are all absolutely beautiful.

"Now, we're going to jump right in today with a temptation." Emilie looks out among the students. There are still so many options, thousands of students. She won't call on me. I'm not special; I don't stand out.

"Speak for yourself. I'm one of kind."

I'm going to hurt my eyes from rolling them at Barlowe so much. *"You're so arrogant."*

"It's not arrogance if it's true."

I don't get to roll my eyes again. Emilie is staring right at me. Shit. "Lilly. Why don't you come over today?" Double shit. I've just been voluntold.

I take a deep breath before standing up. *"Do you want me to come with you?"* Barlowe asks. I'm too nervous to answer with words, out loud or mentally. I shake my head instead.

When I reach the demoness, Emilie says my name again, this time as if she were tasting it. It disturbs me in myriad ways that the professor knows my name. There are thousands of students, and she knows my name. The odds clearly aren't in my favor, regardless of the numbers.

"I see that you're nervous. I promise it won't hurt. In fact, you might even find it pleasurable. I will take very good care of you." I almost forget to breathe and my knees knock together repeatedly.

Emilie addresses the circled students. "Sway isn't only about using your will against others. It's also about being able to show them what they want or what they might be missing. Convince them what you can give them is something that they not only want but need. When you begin to use Sway this way, you will be able to create images to plant in their minds. Dreams, hopes, visions, desires. Our lovely volunteer is about to demonstrate for us."

I don't like the sound of that at all. I fight hard not to let my face go red. I'm not completely successful, especially when Emilie saunters closer. She catches my gaze and holds it. "Do you mind if I touch you?" I know Emilie is using Sway and while I try to fight it, I can't. I nod dumbly.

I think the demoness is going to touch my face, but she plays with a small piece of my hair instead. I hate that I lean in toward the professor's touch. Emilie smiles as if she expected this, which I'm certain that she did.

"Can I kiss you?" Emilie's smile grows even more wicked, which I didn't realize was even possible. I try to force a "no" out, but it lodges in my throat. I know why. It's as Emilie stated. I don't want to say no. I want to kiss the demoness. I've never kissed another woman, and the professor is gorgeous beyond words. I want to know what her lips taste like.

"Focus," Barlowe warns.

"I am focused."

Barlowe laughs in my head. *"Not on that. You leave her to me."*

"That's not helpful," I retort.

Barlowe is going to say something else, but Emilie gets to me first. "Lilly, I want you to close your eyes please." I'm not able to combat the request this time. My eyes close almost immediately. I want desperately to please the professor.

"Take a deep breath." I inhale. "And out." I exhale. "Good. Very good, my dear. Now, I want you to open your eyes."

Her lips touch mine, but it's gentle, a brush only really. There's a strange pull on my very being and I open my eyes. Everything is the same, but I feel more than hear someone walking up behind me. I turn quickly, fear fueling my adrenaline.

Gabe is right there. He's so close I can smell that West Coast wind on him, mixed with eucalyptus and redwood. "Gabe, what you are you doing?" I ask.

"You know what I'm doing." He inches closer, but there isn't much room left between us. He doesn't bother asking as Emilie did. He runs his fingers through my hair, his warm hand finally resting on my cheek. I let him. I gaze into that smile, that sun shining through his golden skin.

Leaning down, he whispers to me. "I don't want to pretend anymore. I want you. I want you now." Butterflies aren't fluttering in my stomach. They are doing nose dives like kamikaze pilots. I swallow loudly, hoping I can get the taste of lust out of my mouth. It doesn't work.

I look past him out at the gathered students. "Gabe, we really shouldn't be discussing this in front of everyone else." He places his calloused hands on my shoulders, shifting me gently but firmly to look only at him.

"Who cares about them? This is about us. Just us. I want to kiss you. And so much more. But we can start there." A burning desire lights up in my core and I know I don't want to deny it anymore. There's something about Gabe that I want.

"I do too," I whisper breathlessly.

"You what?" Gabe's tone turns playful.

"I want you. I don't care if others see. Just kiss me please. Kiss me now." His body is so warm against me as his hands wrap around my back, holding me in place. The first kiss is soft, gentle, but each that follows comes quicker and more urgently. My mouth parts for his. Those calloused hands run all over my body and tangle in my hair.

Oh yes, I think. Fuck yes. I wrap a leg around his to get closer. His hardness bumps up against me. Burning with a deeper desire, I seek to get closer and closer. I'm so focused on Gabe's body I don't feel the hands on my shoulders at first.

I look back and there's Drake. Gabe remains quiet as I face the brooding Descended. The Ascended steps up to me though, his firmness pressing against my ass.

Drake smiles at me. It might be the most beautiful thing I've ever seen. I never thought I would see a smile on that stoic face. Gabe plays with my hair and kisses my neck as I ask Drake. "What are you doing up here?"

"Gabe already told you the answer. You know why I'm here. He wants you. I want you. Neither of us is going to wait any longer. Forget everyone else and fuck me now." His words are harsher, more brutal, and definitely demanding. My core is a bonfire. Words aren't necessary as I grab him and draw him down to kiss me passionately. There's no need for gentle between the two of us.

I'm losing control as Gabe caresses and kisses me from behind and Drake fondles every part of my body from the front. My moans ripen and travel up out of my core and into the world. I want them both. Need them both. Not going to be denied either one of them. Fuck the world.

Gabe reaches around and gently takes my face in his hands, engulfing my mouth with kisses. Drake kneels down between my legs, his large hands on my thighs sliding up and under my school skirt. I look back at him just in time to witness the wicked grin on his face before he disappears under my clothing.

I lock lips with Gabe once more while Drake slips my panties down around my ankles. My moaning is as sudden as his mouth on my nether lips. I groan loudly, right into Gabe's mouth. I don't fucking care. Pleasure is everything. I want more. More Gabe. More Drake. More of this.

I'm getting so close to exploding. I hold Drake's head in place and gyrate against him. That's how much I need it. And just when I'm about to explode, Gabe tells me to open my eyes. The command is so sudden and so strange in a moment like this, that I do.

I find myself staring out at my classmates, including Gabe who is firmly seated, between Eli and Trist. Most of the faces staring back at me look the way I feel. Filled with lust.

Blinking and shaking my head, I turn away. Drake isn't there. It's only me and Emilie, our professor. Magic. Fucking Sway magic. Quite literally in this case, I think snarkily. Everything that just happened didn't happen. Emilie planted an erotic vision in my mind, and I went right along with it.

She's smiling like a cat who caught a big juicy mouse. Her lips are plump and bruised. Apparently, it isn't all just in my head. "You were wonderful, my dear," Emilie purrs. I fume as the professor sashays by, addressing everyone. "Eventually, you will learn to plant entire visions, dreams, or nightmares. But with practice, you can already learn to plant images or ideas and then just let the subject run wild with them."

My fists clench and for a one small moment it's fury that I feel, not lust. Emilie continues though, "Sway is the essence of prophecy, what could be if the subject wants it enough. They can realize it. They can bring it to life."

My mind reels. I don't think the students know what I saw. Who I saw. But Emilie clearly did. The demoness plays off what she figures is a soft spot for me. I want to punch her. Scratch her eyes out.

"That is quite literally the cattiest thing I've heard you think so far," Barlowe chimes in.

I'm humiliated and that pisses me off. *"I can't believe I let her get into my head like that."*

"I get it, but I don't think that's the only reason you're all amped up right now."

I know exactly what Barlowe means, but I'm too furious to admit it. He hears my thoughts though. He understands it's because I'm so close to orgasming, left frustrated as hell, still on the edge. What's worse, when I stare daggers at Emilie, I know that the professor knows too. She did this on purpose, just to torture me.

"Yes and no," Barlowe chimes in again.

"I'm starting to hate that phrase already," I grumble.

"She wants you to know what it feels like, so you know what power you possess."

I want to retort, but the higher thinking part of my brain tells me Barlowe is right. *"You better get used to that,"* he teases.

Emilie saunters by and whispers, "There's no shame in desire, in wanting, to burn. Remember that." I lock eyes with the professor, but this time there's a different intensity present. It is more one imploring me to reflect. "I want you to consider and remember the power that you possess. Consider and remember what you saw in the eyes and faces of your classmates at the end there. Beauty and seduction are weapons unlike any other."

I hesitate, but maybe Barlowe is right after all. Maybe Emilie is teaching me firsthand. *"Of course, I'm right, dumb dumb."* I'm still thinking about it as I walk back to my pillow. Barlowe curls back up in my lap and purrs and I'm pretty sure it's to comfort me more than anything else. Marius catches my eye and extends a hand to squeeze. I take him up on the offer.

Emilie voluntells other students, but I'm so tuned up that I don't catch much of it. I want to be angry, furious even. But all I can think about are those few imaginary moments with Gabe and Drake. My gaze keeps darting over to the two males. More than anything, it's Emilie's words that keep me contemplating. Beauty and seduction are power. And despite what I might feel about myself, about my body, I'm beginning to realize that I have both in abundance. I have power. I just have to decide to take it and use it.

Chapter Thirty
Revelation
February – Purgatory Academy

HELL

    "Ugh. Your vision was so vanilla." Balor huffs.
    "Not everyone loves BDSM the way you do," I shoot back.
    "Ha. That's because you're not doing it right."

Lunch is quiet and awkward. I wasn't the only one who received Emilie's special treatment. Even Gabe's big group of Ascended is relatively hushed. Marius doesn't know what else to say at this point. I'm grateful for that because I don't know what to say either. Even our Familiars are silent. Blackbeard pecks at Marius' food. Barlowe is curled up next to me, sleeping. Apparently, even kitten Familiars need a lot of sleep.

Although I'm not speaking, I'm feeling plenty. My hormones still rage. My almost orgasm aches like hell, my skin all flushed and hot. I try not to, but I keep glancing at Gabe and Drake.

Drake sits with us but is silent as always. He's reading and eating as per usual. But as I watch, he takes a deep breath, puts his book down, and meets my gaze. I want to look away, but then again, I don't want to. I feel Marius staring back and forth between the two of us. There is a lot of staring going on in general.

Drake's face screws up in contemplation before he takes another deep breath and relaxes. Then he speaks gently to me, "I know what Emilie showed you."

I go right on staring. A million metaphorical years later I respond, "How?"

He takes another deep breath. I realize he's giving me the answer. He smells it on me. The arousal.

"Emilie was right. Everything she said, it was true."

I can't believe I'm having this conversation with Drake. "How did you hear her?"

Drake smiles. "She was right about it all. You should consider that."

It's somehow strangely comforting that Drake knows and agrees. It's empowering in a rather peculiar manner. I smile slightly and he returns to his book and lunch.

Chapter Thirty-One
Bait
February – Purgatory Academy

I spar with Marius in War and Weapons. He still isn't a good fighter, but he is less bad if nothing else. Nevertheless, I beat him every time. He's getting tougher though. He rarely shies away from a hit now and even tries to go on the offensive. All Familiars are lined up along the walls. The professors made it very clear they are not to participate today, but that they will be included in future classes. I don't love the way The'slin says that. Then again, I rarely like anything he says.

After sparring is over, the professors give us lessons on various weapons, war history, strategy, and tactics. They start in ancient human history. Apparently, they'll come back to angelic and demonic warfare. Either way, it's all new. They didn't start on any normal class work prior to our third Tribulation. I assume it's because they don't want to waste their collective breath on Nephilim who aren't going to be alive much longer. I can't disagree more. If the professors gave them a bit more training, a little more knowledge, more of them might be alive today. Of course, they don't care about that because they're monsters. Well, The'slin is. Khal'ith seems decent enough. He seeks to temper the demon as often as he can.

As per usual, they select several students to fight each other at the end of the class. My gut twists when The'slin calls Marius and Adam up to fight. My Descended friend is the color of a corpse as he shuffles forward.

"Drake," The'slin calls. Fuck. This can't be good. The demon has some sort of strange obsession with forcing Drake to fight. Perhaps it's that he refuses, and the demon loves control. Then again it could be because The'slin believes Drake is the End of Days. The results are the same either way, other students being tortured for it, my friend first and foremost.

I don't blame Drake for not fighting, but I also don't understand it. Wouldn't he want to learn? Even if he is a dragon, that doesn't guarantee he'll survive PA.

Drake takes his time reaching the demon. "I'm going to start this fight in a moment," The'slin says to Drake. "We both know Marius doesn't stand a chance, but I'm not going to stop Adam. He only backs off when you intervene."

Adam smiles like a demon and the irony isn't lost on me. It reminds me of a kid at the circus who once threw rocks at the elephants like it was the best game in the world. He didn't like it as much when all four of them charged and almost broke through the fence to trample him.

Marius looks like he's going to vomit. Khal'ith clenches his jaw tight, less than pleased with this entire scenario. He watches intently as The'slin has the two Nephilim bow to each other. Marius, clenched up like a clam, takes up his fighting position.

Some of our classmates call out. Most are either rooting for Adam or teasing Marius. I hate it and shout to my friend to keep his calm and concentrate on the fight. He seems to have heard me because he takes a deep breath and lets it out, at least some of the tension in his shoulders melting away.

Khal'ith calls for them to fight. Adam wastes no time. He mocks Marius with jukes and posturing, bobbing toward the Descended and then backing out of reach. Marius shrinks away the first couple of times Adam does this, but when he finally doesn't, Adam attacks. With his guard not entirely up, Marius isn't able to stop the three straight strikes he takes to the face and head. He shrinks away again, at least keeping his hands up, but he can't escape Adam who grabs the Descended's head between his interlocked hands and brings his knee up into Marius' gut. The pale young man is down on the mats in moments, gasping for air.

Adam steps back and looks at The'slin, but the demon says nothing. Instead, he turns and stares at Drake who doesn't bother meeting his gaze. Adam's face lights up, realizing they really aren't going to stop him. Khal'ith's jaw is set hard, but he says nothing as Adam approaches Marius again.

Marius is on his knees, precious breath struggling to come. Students jeer at him. I call out to him to get up. Adam kicks him in the gut though and my poor friend is down again. "Ball up, Marius. Ball up!" I yell.

He does. Adam kicks and punches at him but has a difficult time hurting Marius. Frustrated, Adam is finally able to pin Marius' arm out and into an arm bar. The Descended screams at the pain and taps out over and over again, but The'slin just stares at Drake.

Some voices are yelling at the demon now telling him to call the fight. I'm not certain, but I think I even hear Gabe calling out. I'm too busy encouraging my friend. Adam has the arm bar deep, and it won't be much longer before he dislocates Marius' shoulder.

And just then Drake steps onto the mat. The'slin grins wickedly. "Let him go, Adam." The Ascended takes a moment longer before releasing my friend, leaving the Descended writhing in pain on the mat. Adam pops up, all excitement to face Drake.

The stoic reported dragon has eyes only for the Ascended as he nears him. He comes to a stop standing between Adam and Marius who is still in pain on the floor. Drake catches my gaze. I understand immediately and rush out to help my friend, hauling Marius to his feet. He leans heavily on me while we both turn to watch Drake and Adam.

The'slin already has them bowing to each other and taking up fighting stances. Adam barely bows, never taking his eyes off Drake. The Descended doesn't bow or look to prepare himself. The'slin calls for them to fight and Adam rushes in immediately. No jukes this time, just anger and a clear, burning desire to hurt Drake. His combos are fast and wicked. And Drake takes each and every one of them. He doesn't bother to block, but allows Adam to hit him, over and over again.

It doesn't take long to understand that he's taking the beating Adam would have continued to give Marius if he'd not gone out there. The'slin snarls. "Drake! If you don't fight back right now, I will sic two students on Marius and make you watch."

Drake takes a few steps back from Adam and stares daggers at The'slin. For a split second, I'm concerned Drake is about to attack our demonic professor. Instead, he turns back to Adam who comes right at him. This time, his strikes aren't fast enough to tag Drake. The Descended dodges out of the way. Adam's attacks become sloppier before finally his back is slightly to Drake because he follows through too far with a haymaker and the Descended pushes him from behind, sending him sprawling embarrassingly onto the floor.

The Ascended jumps back up, furious and coming at Drake in a frenzy. Adam moves so fast, but somehow Drake dodges and shoves Adam to the mats again. While the infuriated Ascended stands back up, The'slin's voice rings out once more. "Drake! This is your final warning. Fight or I will personally see to Marius."

Adam glares, but most of the students aren't calling out anymore. Many stare slack-jawed at the demonic professor. Most of them agree The'slin is taking this too far.

Adam is too embarrassed though and desperately wants to hurt Drake. He wades back in, reckless in his movements. He takes an out of control shot at Drake's head and that's the end of the fight. The strike misses by a lot and Drake responds with a haymaker of his own, completely controlled and completely deadly. It drives Adam to the mat where he lands without moving. Khal'ith counts him out and then checks that he's still breathing. The angel confirms he is. Drake stomps off the mats towards the locker room and class ends.

Chapter Thirty-Two
Small Kindnesses
February – Purgatory Academy

Gabe approaches us before we get far down the hallway. Trist and Eli hang back. "I just wanted to say that I'm sorry that happened. I'm not okay with it. I know we're on opposite sides of a war, but there's still such a thing as honor and I don't approve. I will be having words with Adam about it."

I don't know how to respond. I'm still upset on behalf of my friend, but it isn't Gabe's fault. In fact, he's being kind. Marius speaks up, "Thank you, Gabe. Seriously, I'll be fine though. I can feel my ribs mending already."

I see red when I realize what Marius is saying, that his ribs are broken from that pommeling Adam gave him while he was down. Gabe looks like he wants to say something else but thinks better of it and just nods before heading back to Eli and Trist.

As we walk down the hill, I finally speak up. "Do you think he meant that?" Despite my biochemical responses to Gabe, I'm not completely positive I can trust him.

Marius is quiet a moment before responding. "Yeah, yeah I think he does."

We mistport out the gates and walk down into the fog, our footing sure now after days of traversing the hill. We stop at our typical spot. "I want to thank you," Marius says.

"For what?"

"For supporting me today. For helping me after. For training me. Just for being my friend. I know you took a chance, befriending me." I try to object, but Marius puts up a hand. "I know. I do. I know that I'm weak. I know that I'm developing slower than others. I understand that taking a chance on me was a dangerous thing for you. So, yeah, I'm grateful."

Words fail me so I do the next best thing to express my gratitude. It costs me something, but it's worth the price. I kiss him on the cheek. "I'll see you tomorrow."

I trudge off into the mist until I can't see Marius anymore. I picture the forest near where the circus will be today. Nervousness wells up some, but I focus with Barlowe's help. He understands what I need when I need it.

We mistport safely and I let out a sigh of relief. My dad left me dinner in my RV. I eat it quietly and go to bed early, Barlowe's purrs a lullaby that guides me into dreamless sleep.

Chapter Thirty-Three
Dark Tidings
February – Purgatory Academy

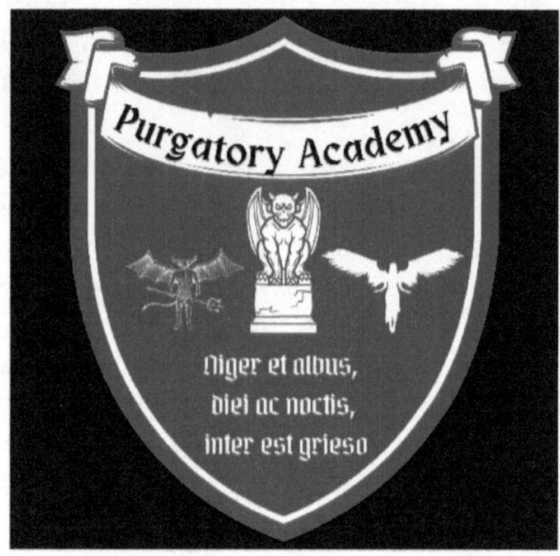

The next morning Marius is surprisingly chipper for someone who just had the crap kicked out of him. When I ask him about it, he says with a smile, "I'm all healed up. It makes me grateful to be Nephil."

"You're just brimming with gratitude right now, aren't you? You ever consider becoming a Buddhist monk?" I tease.

Marius sticks his tongue out at me. "Ha ha. I am grateful though. I mean, come on. Drake saved me yesterday. I need to thank him too."

"It would have been better if he'd helped sooner," I grouse.

"Nah, I understand why he didn't."

I don't bother arguing. I don't want to ruin Marius' good mood. We walk into Sinners and Saints. The bells chime and our professor, Manciel, pulls back his hood to reveal a somber face. "We are about to have a guest in class who needs to relay some important information to you. He should be here any moment."

Students look around at each other, questions dancing on their faces. They don't have to wait long because Gressil marches in through one of the faculty doors of the room. A heavy, smothering feeling settles. It grows even thicker when Gressil is followed by a gargoyle. I haven't seen many of them since those moments in the cafeteria between

Adam and Drake. It's strange to see the stone monster walk through a doorway instead of a wall. There's a lot of side shuffling to get through. If the gargoyles weren't so intimidating, it would have been funny. As it is, most students tense up at the sight. The gargoyles usually only show up when violence occurs. Gressil and the stone sentinel step up to Manciel. The granite giant towers over the faculty members.

Gressil typically looks like an overworked professor or teacher, but today he looks worse, disheveled. "I apologize for the interruption, but it is information of the highest priority. That being said, I won't draw it out. One of your number was found dead this morning, murdered."

Confusion is prevalent among Nephilic faces at this blatant declaration. Students mumble, questions rising up. Gressil doesn't let it escalate, holding up a hand for silence. The students acquiesce, but a restless and nervous air remains. "I understand that you have questions, and I will endeavor to answer them the best I can. While I have no interest in alarming you unnecessarily, I will be blunt. You are all well aware that no violence is allowed here outside of the Tribulations. Our resident gargoyles," he motions toward the stone-faced monster behind him, "make certain of that. That is what makes this so disturbing. Never in the history of Purgatory Academy has there been a murder. There has been the occasional suicide but never murder." Murmuring returns at these words. The gargoyle's face grows even graver at this proclamation as if he were taking it personally. Then again, he might be given that he and his kind are there to make certain this exact thing doesn't happen.

Hands shoot up now, burning questions no longer able to be quenched. Holding up his own hands, Gressil speaks once more, "I know you're all wondering how this was even possible. Many of you want to know who it was that committed murder. The answer to both questions is that we don't know…yet. But we will figure it out."

The gargoyle looks as if he will use his fists toward those ends, and happily. All the hands are down now, but one. Gabe doesn't wait for Gressil to call on him. "Who was killed?" The room grows quiet.

Gressil stares at the blonde as he responds, "It was the Ascended, Adam Melek."

I have two thoughts. First, I had no idea what Adam's last name was. Second, it is definitely that same Adam who bullied Drake and beat Marius yesterday.

Chapter Thirty-Four
Suspicions
February – Purgatory Academy

Hell

"*Now we're getting somewhere,*" Balor rumbles.

An idea floats through the mists of pain in my mind. "*You're investigating the murders. You don't know who did it. It wasn't Lucifer. That's why you're doing this.*" Even with a mental voice, my shock and surprise are clear.

Balor's silence speaks louder than any other confirmation he could have given me.

I don't hear much more of what is said in class. Evocation is pretty much the same. All I can think is that Adam is dead. Not just dead but murdered. I don't want them to, but my eyes keep going to Drake. He just seems like the most likely culprit. Adam bothered him the most by far. And then there's the whole Apocalypse and End of Days and 666 thing. Holy Hell, I sound like one of those true crime fans.

Marius tries to speak to me a couple of times during classes and in-between, but I struggle so much to focus that I don't hear him half the time. Beyond the initial announcement, the faculty don't mention Adam's murder again. I figure it's because plenty more of us are going to be killed either way.

By the time we get to lunch, all any of the students are talking about is Adam's death. Whispers bounce off the corners of the cafeteria and Nephilim huddle together. Many of the Ascended are upset. Some of them are even crying. The two Ascended who were closest to Adam are tucked off in a corner, away from the large group where they're typically attached. Their faces are filled with grief, but also a deep anger.

For all the bullying Adam conducted, he was a legacy from a family of seraphic lineage dating back centuries. These ancient families are close. They carry a collective mourning over his death. It's strange that it hits them so hard. There is no such mourning over those killed in the Tribulations. Again, I wonder how many of those who are dead already actually belonged to any of these old families who raised their children in the knowledge of this entire world.

When Drake enters the cafeteria, silence reigns and more eyes than I can count follow him. Apparently, most of them have already decided who the culprit is. The question remains how he pulled it off. No one is near his old seat now. In fact, the couple tables closest besides my own are also vacant. No one wants to be associated with him.

He doesn't even glance at us as he sits down at his old seat. I understand why he sits there alone. He's trying to protect us from being pariahs as well, a surefire way to get killed here. Rustling to my right has me looking that way. Marius shifts uncomfortably. I can't read the look on his face. He doesn't bother enlightening me either.

He stands up, hands trembling. He sticks them in his pockets to hide it and walks over to Drake. He sits down and it's so quiet even his whispered words are clear across the cafeteria. "Don't do this," he says. "Come sit with us."

Drake doesn't answer immediately. He keeps eating and reading. Marius lays a hand near Drake without touching him. "Drake, please. I trust you. I don't believe you killed anyone. Don't push us away. We're your friends."

The outcast looks up and meets Marius' gaze. "Am I?"

Marius holds that gaze. "Yes."

A muscle twitches in Drake's chiseled jaw. Silence still permeates the cafeteria. And then I realize something. Yes, Drake is the most likely perpetrator. But I don't believe it. He might be the End of Days, but it isn't because he's cruel. If he were cruel, he would never have helped Marius. I find myself standing up and walking over, focused on Drake and Marius, willing my face not to turn red as the entire cafeteria watches me.

"Yes," I echo Marius. Drake raises an eyebrow. "We're your friends," I say. "And there's nothing you can do about it." His lips are so close to smiling, but he holds them down in their stoic pose, like some sort of weird lip yoga. Ugh, what a weird idea. No, I'm the weird one for thinking it. "Now, come on." I head for our original table without looking back. But I hear Marius get up and then Drake as well who settles down next to me.

Marius smiles at Drake who nods before returning to his food. He does glance at me a moment later and I take a chance and wink. Drake gives in and smiles. It's small and without teeth, but it definitely counts.

Slowly but surely sound returns to the cafeteria. People go back to their own groups. They might not have changed their minds, but you can only spend so much time concentrated on hate. At least, I hope so.

For the second time that day, Marius surprises me. "Drake," he waits to continue till he has the Descended's attention. Our friend looks up at Marius. "Thank you."

Drake stares at Marius who blanches but holds his gaze. "You're welcome," he says. "But since we're talking, I think it's important you both understand what you're choosing here. Being my friend isn't doing you any favors. The chances of survival here are low for anyone, but outcasts almost never make it."

Marius bites his lower lip as he considers. "I understand, but my chances were never great anyway."

I open my mouth to refute the statement, but Marius holds up a hand. "We all know it's true. I would probably already be dead if it weren't for you, Lilly. It's not some secret." He's right. But I'm not sorry for my friendship with Marius. I care about him, about both of them. I'm determined to get them through this year.

Marius addresses Drake again, "And I might have died if you hadn't stepped in. Those are not the actions of a monster. You saved me. I can't believe you killed Adam either. You didn't need to bother. It's obvious you could take care of him some other way."

"Just because I could have done it a different way, doesn't mean that I would. Perhaps I lost control." He raises an eyebrow in challenge, waiting for a response.

I don't intend to laugh, but it pops out. The males look at me with surprise. I hide my smile behind a hand. "Sorry, but you have to be the most controlled being I've ever met. You rarely even allow a smile to slip through that wall of stoicism." Marius laughs at that. Drake flashes a smirk just to prove he can. "See?" I say.

Drake shakes his head ruefully. When it becomes clear he isn't going to say anything more, Marius goes back to his food. Blackbeard makes certain that he shares.

I do the same, sharing with Barlowe who finally speaks, *"You have strange friends."*

"I'm going to tell you something that my dad always says."

"And what is this particular piece of wisdom, this gem?"

"Just because others are weird, doesn't mean you're normal."

Barlowe laughs in my mind. *"That's funny. I admit it."*

"He uses it for all kinds of things. 'Just because others are dumb, doesn't make you smart.' It's a way to remind himself and others to be humble and listen."

"I like it," Barlowe agrees.

As I feed my Familiar food, I realize I don't see Drake's kitten. "Drake, where's your Familiar?"

Without looking up from his book, he grabs his backpack. It's black and has quite a few pockets. Sticking out of one of the smaller ones is a little white, kitten head. He dozes, all warm and comfy inside the pocket.

"Ahhh, he's so adorable." I'm proud of myself for not squealing. "I haven't asked. What's his name?"

"Rowan."

"That's beautiful. I love it."

"It's the name of my sister," he explains.

"You named your cat Familiar for your sister?"

He nods, a sad smile but a smile nonetheless playing on his lips.

"Thank you," I blurt.

"I didn't save you," he jokes.

"No, but Marius is my friend and I'm grateful to you."

Drake settles his gaze on me. "You're welcome."

I add one more thing. "I agree with Marius. You didn't kill Adam."

He looks at both of us this time. "Thank you." No smile this time, but I will gladly accept the gratitude.

Chapter Thirty-Five
The Dead Tell No Tales
February – Purgatory Academy

Our last class of the day is Magic Weaving. In retrospect, we weren't ready for it. When we enter the room, Nekleth is not only already there but is accompanied by a couple. The three of them chat quietly as we pile in.

I'm more pleased than I want to admit that Drake sits with us. We guilted him into it by explaining that's what friends do. He mumbled something about bad ideas, but sits with us, nonetheless.

I inspect the couple with Nekleth. They're young looking, but I understand now that means nothing in this world. I've learned in my classes that my own aging will all but stop once I hit my mid-twenties. They could be angels, demons, or Nephilim. In any case, aging doesn't happen or when it does, it's more of a drip. They appear to be in their mid-twenties despite the fact they are both clearly grief-stricken.

They continue to speak softly despite the added noise of thousands of students. When the bells chime, we're all seated, paying more attention than usual, curious about this abnormality in our class structure. Nekleth wastes no time. "Welcome all. I'm sure you have heard the sad news of the passing of one of your classmates." As soon as he says that my suspicions are confirmed. I know who this grieving couple is. Fuck. But why?

Nekleth motions toward the couple. "I'd like to introduce you all to Adam's parents. They have graciously given their ascent for me to use my special skills and gifts." Oh shit. It's even worse than I imagined. He's going to use his necromancy. There's no cold hand on the back of my neck, but it feels that way, nonetheless.

With a grandiose wave, Nekleth gestures toward one of the nearby doors and out rolls a metal gurney. On it under a white cloth is a body. Adam. Adam's body. His mother covers her face and starts crying. Her husband puts an arm around her. I can't believe this is happening. Nekleth is going to bring Adam back from the dead right here in class with his mourning parents present too. Fuck. My pulse quickens, my body near fight or flight mode.

"I will raise Adam's soul and unite it once more with his body in the hopes that he will be able to tell us who murdered him." I hate being right. The gasps and other sounds of surprise might have covered up the fact that Nekleth is smiling the entire time. Others might not have noticed, but I see it. He is getting off on this and it disgusts me.

Adam's father has firm determination planted on his face as if he's ready to do what he must in order to find his son's murderer. That's the real reason the couple is here. Nekleth could have easily done this on his own or only in front of the faculty, but he loves the spotlight. The parents are putting up with it because they are convinced the murderer is in this room and when their son tells them who it was, they will take care of that person. Shit.

The initial shock is wearing off among my classmates. More than a few of them break down in tears. Adam was well-known and well liked among the Ascended. I considered him a complete prick, but that doesn't mean that he deserved to be killed.

"I want to give a grateful thank you to Adam's parents for their courage." Adam's mother continues to cry, but his father gives a curt nod. There's no way this couple is close to Nekleth. Honestly, I can't imagine that the necromancer has any friends at all, regardless of what side of the war they're on. No, this is out of sheer desperation for revenge, at least on the part of the father. For the mother, it might be more about closure.

Speaking to the students, Nekleth says, "You will now witness the full power of necromancy." Jerk off. Barlowe quietly agrees. The professor takes the white cloth off the body. The mother sobs even worse, growing louder and more frantic. Adam's father screws up his face at the sight of his son's body. I certainly empathize with their responses especially since the body is all but nude and rigor mortis set in. He has dark welts and scratches all over. I can't see a killing blow from here, but there are a lot of bruises. There isn't much skin left untouched. However, there is a large set of bruises around his neck. Perhaps he was choked to death.

That seems so unlikely though. From what I'm learning in my classes about my own biology, it would be all but impossible to choke one of us to death. Whoever it is, must have been extremely powerful. Several options pop into my head. One of them is those rogue Familiars. Perhaps with enough numbers, they could have killed Adam. It would definitely explain all the scratches and bruises.

"Those aren't from Familiars," Barlowe corrects me.

"How do you know?"

"Look closely at the wounds, the scratches specifically. They're all relatively the same length and shape. Given that Familiars come in so many guises and sizes, the claw marks would be different lengths and depths."

"You've been a cat for less than a month and yet here you are, Sherlock Holmes."

"Elementary, my dear Watson. Elementary."

I want to tease him that the saying isn't original to the books, but rather to some of the later cinema. I don't get the chance because Nekleth is continuing on with this fiasco. "I ask for your complete silence now. It's unclear how well Adam will be able to speak once I've restored him."

Standing next to the gurney, Nekleth dispenses with much of the theatrics. No hand gestures or mumbling of magical words. He stands there with keen concentration on the body. And then it happens. Students scream. Adam's mother adds her own voice to the chorus.

The body begins to shake and jerk about as if he were having a seizure. Then it stops as quickly as it began. Nekleth steps back. Adam's mother stops her tears and leans forward, still in her husband's arms.

The scariest fucking part happens right then. Adam sits up. The screams double in amount and volume. My gasp is muffled by the hand over my mouth. Plenty of my classmates don't have as much success with their own as panic rears its ugly head.

I catch Marius' horrified face. Blackbeard appears to be comforting him from what I can tell. Trist actually looks like she might cry. I never thought I'd see such emotions from the unfeeling Ascended. But then again, her family may have been close to Adam's. In a strange way, it's a relief to see that Trist has feelings other than anger and judginess. Eli looks even more pained than he usually does. Gabe's face is filled with hurt and for some reason I don't want to admit, it hurts me to see.

I focus back on Adam. It's easier to watch the undead young man than that pain in Gabe's eyes. Adam's eyes are green; his soul is actually back in his body. Returned from the Beyond. Or wherever souls go when they die. All this Heaven and Hell shit, but we still don't know what happens to us when we die. Go figure.

Adam's mother is torn between horrified and wanting to run to her son to hold him. His father is trying his best to stay calm while holding his wife both up and back from their son. There's an animalistic snarl creasing his face. Nekleth wears a smaller than usual version of his evil grin, but I assume that's his attempt at being sensitive to the situation. Asshole. He loves this shitshow. He's in his element.

Moving close to Adam again, the necromancer clears his throat loudly. "I'm going to commune with Adam now. I need absolute silence if you please." I want to smack him just for using the word "commune." It's the kind of word used by the resident psychic in the circus.

"Adam, can you hear me?" It's simple enough of a question. Establish the connection.

The freakiest fucking part is that Adam responds. A rasp of a voice that's still Adam's comes out as a strangled moan. "Yes." The glowing, green eyes don't blink. His body barely moves.

Nekleth, on the other hand, is completely at ease. Perhaps he prefers the company of the dead to the living. It wouldn't have surprised me. Inclining his head, the necromancer asks another question, cutting to the heart of the matter. "Adam, do you know who killed you?" Again comes the rasped moan of affirmative.

His father lets go of his wife and rushes forward, stopping short of touching his son. "Who was it? Who did this? Tell me, son. Who broke the ancient laws?"

Nekleth holds up a hand to Adam's father, requesting patience. The son doesn't answer. I'm not surprised that the undead would only respond to the necromancer. "Who was it?"

Adam struggles with the words, "N-N…No."

The necromancer's face furrows with concentration. That's new. Maybe this is tougher than he lets on. "Adam, who killed you?" Authority filled with magic echoes from Nekleth's command.

Adam's face screws up with some kind of emotion. He begins again but still struggles. "N-N-No."

The necromancer is furious now. His voice rises. "Adam, I command you to tell us who killed you!"

Adam's face contorts with what could only be rage. "D-D-D."

His mother breaks free of her husband, who holds her again, and rushes forward, "Adam, sweetheart, please. Tell us."

I can't stand this much longer. An idea blooms in my mind and before I can consider it longer, I blurt out. "Where is his Familiar?"

Nearly every head turns to stare at me. I breathe deeply, focusing myself, but I know at least some red bleeds onto my face, the heat on the tips of my ears. Nekleth is scowling at me, but the thought is planted. Adam's father regards the necromancer. "We haven't been able to find his Familiar. Do it. Ask him where his Familiar is."

The professor scowls again but he asks, "Where is your Familiar, Adam?"

The emotion on his dead face is profound sadness. "D-D-Dead."

Whoever killed Adam, killed his Familiar too. They were thorough. Nekleth yells at the undead Ascended. "Tell us who killed you!" A vein throbs in the necromancer's forehead.

Adam shifts toward his family and it's clear that it costs him. Any kind of movement seems to be very difficult. I didn't like him in life, but I feel bad for him in death. "S-S-S-orr-y. L-Lo-ve…y-you."

With that his body begins to convulse. Terror rises anew throughout the room. When his body goes limp, the green fades from his eyes and they close. "We need to try again," Nekleth says to Adam's parents. "I can get the culprit from him."

Adam's father is already shaking his head as he holds up his wife who has lost the last of her strength. He takes her gently to one of the side faculty doors, but just as they reach it, one of Adam's friends who laughed so much at the Ascended's bullying yells out. I think his name is Luke. He has dusty blonde, curly hair. He's seated next to the third member of their little trio. He is a brown-haired skinny guy by the name of Matthew. He nods at Luke's words. "He was going to name Drake as the murderer. We all heard it. He kept saying the letter 'd.'"

His words bring about a brand-new cone of silence in the lecture hall. All eyes turn toward Drake. Even then, the Descended remains unperturbed.

Adam's father, leaving his wife leaning on the wall, takes a few steps toward Drake. Shit. A not-so-subtle light begins to glow like a halo around the Nephilim's body. He stops though. Standing in the corner is a gargoyle who sensed the man's intentions. Nekleth looks back and forth between the two. Shaking his head, he says class is dismissed. The gargoyle lingers with Adam's parents while the students file out.

Chapter Thirty-Six
Shapeshifting
March – Purgatory Academy

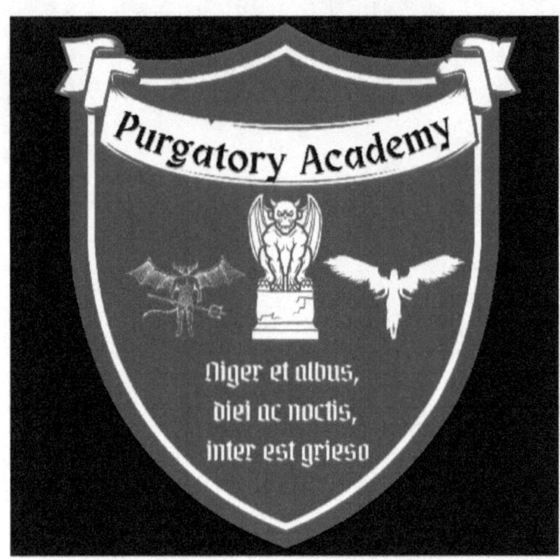

March arrives. With it, the fourth Tribulation. The professors give us no insights into what it will be. They only inform us that our Familiars will not be allowed to accompany us.

Barlowe grumbles about it when I wake up the morning of the Tribulation. My Malak waits at the foot of the bed with a pile of clothes in hand. *"What's the point to having a Familiar if they don't allow me to protect you when you most need it. Also, I'd really like to shred this Malak for you. Can I at least do that?"*

"Good morning to you too, Barlowe," I yawn. I get up and kiss the Familiar on the top of his furry little head. The cat purrs in response.

"Good morning," I say to the Malak as well while I scootch by to the bathroom.

When I come out, the clothes are on my bed and Barlowe is sitting on them. *"Thanks for guarding my clothes,"* I tease.

"You're welcome," he responds most seriously.

Picking up the pile, I see they're normal workout clothes with one exception. I inquire with the Malak, "Did you know there's a hole in the butt of these pants? I'm not sure if you're aware, but I don't need that. I already have one." Barlowe laughs in my mind, but the Malak doesn't respond.

I sigh. "Fine, I'll just wear black underneath. We wouldn't want my bare ass sticking out in life-threatening situations."

"I'm not sure all of your classmates would agree with that assessment."

"Shut it."

Thankfully, I find a pair of black panties. I hope no one notices. Probably not, given they will be too busy fighting for their lives. I have a banana, but even that is difficult to finish as the nervousness sets in. My Malak doesn't bring me anything this time, but the three of us do depart together. I almost say something to my escort before mistporting inside the gates with Barlowe but think better of it. What could I say? Here's hoping I'm not dead when this is over. Meh.

Marius and Blackbeard are waiting for us. No sign of Drake. "Good morning," Marius says.

"Good morning. Good day to die." Blackbeard is helpful like that.

We don't exchange any more words or pleasantries on our way up. Gressil meets the collected Nephilim at the front doors and without a word we go in. I don't love the fact that after all our winding through the hallways, we come out in the courtyard again. I don't associate it with good things.

"Hey now. I hatched to you here," Barlowe reminds me. It's a good point. When I think of those moments he hatched to me, I feel a bit lighter, calmer.

There are no Familiar eggs in the middle of the courtyard this time, only Gressil and the other faculty members. However, there are ladders staggered across the courtyard leading up to the roof. Gressil states the obvious. "You will be climbing up onto the roof."

Okay. Terribly helpful. Gressil continues, "From there you will shapeshift and bring out your wings. Your objective is to fly across the Ossa Forest to the other end. If you crash in the forest, you will need to walk the remainder of the way. That is the sum of your fourth Tribulation. Please remember that Familiars must remain here. I wish you all the very best." With that, the dean of students and the professors mistport away, presumably to wait on the roof for the Nephilim to climb up.

Marius and I head up a ladder. Once we're at the top, I see that we're on a flat part of PA's roof, the spiraling towers hovering over us to the left while the Ossa Forest of bone trees awaits just below on the right.

I finally spot Drake headed our way. He nods. It's a small comfort, but I feel better. I take stalk of my surroundings. I've never counted the castle towers of the school before. There are nine in total. I wonder what they're used for because we don't have classes in them.

Now that we're up here, I realize just how daunting this task is. I'm not alone. There is plenty of trepidation among the students. Gressil speaks, his voice somehow magically enhanced so we can all hear him over the light wind that blows at cross angles through the slopes and spirals of the school's roof. "You need only reach within and find the other form that each of you possesses. As always, allow your imagination to guide you toward the reality. There you will find the kernel and there you will be able to make it grow. Again, I wish you all the only very best." I don't have the first clue what the fuck he's saying. How in the world am I going to grow wings using my imagination?

"It's as he said. You tap in using your imagination like you do with any of your powers."

"Barlowe, I don't think you're allowed to help."

"False. I'm not allowed to come along physically. No one said anything about telepathically."

I have to smile. Barlowe's right. I walk over to the edge considering it. Marius joins me. I ponder the forest. The portion of the roof where we stand is a little taller than the trees of the forest. There's no way I'm going to be able to fly over the expanse of it. I can't even see the end in the distance.

"Do you understand they have set you all up to fail on purpose"?

"You can see this?" I ask Barlowe.

"I experience everything you do, at least to some degree. It depends on how powerful your thoughts and emotions are and how well I can or want to distance myself."

"Nice to know. Who wants privacy anyway?" I grumble.

Barlowe laughs. *"None of you have shapeshifted yet. That means that even if you accomplish it today, you will have to fly over the forest. It is much too far for you to glide. You will have to flap. And the mechanics are more difficult than most realize."*

"Great. How do you know so much about this?"

"I told you. Stop making me repeat myself. I was in that egg for a very long time. I wasn't deaf though. Nor was I idle. Now, pay

attention. It's going to sound crazy, but once you have shapeshifted, your best bet is to jump from one of the towers. That will give you space to glide above the tree lines which you do not have here."

"You're right," I agree. *"That does sound crazy."*

Marius looks more terrified than when they announced he was going to fight Adam. Behind us Gabe, with the help of Eli and Trist, is gathering others up. They're headed toward the sloped portions of the roof where they can climb up the towers. I wonder how they expect to climb, but then I see the daggers that many of them have. They were prepared because their families prepared them. I'm getting pretty tired of this unequal shit.

"Has Barlowe been giving you pointers?" Marius asks.

"More like instructions or commands," I grunt.

"Blackbeard says we're better off launching from the towers."

"Barlowe agrees as do practically all the Ascended from the looks of it. How do we climb that?" I ask. "I don't have daggers. You?"

"Nope."

Drake joins us, peering out over the forest. "Close your eyes," he commands us. We exchange a glance at his brusqueness, but we follow his instructions.

"I want you both to focus on your nails. Imagine them growing long, so long that they're claws. So strong that they're daggers."

I suspend my disbelief and go along with his instructions. And somehow, I feel growth in my nails. I open my eyes to find them growing till they're about six inches long. They turn black and are hard as hell. I look over at Marius and he has the same.

"Good," Drake says. "You should be able to drive those into the roof as you climb."

"How did you know we could do this?" I ask.

Drake shrugs. "Nearly all Descended have the ability. When you get to the top, you want to use the same process to grow your wings. Don't try to flap in the beginning, just expand them and jump. Soar. Glide. That will be difficult enough. Understand this though. You won't make it. When you go down, stay together and move as fast as you can."

"What about you?" Marius asks.

Drake ignores the question. "You should practice now before you go up. There's not a lot of room up there as is and it's going to be crowded."

I stare up at the towers. There's a slow trickle of Nephilim climbing them. It isn't everyone though. A few remain baffled or stunned, sitting on the roof. "This time when you close your eyes, I want you to imagine there's a flower in your chest. Let it be a seed first and then imagine it splitting open, growing, and finally blooming."

Drake and flowers. It seems like a strange thing to do, but I put my trust in the dragon apparent. Marius already has his eyes closed. I do the same, envisioning the seed and as it grows and blooms, I make it a rose. But not a red rose. No, I make it a black rose, a symbol of the person I am. I might be Descended, the spawn of demons and devils, but I'm beautiful and I'm powerful.

As I accept that idea, these lovely stirrings swirl all around my body. They're concentrated between my shoulder blades, my tail bone, and in my scalp just above my hairline. My bliss is interrupted by Marius' exclamation. My eyes fly open to check on my friend, but my mouth hangs open in shock at what I see. He has the same look on his face and because of that I'm able to clearly see the two long canines protruding from underneath his upper lip. Sprouting from his back are two huge bat wings, leathery and a dark gray so deep it's nearly black. The surprise on his face quickly melts into a smile of pleasure.

"Marius, you…you have wings."

I've seen him happy plenty of times despite our circumstances and his struggles, but this is more akin to joy. "I knew this would happen, but I never imagined it would be so…"

"Empowering," Drake comments.

Marius agrees, "Yes."

"You look so badass," I say.

"Me? Have you seen yourself?" Marius responds.

What? And then I realize what I felt was my shapeshifting growth. There are wings on my back and with some concentration I'm able to arch them around me so I can see them. They're just like Marius' but they're a shiny black.

"That's not all," Marius says. He points at his own head. Huh? I bring my hands up and the tingling I felt on my head makes more sense. There are two horns growing out of my scalp. They're ram horns, curling around like I've seen on some of the gargoyles. Holy shit.

"I have horns!" Marius laughs. I glare at him.

"They're beautiful," Drake says.

I can't fight the fluttering butterflies this time. They're in my chest and far too happy to pay attention to me. "Thank you," I whisper.

I feel my own fangs protruding as I smile. "Oh shit."

"They're beautiful too," Drake says immediately.

I hold his gaze for a moment, but finally have to look away. Wings are sprouting everywhere. Some are black and leathery like my own. Others are gray or white with feathers. Those must be the wings of the Ascended. Some of my classmates are already launching from the spiraled towers, gliding over the bone forest. A few crash right away. Others make it farther. None of them get anywhere close to crossing the entire forest.

The horror I'm watching is interrupted by another one. Apparently, the tingling at my tail bone wasn't finished because there's a loud tearing sound in the back of my pants. My eyes widen and I turn, trying to get a glimpse of my own ass.

As I do, something hits me in the eye. "What the fuck!" There's something whipping about, attached to my tail bone. It almost gets me in the other eye a couple of times, but finally I'm able to catch it in my hand. I grab it so hard I give myself a hard tug on the ass. Then it becomes clear what it is. A tail! I have a fucking tail! Obviously, that hole in my paints wasn't big enough because there's plenty of tearing back there.

It whips about with a mind of its own in my hand, but I'm able to see it a bit better once my eye stops hurting quite so much. It's long and leathery to the touch, all black and at the tip is an arrow shape that flaps back and forth like a pair of tiny wings. I try to make it obey me the same way I would my own hands, arms, or legs. I certainly can't let go. My eye still hurts.

I pinch the arrowhead tip between two fingers. It isn't hard like bone, but rather flexible. I'm guessing it's cartilage. The very tip of it looks sharp. I take my index finger and push at it. I pull it away almost immediately. A sharp pin prick of pain pierces my finger, and a small welling of blood arises. That damn tail is sharp. I really will have to be careful with it.

I realize Marius and Drake are staring at me. Marius' stare is that of a person trying not to laugh at a friend. He's losing that particular fight. On the other hand, Drake is smiling … with awe? I meet his gaze again. He reiterates, "It's beautiful."

I shake my head. "Maybe, but how the hell do I control it?"

"You just tell it what to do. It doesn't have a mind of its own."

"All evidence to the contrary," I retort.

"You do the same thing you always do with magic. Imagine it into being. It already exists technically, but the envisioning of it will help you bring it into your awareness."

I'm not certain I understand what Drake is saying, but I close my eyes and imagine a connection between myself and the tail. And sure enough, it's there. Taking a deep breath, I let go and tell it to move to the ground. Sure enough, it obeys.

A smile blooms on my face. Drake speaks, "You should both shift back to your human forms. It will be easier and safer when you climb. You don't want those currents up there lifting you away." He points.

Sure enough, there are more than a few Nephilim with their wings out, trying to climb up the towers, but the drafts keep pulling at them. In some cases, they are ripped off, tumbling back down. I even see a couple pulled right over the edge and into the bone trees of the Ossa Forest, disappearing quickly amongst their own screams. All I can do is wince.

I clear my head from these scary images and close my eyes to concentrate. I imagine my wings contracting and shrinking back into my back, my tail back into my ass, and my horns curling in on themselves into my scalp. The same tingling occurs and soon enough they're all gone, my claws and fangs the only things left behind. I don't know why I kept the fangs, but something about them makes me feel more confident, more badass.

It gives me enough confidence to look at Drake once more and ask a question I've been dying to know the answer to, "Why do you keep your distance from everyone? You know that we're all better off cooperating. And yet you don't. Why?"

Drake stares at me. "Why are you asking that now?"

"I might be dead soon. I want to know before I die."

Drake sighs. "Two reasons. As I'm pretty certain you're aware, many believe I'm going to bring about the end of the world. They call me dragon. End of Days. 666. Now they think I'm a murderer as well. There's no point in endangering others by making them my friends."

I'm only just beginning to realize how good Drake secretly is. He doesn't want others to be hurt or die because of how he's viewed. He helped Marius and refuses to hurt others when he finds it unnecessary. "And the other reason?" I ask.

Drake shrugs. "Like you said, most of you will be dead soon enough."

That I understand perfectly. I struggled with the same after watching Rodrigo turned to goo and then trying to decide if it was worth it to get to know Marius when he might die any day. But I made my choice. I chose Marius as a friend and won't go back. "Well, you've screwed that all up now," I tease Drake.

"Oh?"

"Yeah. Now we're friends and you can't get rid of us that easily."

Drake smiles again. I could definitely get used to the sight. "It's one thing to sit together at lunch, but to be my friends, it will endanger you."

"Yes, because this place is so safe." Sarcasm joins my eyeroll to prove my point.

Drake shakes his head, giving in. I know he has because he changes the subject. "When you get to the top of one of the towers, you shift inside the railing, so you don't get swept away. Keep your wings tucked in till it's time to jump and then unfold them fully. Glide as long as you can. Find the currents that will carry you. Stay as close to each other as possible. When you crash into the forest, it will be much more dangerous than you know."

"Why?" Marius asks.

"The skeletons."

"The skeletons…" Marius hasn't decided if his words are a question or a statement.

"They might not seem like much, but bones don't break easily. And they will have the numbers."

Marius looks like he's going to be sick. I don't feel much better. Drake marches toward both of us. "Listen to me. You have to climb one of the closest towers. They'll give you a chance to get farther along on your glide.

"Wait, why are you talking as if you're not coming with us?" I ask.

Drake glances over at Gressil and the faculty members. They're all staring at us. Or more accurately, at Drake. Everyone is always so curious to know what he's about. He walks to the edge of the roof overlooking the bone forest. He smirks at me. "I'm not going that way. I will find you though." And with that, Drake drops right over the edge of the roof. We run over. It's at least thirty feet up, but he lands on one knee, stands fluidly, and marches into Ossa Forest. Holy shit. He might be smoking hot, even crazy smoking hot, but he's definitely just plain crazy too.

Gressil's jawline tightens in tension. Many of the faculty members don't hide their feelings either. There's anger, surprise, even shock.

Marius and I share a grimace. I shudder to think what some of our professors would do to Drake if they were allowed. I shake away the thought. It's time to climb up the tower. We head toward one of the closest ones as Drake suggested.

It's strange to see the other forms of our classmates. The longer I watch, the more I see the differences though. The angels stand out easily enough, what with their feathery wings. The incubi and succubi are more difficult to tell apart from the vampires. It's really the tails and horns that do it. The vampires have wings and fangs and claws, but not these extra features.

As we arrive at the slope of the tower, I inspect my nails more closely. At first, I feel like one of those women who has long, glue on nails. I've never had anything against the idea but wasn't interested in it either. I don't understand how they can do anything with them that long…text, eat, whatever. But as I run them along the shingles of the school, I understand these are nothing like those fake nails. Plenty of my classmates are using them to dig holes into the roof.

Cocking back a hand with my fingers close together, I drive it into the shingles. Sure enough, it sticks deep. "I don't think that's the problem," Marius says next to me.

"Oh?"

"It's our feet. There's no grip at this ninety-degree angle straight up with these shingles."

I study others above us. Marius is right. Plenty of them are struggling. "What if we follow the path of some of the others? The divots they've created aren't much, but it's better than nothing."

"Fair enough," Marius agrees.

Up we go. It's slow going, but we make progress little by little. More than once, others topple back down past us; thankfully, none fall into us. Some have their wings out already and are pulled off the tower wall by gusts of wind. A few land on the roof, but more end up in the forest like we saw earlier. Their wings are like parachutes, dragging them along.

Even among the Nephilim who make it to the railings of the towers, many of them flap and plummet among the trees of bone. None of them land gracefully. I know my senses continue to increase in depth and ability because I actually hear bodies thud, grunts of pain, and even breaking bones.

Marius follows me up the best he can. There are a couple of times he has to stop and rest, but he grinds it out. I'm proud of him. He's getting stronger. Weeks ago, he wouldn't have been able to do this climb. Finally, we near the top. Others are piled up inside the railing. None help us, but they do stand back as we climb over. We sit down against the wall of the tower, breathing heavily.

Around the corner from us is a door. The normal way to get up into the tower. The safe way. Not the way we came.

We lay there for several minutes catching our breath. "We should get going," I finally say.

Marius is still breathing so hard all he can do is nod. I stand up and offer him my hands, careful of my claws and his. I struggle to pull him up. He's definitely exhausted. At least he doesn't weigh very much.

The gusts of wind are worse up here. A couple of Nephilim who stand on the railing lose their balance before they can jump properly. They fall far and hard. Most of them live, a few don't. One vampire is taking too long to spring from the railing. The gray-feathered Ascended shoves him. His friends laugh while the Descended screams all the way down.

Of course, when it's the asshole's turn, he takes forever too until he jumps out of shame from all of the jokes his friends throw at him. He glides for a bit but cries out as he slams into one of the bone trees. Neither of his friends does any better. It's awful to watch, but all we can do is prepare ourselves the best we can.

"Let's jump together," Marius suggests when we're up. I cock my head to the side in question. "At least we'll go down together that way like Drake said," he explains.

"Alright." We close our eyes and will our wings out. I don't shapeshift my horns or tail into being. The wings are difficult enough to control. The wind whips at us, but both Marius and I tuck in tight. We climb carefully up on the railing, crouched down holding on to it like a pair of gargoyles. "On three," I say. "One. Two. Three."

We jump. Well, it's more like we fall forward. I do as Drake suggested and flare my wings out wide. I don't fight it as a gust of wind pulls me up. From the corner of my eye, Marius is next to me doing the same. A current of wind captures us both and pulls us forward.

It's only seconds before we're over the Ossa Forest. As we glide, we catch glimpses of Nephilim fighting for their lives here and there as numberless skeletons drop like rotten fruit from the trees to face and chase them. It scares the hell out of me, but I refocus myself on my soaring.

I understand already that even with the current pulling us forward, I will have to flap my wings soon. I make eye contact with Marius. Over the wind, I yell. "I'm going to try to flap just once." He nods, never taking his gaze from me, face screwed up with worry.

Breathing in deeply, I concentrate on my wings and having them flap together in unison. I focus in on the muscles that run through them as well as my back. My wings obey and I surge forward a little bit. The success surprises me so much, I almost forget to spray my wings back out again to glide. It's a shaky moment, but I pull it together.

Looking over at Marius again, who is slightly behind me now, I see him smiling. Holding up a hand, he motions that he's going to try it as well. He flaps his wings, but it isn't together. One wing goes before the other and dread fills my stomach as I hear him scream and watch him plummet into the trees below.

I panic and try to slow down, but I lose control as well and fall from the sky. The bleached white of the trees rushes toward me if they were reaching for me, promising a misty grave below, adding our own skeletons to this bone garden.

I don't remember a lot after the first couple of branches pummel me. Stunned, I wake up and shift sluggishly. Pain flashes in my head, but as I investigate the rest of my body nothing appears to be broken or permanently damaged. I stand up gingerly and try to reorient myself. I almost call for Marius, but then reconsider. I don't want to make any more noise than I have to; no need to inform the skeletons of my location. I wonder how I'm going to find Marius though.

He answers that question for me, "Lilly! Lilly, are you there?"

Shit. He's going to bring the skeletons right to him. I run toward the sound of his voice as he continues to call. The trees are thick though and the mist even heavier. I almost run into low hanging branches repeatedly. Thankfully, I'm not impaled.

The other problem is that sound echoes off the trees. Marius' voice comes from one direction, but then another the next moment. My wings get scratched to hell by branches and finally I stop to retract them into my back. My adrenaline quickens the process.

Marius continues to call, but his voice is more frantic. I have to hurry. It's a few more minutes of struggling through bone and mist, but he sounds closer. I run into a clearing where the trees aren't as thick and there's Marius.

He's banged up, but alive. His wings are retracted already. We rush to each other and hug. "Oh, thank the devil," Marius says. The amount of relief I feel is surprising, but I don't stop to consider it. I just hold my friend harder.

Finally pulling back, I say. "Why would you call like that?"

He cringes. "I didn't know what else to do. I knew I wouldn't survive alone so I did what I could."

"How did you even know I fell too?"

"I just, I knew…I didn't believe you would leave me behind."

I manage to hold back the tears of gratitude for my friend. "Well, you were right," I say. "Now, let's get the hell out of here." Marius nods and we turn back the way I came.

"Are you certain we're going the right direction with all this fog?"

"I may have blacked out from the fall, but I definitely recognize the tree that did the honors. It was back this way." Marius follows, trusting me. "Have you seen any skeletons?"

He shakes his head. "Not yet thankfully."

We hurry in silence for several minutes, going as fast as we dare through the Ossa Forest's heavy mists. But then we hear the screams. With the intensity and number of them, it's difficult to know where exactly they're coming from. The terror rebounds off the trees, swallowed up in the fog.

We stumble into another clearing where the mist isn't as thick, but the number of boney warriors more than makes up for that. In the middle of the sea of skeletons are five Nephilim, battling for their lives. None of them has their wings out, but I'm able to discern their kind from their other attributes. Three are Ascended and two Descended, brought together out of a sheer need for survival. Two fight closer together, a man and woman. The man has horns, so he must be an incubus. They're lashing out at the skeletons with their claws. The trio near them has no claws but yields large pieces of bones they must have ripped from nearby trees or perhaps even from the skeletons they destroyed already. There is quite the pile.

As I consider them, some of the skeletons turn to face us. I don't think; I just respond. I slash out with my claws, ripping ribs away from the closest skeleton. It isn't concerned though and soon there are several more coming at us. I do my best, slashing and clawing. Marius does the same. He's hesitant at first, but survival instinct makes up for a lack of skill. Still, we're being backed up away from the clearing. We have to use the trees as cover.

The problem is we're all making so much noise that more trees are dropping their skeletal fruit among us. We're not going to last long like this. We have to change tactics, and quickly. Over the din of battle I call out, "We have to work together. Form a circle!" There's a good chance it's already too late. The two little islands of Nephilim are scratched and bleeding and more skeletons are dropping or moving in on them.

The Ascended understand though and push their way toward the two Descended. They stand back-to-back-to-back in a loose triangle. The Descended fight to work that way as well, but their going is much slower. Marius and I try to do the same, but it isn't working. We both sustain multiple lacerations. Bone can cut pretty well when it wants to. Teeth gnash at us. The skeletons only fall when we smash the skulls. Anything else still attached continues to fight.

The Ascended reach the Descended and they form a small circle of five and wade their way toward us; Marius sustains a bite on the forehead before I'm able to smash the skull with a strike of my clawed hand. There's blood, but he wipes it away with a thumbs up to let me know he's okay. Somehow the group is able to reach us, and we form up together.

"We have to make our way toward the edge of the forest," I say. Fuck's sake I have a brilliant military mind. The number of skeletons is growing and it's only a matter of time before we are overwhelmed. Claws lash out, tearing flesh. One of the Ascended is pulled from our circle, lost amongst his own screams and splattered blood.

Blanch bone scrapes and scratches everywhere. Another Ascended is pulled from our group and falls screaming under the weight of bones, tearing her apart little by little till there's nothing left to heal.

We work together to seal off the holes in our circle, but we're pushed up against each other's backs and have nowhere to go. In that moment I understand I'm going to die like this, ripped apart by skeleton hands and grinding teeth. Panic claws at me just like these boney guardians.

Just when my hope is all but dead, a deep baritone rings out. "Use your magic!" There he is. Drake. I catch small glimpses of his dark visage among the white bone. "Do it or die!" he roars.

I have no idea how he found us, but he's right. Fear fuels magic if focused. The remaining Ascended cups a bright light in his hands and shoots it at the skeletons. It burns through them, breaking spines, skulls, and more as it flies. The incubus uses a lash of what looks exactly like shadow, smashing the skeletons to little bits. The female vampire holds two swords, but they appear to be made of solidified blood. She crushes skulls left and right with them.

Marius doesn't manifest anything. I try to unleash my own magic, but nothing arises. I swallow my panic, but it rushes right back up my throat.

Drake is somehow cutting through the bones. He isn't using weapons. But his every punch and kick smashes entire skeletons. He picks them up and wields them as weapons against the others. How can he be so strong?

He reaches us and slips into our circle. Even with our magic, we're barely fending off the undead. Drake speaks at my back, "Channel your magic."

"I can't," I shriek.

"Yes, you can," he answers. He pushes to my side, grabs my shoulders and wrenches me toward him. Before I know what he's doing, he slaps me hard in the face, snapping my head to the side.

I see red. The red of anger. Of fury. What the fuck. I whip my head back to snarl at Drake, but he oh so calmly looks at me and says, "Use it."

I feel it then. The power surging. It's awake. Holding out my hands, pointed at the skeletons in front of me, I scream out my boiling rage. Twin streams of glowing, green fire shoot through the ranks of bone soldiers. So hot, it melts them right then and there, piles of ash left behind with tiny motes of emerald flames dancing on them.

My fury drives me in a small semi-circle, destroying at least half of the gathered bone warriors. And just as quickly as the flame erupted from my hands, it flickers out and dies, spent too quickly.

"Run," Drake commands. I've cleared a path from the skeletons and he turns to face the remaining ones. The Ascended and Descended take off running as fast as they can toward the edge of the forest. Marius comes over to prod me forward.

My legs carry me. I turn back to find Drake who holds my gaze for a small moment before continuing to smash skeletons. We run on, fueled by both fear and fury. We're not chased though and a few seconds later there's a huge explosion that shakes the very ground. I know it comes from where we'd just been, but Drake doesn't follow us.

I close my eyes for a moment and turn to run full on, desperate to get out of the forest as much as I am to run from the shame that will always stay with me. Shame that I let Drake stay behind. Shame that I didn't remain to help him. Shame that worms its burning way into every crevice of my being.

But then we're there. The edge of the forest. Gressil and the faculty meet us, waiting patiently and completely unruffled. There are Nephilim present as well, most of them bruised and bleeding. Among them, not a hair out of place, is Drake.

Chapter Thirty-Seven
Another One Bites the Dust
March – Purgatory Academy

Screaming continues to flow out of the forest for some time. The stream of survivors is considerably lower. They stumble out alone or in pairs. However, Gabe and his lieutenants lead a large gathering out. They're pretty beat up, but not nearly as badly as others. The light is definitely fading which answers a question I've had for some time about whether there is night in Purgatory. I really don't want to be around to find out more about it though.

I keep looking over at Drake who stands alone. I can't believe it. He walked out of the forest without a scratch on him. Not only that, but he's there when we arrive. Even though we'd been running for our lives. Even though he stayed behind.

Instead of standing here lamely, sick to my stomach listening to the screaming that's finally dying out alongside the dim light in the sky; I motion to Marius to let him know my intention. He makes to go with me. When we get to Drake's side, he gives us a tired smile and a bit of warmth seeps back into the world for me.

I have to know how he survived *and* arrived before us, but Drake looks as if he's about to say something. Just then a Malak mistports near Gressil and hovers the rest of the way to the dean of students. We watch as the two speak, the Malak leaning in close. Gressil's eyes widen for a moment. He pulls away and speaks loudly and immediately, "Any who are going to come out, already have. We are returning to the school immediately. We must hurry. Another student has been murdered."

Without waiting for responses, he sets a brisk pace back to the academy, skirting around the forest. My head reels with emotions. I quick march next to Drake and Marius and I can't help but feel a mixture of bewilderment and anger. How many students have just been killed in the Tribulation, but no one does anything about it? And yet, now we're rushing back to PA because one student is murdered outside the rules of the school. It's all so fucked up.

On top of that I have those moments in the Ossa Forest to consider. Drake saved us. I don't understand how he can be that powerful. And I sure as hell don't understand how I conjured that green fire. Most of us are still struggling to weave magic, but I haven't seen anything like my emerald flames.

We reach the school and there is the body, right next to the forest. Most of the students walk by and wait while the faculty and Gressil move that way, but one of the Ascended makes a run for the body, clearly identifying it. The Ascended is Matthew and the body was his friend, Luke. They were Adam's two friends. Now only Matthew is alive from the three.

I'm close enough to see Luke's body is bruised and scratched the same way Adam had been. That alone tells me it can't have been the skeletons. They ripped and tore till there were only gory bits left. Whoever this is, choked the Ascended to death. That shouldn't have been possible.

Matthew sees us standing there, tear streaks down his cheeks. He screams at Drake, face red with fury. "He did this. He killed Luke. And Adam. Keep him away from me. He's taking out the Ascended one by one." Gabe approaches with Trist and Eli in tow and tries to calm Matthew down, but he can't be consoled.

Faculty come forward and motion the students on, but Matthew and the Triumvirate along with a few other Ascended remain behind with the body. There are more than a few students who stare at Drake as they continue by, trailing whispers about how he could have done it. He did walk into the Ossa Forest alone. He could just as easily have walked back out again and killed Luke when no one was around.

It's absurd, but people don't think straight when they're afraid. And it's fear that is going through the students right now. It's crazy people are so upset about this, but no one seems to mourn, at least in the moment for who knew how many of our classmates just died in the bone woods. Expectations, they're a real bitch.

We're brought to the front of PA and reunited with our Familiars. Gressil mistports there moments later and informs us the Tribulation is over. We're free to go home. He mistports away again, no doubt to continue to investigate the murder. Most of the students drift off, stunned.

Drake wanders off without a word. I don't know what to say to him anyway. Marius and I mistport out, hug briefly, and mistport home. As I melt away, relief that we survived washes over me, but I mourn for all those who didn't.

Chapter Thirty-Eight
Stirrings
March – Purgatory Academy

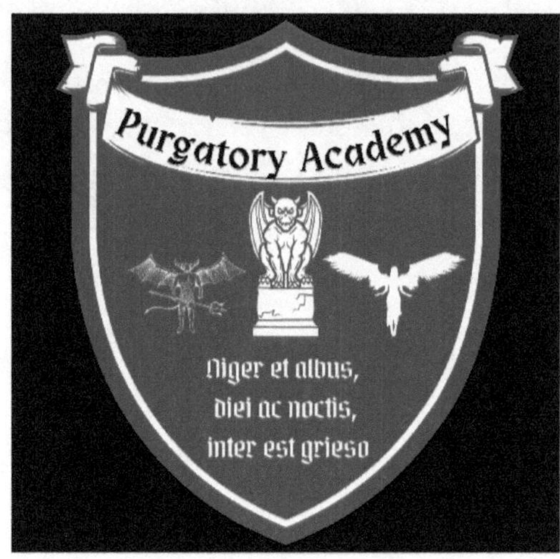

My Malak is one of the last beings I want to see when I mistport into my RV, but there the fucker is. We stare at each other. Well, I stare at him. I can't see into the depths of that stupid hood. He could be sleepwalking for all I know. One robed arm reaches toward me, a folded piece of paper peeking out. I take it gingerly and open the written note in a spidery hand:

Because of today's murder, we have decided to cancel the Spring Equinox celebration.

The note is signed by Gressil. I don't bother asking the Malak what the dean of students is referring to; instead, I toss the note on my bed, but when I turn back my Malak is gone. Good riddance.

It's pretty late when I finally crawl into bed. I try to eat some of the dinner my dad left for me, but my appetite's spoiled; Barlowe is more than happy to finish it off. Despite my exhaustion, I struggle to fall asleep. Barlowe curls up next to me and his warmth and purring ultimately lull me into slumber.

The only good thing about the Tribulations is that they are on Fridays, always Fridays. That gives the survivors the weekend to rest up and prepare for another week of grueling schooling, while waiting with bated breath for the next Tribulation. Unfortunately, I'm not able to sleep in. My thoughts crash down on me with abandon. They swirl around so many different directions.

There are the normal things from Purgatory Academy. The Tribulations, the classes, the divide between the Ascended and the Descended, the chasm between the ancient families and the newbies like me who know shit all. That last one is the one that bothers me the most. I'm at such a disadvantage compared to those old families and I'm not alone.

Of course, there were the two murders. There's clearly a connection between them. They were both Ascended, but more than that they were friends. There has to be something there. It doesn't look good for Drake. It's possible he killed them, but it would have been so fast from the time he waited in secret till everyone was gone and then came and helped us in the Ossa Forest.

I know my own feelings are blinding me to the situation some. I don't want to admit it, but it's true. I have a thing for Drake. Of course, I have a thing for Gabe too. I don't want to admit that at all either. Gabe is that sort of old school chivalrous and despite wanting to be a modern, independent woman, I respect that…well, I'm turned on by it at least. Drake is just brooding hotness with what just might be a gooey center. They're both a bad idea. The Golden Boy and the End of Days. And that's part of their appeal. My libido agrees.

I push the lust away, but my thoughts turn to that first day at PA. Gressil whispered that he knew my mother. I've been so busy studying and just trying to stay alive that I've not given it as much thought as I wanted.

There's also the green fire I shot out of my hands in the Ossa Forest. I'm learning about all kinds of magic the Nephilim possess, but nothing has been mentioned of it. Fire yes, but not my kind. Considering all of this is giving me a headache.

I'm unable to stave off the growing need in my loins. A thought flashes into my mind. Well, it's more of a vision. Well, a vision of a vision. It's that dream Emilie gave me of Drake and Gabe. That's a much nicer thing to think about, to consider, to want. Ache develops between my legs. It builds and builds, and I can't think of anything else. My fingers slip underneath my pajamas and panties.

"What are you doing?" Barlowe's voice scares the shit out of me. I completely forgot he was curled up right next to me. He laughs in my mind.

"It's none of your business," I snap.

"Oh please. My question was rhetorical. I know exactly what you're doing...and thinking, for that matter." My face burns with embarrassment. *"There's no point in being ashamed about it. It's natural. On top of that, as your powers grow, so too will your needs. Shame will only get in the way. Denial of that shame's existence is even worse."*

"That doesn't mean I want to do anything like that in front of you," I grumble.

"I can go away."

"Don't bother. I should get in the shower." I stand up and walk into the bathroom, closing the door behind me. I get into the shower, the water warm and lovely. My comfort only leads back to those same thoughts. In my mind's eye, I see those hard bodies, those callused hands, those beautiful eyes and gorgeous smiles. How they pressed up against me.

My eyes close and I pick up where I left off. I imagine Gabe behind me in the shower, his hard cock pressed against my ass while Drake kneels before me and uses his tongue instead of the fingers I slide inside. It feels so good and I tell Drake to go faster. Gabe kisses me from behind. Apparently, my imagination is pretty good because I don't last long before I burst right there in the shower on my own fingers.

It's an intense one and I have to lean back against the wall to prop myself up, my legs weak. Barlowe was right. I should embrace this a bit more. It's nice, very nice. But that doesn't mean I'm going to do it in front of my creepy cat Familiar.

I dry off and dress. Looking at my phone, I'm shocked to find it's almost dinner time. I don't feel hungry, but I know I should eat. Plus, I miss my dad. It's Saturday though and he'll be doing his show with the elephants soon. I decide to go out instead and wander about a bit.

"Want me to come with you?" Barlowe asks.

"No. I'll be okay." Barlowe puts his head back down on the bed and falls asleep.

There's a hustle and bustle about; the carnival is already open for the evening. I decide to eat some crappy carnie food that's delicious, nonetheless. I might even say hello to some of my friends in the circus. I haven't been around much lately and that sounds nice.

I have an elephant ear first. They're deep-fried goodness. They aren't even remotely healthy, but they are so delicious. I wash it down with a lemonade. Too much sugar, but oh so tasty.

I don't stop to play any of the rigged games, but I wave to some of my buddies as I pass. They always wave back, genuine smiles gracing their faces. I wander for hours. There's something about the carnival that's strangely comforting. As an introvert, I need a break from people, but walking among them without talking is somehow soothing and connecting.

I meander about, occasionally sitting to watch. It's crazy how this used to be my entire life, but now it's only a small piece. It hurts, but it's also liberating to know there's so much more. My wandering takes me to the Freak Show at the edge of the carnival. Some of my closest friends work there.

There's a group of four college students in front of me as I enter the large, worn black and white tent. The young men are enjoying themselves on a Saturday night, being generally loud and obnoxious. One of them sees me as I sip at another lemonade. Our eyes meet and I smile coyly over my straw. He's handsome in a jock sort of way. Taller than me with short curly red hair; I appreciate finding another redhead like me. I keep my distance. Furtive looks are one thing, but I don't want to talk or even flirt. He keeps looking back though.

The jocks, because they definitely are, stop in front of the second to last of the performances in the Freak Show, the Bearded Lady. Carmilla was my mom's best friend. Now she's a sort of part-time surrogate aunt to me since my mother's death.

The beard Carmilla wears is fake, but the curves she has are quite real. I don't understand how she can still look that way. There's a reason her booth is one of the last ones. People tend to linger. The Bearded Lady definitely gets better tips than most. The college guys, who are about my age, act more like boys as they hoot and holler at Carmilla while she does her belly dance performance for them.

I dawdle, but the redhead continues to cast glances my way. The other three are completely mesmerized by Carmilla's exotic and erotic dance. It's impressive the directions she can bend her body. The college guys are putting quite a few dollars in her tip jar, obviously their beer money. Still well spent from the looks on their faces.

There's a sign at the opening of the Freak Show tent stating that there's no photography allowed, but one of the guys tries to sneak his phone out. Carmilla dances toward him tsk tsking sensually with a finger waggling. The others laugh and tease him for getting caught as he puts the phone back in his pocket.

The redhead's gaze lingers this time. I consider scooching past, but he's staring now, even as his buddies finally walk over to the final act. My friend, Wally, plays the role of werewolf there. Wally the Wolfman he's called. Now that I'm at Purgatory Academy, I wonder if werewolves actually exist.

Wally is good at what he does. He howls and growls with extra hair plastered all over his body. He runs around on all four and sniffs things. His movements and makeup are just good enough to make a person wonder if it's legit. That idea pretty much describes most of the acts in a circus and carnival. The most convincing part is his howl. Even the other carnies suggest he could be a real wolf.

The carnival should be closing soon. The redhead finally screws up his courage and approaches me near the Bearded Lady's small plank stage. Hands in the pockets of his tight jeans with a dark flannel, it's a reverse sort of Freudian moment. I decide not to touch that thought.

My time in the shower has taken the edge off, but that's about it. It isn't the same as being wanted, needed, coveted. The redhead slides a hand out of a pocket and waves nonchalantly as he approaches. "Hey, I'm Jared," he smiles.

I smile back almost automatically. That isn't something introvert me would have done a year ago, or even six months ago. "I'm Lilly," I respond.

"Listen, uh, I don't mean to be too forward here, but I just wanted to say that I love your red hair."

A throaty laugh ripples from me. I've never done that before, but it feels good. I feel…sexy. And Jared is obviously enjoying it. "Yes, you did," I say, smokiness pouring from my voice. Jared wears a confused look. Patiently, I explain. "You did mean to be forward."

He laughs this time and runs a hand through his red curls. "Yeah, okay. You caught me."

Leaning toward him I whisper, "I liked it." Part of my brain asks what the hell I think I'm doing, but the rest of me isn't really paying attention to that logical slice.

"Oh really?" he teases. "I'm happy to hear that. We redheads need to stick together."

"Hell yeah we do," I confirm. I shift closer to Wally the Wolfman and Jared's friends but walk slowly enough to invite him to come along. I could swear concern creases Wally's muzzle for a moment.

Jared's buddies notice he's talking to me and smirk at one another before going back to watching Wally run around and howl. I continue on by and Jared keeps right on following. At the end of the Freak Show tent is a lone folding chair.

A need burns through my body. I turn back to Jared, "Did you mean it?" He gives me a confused smile. I explain, "That redheads should stick together."

The confusion washes away but the smile remains. "Yeah, absolutely," he asserts. I twirl around touching my own skin. It's tingling and wonderfully warm. I feel so good and want to feel more. I cock an eyebrow at Jared and say, "There are a number of ways we can stick together." The husk in my voice is heavier.

"What did you have in mind?" he asks.

I motion for him to continue to follow me, leading him over to the chair. Taking his hand, I push him down gently. Embarrassment written on his face, he looks about, but his friends are around the corner, howling with and cheering on the Wolf Man.

No one else is present. I give it little thought beyond the fact that it serves my desire to be alone. I waste no time in straddling him, running my hands over his face and hair. His eyes are big with surprise. "Don't worry, I'll take care of everything," I promise.

Jared tries to nod, but I swallow up his movement with a kiss. I don't start slow either, but with a hunger I never realized I possessed. He tastes of carnival popcorn and watery beer, but I don't care. I feel wonderful. I feel alive.

He obviously feels good too because he grows under his jeans. My own core burns with desire. I want more, need more. Grinding against him, I moan as we kiss deeper.

"Maybe we should find somewhere more private?" Jared suggests, breathless.

"No need," I murmur as I keep kissing him.

"My-my friends are just around the corner," he tries again.

Frustrated, I pull back and stare into his eyes. I barely have to call up my Sway to take hold of him. "Don't worry about your friends. Just be here with me. Only this matters."

Jared's eyes glaze over, and we go back to kissing, more urgent than ever. He is achingly hard, his face filled with need. I smirk and slide down onto the ground, kneeling in front of him, reaching for his zipper.

It's in that moment Carmilla, Wally the Wolf Man, and Jared's three friends come around the corner. It's clear that the college guys got a bit out of control. I can tell from the scowl on Carmilla's face and Wally walking right behind them.

"Lilly?" Carmilla says, confusion in her voice. Jared's friends stare, slack jawed but Wally glares at him.

"What?" I snarl at Carmilla in a voice neither of us has ever heard before.

"Lilly?" Surprise laces Carmilla's voice this time.

"Keep walking, Carmilla. We're fine." The snarl is still in my voice. I don't know where it comes from.

Carmilla walks toward us, and I stand, taking up a fighting stance, which has the Bearded Lady stopping and Wally the Wolf Man stepping up next to her. The little bit of distance wakes Jared up. He blinks a couple of times, and his friends rush forward to gather him up. Wally motions for them to leave immediately. None of them argue as they flee the Freak Show tent.

Wally stares at me. "I'll go make certain they get out the gates." Clearing his throat, he marches out.

The Bearded Lady lingers behind. "You ruined everything," I all but shout petulantly.

Carmilla blinks and steps forward slowly as if approaching a predator. She keeps her gaze locked with mine. Her face opens up with realization and her hand comes up to gently caress my face. I practically purr at the touch. Jared is gone from my mind and thoughts of Carmilla flood me. The woman is beautiful behind that fake beard. She wears so little too, showing off her lithe body. My hand reaches for the older woman's hips, searching to bring her closer.

"Lilly!" Carmilla's voice is filled with sharpness as if she'd said it several times and not been heard. I take a deep breath, shake my head, and try to come back to myself. What in the world is going on? This isn't the kind of person I am. There's nothing wrong with that, but it isn't me. That's not to mention my personal history that I refuse to delve into now, or ever. The realization slams into me and I slump down. All the desire and lust, the arousal, finally seep out of me. I'm left feeling weak and unfulfilled, like there's an itch I can't scratch and even though it isn't there anymore, I still feel the phantom of it.

Carmilla doesn't reach out this time. "Sweetie let's get you home. I'll go with you."

I barely remember the walk, fog filling my mind. We make it to my RV and Carmilla gets the keys from me. "We need to get you inside. You need some sleep. You'll feel better in the morning."

As the door opens, I turn to Carmilla with a sudden realization. "Are you going to tell my dad?" I'm twenty years old, but I still care what my dad thinks of me.

Carmilla chews her lower lip as she considers the request. "You know, I rarely remember you getting into trouble as a child. You were always so well behaved. Even when…" Her words trail off, but I know what the older woman was about to say. Even when your mother passed away. "I think we'd just worry your father if we told him, so no. I'm not going to say anything to him." She pauses for a moment. "Darling, are you okay? I haven't seen you in a while, but when I finally do, you're…well, different."

I don't answer right away. "Life has been…complicated lately."

The Bearded Woman nods. "Life has a way of doing that. But if you need anything, please let me know. I'm here for you. I'm happy to listen."

"Thank you." I climb up in my RV.

Barlowe is waiting for me. *"That was a close one."*

Shaking my head, I walk past the cat and plop down on my bed, falling backward on it. "Ugh," I rub my temples. "How did you know?" I ask out loud.

The cat Familiar scoffs in my mind. *"You know the answer to that. You weren't that far away. I see and feel what you see and feel."*

"Great," I respond. *"You're such a voyeur,"* I tease. *"Why didn't you help me?"*

"I'd have to believe what you were doing was wrong for me to help," he responds.

"Ugh."

His laughter echoes in my mind, but he curls up next to my face, immediately purring like a tank. I lean against him, appreciating the warmth his little body provides and the soothing vibes his purring gives off. Of course, he has to ruin it right away. *"Your dad came looking for you."*

"Why did you let me lay down before telling me?"

"You obviously need to get some sleep. You can talk to your father tomorrow."

A deep sigh escapes me, but Barlowe is right. My dad was probably just checking in on me, but I miss him. I need a dad hug badly. It's more than that though. He's also the only normal thing in my life anymore and I desperately need more normal in my life. I'll go find him tomorrow. Right now I need more sleep.

I slip into pajamas, but although I sleep, it isn't deep. That need still gnaws at me. It's unfinished, unfulfilled. I wake up in the morning to knocking at my door.

It's my dad, holding a pile of steaming crepes. A smile spreads across my face at the sight and my stomach grumbles at the fragrance. He has two thermals as well. His is filled with coffee and mine with chai tea latte. I get a sweet whiff of the cinnamon as he opens mine and passes it over. I'm reminded of Drake for a moment but brush it away.

Barlowe saunters in, stretching all four of his legs and jumping up on the table to await his portion. He's still a kitten, but he has hops already and is growing quickly like a real kitten would.

"Good morning, Barlowe." Dad commences to rub and pat the Familiar all over his furry body. Barlowe, for his part, purrs up a storm, before finally laying down on my father's lap.

"I enjoy the calluses on your dad's hands."

I snort mentally. *"That comment might not sound as innocent as you think it did."*

"Who says I meant it innocently?"

"Gross." Dad makes certain to give the kitten a couple of spoon scoops of cream from the top of the crepes. Barlowe purrs louder before falling asleep. Only then does my dad start eating his own crepes. He's always putting others before himself. Me, I'm halfway finished by that point.

"How are you?" he asks.

I don't look up as I tell him my half-truths. "School is keeping me pretty busy. It's tough to maintain everything."

"How about today?" he asks.

"I don't have anything due tomorrow. What did you have in mind?"

"Want to help me with the elephants before tonight's shows?"

"I'd like that very much."

"Great," he says. "I'll take this with me and meet you over there."

Barlowe doesn't love having to get up from his warm spot, but he does it without verbal complaint, just grumbling. Kissing me on the forehead, Dad leaves. I hop in the shower and dress in boots and jeans with a hoodie, comfy clothes for helping him.

I open the door and Barlowe darts out with me. *"Where are you going?"* I ask.

"I'm bored to death in your RV. It's time to explore. Plus, you really need to get a cat door in that thing. I don't like closed doors."

I'm getting used to snorting mentally. Barlowe provides me with plenty of practice. *"I'll get right on that."*

I'm still thinking of the idea of a cat door when we arrive at the elephant enclosure. Dad sees the humored look on my face. "What's so funny?"

"I had this silly thought about putting a cat door in my RV for Barlowe."

Instead of laughing, my dad's face gets pensive. "I think I could manage that."

I chuckle. "I'm sure you could." I begin helping with the elephants. Barlowe follows me. The elephants are extremely curious about him. They surround him, each of their trunks touching him. And he loves it. Flopping over in the dirt, he lounges while they pet him with their trunks.

We work in silence, but it's a companionable quiet. The physical labor is soothing. It's good to be normal for a little while.

When we finish up, Dad hugs me long and hard before heading back to his RV to shower and change for the evening's performance. Barlowe and I walk back to our RV as well. I consider watching the show tonight, but I'm exhausted still. It isn't so early that I can't go to bed already.

As I lay there, my thoughts sadly return to Purgatory Academy and everything I have to face yet. I'm just going to have to deal with it. My musings steer me toward the green fire I conjured in the Ossa Forest. I consider attempting it again but decide against it. I don't want to burn my RV to the ground.

My thoughts wander toward Drake and Gabe, but I'm too tired to entertain any fantasies. I'm grateful for that. More than anything else, I ponder the murders. My life is filled with so much death. And with each new Tribulation there's a chance it will be my own.

"It hasn't all been bad," Barlowe chimes in.

"No?"

"Of course not! You have me!"

I don't want to give Barlowe the pleasure of knowing I find that funny even if he tells the joke way too much, but I laugh out loud, nonetheless. *"True,"* I admit.

"There's Marius too. But mostly me."

I laugh again while we curl up together. But as I enter that state between waking and dreams, my mind turns to the murders once more. And a plan begins to form.

Chapter Thirty-Nine
Captain of the Guard
March – Purgatory Academy

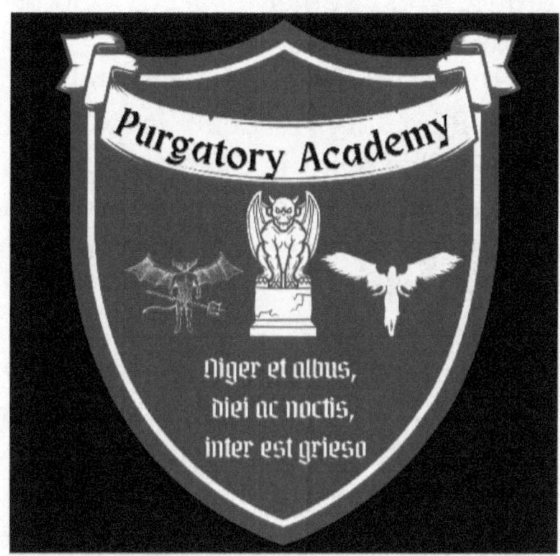

The next morning Marius and I stare at the glowing red numbers of the surviving Nephilim. The Ascended numbers fell from 903 to 843. The Descended dropped from 1012 to 946. The most horrible part about it all is my first thought. I figured more of us died during that Tribulation. The numbers didn't lower that much though. I hate myself for thinking that way. This isn't math. This isn't statistics. These are living, breathing beings. Each one of them had wishes, desires, dreams. But they were snuffed out. And the comparatively small number of them makes no difference. I scold myself internally for my callousness.

My second train of thought pisses me off more. Even though there are more Descended than Ascended, it's obvious that the last two Tribulations hit the Descended harder. I continue to contribute that fact to the have's and have not's in this world. There are more Descended left unknowing of this existence. I've seen it among my classmates, spoken with them. They aren't prepared to survive here. Plus, the Ascended have natural leadership in Gabe. The Descended have nothing of the sort. I can do something about this last point.

There is a surprise waiting for us in our Angelology and Demonology class. Neither of the professors are present. Instead, there's a gargoyle. Nervous silence permeates the classroom as the bells ring out. The room is even smaller now which makes the hulking gargoyle seem larger than he already is.

In that now familiar gravel of a voice he speaks, "I am the captain of the guard here at Purgatory Academy. I am here today to teach you about gargoyles, my kin. It's the goal of your professors in this course to introduce you to other denizens who reside here beyond the angels, demons, and yourselves.

"Gargoyles, like your Familiars, are natives of this plane of existence. Our goal at Purgatory Academy is to keep the peace, as I'm certain you are aware at this point in the academic year. The one thing that you should know about us is that we are a private and secretive kin. I'm not going to divulge all sorts of information about my kind. However, you are welcome to ask questions." His voice suggests nothing of the sort.

My plan is formulating even more as I consider the giant stone creature. Raising my hand to the absolute mortification of Marius, the gargoyle grunts his acknowledgement. All heads swivel my way as I speak, "Are there any updates on the murders?"

The room was deathly silent before. Now it is death. The anxiety is so thick I might have just choked everyone to death on it. I breathe through it, not allowing my face to turn red with embarrassment. This is too important to allow my anxiety to get in the way.

The stone of his face shifts some, but I can't read it. Admiration? Irritation? The look he uses right before he rips your face off? "The investigation is ongoing."

Wow. He has the television crime show answer ready and waiting. Impressive. Feeling like a journalist for some stupid reason, and obviously having a death wish, I speak up again. "How were the murders even possible since you are able to stop violence before it begins?"

The temperature in the room drops to subzero. He grinds out his response. "The investigation is ongoing. Now. Are there any *other* questions?" There aren't. The gargoyle grunts. "Then you are dismissed early."

I sweep the room to find Marius, Gabe, Drake, and several others staring at me. I ignore them all. I'm not giving up that easily. Standing up, I make my way toward the gargoyle who is marching toward one of the faculty exits.

Eyes are following me, but I keep my own on the gargoyle. Hurrying forward as he stomps out, I call to him. "Captain!" Instead of going out the door, he's standing in front of the stone wall next to it. The rippling is already taking effect as he waits. I call again. "Captain!" He hears but ignores me.

I come up short of putting my hand on the behemoth's shoulder as he turns toward me. A growl reverberates from his chest, and I snatch my hand back before he rips it off. When he realizes I'm not a threat, the rumble fades away and an arched brow replaces it. I put a hand to my mouth to hold in my laugh. I didn't expect that at all. Stony eyebrow arch. Nice.

The captain seems to realize what I'm thinking. It makes him smile. Or at least I think that's what he's doing. The shark teeth don't make it easy to feel safe. Shaking his head a bit he says, "Let me guess. You want to help."

"I have a plan," I whisper. The look on my face must convince him to take me seriously. He shifts away from the wall and the rippling stops. I take that as my cue. Leaning in, I explain.

When I'm finished, the gargoyle stares at me long and hard before he responds, "I appreciate you wanting to help, but this investigation is the responsibility of the gargoyles."

Keeping his gaze, I retort. "Or maybe you need to help me."

The captain huffs a short laugh. "Sway doesn't work on gargoyles. It's part of the reason we're so good at our jobs."

I shrug. "It was worth a shot."

"There are only two ways to get a gargoyle to help you."

I wait for him to explain, but he doesn't. "Okay. What are they?"

Turning back to the wall, it ripples anew as the captain speaks. "If you don't know what they are, then you're not ready to ask for help from gargoyles." He melts into the wall.

A sigh of frustration escapes me, and I turn to find Barlowe waiting for me. *That went well.*

Shut it. I don't look back to see if my Familiar is following me out of the room. His mental mocking laughter is proof enough.

Chapter Forty
Making Plans
March – Purgatory Academy

Marius waits for me outside the classroom and we walk together to our next class, Temptations and Fortitude. He holds off till we're away from the classroom before he begins bombarding me with questions. Blackbeard echoes his inquiries out loud like the good, annoying parrot he is. Barlowe puts a stop to it when he jumps and nearly knocks Blackbeard down. Luckily, Marius lunges backwards so he misses, barely.

I'm too busy berating the kitten Familiar to answer Marius' questions before we reach our next class. Emilie is already there. Today she's wearing a one-piece bunny suit, like from the old Playboy magazine years. She even has the bunny ears. It's ridiculous, but as always Emilie makes it work. I know it's all old school because there are plenty of circus men who still prefer the magazines. They say it's more natural and no one can trace it like with a phone. Good old carnie paranoia mixed with healthy hormones.

"Hello, my sweetlings," Emilie's golden voice sings out. "Today we will be pairing off again to work on your Sway." Nervous groans echo all around, but the demoness ignores them as she immediately begins calling out the pairings. The professor apparently thinks she's not only sexy but also funny because she has Gabe and me working together again. Before Barlowe can follow me over, Emilie informs us that our Familiars need to remain behind.

Gabe and I meet about halfway across the room. While Emilie might have been playing games with the two of us, it actually works to my advantage because this is the next step in my plan. "Hi." I pour cheeriness into my voice with just a dash of Sway.

The Ascended looks as if he's trying not to smile back, but he loses. "Hey."

I'm not certain how to broach the topic and that makes it a bit weird. "Crazy year, right?"

He responds, "Yeah." Lame questions warrant lame answers. Fair enough.

"I, um, I wanted to tell you that I really admired how you handled the last two Tribulations. You saved a lot of lives. You know that, right?" Gabe's face screws up uncomfortably. "You don't like compliments any more than I do, do you?" I ask.

He fidgets. "I suppose not. I didn't do it, you know, to stand out. I did it because it was the right thing to do."

"I appreciate that about you."

"You do? You? A Descended?"

My raspberry is particularly fresh with spit. "I mean, I'd prefer if we all worked together, but I get that we're supposed to be enemies and everything. Still, we're all just trying to survive." Gabe is silent, contemplating my words, and perhaps wondering if they're some kind of trap. "I understand. You don't know if you can trust me because I'm Descended," I continue.

Gabe looks as if he wants to argue the point but can't come up with any logical answers. "Can you be? Trusted, I mean?"

I look into his eyes. They really are a beautiful blue. Like the ocean, I'm pretty sure I would drown in them if I stayed too long. Shaking my head, I say, "Yes. But you have to be the one to believe it."

"How do I do that?"

"Well, there is one way."

"I'm listening," he says.

"You can help me."

"I can trust you by helping you? How exactly does that work?" The incredulity is written all over his face. This is my chance though. No time to be bashful about it.

"I want to stop these murders," I blurt out. I must have said it pretty quickly because he stares blankly at me for a moment. I decide to repeat myself, "I want to st-"

"I heard what you said. But why? They were both Ascended. Why would you care?"

I don't want to admit how much it hurts to hear him say that, the pain as sharp as a knife. "I know we Descended are supposed to be monsters, but I'm not. There are a lot of things about this place and this world that are fucked up, but I don't think it's okay that someone is going around murdering students, regardless of who they are."

Gabe takes in my words. He knows how I must have felt about Adam, who was quite the bully. His friends aren't much better and one of them is dead now too. "Adam and Luke were my friends. We grew up together. I wasn't proud of everything they did, but I cared for them."

There's a vast pain in those sea blue eyes. "Look, I might have only seen the ugly things about your friends, but that doesn't mean I wished them dead and I sure as hell had nothing to do with it. It has to stop."

"How do we go about doing that?" he asks.

"I've been considering that. I think the first thing we need to figure out is if there was anything they shared. I know they were friends, and they grew up together, but I'm talking secrets or something like that. The best thing to do would be to interview their families. But obviously..." my voice trails off.

"It would be better if that came from an Ascended, especially a friend," Gabe finishes. We stare at each other for a few more moments. I wonder what his lips would taste like. Gabe breaks the spell by looking away thoughtfully. I can't decide if I'm grateful or bummed about it. When he finally looks back, he says, "Alright, I'll consider it."

It's more than I could hope for so I just nod. "We should probably practice before Emilie comes around and uses her Sway on us."

Gabe actually shudders at that. "No thank you. You're bad enough as is."

I hear the joking in his voice, but I still pretend to be insulted. "Hey, what's that supposed to mean?"

He gives me that bulbs bright smile. "You do realize your Sway is more powerful than most others in our class?"

I draw back in surprise. "It is?"

"*You are,*" he emphasizes.

"How can you tell?" I ask.

"Are you kidding me? You were the first to get your egg to hatch and your Familiar was completely docile."

I laugh at that. "I can't wait to tell Barlowe how *docile* he is." I'll have to consider the fact later that he noticed I hatched my egg first.

"I'm serious. Even now I'm wondering if you Swayed me into considering this crazy idea of working together."

The tone of his voice invokes a desire to be more playful with him. "Trust me. If I used my Sway on you, you would have said yes immediately." Fuck. What am I saying?

"Is that right?" The challenge in his voice is evident and he moves subtly closer to me.

"Mmmhmm," I whisper. The stare we share now can't be anything else but lust. Focus, I tell myself. "It doesn't feel that way."

Gabe's forehead wrinkles in confusion. "What doesn't?"

"My Sway. I don't feel that powerful."

"Well, our powers are complicated in the beginning. They sneak up on us as we mature. It's not all at once. If you ask me, it's better that way. We'd probably all kill ourselves if we had them immediately."

It makes sense. "Even so, I'm not sure I'm handling mine all that well," I admit.

"I don't know about that, but I will say this. You are not at all what I expected from a Descended succubus."

"Exactly how many succubi have you known?" He shakes with silent laugher. "Well, to be honest, you aren't what I expected from someone referred to as the Chosen One and the Golden Boy," I tease.

He cringes at the joke. "My family has…high expectations." I wait for him to share more, wanting to give him space and time to do so. "I'm a leader. That's what I was born to be." No trace of satisfaction or arrogance laces his voice as he says the words, just resignation.

"That must be difficult," I sympathize. I mean it too. That has to be tough.

Gabe rolls his shoulders. "It is at times."

Trying to look for the positive I say, "But at least you're not alone. You have two other archim with you."

His face lights up at that. "True. We grew up together, being groomed for what we'll become." We share a companionable moment of silence before he continues. "Listen, I will talk to Trist and Eli and let you know at lunch. Okay?"

"Deal," I say.

Chapter Forty-One
Making Alliances
March – Purgatory Academy

I start talking as soon as I sit down at lunch, "Do either of you know anything about gargoyles?"

Marius and Drake are already eating. Marius finishes chewing before he speaks because he's polite like that. "Not any more than anyone else. It's like the captain said in class, they're secretive. What did you say to him? You didn't tell me anything in the hallway earlier."

"I told him I wanted to help with the investigation."

Drake scoffs. "I'm sure he was quite receptive to that."

I make a face at him. "Yeah, but there's no need to be snarky about it." Drake sticks out his tongue at me. I'm so surprised by the familiarity I don't know what to do at first. "Did you just tease me?"

Drake winks at me and goes back to eating. I glance at Marius and his mouth is hanging open. Shaking my head, I continue on. "Anyway, when I talked to him, he said that there are only two ways to get help from a gargoyle. He wouldn't tell me what they are."

"I thought you said you wanted to help him, not get help from him." The teasing is in Drake's voice this time. I roll my eyes and shove some food in my mouth to take a moment. His teasing is a lot hotter than I'd like to admit. Stoic is sexy in its own way, but Drake opening up is even better. I'm just about to say something again when he speaks. "I know what he meant. I'll take care of it." Marius and I both stare at him. He doesn't bother explaining further. Back to stoic it is.

Marius jumps in, "I want to help too. It's the right thing to do." I hold out a hand to him across the table to show my gratitude. He squeezes it gently and goes back to his food.

I'm about to say more, but I'm distracted by the fact that Gabe is walking over to our table from his big group of Ascended, Eli and Trist in tow. Everyone is staring. Behind them, I glimpse Matthew, the third member of Adam's trio of friends. Every one of his facial features is distorted with anger.

They don't sit. Gabe clears his throat while Eli stares at the ground and Trist looks like she is ready to rip all our heads off. "We're going to help," Gabe declares.

I try to give him as good a smile as I can with Trist all but ready to attack. "Thank you. That means a lot."

Trist scoffs, "The only reason I'm doing it is because I think it was one of you." She stares at Drake, who keeps on eating.

"Keep your enemies closer," I say. "Got it. Nonetheless, we're grateful." Gabe catches my eye and nods ever so slightly before they walk back to their group, the entire cafeteria still silently watching.

Chapter Forty-Two
Keeping Alliances
March – Purgatory Academy

Marius and I spar lightly together after our warmup in War and Weapons; he's getting better. Once we finish, the professors bring us all in for the fighting section of the class. "Drake!" The'slin calls.

He walks over without a care in the world. The'slin grins at Drake before calling out again. "Trist!" Fuck. Trist stalks forward, a shit eating grin on her face. She stands across from Drake, staring at him with pure delight.

The'slin makes eye contact with Drake. "If you don't fight her, I will sic her on one of your friends." Trist's grin grows wider. Drake scowls, but he nods his understanding to the demon.

Khal'ith has them bow and take up their fighting stances before calling the fight. Trist goes right at Drake with several combo punches, but he blocks or dodges each one. She hangs back for a moment, and he steps forward throwing a couple of punches that are ridiculous. Everyone knows it as evidenced by their laughter. Trist and The'slin are the only ones who don't find it amusing. They both glare.

Trist springs forward with a haymaker and connects with Drake's jaw, hard. He steps out of reach again and throws more mock punches. She runs at him, punching him in the face with a couple of sharp jabs. She's furious, but Drake springs out of her path repeatedly.

The'slin storms forward, fury written all over his face. He roars at Drake, "Keep this up and I will call Lilly up here to fight Trist instead."

Drake stares at the demon. And snorts. "Good luck with that. Lilly can take care of herself just fine."

The demonic professor takes a step toward Drake but then stops in surprise when Khal'ith's clear laughter rings out. He whips about to face the angel, but his counterpart shrugs back at him, amused.

Letting out a big breath, The'slin says to Drake. "Do you know why I push you so much?"

Drake doesn't even twitch. "I don't give a shit." Then he walks away. The demon takes a couple of steps that direction, but Khal'ith moves into his path.

All I hear in my mind as Drake comes to stand along the wall again is how he knows I can take care of myself. The words, and the thought, make me happier than I want anyone to know.

Chapter Forty-Three
Secrets Shared
March – Purgatory Academy

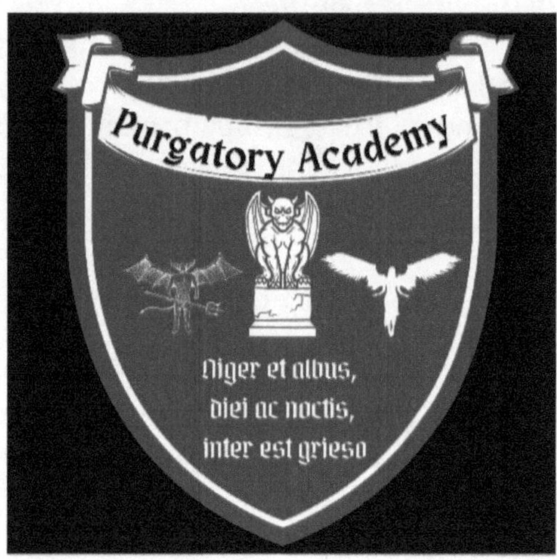

That evening Dad surprises me with dinner in his RV along with Carmilla. It's nice to feel normal for a while, but I'm beginning to realize it will never last for me. Not really.

Carmilla is unusually quiet during much of the meal. My father senses it and being the sweet person he is, carries the conversation. The Bearded Lady, who is sans beard this evening, side eyes me quite a bit.

When we're finished with dinner, my father stands to clean up. Carmilla says, "Sam, I hate to leave you alone with the dishes when you already cooked, but do you mind terribly if I steal Lilly for a little bit?"

He doesn't bother turning toward us as he responds. "Of course not. I've got this."

"Walk with me?" Carmilla asks.

I kiss my dad on the cheek before bidding him a good night. Carmilla steps out first and the two of us head for my RV in silence.

When we reach it, because it isn't that far from my father's, I say to Carmilla. "We haven't spent time alone together in a while. It used to be a regular thing."

"You've been quite busy the last couple of months." There is no accusation in Carmilla's voice, just observation of a fact.

"True." I hesitate but forge forward. "But you were already drifting away." I don't know where the words come from, but they're true at least from my perspective. Carmilla stares, a look of complete shock on her face. I continue, "I always assumed you didn't want a redheaded reminder of what you'd lost when my mother died."

The look of shock melts into one of utter horror. "Oh sweetie, of course not." The last word fades away and I see the truth of her fear. I not only lost my mother when she died, but also my de facto aunt. And if I'm being absolutely honest, I lost at least part of my relationship with my dad too. We never speak of my mother and that is a death in and of itself.

Carmilla sits down on the steps in front of the door to my RV. Blowing out a big breath, she says, "I loved your mother so much."

"So, you didn't want the reminder any more than my dad does."

The Bearded Lady gasps and her eyes fill with tears. Her voice breaks before she can speak. Trying again, she says, "No, that wasn't it at all."

Hands on my hips, and suddenly angry, I say, "Then why?"

Exhaling deeply again, Carmilla asks, "Do you know how special your mother was?"

Huffing out a less than pleasant laugh, I respond. "I'm learning more about it every day."

It's Carmilla's turn to laugh. "I bet you are." The statement and tone catch me off guard. "You do remind me so very much of your mother."

"I'm getting an inkling of that too," I say. And then it dawns on me. It has been right there in front of me the entire time, but I was just too dense to see it. I peer closer at Carmilla. She's still such a beautiful woman. She has aged so well, but as I step closer, I realize it for the very first time. Instead of saying anything, I reach out gently and pick one of the small wrinkles of skin off Carmilla's face. It peels right off.

The older woman doesn't move. "Did you know that your mother and I attended the same college?"

"A private one, yes?"

"That's right." Carmilla smiles and there they are. Elongated canines the likes of which only a Descended Nephil could have.

I'm completely prepared to be angry at the older woman, but seeing those teeth all I can do is laugh and smile back, sharing my own fangs. "What didn't you tell me?" I ask, nearly bouncing up and down with excitement now. Talk about an emotional roller coaster. "Why didn't my mom tell me?"

The fangs disappear. "Your mother and I both held out the ridiculous hope it would somehow skip you. It's been known to happen. But as I look back on it now, I understand how naïve we both were, given her family lineage."

"Is it an ancient family? I know I'm from the House of Lillith."

"It is indeed."

"What about your house?"

Carmilla reaches under the folds of her shirt and pulls out a chain necklace with a ring just like mine. Showing it to me, I see the symbol of the House of Cain, his visage stamped there along with the words, encapsulated in a ruby gem. "Your mother helped me a lot when we were at PA. She was my best friend."

Carmilla is a vampire of the House of Cain. I let the thoughts, the memories of my mother wash through my mind. "I miss her so much."

"Me too," Carmilla whispers, her eyes closed as if she could get them to reabsorb the tears that fall as soon as she opens them.

I reach for her and we hug, crying together in silence for a couple of minutes more. "Why did you two never tell my dad the truth?"

"Simple. We wanted to keep him safe. Plausible deniability. He wouldn't have to lie if asked. All that."

"Was there anyone in particular you were keeping him safe from?"

"Your mother's family," Carmilla explains. "Your mother and I were best friends at PA because we grew up together. The thing that bonded us more than anything else though was that we both hated our families with an abiding passion. Keeping each other alive through our year at Purgatory Academy only solidified that friendship. Both of our families are filled with monsters, but if I had to choose, I'd say her family is worse."

Confusion washes over me. There's a family out there I'll never know, but perhaps I don't want to from the sounds of it. We sit in more quiet before I change the subject. "Can you tell me anything about the Tribulations?"

Carmilla stares into space. "No. I can't."

Anger juts up suddenly. "You want to tell me all those old fucking families don't tell their children exactly what they will be facing in the Tribulations?"

"That's exactly what I'm saying."

I can't believe what I'm hearing. "What would stop them from that?"

"When you leave, a spell is placed on you. You can't talk about it with anyone other than someone who has already lived through it."

"What happens if you do tell?"

"You die."

I don't know what to say to that, but my anger hasn't cooled down yet. "I still say ancient families have advantages I never did because my mother and you told me nothing about my heritage."

Carmilla doesn't respond immediately. "You're right. Hindsight is twenty-twenty though. It's easy to see now that we were wrong."

I want to be angry still, but when I really consider it, I get it. They were doing what they believed to be best for me. I can't fault them for that. "I understand," I say finally.

"I can tell you this little piece of wisdom though," Carmilla says. "Make friends. You're much more likely to survive if you do."

"I have." I think about Marius, but also Drake and Gabe.

Carmilla senses something in the faraway look on my face. "Friendships are important. Anything deeper than that can be dangerous." I don't respond. "I should let you sleep. We'll talk more. I promise."

I smile at the thought. "I'd like that." We hug long and hard before I head back into my RV. There is a lightness in my heart that hasn't been there perhaps since my mother died. It's nice to have it back.

Chapter Forty-Four
Imps and Sway, the Sexy Way
March – Purgatory Academy

My Sinners and Saints class the next morning flashes by. My thoughts are all over the place but mostly steer back toward my conversation with Carmilla the night before.

Evocation doesn't let me drift though. Ren'el calls me third to come up and take my turn to call an imp from Hell. The first student, an Ascended with a Middle Eastern complexion and a thick Arabic accent, struggles both calling the imp up and sending it back down. The imp even gets away for a bit, pissing and shitting on the heads of students. Ren'el finally steps in and catches it, sending it back immediately.

The second student does a bit better, but not by much. It just means that the Descended female, who curses quite a bit in Spanish, calls the imp up, but struggles to keep it under the dome. She figures it out though and sends it back. At least, no one is defecated on this time.

Then my name is called. Nerves shake my knees as I walk over to the nine-pointed star. Ren'el motions for me to go ahead. At this point, it's expected that we know what to do. She hands over the athame. I prick the tip of my finger, letting a few drops drip into the star.

The nice thing about going so late in the process is that I have plenty of time to consider what I'm going to do. My decision is made out of sheer belligerence, but I'm not going to show my hand yet. Instead, I close my eyes and call to the imp, whispering the entire time. Three times I call, swelling my Sway to a crescendo.

I sense it happening, the conjuring working. Opening my eyes, the mist in the little globe is already fading and left behind is the black imp. As with every time they're called up, the creature punches, kicks and rages.

But I have already decided what I'm going to do. It's Drake who gave me the idea. He didn't bully the imp. He showed respect.

I kneel down and sit back on my heels, leaning forward over the tiny dome. I unbuttoned my shirt some before I came over and made certain my cleavage was showing. I don't allow myself to consider that I'm showing it off not only to the imp, but to many of my classmates. I focus on the imp.

Giving the little guy the biggest smile I can muster; I really hope it's a guy. Or at least a bisexual female. I don't speak Impish like Drake, but I'm pretty sure a combination of English, my tone, and some body language will bring across my point.

"My but you are a handsome male." I take a chance on the sex of the imp. His angular little face perks up at my compliment. His thin mouth splits open, showing off his shark teeth. He licks his lips with a black, forked tongue and presses his hands against the dome as I continue to sweet talk him.

It's only moments before the hard shell around his crotch splits open and a penis slides out. Yep, he's definitely a male alright. He presses hard against the dome now. I keep my smile pasted on my face. "Listen, I need your help. Could you be a good boy? My sweet helper?" I pour Sway and sensual sweetness into my voice. The imp nods incessantly. "That's wonderful. You know," I get down on all four letting my cleavage be even more evident, "I always take care of my special boys." I finish with a whisper and a wink. His shark smile widens, and his black sex stands up straight and strong. "I need you to go home to Hell now. I know you were brought here against your will. But when you do…I want you to think of me."

The imp grabs himself hard even as the mist rises in the tiny dome. He's stroking quite quickly as he disappears. Getting back up from my knees, I'm surprised to find most of my classmates staring at me with the same look the imp wore – lust.

When I spot the Triumvirate, Eli appears more shocked and surprised than anything else. Trist looks pissed off as per usual; she stares daggers at me. What's new? A flood of emotions flash across Gabe's face, each one as intense as the last. Lust is among them and no small amount of gratification flickers through me.

I still find myself searching for Drake, despite my gratification over Gabe. When I find him, I wish I'd remained content with Gabe. Drake's face reveals nothing, stoic as ever. For the first time since I met him, I hate it. I hate that look of complete and utter indifference.

"Impressive, Lilly. You may take your seat," Ren'el says. Most of the class continues to stare as I head for my chair, a strange mix of satisfaction and embarrassment following me the entire way.

"Good job," Marius whispers as I sit down. He's smiling mischievously.

"Shut up," I whisper back.

Marius snickers in response. Plenty of students are still casting furtive glances my way when class lets out. One thing is obvious after that session; my Sway is getting pretty damn good.

I mention as much to Marius on our way out. "Sway tends to be more powerful among succubi and incubi," he responds.

"I hadn't considered that. I wonder if I should talk to some of the others. Get some tips on how to control this better."

Marius gives me a side eye. "Are you struggling with something in particular?"

I can't bring myself to tell him about what happened at the carnival. Instead, I go on the offensive a little bit. "Marius, why don't you spend more time with other Descended? You come from an ancient family, but you spend your time with me."

Marius cringes. "Is that so bad?"

"No, I'm grateful, but I just wonder why."

I've never seen Marius angry, but it flashes across his face now. "I know them, but they aren't my friends. There's a difference." He doesn't say more. And I don't ask.

Chapter Forty-Five
Pravuel
March – Purgatory Academy

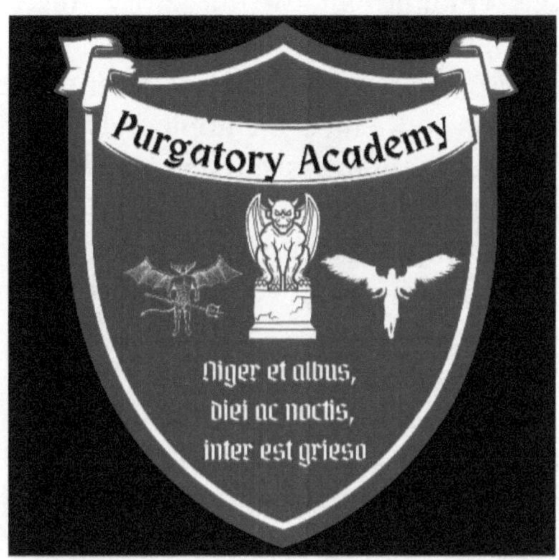

We never make it to the cafeteria. Drake intercepts us in the hallway. He throws a green apple and a bag of my favorite chips to me. Marius gets an orange and his favorite snack. He hands us each a bottle of water. Warmth blossoms in me that he knows what I like to eat. Of course, he knows what Marius prefers too, but my joyous emotions tell me to overlook that little insight. Then I notice Drake has a black eye. I'm about to ask about it, but he doesn't give me the chance. "We need to eat while we walk." Marius and I share a glance and nod. I motion for Drake to lead the way. I don't know why, but I throw in a flourished bow and sweeping hand. He smirks at my theatrics and butterflies flutter in my stomach. I'm not getting used to them, but they are familiar at this point. I enjoy his smile way too much. Of course, they are a rare commodity and perhaps I should get all the joy I can out of each one.

"Our Familiars will need to stay behind for this," Drake says. His white kitten meows sadly at that. Blackbeard jumps nervously from one foot to the next on Marius' shoulder before he apparently is able to convince the Dracula parrot to hop down. He doesn't get too close to Barlowe whose own words of unhappiness are more than a little colorful. I promise him we'll be back before the start of the next class.

Drake sweeps passed at a clipped pace. I get a whiff of him. My core warms at it. I shake my head though. No, I need to concentrate on the task at hand. Whatever that is. "Eat while we walk," he reminds us.

I stick my tongue out at his back as Marius and I rush to catch up and keep pace. Drake's shoulders shake with silent laughter. I look at Marius, but he just smiles and keeps peeling his orange while we walk briskly through the winding halls of Purgatory Academy. I try to pay attention to our surroundings, but it doesn't work well so I bite into my apple, enjoying that sour tang. My sense of orientation was never very good anyway. Might as well enjoy the apple.

Eating proves a challenge at this pace. I lose sense of time as I finish the apple and start in on the chips. I take a drink of my bottled water as we come to a stop in front of the largest oaken doors I've seen yet in PA. They're always fucking wooden doors. Nothing good is ever behind them.

Drake opens them without preamble. I take in a breath. It's a chapel. I know from our classes that there are three of them here in Purgatory Academy, but I've never visited one. One of the chapels was built for use by angels and Ascended, one for demons and Descended, and one for the denizens of Purgatory itself, such as the gargoyles. If I remember correctly, they only hold services here during the equinoxes and solstices. Other than that, the chapels are used for individual contemplation or meditation.

I haven't spent much time in church or other religious edifices, but I feel that quiet regard that always seems to accompany sacred spaces. This one is filled with wooden pews and stained-glass windows that filter in the watery light of Purgatory. Chandeliers assist that weak light, gently brightening the dark corners of the stone walls. Incense lingers in the air. There is an altar in the front of the chapel. It's a plain slab of stone large enough for a body to occupy. My professors suggest when demon lords and archangels do visit Purgatory Academy, they come here. No one knows what they do in solitude. It's above their pay grades.

Drake makes for a corner to the right of the altar and pews. Marius follows him immediately, but I meander a bit. The stained-glass windows depict Death in black robes just like those the Malakim wear, a scythe in both robed hands. The other three Horsemen of the Apocalypse are present as well, each on their horse and holding their own items of power.

Marius floats back to gather me. I follow him to the corner to find Drake waiting in a little alcove. He's standing next to a small stone artwork piece of a gargoyle. It's a miniature reminiscent of the captain of the guard at PA. I watch as Drake leans in toward it and whispers something even my Nephilic hearing can't decipher. Turning back to us he says, "Our escort will be here in a moment." Marius snickers, but I just roll my eyes at his immaturity.

The wall next to the mini gargoyle begins to make its pebble dropped in a pond movement and the captain of the guard steps out of it. He turns to Drake as soon as he sees him and gives him a toothy grin. Like imps, the gargoyles have shark teeth. When I really consider it, it's a bit creepy the similarities I find between the bulky, stoney fleshed gargoyles and the slim and leathery, diminutive imps.

Turning to Marius and me, Drake says, "I'd like to introduce you both to the captain of the guard here at Purgatory Academy. Lilly, I believe the two of you have already chatted and we all heard him speak in class." Motioning to the two of us he turns to face the gargoyle. "Lilly of the House of Lillith and Marius of the House of Cain."

The gargoyle holds up a clawed paw. "There's no need to stand on ceremony. Miss Lilly, it's good to see you again. Mr. Marius, it's a pleasure to meet you." His cordial voice goes against the gravelly sound of it and the gruffness of his presentation in class before. "You know me by my title but given the circumstances, I don't think it inappropriate to share my name. I am Cuddlebug."

I don't mean to stare, but I don't know what else to do. Marius puts a hand to his face. And then two, hiding the laughter near to boiling over. "I-I'm-I'm sorry. What, uh, did you say your name was again?" I hope the laughter isn't evident in my voice.

All shark teeth smile, he repeats his name. "Cuddlebug."

Marius twists away, his face now completely hidden in his hands, small snorting sounds popping up. I hold my breath, hoping it'll help. Drake has an arched eyebrow of inquisitiveness, watching and waiting. I make the mistake of looking at Cuddlebug again. He appears almost expectant. And that is all it takes for both Marius and me. Simultaneously, we burst out laughing, doubled over because we held it in so long. Tears stream down our faces. Marius attempts to apologize, but it comes out as more of a wheeze.

Cuddlebug chuckles, his stoney shoulders shaking. "Excellent. I was concerned for a moment there that you weren't going to laugh at all."

We both stop laughing at his explanation. It makes Cuddlebug smile even wider. Drake's eyes twinkle, I'm certain of it. The gargoyle nods to Drake as if to suggest that he explain it to us. Clearing his throat, the Descended does. "In gargoyle culture, parents give their children funny names in an attempt to make others laugh. The amount you laugh is a direct correlation to how funny the parents were in choosing the name for their child. The fact that you laughed so much so sincerely is a great honor to Cuddlebug's parents."

"Yes, my parents will indeed be happy to hear how much joy they have brought to your lives," Cuddlebug adds very solemnly.

I try to wrap my brain around that. Marius appears to be doing the same when he asks, "What if someone didn't find it funny or didn't laugh?"

"That's okay," Cuddlebug says. "You don't bring shame on a family for that, but they don't gain honor either."

I'm still catching up. "So, do people, or, uh, gargoyles ever fake laughter to make you feel better?"

I didn't think the captain's face could show so much horror, but it does right then. "That's the worst thing anyone could do. To fake their laughter would indeed be a great dishonor to all involved."

I nod, not knowing what to say. Drake saves me though. "Our time is short. We should go."

"Where are we going?" I ask.

Drake motions to Cuddlebug. "You already know that Cuddlebug, as the captain of the guard here at PA, is in charge of the murder investigations. You wanted to help, and he's agreed."

My eyes get real big. I don't know what is more impressive, that Drake convinced the gargoyle to let us help or that he said the captain's name without a trace of smile or humor. I ask at the same time as Marius. "How were you able to do that?"

Cuddlebug smiles. Drake shrugs. "It isn't important. What is, is that he's accepted."

It's the strangest thing to see a gargoyle arch an eyebrow, but this is my second time experiencing it and I feel like an old pro now. Apparently, he decides he'll explain if Drake won't. "As I've mentioned to Miss Lilly already, there are only two ways to get a gargoyle to help you. Since Mr. Drake has already achieved that goal, I'm content to share with you both what those are. First, a gargoyle will agree to assist you if you are able to make them laugh. As you may have already surmised, laughter is considered the highest of virtues among our kind.

We are stoney and stoic by nature so when you are able to make us laugh, it is the greatest of compliments. The second way is to defeat one of us in single combat."

I glance at Drake's black eye. It must have been bad if it's taking that long to heal for a Nephil. Marius' eyes get super wide, clearly wondering which it was. I have to know. "Which one was it?"

Cuddlebug resumes his stoic face. Drake does the same. "I will say this. Mr. Drake is as stoney and stoic as a gargoyle. I'm half convinced he has gargoyle ancestors somewhere in his bones and blood." I understand the statement for the compliment it is.

Drake clears his throat. "Part of the agreement is to take us to Pravuel."

I don't understand, but Marius gasps in surprise. "Are you being serious?" Drake and Cuddlebug both nod solemnly. It's really annoying to know so much less about this world. I wave a hand in a please keep explaining it sort of way. Marius answers. "Pravuel is the Historian for Purgatory Academy. He's an angel, a seraph. He works with an entire team of other beings, both angels and demons, all who record everything that occurs on the grounds of PA."

"Wait," I interrupt. "How does that work?"

"The Historian and his staff are given the gift of a form of omnipresence. They see everything that is happening here all at once as if it were present in front of them. As they do, they write it, recording it all down."

The number of revelations I'm getting are going to make my head explode. "That's crazy. Why even bother?"

Marius shrugs. "All I know is that if anyone knows who is committing the murders, it's Pravuel."

I consider this. "Can he see anything outside of PA?"

"No, his omnipresence is relegated to the grounds of the academy."

I'm super tired of having my head reel so much from so many new pieces of information. There's always something fresh and scary in this world, or worlds, whatever.

"We need to head there now," Drake reiterates. Marius joins me in looking around as to where exactly we're supposed to be going. Drake explains, "Pravuel's office is in a place where the only way in is by stonewalking."

"Shit," Marius swears.

My annoyance at not understanding is ratcheted up even more. "I have no idea what you're talking about," I say through clenched teeth. "What is stonewalking?"

Cuddlebug speaks up. "This is how we gargoyles travel among the grounds, how we get from Point A to Point B." I forget to breathe. He's referring to that stone rippling trick they do. I was afraid of that. Cuddlebug grins at the look on my face. It does not reassure me. "Miss Lilly, I promise you will be just fine as long as you all stay together with me." I'm trying to figure out what question to ask next, but he continues. "The gist of it is as long as you remain in contact with me, you will be safe. I will open the stone. Mr. Drake will follow me with his hand on my shoulder. Each of you will hold hands and everyone will be safe."

I don't love this idea. Marius' face agrees with me. Cuddlebug stands before the stone wall where he just came from. The rippling begins. Drake places a hand on the gargoyle's shoulder. Looking back at us Cuddlebug says, "Whatever happens, don't let go."

"What happens if we do?" I ask.

"You will be stuck in stone." Now I'm positive I don't like this idea. Marius' face still agrees.

"Is there any way Pravuel could meet us somewhere else?" Marius asks.

"The nature of Pravuel's job as Historian keeps him occupied almost constantly as you can imagine. He can only take breaks for the barest of necessities. That's the reason for the team of others who help. The fact that he has agreed to meet with you at all is quite the honor. Frankly, it's unheard of."

That gives me a couple of thoughts. First, Pravuel must be concerned about the murders too. Second, I have to wonder again how Drake made this happen. Did he make Cuddlebug laugh or was that black eye from their fight? I try to imagine Drake beating Cuddlebug in single combat. I can't see anyone doing that, honestly.

Drake holds out his hand to me; warmth glows under his calluses. My body always seems to be a bit on the cold side, leaving my extremities like popsicles. That's what my dad tells me all the time anyway. His hand engulfs my own as I grab Marius' which is closer to my own in size and lack of heat. The calluses on Drake's hand have less than pure thoughts popping into my head.

Cuddlebug turns back to us one last time. "You will be able to breathe and see while we stonewalk. Just focus on holding on."

That doesn't stop Marius or me from taking a deep breath as we approach the wall. Cuddlebug walks straight into the rippling motions of stone. Drake doesn't hesitate in following him. Logically, I know I'm not going to hit the wall, but I still brace myself. Of course, I don't hit it. It's more like melting into it.

It's easily the strangest thing I've ever experienced in my life. For one thing, it's a continuation of rippling like when the gargoyles enter or exit the stone. Every movement sends the ripples floating away from us. It's like witnessing what I imagine radar looks like to bats or in a submarine.

Our movements are slower. The semi-liquified state of the stone is denser than normal walking would have been. It's more akin to shuffling through molasses. Cuddlebug never loses his rhythm though, guiding us through the stone.

I definitely lose my sense of direction. All I can see is the dark gray color of stone. And yet somehow it is floating in front of me as if watching a fly get caught in honey…except I'm the fly.

I'm just beginning to get concerned I will indeed need to breathe when Cuddlebug disappears from view. Then Drake's gone. And finally, I lead Marius out of the walls too. I take a deep breath, grateful to feel air enter my lungs.

Marius releases my hand and all but keels over, his head between his knees, his hands on his thighs propping him up. Cuddlebug rumbles. "I told you, you don't need to hold your breath." He shakes his head in irritation at the irrationality of Nephilim. My face is red both from embarrassment and a slight lack of oxygen. Cuddlebug huffs with resignation. "I suppose it is to be expected from those who aren't made of something more solid."

Marius stands back up again after a few more deep breaths. I place a comforting hand on his back, and he gives me a grateful nod. Then we both turn to take in our surroundings.

Standing behind a giant desk of exquisite mahogany with the sides etched in detailed patterns, is an angel. He's tall, but not quite as tall as Drake and certainly not Cuddlebug. He wears a light brown Armani suit with a vest and a tie that seems to glint gold in the light of a nearby fireplace. His skin matches the tone of his suit, and his very person seems to glow with vitality. His hair is a curly brown, cropped short and close to his scalp.

He smiles pleasantly, a warmth almost emanating from it. He's a handsome man and quite well shaped; that much is evident under the impeccably tailored suit. I didn't expect the Historian to be so…buff.

His wings are a pristine white with a glow all their own. They're quite the contrast to the more muted and calming colors of his clothing and person. It's strange to see him with them actually. None of my angelic professors wear them while they teach. In fact, I haven't seen any of them with their wings exposed.

"Welcome." His voice is nearly as deep as Cuddlebug's.

The gargoyle motions to each of us. "Pravuel the Historian, allow me to introduce to you three of our current Descended students." He holds out a clawed paw toward Marius first. "Marius of the House of Cain. Lilly of the House of Lillith. And Drake of the House of Lucifer."

I've never heard anyone actually refer to Drake by his house. A chill runs through me at the sound of it, as if hearing it out loud somehow makes it more real. Even the seraph shifts in slight discomfort at the mention of the Dark Lord.

Cuddlebug waves a hand toward the angel. "Allow me to introduce the three of you officially to Pravuel the Historian of Purgatory Academy."

The angel nods his thanks but is silent for a moment as he takes in the three of us. "Marius Lamia, I welcome you personally. Many members of your ancient and esteemed family have come through the halls of Purgatory Academy. Many of them failed and many succeeded. I wish the latter for you." Marius doesn't seem to know what to say and instead awkwardly bows halfway before straightening, realizing that might not be the right answer.

Pravuel is too polite to mention it and instead faces me directly. "Lilly Foxflame, you are as beautiful as your mother Laurana. She was one of the most famous succubi to grace these halls. Some would prefer the word 'notorious,' but I found her to be both brave and intelligent beyond her years." That's the second time someone has mentioned my mother here and I have so many questions.

The angel moves on to Drake though and I keep my mouth shut, too curious to hear what he will say to the child of Lucifer. In fact, he says nothing. He only takes in the Descended. And Drake does the same in return. It becomes a bit uncomfortable, the silence stretching on between the two of them.

Then the angel smiles thinly. "Drake Tepish. Child of one of the most ancient and powerful families of Hell. And a son of the Dark Lord Lucifer himself. It has been decades since last one of your ilk has walked these halls."

I try to distract my discomfort with funny thoughts about how seriously the angel takes his role as Historian with all the knowledge he has of us and our families. It doesn't work very well. They break their stare as Drake gives the slightest of nods.

"I welcome each of you once more. Please be seated." I look around the room. Beyond the ornate desk where Pravuel stands, the bare wall where we emerged, and the healthy fire, it is wall to wall bookshelves filled with books.

Cuddlebug walks past us back to that same wall. The rippling begins anew and in short order four chairs slide out of the stone. Three of them have a back for leaning a bit but the fourth is more of a bench. All made of stone, they are almost as ornate in design as Pravuel's desk. The gargoyle sits the three backed chairs in front of the desk and then brings the bench to the side. He sits on this one, obviously needing it with his wings far too large to accommodate one of the chairs.

I sit down in the chair closest to the fire and farthest from Cuddlebug. Marius sits next to me and Drake takes the final chair, closest to the gargoyle. I take the opportunity to look around more.

The books draw my eye. One is open on Pravuel's desk; they're not normal books, made from paper. The pages are made of precious metals, so thin they are used just like paper ones. I see gold and silver among others, glinting in the fire light all across the bookshelves.

"They are enchanted," Pravuel explains. "We etch the histories of Purgatory Academy into them. With the proper enchantments, they last much longer than any paper book ever could."

"They're beautiful," I answer. "There are so many."

"This is but a small portion of the entirety, I assure you. The students have a library here on the grounds, but we have archives where we deposit the histories." Curiosity blooms inside me with this newfound knowledge. There is a library? Where is it? How big is it? I must have missed it on my map the first day of school. Unfortunately, my curiosity is thwarted once more. Pravuel sits in his chair, interlocking his fingers on the desk. "I apologize for rushing our meeting along, but I do need to return to writing as soon as possible."

Cuddlebug grunts toward Drake as if to say this is his show. For a moment I think the angel and Descended are going to have another staring contest, but then Drake speaks. "Historian, we are grateful you have taken this precious time to speak with us." Pravuel nods at the formal pleasantries. "As time is of the essence for both you and us, I will move straight to our questions if it please you." Pravuel inclines his head once more. "We would like to inquire if you know who is murdering Nephilim."

Pravuel doesn't even hesitate. "Yes." I hold my breath waiting for the angel to go on, but he doesn't.

Marius can't wait though. "Who is it?"

The seraph addresses my friend. "Sadly, I'm not allowed to intervene to that degree. I am the Historian. I cannot meddle in the affairs of those present here. I would help if I could, but in this regard I'm afraid I simply cannot."

Marius' face registers shock, but Drake is nodding as if he expected this. I don't understand. I want to ask if he knows he can't say, then why did he bother to meet with us. I almost stand up in anger. We need to stop this.

Drake continues though, "Is the being responsible for the murders here at Purgatory Academy?"

Pravuel smiles at the shrewdness of the Descended's circumventing question. "That's very good, Drake. Very impressive. Do you know that I'm physically incapable of intervening? The magical weaving that allows me to be omnipresent here keeps me from helping too much. I can always feel when I can't. But you found a loophole." I'm sitting on the edge of my seat now, waiting for the seraph to tell us more. "Yes, the culprit is a current member of the community."

"Are the killings occurring on the grounds?"

Drake has Pravuel's complete attention now. Everyone else's too. "Why would you ask that question?'

Drake shrugs. "It crossed my mind that the killer could have taken the students somewhere, killed them there, and then brought the bodies back. It would explain why the gargoyles have not been able to stop it."

"Bravo," Pravuel says. Even Cuddlebug looks impressed with Drake's logic. "Unfortunately, this is not the case. The killings occurred here on academy grounds." Drake frowns. I assume that means he's frustrated. Pravuel places his hands on the desk. "Do you have any other questions?" Drake looks at Marius and me, but I don't have any and neither does my friend. Pravuel notes it. "Thank you for your visit." He stands up again, indicating that our meeting is at an end.

We wait as Cuddlebug gathers up the chairs and slides them into the wall as if they never existed. Pravuel speaks one last time before we depart. "I have considered another option and it would appear that I can share it without breaking my spell. Check the library. Look for information there." I mouth a quiet thank you to the angel who nods in turn before picking up his pen to etch more history into the open book before him.

I'm not thrilled about going back out the way we came in, but I don't see any doors in the room. We line up in the same order we did on the way in. As we enter the stone, I look back at the angel one last time. He's watching us intently, but I can't read the look on his face.

Despite what Cuddlebug said, I still hold my breath on the way back. Thankfully, this time neither Marius nor I keel over from it. Drake turns to Cuddlebug as the wall stops its rippling. "Thank you. We're grateful."

"You are most welcome, Mr. Drake. If you learn anything new about the murders, please let me know immediately."

"We certainly will," Drake agrees.

Cuddlebug sizes the Descended up. "You know, you aren't at all what they make you out to be."

Drake smiles. "I'll take that as a compliment." The gargoyle chuckles.

"Cuddlebug, thank you. I want you to know we're all grateful," I say. I don't know why I do it, but I reach up on tip toes and kiss the gargoyle on the cheek. His skin is hard and cold as stone, as expected. He doesn't seem to know what to do with that so instead he turns with one last look at me and melts back into the wall.

Chapter Forty-Six
Don't Play with Fire
March – Purgatory Academy

The three of us jaunt quickly to Magic Weaving in silence. There's a lot to take in. As is so often the case at PA, I don't have time to consider anything besides when I go from class to class because we're too damn busy. Our Familiars waited outside of the chapel for us and follow along. I don't need to fill Barlowe in because he listened silently while we were with Pravuel. He remains uncharacteristically quiet and that concerns me more than when he speaks.

Our Magic Weaving class is focused on opening up and developing our powers. As we do so, Nekleth walks about. "The Tribulations are intended to weed out the weak, yes. But they also drive you to use your powers through sheer survival instinct and desperation." Hello, Ossa Forest.

I "practice" with Marius and Drake. I think of it that way because Drake refuses outright to bother. Marius is getting nowhere and he's plenty frustrated about it. When I begin to work on mine, Drake whispers, "Don't show anyone your green fire."

I've barely had time to consider it since I used it in the Ossa Forest, but I have a sneaking suspicion it might be growing stronger in my veins. Perhaps Drake is right. I should figure out what it is first. How can I be expected to trust the likes of Gressil or other members of the faculty when they stand by and watch us butchered in Tribulation after Tribulation. I witness small bursts of magic from my classmates. Fire and ice and darkness and light. They pop up around the classroom, but there's no green fire.

On our way out of the class, I rush to catch up with Gabe. Barlowe pads after me. The Ascended stops in the hallway while Eli and Trist hover nearby. I fill him in on what we learned from Pravuel. He listens intently.

It's difficult to ignore the stares and scoffs we receive from classmates as they pass by. Most of it's reserved for me. The snarkier part of me thinks it makes sense since I'm the harlot succubus tempting the gallant Golden Boy.

"Thank you for sharing," Gabe says as he returns with his puppy Familiar to rejoin Eli and Trist. The female looks as angry as ever. Eli, for a change, has an open look on his face. He gives me a thumbs up. Huh, well look at that.

Chapter Forty-Seven
Death Comes in Threes
March – Purgatory Academy

I'm losing sleep and stop seeing my dad. Barlowe is my only comfort at home. School is consuming my life. The following week we're informed in our first class that another student was found dead that morning. It's Mattew, the final friend of the three who bullied Drake. While there is still shock, the anger and paranoia are what are really building among the Nephilim. Many of them give each other looks of suspicion and disgust. Drake definitely receives the most.

It's the first day, but certainly not the last, where fights break out among the students. They begin in the hallways in between periods but soon escalate to lunch and even classes. The gargoyles intervene quickly and efficiently, but the fighting doesn't stop. Weeks pass like that.

Our professors are running us ragged with information and practices, partially because that's the nature of PA, increasing the stress to see how we respond, but I figure it also has to do with keeping the students from having an outright riot.

With that kind of environment, it's not wise to chat with Gabe in the open and we haven't found time to get to the library yet. Pravuel suggested we search there, but he didn't give us any more information than that. I also want to follow up with Gabe about reaching out to the families of the murdered Ascended.

Then one day while walking to lunch, Gabe's Golden Retriever Familiar pads over to Barlowe who immediately has his hackles up and is spitting at the puppy with paws too big for his body yet. The puppy sits down though, nervous energy making his tail wag like crazy. Barlowe shrinks back down to his normal size and stares at the puppy.

Finally, Barlowe returns to me. *"Yeller here wants me to tell you that Gabe is going to speak with the families of his deceased friends. Eli and Trist will help him."*

Gabe delivered a message through his Familiar. It's a genius way of communicating so no one will know. *"Please have Yeller tell Gabe thank you. Let him know we're going to the library soon to search and they're welcome to join us."*

Barlowe turns back to the dog and stares again. After a few moments, the puppy barks at the cat who hisses once more, but he's running off down the hall already, slipping occasionally on the worn stones with those too big paws.

Gabe doesn't send Yeller over during lunch because there are too many eyes, but he does send him right after as we head for our last class of the day. Through our Familiar messaging Gabe lets me know they will reach out to the families tonight and they can head to the library together right after school. I relay the information to Drake and Marius.

Hours later, all six of us are standing in front of the open library double doors. On both there's a sign that reads no Familiars allowed. *"I'm not waiting out here,"* Barlowe growls.

"I'll be fine. Maybe they're just afraid you'll use the books like kitty litter." He doesn't laugh. Can't win them all, I suppose. The six Familiars fly, walk, and slither away to wait for us outside the front of the school.

The library beckons me forward. I love libraries. It's the one place I always made certain to visit when the circus moved to a new town or city and I've visited some beautiful ones. My dad always did what he could to get me a library card in each new place. I have a small tin canister with Wonder Woman on the top of it where I keep all of them.

I've never been in a library like this before though. It's …well, it's just different. In a good way. In a beautiful way. As we wander about at first it doesn't seem that large. The floor is circular in shape with a reference desk to the left of the open doors. Stacks of books on bookshelves eight feet tall hug the walls of the circle. Cushioned among the shelves are huge, marble columns. They look marble anyway, but they're a darker color. On closer inspection, they are a shade of blood.

Next to the reference desk is a set of stairs and that's when I realize how magnificent the library is. It moves upwards. Circular floor after circular floor waits above us. I'm still looking straight up into the darkness when I lose count of the floors. Then it dawns on me why it's built the way it is. Yes, there are stairs for walking up, but it's also structured with wings in mind. You could fly up there into the darkness and find what you need. It must be housed in one of the many spirals that dots Purgatory Academy. It's daunting and dazzling.

"Where do we start?" Marius asks in a hushed library tone.

That's a great question. Drake speaks up, "Pravuel said we should search here. That was all he said though."

Trist mutters something like, "Thanks Captain Obvious."

Drake ignores her. "I think we need to speak with the librarians. They might be able to give us more direction."

Librarians? It makes sense, but for some reason it's strange to think there are librarians in this place. But even as he says the words, a glow appears behind the reference desk. We all turn in unison to get a better look at the apparition coming into focus.

My brain wants to make the argument this shouldn't be possible, but I've been at PA for almost three months now. I tell my brain as much. It finally agrees when the grayish white radiance becomes a lightly glowing man smiling contently with fingers interlocked. He wears a full beard that must have been dark in life and thinning hair parted to the side. He's dressed in a dark gray, three-piece suit with a button-up vest and an old school tie.

"Good evening." His voice is pleasant enough, but there's something about him that makes me uncomfortable. "How may I help you?"

Gabe and Drake turn to me as if I'm the one who should speak with him. Great. Stepping in front of the others, but not quite all the way up to the reference desk, I say. "We're looking for information." Damn, I'm smooth.

His smile widens. His eyes are dead though. That doesn't make much sense given the fact that he's dead, a ghost, or maybe it does because he is? Ugh. "That's why I'm here. What, may I ask, are you looking for?" His eyes slide up and down my profile. I don't care for that at all.

Taking a deep breath, I explain what we learned from Pravuel. The ghost listens intently, even when his eyes continue to take in my body. I ignore the creepy feeling emanating from him. When I'm finished, he gets this thoughtful look on his face. "The Historian is correct, of course. Here's what I suggest. This library has books on the deaths of every being who died here. Theoretically, there are paper book copies here of the metal versions of what the Historian and his staff record." The smug smile he gives me is supposed to be charming, I assume. But he does have a good idea.

"Where would we look for these books?" I ask.

"Well, that's the nice thing. The books here are organized by year. The oldest books are higher up." He points upwards with a finger. "That means the newest books are here on the ground level."

"And where would this section be?"

"That's the challenge. There are no books here only about the deaths of students. They are the histories of the school. The deaths are written into them so you will have to sift through much of what is here on the ground floor to find those deaths."

My mouth drops open. "Okay, well then, thanks. We'll get started."

He smiles like it's no big deal. "Please let me know if you have any other questions." Then he fades into nothing.

"We should split up, right?" Marius suggests. "We can cover more ground that way."

"I'll take this section here next to the reference desk," I point.

"I'll take the one next to it," Gabe says.

The others divvy up the rest of the ground floor and start looking through the titles. I read pages and pages till my eyes grow blurry. One by one the others announce they need to head out for the evening. Drake and Marius leave after Eli and Trist, but they both linger for a moment. Protective boys. Sheesh. "I'll be just fine," I say. "I'll see you guys tomorrow."

Gabe is seated with several volumes at one of the nearby desks. I take mine over to him. He glances at me, glossy eyed, and continues to read. We sit like that for another half hour before he says he needs to take a break. I grunt as I turn another page, mental numbness well formed in my brain.

"How's it going?" I jump at the closeness of the voice. The librarian ghost is standing right behind me, far too close. "Have you found anything yet?"

I try to sound as casual as I can. "Not yet."

"Perhaps I could help you a bit more," he suggests.

"Oh, how is that?" I ask. His lack of blinking is disturbing.

"You know, you are so beautiful. I love the red of your hair. Colors fade for us ghosts." His spectral hand reaches out and plays with a strand. I actually feel the cold, otherworldly touch of his fingers and shiver. I might be a succubus, but I'm not about to be turned on by a pervy old spirit.

"Thank you for the compliment, but I need to get back to my research."

"Are you sure you don't want some extra help?" His hand moves to the small of my back and the cold that radiates there almost hurts.

"Actually, it's pretty late and we've been here for hours. I think it's time I left." I hate how grateful I am that Gabe returns right then. The librarian backs up a step. "Should we reshelve the books or…?"

Gabe gathers a sense of the room and comes to stand next to me, facing the ghost. "No, don't worry about it. I will reshelve them myself," the spectre says, smiling.

"You ready?" Gabe asks, without taking his eyes off the ghost. I stand as answer, the two of us walking out together.

I make it out of sight of the doors of the library before I allow myself a moment, leaning against a wall with a nearby flaming sconce. Gabe speaks up almost immediately. "He was being creepy, wasn't he?"

I nod breathlessly. It reminds me too much of past experiences I never want to consider again. The Ascended reads a trace of this on my face but gives me space; I appreciate it. "I'm okay," I assure him as much as myself. I stuff the memories down, not allowing them to resurface.

"Are you sure? Do we need to go back and have a conversation with that librarian?"

I chuckle. "Are you going to preserve my honor by beating the shit out of a ghost? A dirty, wicked succubus like me."

Gabe rolls his eyes. "I've seen you fight. I know you don't need my help."

"Maybe I like the idea of getting you to do what I want," I tease.

Gabe shifts closer. "And what is it you'd like me to do?"

My breath hitches, but I play it cool. "If you have to ask, then you aren't ready."

Gabe doesn't say another word. He leans in and hovers near my lips. I don't move or breathe. He comes the rest of the way and tastes like mint. I love it and want more. Soon we're tucked in a dark corner of the hallway, our breath mingled together into one. His hands rise to frame my face while my own wrap around, pulling him closer.

He groans as our hips meet. I grind against him, forgetting my surroundings completely and loving the feel and scent of him. His hands roam all over my clothes and my bare thighs. My core heats at his touch. His groans change tone though and gently he pulls back, extraditing his hands from my hair. Reluctantly, I release him. "Sorry about that," I say. I don't believe my own words.

Gabe takes in a deep breath and lets it out. "Me too." He doesn't sound sorry either.

Trying for normal conversation I say, "We'll need to return to the library to keep looking."

He agrees. "Yeah, I-I'll, uh, talk to the other two."

"Me too," I agree. I adjust my school uniform, trying to put everything aright.

Gabe is weaving down the hall, but almost trips, waving without looking as he rushes away.

"Oh good," I say. "Things aren't awkward now."

Chapter Forty-Eight
Silver
April – Purgatory Academy

The next Tribulation ambushes us, literally. On a Friday morning in April, Gressil meets all the students at the front doors. I'm tired of seeing him already. He leads us through the hallways on a route that I now know well. Out into the courtyard we come again. I wish that Barlowe were with me, but we're all instructed to leave our Familiars at home. I'm beginning to wonder what the purpose of a Familiar is if we never get to have them around to actually help. The faculty and each surviving Nephil's Malak is present though. Definitely not as good as having Barlowe here.

Gressil tells us to spread out in the courtyard and my Malak approaches. Each does the same with their own Ascended or Descended. I haven't attempted to speak with mine in weeks. I'm far too busy and too focused on survival and my own investigations.

I stare into the depths of those robes but see nothing. "Today's Tribulation is one of endurance," Gressil explains. He snaps his fingers and en masse the Malakim lift one robed hand and blow some kind of dust into the eyes of their Nephil.

I cry out in pain as soon as it hits my eyes. Whatever it is, it burns horribly. I'm not alone. There's screaming everywhere. A limb slams into my stomach. I don't know if it's a fist or a leg, but it takes the wind right out of me. And then I feel chains being wrapped around me. Where they touch my skin, it burns. I scream more, louder.

I try to focus through the pain. My Malach props me up against one of the columns in the courtyard. Similar situations are occurring all over the cobblestones, students chained up writhing on the ground and yelling out in pain.

The burning is subsiding in my eyes though. I blink away tears which burn as they drip down my cheeks, searing me somehow. My Malak stands over me, motionless.

Gressil's voice rises above the collective shouts of pain. "As I'm sure you all know, Nephilim are susceptible to silver. Your Tribulation today is, as I mentioned earlier, about endurance, namely enduring pain. Now, you may be thinking it's painful with the silver shavings blown in your eyes and being chained with the same, but that is only the beginning. The true test, the actual Tribulation, is to have liquid silver pumped directly into your veins. All you have to do is endure it, survive."

My Malak moves forward and there's the pressure of a large needle into my left arm. I don't plead, but I do wish again that Barlowe were here at least to comfort me. We're so far away I can barely sense the connection we share.

The Malak pushes the plunger, and a terrible pressure grows under the skin of my arm. My sight is better already despite those fucking awful silver shavings. I watch the last of that silvery glow of molten metal enter my veins.

Then the real pain begins just as Gressil promised. It spreads like a wildfire as my blood stream sweeps it along to every corner and crevice. Strictly speaking, the Hell Fire I endured on my first Tribulation burned hotter, but the silver is more like that icy hot that people put on sore muscles; except it never quite stops. It expands and burns and burns in that cold, dead sort of way.

I screamed before, but now my cries must be defined as blood curdling. I acknowledge them as such because I actually taste my own blood coating the back of my throat. It drowns out everything else. I scream till I'm hoarse. I fight futilely against the chains, but it's all to no avail. All I can do is what Gressil said, endure.

The silver is everywhere in my body and there's no way I can escape from it. Even as I think it, the pain becomes too much. Finally, thankfully, blissfully, I lose consciousness.

When I wake up, Drake is standing over me. The chains are gone, but I'm still leaning against the column. "You're going to be okay," he whispers in a way that suggests it wasn't the first time he said it.

"How are you healed already? I feel like my whole body is going to melt into a puddle." My voice is that of a person who smoked for thirty years on a daily basis. "Didn't the silver burn you?"

"They didn't silver me," he says.

I'm conscious enough to understand what I just heard doesn't make any sense. "Wait. What? What do you mean they didn't silver you?"

"I mean I wasn't silvered," he says as he helps me stand up, still leaning against the column for support.

"How is that possible?"

"My Malak and I had a disagreement about it. I won't be seeing him for a while."

My head is still spinning. "Why not?"

"He had an accident and will need time to heal. Now, let's concentrate on getting you better."

Holy Hell. My brain is finally catching up. His Malak attacked Drake like each of them did with their own Nephil. But he was able to fight off his guardian.

"It's safe now so I'm going to leave you here for a moment while I go get Marius. Then I'm going to get both of you out of here. Okay?"

I mumble assent and go back to focusing on stopping the spinning. I'm close to getting it when Drake brings Marius over, baring much of his weight on his shoulder as he half carries the pale vampire.

Without a word, Drake brings my arm up and over his other shoulder. The loopiness remains, but I can't ignore that glorious scent of cinnamon and campfire that wafts off Drake. I'm pretty sure Marius is worse off than I am. He struggles to walk at all. My legs work, but not in a straight line.

Drake mistports all three of us out the gates without a thought. He sits us both down on large boulders while the mist caresses our faces. "Okay, since I don't want either of you ending up a melted goo of bone and blood, I think it best that I mistport you both home."

Marius and I both fumble for our phones to show Drake a picture of where we want to go. We came up with the idea earlier in the year so that we could mistport to each other, especially given that the circus moves so much. It's the one way that our phones are worthwhile here in Purgatory. No cell signal, but we can use the cameras.

Drake commits both to memory. "Ladies first. Marius, you stay here, and I will be right back for you."

"Mmmmkay," Marius mumbles.

Drake helps me up and has me lean on his shoulder again. That cold in-between feeling hits me as we fade away and then appear next to my RV. Barlowe cries for me from inside. "You have your keys?" Drake asks.

I fumble for them, but he takes them and gets the door open. The black blur of Barlowe is standing there meowing and waiting for me. Drake helps keep me steady till I'm up and in, but he doesn't enter. I turn to look at him. "Thank you, Drake."

He gives me a small smile and mistports away to collect Marius. Barlowe bombards me with mental questions, but instead I open my memories to him so he can see for himself. I have enough presence of mind to lock my RV door, but that's it. I lay down on the bed, over the covers, and Barlowe curls next to me. His purring puts me to sleep. I don't dream; small mercies.

Chapter Forty-Nine
Lenny
April – Purgatory Academy

It's Sunday evening and I still feel the silver in my body, but it doesn't burn anymore. It's more like a heaviness as if solidified, weighing me down. I'm seated in my booth when my Malak appears next to the foot of my bed where he always does. For a moment, I allow myself to consider how it's possible he's able to know where I am every time. I didn't give him anything when we moved on to Texas. My anger at his presence takes over quickly though.

"What do you want?" I don't expect an answer. I've never gotten one before. Sure, he gave me a couple of small kindnesses in the past, but none of that makes up for what he's done to me. He placed the Hell Fire in my hand. He attacked and tortured me with silver. My anger rises at the thought of it and a scream of fury claws its way up out of my throat.

But it dies right there because my Malak throws back his hood. There are a lot of things I imagined under that robe. They ranged from a skeleton to rotting flesh. That's why what I see shocks me. It's just an old man.

He has bushy white hair with stubble the same color. His eyebrows look like they might have been red or brown when he was younger, but they're mostly white now too. There are tears in his red rimmed eyes. "I am so sorry." His voice is gruff. My anger evaporates at the sound. He says it over and over again. He sits down hard on the edge of my bed and the tears pour like rain. "They made me do it. I had no choice. I have no choice."

Shock pushes its way through my entire body. My Malak is a man. And he's sorry for what he has done to me. It's a lot to take in, but apparently, it's a worthy distraction from my own trauma and trials because I find myself wanting to help him, comfort him.

Part of me knows that is just plain stupid. The being in front of me is extremely powerful and deadly. He's my keeper. But now he is humanized with his hood back. Perhaps that's why they all wear them, so they won't be viewed as familiar.

I edge forward and lean against a wall near the end of the bed but still just out of reach. For a moment I consider giving him a tissue. That's snot coming out of his nose. He's definitely an ugly crier.

I take a step toward the bathroom for toilet paper, but he holds up a hand, waving me back. His sobbing is slowing down. He uses his sleeve to wipe it away. When he does, I get a glimpse of his hand for the first time. They're…hands. I don't know why, but somehow it makes him even less scary than the sobbing does. He almost appears…fragile.

He turns his puffy eyes toward me. Absently, I notice that they're the same color as my own. They even glow a brighter green the way mine do when I cry. It's the one beautiful thing about his rugged, ragged face. He looks back down and whispers an apology once more.

"I think that about covers the apologies," I attempt to joke. Even to me I can hear how awkward it sounds. I blurt out trying again, "I'm just relieved you aren't a skeleton or a zombie."

That gets a laugh. "Trust me. If you knew more about what we Malakim are, you would understand we are much worse than either one of those things."

"How so?"

"We are messengers of either Heaven or Hell, but we work primarily here in Purgatory. We belong to the three worlds, the three planes of existence all at once in some strange way."

I don't see how that makes him dangerous, but I decide to focus on the positive. "At least you stopped crying."

He huffs another laugh. "There is that." He gets very serious as he looks at me again. "You remind me of my granddaughter."

I push off the corner. It brings me just a fraction closer to him. "What's she like?"

He takes a deep breath as if preparing himself. "She was like wildfire, untamable. But I loved that about her. She was extremely inquisitive. She always wanted to understand everything no matter what it was. She was also filled with kindness. That's where you remind me of her. Here you are trying to make your torturer feel better." A fond smile sprouts on his face, his eyes seeing something or someone who isn't present.

"You said she was. Past tense."

"She was taken from me."

"By whom?"

"I can't say." He shakes his head, eyes cast down. He's afraid.

"Is she…?"

"Dead? Yes, but as I'm sure you're beginning to learn in your time at Purgatory Academy, that mortal life is only a small portion of the soul's eternal journey. There is much that can happen to one afterwards."

"So even after death someone is holding her?"

"Torturing her to be exact," he whispers, the words filled with pain.

"That's awful."

"It's the reason I'm here."

"What do you mean?" I ask.

"Being a Malak is a great honor for which many an angel and demon vie. I'm not one of them. This position was…forced on me."

"And your granddaughter is being held hostage and tortured to keep you in line?" I guess. He bows his head, but the action is enough to tell me it's true. "And what happens if you don't fulfill your role?"

He looks me straight in the eye, tears threatening anew. "They would destroy her immortal soul."

What is there to say? A change of subject is probably the best I can do given the circumstances. "So, you said that most of the Malakim enjoy their work?"

"They all have their own reasons, I'm sure. But there are more than a few demons, and angels for that matter, who enjoy watching the students compete and die in horrible ways. Most root against the other side, naturally. However, there are plenty who love bloodshed regardless of who it is. Even their own student."

"That's terrible." The more I learn about these worlds, the more I hate them. I long for the simple days of the circus. Working with the elephants and my father. Using my hands in the dirt, not blood and fire.

"It is, but immortality has its challenges."

"I find that hard to believe," I say.

"Nonetheless, it's true."

"Like what? What's one challenge?"

"Simple. Boredom. You have eternity. Eventually, you grow tired of the same old and you come up with all kinds of ways to preoccupy yourself."

"Like torture?"

"Exactly."

"Is the position of Malak a high one?"

"It is coveted, yes. But not nearly as much as those of faculty and dean here. The positions are granted to the most faithful and the most dangerous. Being a Malak is often a steppingstone toward those positions."

"If it's such an honor, why were you forced into it?"

"It's a punishment."

"For what?"

"Disobedience."

I want to ask more, but I'm concerned I may have pushed him too far as it is. Instead, I stick out a hand. "Hello," I put on my best smile and even push a bit of Sway into it. "My name's Lilly."

The Malak barks out a laugh. He takes my hand and shakes it. "Lenny."

"It's nice to meet you."

"You too," he responds. The warmth of the moment doesn't last long though. "You should know that I still have to do my job, whatever it is they want me to do."

"I understand."

His hands rise to grab at his hood, but before he cloaks himself in shadows, he says, "You should get some sleep. I'll see you dark and ugly in the morning."

"Don't talk about yourself like that," I joke.

He huffs one more laugh before he puts the hood back up. The mist rises to engulf him, leaving me feeling even more alone than usual.

Chapter Fifty
Desperate Times
April – Purgatory Academy

At lunch on Monday Gabe stands up from his table with Eli and Trist following him. Eli looks nervous and Trist mad. Both are pretty typical. Gabe doesn't seem to care at this point that everyone is watching them. He meets my gaze.

He sits down next to Marius, across the table from me. Eli and Trist sit down on Gabe's right. Eli stares at his lap while Trist glares at Drake directly opposite her.

Speed is of the essence. I lean forward whispering, "How did it go?"

"How the fuck do you think it went?" Trist less than whispers. "We had to talk to the parents of our friends. Our dead friends, you stupid fuck-"

"Trist, that's enough." Gabe's voice is quiet but made of iron. It brooks no discussion. She shuts up but her scowl goes nowhere. "It went as well as it could," Gabe says quietly.

The hurt in his voice is evident. I feel terrible for having asked them. "I'm sorry," I say.

Trist opens her mouth, no doubt to say something else horrible. Gabe gives her a look and she closes it again. "We didn't learn anything that can help with our investigation."

I try not to let the disappointment show on my face. Marius is less successful. Drake doesn't seem surprised; not that he ever does. In fact, he speaks up. "There are things we can still do even if we don't know yet who the culprit is."

Trist gives him a look that says she is already certain who the murderer is. Eli actually looks up out of curiosity. Gabe tenses but asks. "Such as?" His voice is tentative, careful.

Drake explains, "We need to convince all our classmates to stay in groups at all times when here. Pairs may be sufficient, but ideally everyone will be in trios if not more no matter where they're going."

I can't keep the surprise off my face. He comes up with such great ideas, thoughtful and effective. I glance at Gabe to see what he's thinking. I find him staring at me, a gravity pulling me toward him. "What do you think?" I ask to break the tension more than anything else.

He considers his de facto lieutenants before looking back at me. "It's a good idea." It sounds like it hurts him to admit it.

I study the other two Ascended. Eli nods like he thinks it's the best idea anyone has had in some time. Trist still looks pissed. "I hate that it was this...Descended's idea, but...it's a good idea." That must have hurt.

Gabe says, "We'll talk to all of the Ascended."

"We'll do the same with the Descended," Marius speaks up, a new confidence in his voice.

Chapter Fifty-One
The Eternal Fire
May – Purgatory Academy

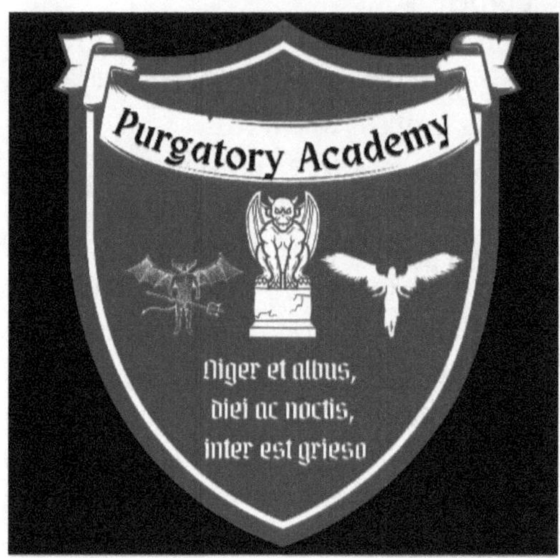

While there are no murders in April, organizing the Ascended and the Descended and convincing them of the importance of staying in groups takes a lot more effort than any of us realized. For the Ascended, Gabe and Trist do most of the work. Eli is primarily there for moral support. I actually have to tell Drake not to help because even the majority of the Descended are afraid of him or at least don't trust him. He agrees in his typical stoic fashion.

That means that Marius and I are left to do most of the compelling. My friend isn't well received by our classmates, but something about this brings him to life. He's becoming more confident, and he often takes the lead when we go to speak with our Descended classmates. It's wonderful to see his personal growth. It gives me hope he'll survive the year even if I'm afraid to embrace said hope.

It takes weeks to get it all done, but there are no more attacks. Our plan is working so the six of us finally find a time to return to the library. I'm nervous about it. That librarian is creepy as fuck. But I also have anxious thoughts about Gabe. It has been weeks since we made out near the library. Thinking about it has me hot and bothered all over again.

I shove all the good feelings down because we're entering the library, and I need to focus on the task at hand. Yes, no more murders have occurred since we got everyone to move around in groups, but that isn't a guarantee.

There is no sign of the pervert librarian, so we go back to the spots where we left off weeks before. Hours later none of us has found anything. I'm looking through the stacks when something catches my eye, although it has nothing to do with our search.

The book is an older leatherbound called *The Eternal Fire.* I skim it and according to the author, Archibold the Archdemon, the Big Bang Theory occurred because the Eternal Fire erupted, creating the multiverse. However, when it exploded and brought existence into being, it shattered into four pieces. Each section flew off into different corners of the multiverse. As part of the Eternal Fire, they all created a plane of existence, but because each was part of the original whole, those worlds overlapped with each other and were forever connected.

Each is a creative force named after the world and plane of existence that it shaped. The four pairs are Hell and Hell Fire, Heaven and Celestial Fire, Purgatory and Ghost Fire, and Earth and Eerd Fire. Two of the fires were lost to time, but they are said to possess incredible power. I'm lost in the reading, enthralled by the topic. However, it's when I get to the color of each of the fires that I stop dead in shock. Archibald states that the Eternal Fires all possess their own unique color of flame. Hell Fire is a royal purple, Celestial Fire a gleaming gold, Ghost Fire a bone white, and Eerd Fire a glowing green.

I read that last part five times in a row but still don't completely believe my eyes. The Eerd Fire is green. Suddenly, I get a sense of being watched, my neck tingling. I glance around, but no one is paying me any attention. I take a deep breath and concentrate on the task at hand. I can come back to the weird green fire thingy later on. But that feeling remains and we still find no answers.

Chapter Fifty-Two
Acts of Kindness
May – Purgatory Academy

The circus has moved around Texas a couple more times. Their next move will take us farther west. When I mistport home tonight, I'm greeted by a wonderful surprise. Barlowe is too because the gift is as much for him as it is for me.

My dad built a cat door for Barlow in my RV. The Familiar cat is pure excitement. He makes certain to show his appreciation first though. He twines himself back and forth between my dad's legs. My father laughs. "You are most welcome. I'm sure you want to try it out. No need to wait. Go on."

Barlowe rushes off. My father wears a surprised look on his face. "That cat is so smart. Just like your mother's fox."

I don't bother trying to argue. "You have no idea."

Concern flickers through my father's eyes, but he lets it slip away and smiles at my comment. I look back to the cat door. It's on the top of my RV. On the side, my father has somehow installed flat, wooden steps for Barlowe to jump up and onto the roof of the RV. That's exactly what he does.

The door itself is similar to a closed chimney on the top of a house. There is a large red button next to it which Barlowe understands because he presses a paw on it and the door slides in. The Familiar crawls in immediately. I love that he is clearly a tree cat, or tree Familiar.

"Shall we go look inside?" my dad asks.

I'm all smiles. "Absolutely."

We step up into my RV. To the right is a sort of carpet and wooden shoot my dad built. The angle isn't too steep and Barlowe keeps appearing and disappearing from it and then jumping on it to sharpen his claws.

"Ah, does somebody have the zoomies?"

"Don't belittle this for me, " is Barlowe's only response.

I laugh out loud. "He loves it. Thank you, Dad. It's wonderful."

I hug my father long and hard, trying not to cry at his generosity. We sit down and watch the cat play with his new door/toy. The longer we sit though the more my mind wanders.

"Dad?"

"Hmmm?"

"Can I ask you a question about Mom?"

"Of course."

"Are you sure? I know you don't like talking about her."

His mouth falls open. "Sweetheart, I love talking about your mom. Yes, it hurts, but it should. It hurts because I lost someone I love. I would be more concerned if I felt nothing at all. It will always hurt and if the day ever comes that it doesn't, that is the day I know something is wrong."

I've spent years trying to spare my father because I saw how much it pained him. Two emotions war for my attention. One is a profound sense of relief. I can talk to my dad about my mom. One is a deep sense of sadness that I assumed so much instead of talking to my father about it openly.

Tears threaten, but the relief and a third emotion, sweet joy, win out. "I'm so relieved to hear that. I have so many questions."

Dad laughs. "Fire away. Just remember that if I'm sad, that doesn't mean I don't want to share about her."

"Did you ever meet Mom's family?"

I remind myself my dad is okay with this even though his face clouds over immediately at the mention of my mother's relatives. "I never met any of your mother's family. Only Carmilla. They weren't actually related, but the two were thick as thieves when I met your mother. They were sisters in all but blood."

"Did she really never talk about them?"

My father's cloud darkens. "She did once," he admits. He doesn't elaborate immediately. "Like I've told you, I used to ask her about them, but she always did what she could to avoid the subject. Finally, when she realized she needed to give me some kind of answer, she explained that she wasn't close to her family. She said they loved her in their own way, but it was a selfish way. Because of that, she'd chosen to leave them behind and start her own family. A happy, healthy one. And then we had you. It was…perfect."

"All of them?" I haven't asked around about my family, but I've considered them often.

"Almost. She was close to her grandfather. She said that it was him who raised her to a great degree. It was her grandfather who encouraged her to live her own life. She said that he was the one who gave her the courage to leave her old one behind and start anew."

It makes me happy to know that my mother had someone at least. Barlowe has finally gotten the zoomies out of his system. He jumps on my dad's lap and curls up to sleep, purring all the way. My dad and I share another smile.

"Should we order a pizza?" he asks.

"Yes please!"

Chapter Fifty-Three
Temptation
May – Purgatory Academy

Our sixth Tribulation arrives quickly as the year at Purgatory Academy begins to slip away. Gressil picks us up at the front doors sans Familiars as per usual. My stomach does loop de loops. Few Nephilim actually died during the Silvering Tribulation, but that doesn't make me feel any better about the chances for this one. I'm surprised to find Gressil taking us a different direction. I figured we would head for the courtyard again, but I should have known better than to expect anything here.

Instead, the dean of students takes us to the classroom of our Temptations and Fortitude professor, Emilie. He waits at the door and has us enter, "Take a seat, everyone." The faculty are all present, standing around the middle of the room. Emilie is there too, but she's seated on a stool.

Today she's wearing a canary yellow one-piece minidress. She has her legs crossed, but that just showcases them more. Her "fuck me" pumps move to a rhythm only the demon can hear. She smiles the entire time and makes eye contact as often as she can. Plenty of my classmates are willing to oblige her on that front.

As soon as everyone is present and seated, Emilie speaks up. No waiting for Gressil, I notice. "Hello my darlings. I'm so happy to see your lovely faces. Today marks your sixth Tribulation. This has to be one of the most straightforward tests you will experience here at PA. Here are the rules. I will tempt you. All you have to do is resist me."

Before I have time to be scared, Emilie raises her hands, and the lights go out for a moment. They're back on just as quickly. I shake my head. I can't remember where I am. But it dawns on me.

The Tribulation is over and I'm back in my RV. I'm home and feeling nothing but a whole lot of relief. Stretching under the covers, I pull them back and realize I'm naked. I forgot I undressed when I got home.

A quiet "oh" slips from my mouth. Standing at the foot of my bed are Gabe and Drake. They're both wearing black silk pajama pants but no shirts. Their physiques are on full display, and I don't mind one little bit.

Gabe's chest and stomach are so tight with muscle, every little movement sends ripples through them. His thighs are so large the pajama pants are tight around them. That same tightness shows other rather large assets hiding underneath as well.

Drake's shoulders are broader, but he's just as defined in muscle. He is also a bit taller than Gabe, but both of them tower above me. Of course, I'm lying in bed naked. There's no shame though. If anything, I'm excited. I get back to my staring, but I don't know where to look first or longest. I just want to drink them up.

They both read my mind and smile wickedly like a pair of twins, one golden and angelic, the other dark and devilish. My mouth goes dry. Stalking forward, Gabe's movements are lupine, his grin wolfish. Drake's advancement is more feline, but one thing is for certain. These are predators.

Gabe comes around the left of my bed, Drake on the right. I really don't know where to look because I have to turn my head to take either of them in this close up. They sit gently down on the bed, but it sinks with their muscled weight. Neither of them bothers waiting, their rough hands reaching out to caress my face, my hair, my bare shoulders.

I all but purr at their synchronized touching. They slip under the covers on either side of me. I turn to Gabe first. He takes my face in his hands and kisses me tenderly. My lips. My cheeks. My neck. They are teasingly gentle. Drake runs his calloused hands all over my back and kisses and nibbles at my ears and the nape of my neck. Goosebumps rise on my skin.

I roll over to face Drake and the Nephilim gentlemen switch their duties. He kisses me with more passion while Gabe's nibbles are more urgent. Their hands roam all over my body. It's luxurious. They pull the covers down and press their hard bodies against my soft skin, the warmth among us creating a sort of seductive cocoon.

Drake's wandering hands reach my pebbled nipples, but he gently guides me on to my back. Gabe and he both take a breast in their mouths and begin teasing them. I can't tell which one I enjoy more. Gabe's tongue circles my nipple before lightly popping it into his mouth, suckling it. Drake doesn't bother with teasing but rather takes the entirety in his mouth and sucks hard till it almost hurts. Then he stops and starts the process again. It's sweet and painful all at once. Combined it's a sensuality I've never experienced in my life, but I know that I want more.

While the Nephilim worship my breasts, I sense more than see them both taking their pants off. I know enough about sex to be impressed at how coordinated they are while they do this.

I definitely know when they're done because twin hardnesses press up against my hips. I can't stand it anymore. I need them. Both of them. I reach down and grasp them each firmly in a hand. Gabe gasps in pleasure while Drake growls his own.

Light and dark move back up to my mouth. Drake takes me first this time, but Gabe is impatient, sucking at my neck and earlobe. I turn toward him to play. Drake bites me in the shoulder and clamps down, sucking hard as he does. I moan with the pleasurable pain. His fangs elongate ever so slightly to pinch at my skin. It isn't enough to puncture, but it's close. I understand he's marking his territory, that a keepsake will show up on my shoulder later on.

Gabe's fingers cup my breast and pinch my nipple. His cock pushes hard against my mound, and I begin grinding against him. Drake's hardness is against my ass. I find a rhythm that allows me to move against them both.

Passion burns like a wildfire, spreading throughout my entire body. I can't stand it any longer. Pressing my hands to Gabe's face, I command, "Take me now."

He doesn't hesitate. I guide him and he slides into me. Fuck yes; he fills me up just as I imagined he would. We gyrate together and Drake continues to grind against me from behind. Fuck. He's even larger than

Gabe and I want to feel it. I kiss Gabe and slide up off him. He growls but follows my lead.

I turn to face Drake, kissing him desperately. I don't need to say anything. He knows. He slips into me and there's a stretching sensation. It's painfully sweet, but I love it. Turning my head slightly to Gabe I say, "Do it."

I stick my ass into his hard cock. Drake waits inside me while Gabe moves slowly. I'm so turned on I'm pretty sure it's going to work even though I've never done this before. My own wetness on Gabe's cock actually helps and I moan as he enters me.

It's difficult to have a rhythm among the three of us, but we figure it out. I'm so close to coming. Their hard, erratic breathing tells me they're almost there too. That thought alone drives me to the edge. "I want us to all come at the same time," I say. "I'm going to count down from ten and I want you to both release when I get to zero."

Both of the Nephilim groan their agreement. Their thrusting grows faster and more urgent. I have to start counting otherwise I'm not going to make it. "Ten. Nine. Eight. Seven. Six."

They hold me tight, so they don't lose their rhythm. They're both growling and grunting louder and louder now. I kiss Drake as deeply as I can. Pulling back, I continue counting. "Five. Four. Three. We're almost there." I barely get the words out. They're both near yelling.

"Two. One. Zero!" I scream out as ecstasy rolls over me wave after wave. Gabe shakes uncontrollably as he shouts. Drake clamps down on me with his entire body before he lifts his head and literally roars, the vibrations shifting through my very bones.

We lay in each other's arms, exhausted and spent. Sweat drips from my forehead down my cheek. I reach up to wipe it away, but when I do, I glimpse it on my fingers. Red. It isn't sweat. It's blood.

I look back up at Drake, but he isn't there. Instead, I'm horrified to find my surroundings have changed. I'm back in Emilie's classroom and one of my Descended classmates is being stabbed over and over by one of the Ascended. Blood from the Descended splatters my face and drips down my cheek. When I attempt to wipe it away, I just smear it in.

I try to blink away the horror to register what's going on, but the horror is real. My threesome was a vision of some sort. Fucking Emilie. The female Ascended in front of me swipes the knife across the neck of the male Descended, thick rivers of blood pouring down.

It isn't only the bloodshed that horrifies me. It's the Ascended's eyes. They're glazed over as if she's dreaming. Fuck. We're all trapped in our own visions of desire, conjured from that bitch demoness Emilie.

The scene in front of me isn't isolated. It's a horror movie in the room. Whatever the Nephilim's deepest and most desperate desires are, they're playing them out. It's shocking to find how many of us long for murder.

The female Ascended in front of me is sawing the head of my Descended classmate off. I turn away but the rest of the room isn't much better. That's when someone grabs my shoulder from behind. Without thinking, I lash out with a haymaker. Thankfully, Drake ducks it and grips me by both shoulders, making me look into his eyes. His completely clear and aware eyes. He isn't enthralled by Emilie's Sway visions.

He already has a dazed Marius with him. He pulls me up roughly and pushes both of us toward a corner of the room. We pass what I figure must be five or six bodies of our classmates. It's difficult to be certain given how dismembered and eviscerated they are. There's blood everywhere.

As Drake hurries us into the corner, he turns to face the room. Some of the shock of the scene begins to wear off and I realize Drake has blood all over him. It makes sense. I bet more than a few of our classmates wanted nothing more than to kill him. Shit fuck. Had the visions captured him too and led him to kill, I wonder. Emilie is so much more powerful than I've given her credit for; this is fucking crazy.

Murder plays out in front of us everywhere. It isn't the only thing happening though. There are plenty of Nephilim having visions much more akin to my own. Their gyrating movements and moans of pleasure are pretty good indicators.

What I don't see a lot of are students who aren't still captured in their visions. "Drake," I yell over the chaos. He cocks his head to the side but keeps his gaze on our classmates. "We have to help them. We have to wake them up." His shoulders slump in resignation and his head nods slightly.

That's when Trist comes screaming at Drake. I shouldn't be surprised it's one of her deepest desires to murder him. At least she doesn't have a weapon. "Don't hurt her." I can't believe I'm saying that, but even that bitch of an Ascended doesn't deserve to be harmed…too badly when she's under a trance like this.

Trist throws a punch at Drake, but he ducks easily and grabs her from behind. She struggles and tries to hit him in the groin, but he chokes her out pretty quickly. He drags her unconscious body over to us. "Watch her," he commands.

Before I can ask what he's going to do, he makes his way toward the faculty gathered at the middle of the room. Strangely enough, no one is attacking them. I'm certain that has something to do with how Emilie has used her Sway on the students.

Speaking of the demon professor, she has a huge smirk on her face. Marius has to stop me from going over there. "Drake's got this," he shouts over the havoc.

We watch his progress. Several students attack him, but he either dodges them and pushes them away or chokes them out the way he did Trist. It isn't long before he makes it to the professor.

He must have been yelling because I can hear him from there. "You have to stop this."

Emilie's smile doesn't falter even a little bit. I can't read her lips but I'm pretty sure it's something like, "Why would I do that? If you can't control yourselves and fight off Sway, how will you ever survive out there in the world?"

Drake takes a menacing step closer, but the professor only leans in with a predatory smile on her lips. He growls at her. And I mean, he growls. It's like he's a beast. Or a dragon...I feel it from here. It reverberates throughout the room.

Instead of being frightened, Emilie appears turned on. There's a lust in her eyes that I've never seen. A strangling sort of jealousy rises in my chest and Marius has to grab me with both arms this time to keep me from marching straight up there.

Drake doesn't back down. He takes one more step and Emilie puts her hands up in surrender, still smiling. The demoness winks and snaps her fingers. And just like that the anarchy comes to a halt. Glazed eyes begin to defog. The worst is yet to come though.

As students begin to realize what they've done, the wailing starts. Many rock back and forth in shock. Others mumble or even slap themselves as if hoping this is a nightmare and they will yet wake up.

Trist is still out cold. Gabe spots us in the corner guarding her. He motions to Eli and the two of them rush over. The blonde doesn't say anything, but he nods his appreciation for guarding Trist. I return his acknowledgement and move out of the way. He picks her up in his arms and stalks off, Eli trailing with shocked tear streaks on his face.

Drake leaves Emilie standing there, still smiling. Walking over to us takes a while because of all the blood and body parts strewn everywhere. When he reaches us, our eyes meet. For a moment, I'm in that Sway vision from Emilie again. I refuse to let it take root here and now though. "We should go," Drake says.

I take in our classmates. I want to help, but shock is beginning to settle in, heavily. Drake sees it too because he motions to Marius who puts a friendly hand on my back to usher me forward. When did he become the strong one? I allow them to lead me from the room as gargoyles appear to clean up and take away the bodies. The faculty don't bother but disappear through the staff doors leaving the Nephilim to collect themselves.

My mind wanders as we leave. Finally, it latches on to something. "Marius, did the Sway work on you?"

My friend has an arm around my shoulder to keep me propped up but at my question his entire body shudders. "Yes, but I'd rather not talk about it."

"Agreed," I say. We continue on a bit longer before I speak. "Drake, did it work on you?"

"For a second," he says after a moment's hesitation.

"Just a second?"

"I realized relatively quickly that it couldn't be real," he explains.

I desperately want to ask him what he saw, but I know he wouldn't appreciate me prying. Instead, I let my mind wander a bit more. I'm only capable of clutching to dark thoughts though. Of course, that might have been because the world in which I reside now may be gray in color but it is dark in nature. Not for the first or the last time I have to wonder what the point is of trying to stop murders when the faculty are willing to allow us to be butchered during the Tribulations.

Chapter Fifty-Four
Friends
May – Purgatory Academy

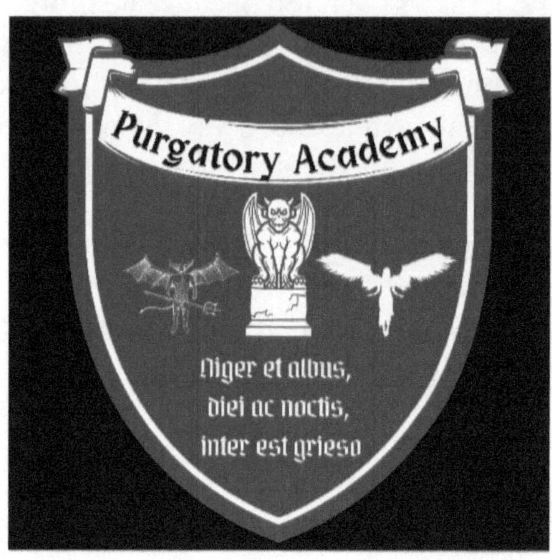

HELL

"Emilie doing her best work, as always."

"I want to disagree with you, but I see your point." I'm mumbling now even when only speaking mentally.

"Of course you do," Balor responds.

Marius and I stare dejectedly at the glowing red numbers on the side of PA. The Ascended numbers fell from 843 to 722 while the Descended numbers are down from 946 to 823. I had nightmares all weekend long about our last Tribulation. I can't imagine they will stop any time soon. More and more I understand why they're called Tribulations.

Like most of our classmates, Marius and I drift through the week. I try to focus, but disemboweled bodies fill my waking thoughts. They flicker in my vision even when I just close my eyes for a few moments to take a breather. The majority of us are walking around like zombies. We move but we aren't fully alive. Barlowe tries repeatedly to pull me out of it with jokes both raunchy and insulting in nature. Even that doesn't work.

Gabe is distant. He doesn't approach us at all. Eli keeps his head down more than usual. And Trist is the worst of all. She no longer stares daggers. She's just sullen, rejected. I hate that I feel any sense of pity for the Ascended, but I'm also relieved to feel anything at all.

One thing I do understand is that any small amount of trust the six of us developed was completely obliterated by Emilie's Tribulation. It showed us all how deep our distrust runs. Fear rules now. It's palpable in the air.

At lunch on Friday, Drake has enough. He sits down and starts in right away. "Alright, I gave you both a week to get over it, but you're clearly not going to without help."

Surprise is splayed all over my face; Marius' too. "How do you expect us to get over something like that so quickly, or at all for that matter?" I ask. There is no temper to my words, only bafflement.

"Because you have to in order to survive." His words cut like a dagger straight between the ribs. His voice softens though as he continues. "Look, this was no one's fault. It is what it is. This is Purgatory Academy. If you let them keep you dejected like this, you won't be able to focus. If you can't focus, you will slip up. Slipping up here is akin to death. It's as simple as that. If you want to prove to them that you are more than what we all saw in those visions, then fucking focus and wake the hell up."

These last words are filled with an anger that almost vibrates. It reminds me of the growl he made when he threatened Emilie. The glaze over my mind and heart break up a little, but there's still so much. I glance at Marius, and he appears to be in the same sort of place.

Drake recognizes it and grits his teeth. "Look, growing up with the shadow of belief about who and what I am following me around constantly was difficult to say the least." We're listening now. Drake never talks about himself, let alone his childhood. "It was a lonely fucking existence. But I learned to deal with it. I read a lot." He picks up his copy of Tolkien's *Lord of the Rings*. Marius and I are both wide awake, wanting to hear more about Drake's life. He sees it and takes a deep breath. "My point is simply this. I got the fuck over it. I moved on. Because if I hadn't, I would have died. I had no one. No family that really cared about me. No friends. Nothing. And now…You are both…" His voice trails off.

I reach across the table and put my hand on his. We lock eyes. Tension grows, but Marius cuts through it by laying his hand on top of mine. Drake huffs a laugh. "Now I have friends. Two of them," he clarifies. "And while I've never had friends before I know enough about it to understand I need to be there for both of you. So, wake the fuck up because the three of us, we're graduating from this bitch."

Marius laughs out loud and it's such a glorious thing to hear that I join him. Drake doesn't laugh but he does smile. It's like a rainbow after dark skies.

"About fucking time," Barlowe says.

"Yeah," I agree. *"About fucking time."*

Chapter Fifty-Five
Creation Story
May – Purgatory Academy

Two more Ascended are killed at the end of May. They're found together with the same bruising patterns and just as much confusion about who might have done it. Drake's words wake me up, but this has me infuriated anew. Friday I don't go home after school. Instead, I head to the library. I haven't been in a while, and I'm determined to figure this all out. Barlowe lopes off to hunt mice in the shadows of the stacks above despite the rule against Familiars.

I've been there for a couple of hours, pouring over volume after volume when the librarian shows up. I've already considered what I was going to do if he did.

"Good evening, my dear," he draws.

I pour Sway into my words. "Hello, it's nice to see you again." My smile is as big as I can make it.

He beams at my openness. I figured as much. A little bit of charm and he's going to assume that his own is quite impressive. "Still searching?" he asks.

I pout. "Yes, but it's not going well. Any suggestions?"

He chuckles. "I see what you're doing. You're quite inept, I must say."

Warm flames of embarrassment heat my cheeks. "I-I, um, don't understand what you mean."

"You don't play dumb well either."

Anger replaces the humiliation. "Excuse me?"

He laughs harder. "On come now, my dear. No need to be insulted. I've seen much worse."

Apparently, my Sway isn't working as well as I thought. "Can you help me or not?" I snap.

The librarian strokes his semitransparent beard thoughtfully. "I could, but it will be for a price."

My eye roll is almost automatic. I twirl a hand to indicate to him that he should continue.

Smirking he says, "For starters, you can flash me."

"What?" My voice echoes in the library.

He shrugs as if to say that's the deal.

"How do I know that you actually know anything?" I ask.

"You don't."

"That doesn't sound much like a deal," I counter.

"True, but you're the one desperate to find what you're looking for."

"That may be, but I'm not that desperate."

The librarian shrugs again and turns to walk away.

I grind my teeth. "Fine. You win. I want the information first though and then the flash."

"Well, I've never been able to say no to a beautiful face." Or tits, I think. "There is one book that might be helpful to you." I don't love the use of the word "might." "The book is called 'A History of Creation Stories.' You should write the call number down." He gives it to me, and I write it on a piece of paper.

"Is that here on the ground floor?"

He points toward the circulation desk, "I pulled it for you already."

I rush over and find it. It's a heavy, dusty leatherbound piece, the title dark and shiny on the front. I walk back over with it and sit down. Unfortunately, the librarian is still there.

"It's time to uphold your end of the deal," he leers.

Mumbling, I stand up and unbutton my top as quickly as I can and flip down my bra for him to see.

He cat calls and whistles. I count to ten and then put them away. And that's when things get way worse. Standing in the entrance of the library and staring right at my chest through the translucence of the pervert ghost is a slack-jawed Drake.

The Descended male recovers quickly and storms forward as I pull my clothes together as best as I can. The librarian realizes we're not alone and when he turns to face Drake, his entire phantasmal body tightens up with fear.

Drake doesn't just storm though. He is a storm, sweeping toward us in his rage. The intensity of it in weighs on my bones. It's like he has his own gravity.

The librarian wishes me luck and fades away into nothing before Drake can reach him. It isn't by much.

My friend looks around as if he can still see the librarian. But finally, he faces me. The storm has calmed, faded. Instead, he wears an inquisitive eyebrow high on his forehead.

I shake my head, red in the face with embarrassment again. I try to explain, but just go with, "Don't ask. I've got a lead at least." I hold up the book to show him.

Drake sits down next to me, looking at the book as if to tell me to lead the way. I'm so grateful to move on to something else besides the fact that I flashed a perverted old ghost to get this book. I slide it over and open it.

It isn't easy to concentrate on the book with Drake so close. The mix of the old leather book's smell with his cinnamon and campfire scent are strangely alluring. Old books and campfires. Sexy. I force myself to turn to the first page. We read silently together for a while and it's soothing.

The further we read the more confused I become. The book is a unique blend of a genesis story with scientific explanations from the perspective of divine and hellish beings. It provides much of the same information I read in the other volume on creation.

This book goes into greater detail though. The authors of the book hypothesize that dark matter is part of how the four worlds overlap and interact with one another so closely, but humans aren't aware of it most of the time.

When we read about the Eerd Fire, Drake looks at me and I at him. Neither of us speaks though. I can't decide if that's a relief or not. We keep on reading.

The book explains that in the beginning the only one of the four planes of existence that was inhabited was Heaven. The Divine ruled there then as the Divine does now. In that world there is light and music.

Nonetheless, from its founding it was hierarchical in nature with the same three levels of angels as there are now: the archangels, the seraphim, and the cherubim. While they were shaped like humans, they had feathery wings of whites and grays. They were nearly all warriors and wielders of powerful elemental magics. Immortal and eternally young, they were extremely difficult to kill. This part was nothing new, but we continue reading.

Finally, we get to a paragraph that discusses how silver can hurt or even kill Nephilim. It says magic can as well, but the most powerful weapon against our kind are the four eternal fires. And it is those four flames of eternity that may have led at least partially to the War in Heaven and the inhabitation of the other three overlapping worlds.

The book leaves that little breadcrumb of foreshadowing and continues on with Heaven and its budding empire. There were only nine archangels: Lucifer, Michael, Remiel, Gabriel, Raphael, Azriel, Uriel, Sariel, and Ariel. At some point the Divine decided to create humans and place them on Earth which they discovered and explored. It was decided that humans would not have wings or be granted magic and immortality. The choice was intended to make certain their kind would be weaker and more prone to worship the angels and the Divine.

My head reels from the idea that the Divine was so…corrupt and selfish. The archangels were put in charge of the population of Earth. The goal was to have them worship the Divine and the Heavenly Hosts. Then the piece shared the most controversial bit of information yet. The authors state that it was Lucifer who advocated for humans to have free agency. He argued that it would make their worship greater in power because they would give it of their own volition.

This suggestion, which grew into a movement among the angels, angered the Divine greatly. Deity wanted to enslave humanity from the beginning, the book states. Lucifer's support grew among the other angels though. Despite this, the Divine ordered that humanity be enslaved, but Lucifer led a protest to the palace of Deity to plead on behalf of the humans.

However, the Divine was angered by what was considered the presumption of Lucifer. Deity banished the Light Bringer and one third of the Hosts of Heaven, the entirety of his followers. They were cast away into Hell.

Lucifer was so angry about his banishment that he vowed to go to war against the Divine. He understood what needed to happen to stop the tyranny. He set out to assassinate the Divine so war could be avoided. There was only one other archangel who fell in the Fall with him, Remiel. The two of them snuck back into Heaven to murder Deity.

However, a trap was set for them by one of the other archangels, Gabriel. Unbeknownst to Lucifer, Remiel contrived with Gabriel to betray Lucifer with the understanding that Remiel would be allowed back into Heaven.

Lucifer, enraged by the treachery, killed Remiel. Humanity was yet young at the time, and none had died. In this moment, death entered existence among the four planes of connected reality.

Eventually, Michael took on Lucifer in single combat and was able to defeat him before casting him back down into Hell. In the meantime, the Hosts of Hell were ambushed. With Remiel's death, others died as well. Among them was another story that would become infamous, if not accurate. Cain, one of Lucifer's top lieutenants, discovered that his own brother, another seraph among the Fallen, had also betrayed them and allowed part of the Hosts of Heaven into Hell. Cain slew Abel in single combat and in his rage, drank the blood of his brother, becoming the first vampire.

In fact, with time various changes came to the Fallen. To this day, no one knows what the reason is for this. Some believe it was because of their transgression and rebellion against the Divine. Others believe it was because of their new home, Hell, shaping their very nature to be something different, twisting their very forms.

With the entrance of death into existence, Purgatory was given to the entity Death. No one knew where the being came from, but Deity gave Death the responsibility of keeping the dead till they were judged and shepherded to either Heaven or Hell. Purgatory grew as a kingdom between the mortality of humans and the ongoing war between angels and demons. New species also sprang up in Purgatory. Again, no one could explain why but it was happening.

As the war continued, Lucifer saw that he and his Hosts would never win. However, they did make the cost of the war high for Heaven. Having done so, Lucifer was able to broker a cease fire with the Divine. Part of the agreement was that their war would only continue as a proxy, a cold war of sorts where they would vie for the souls of humanity. In order to do so they also agreed they would mix with the humans more than they already had and the children and descendants of these dalliances would attend Purgatory Academy where they would be trained to be influence pushers.

We knew this last part from classes, but it still gave me so much to consider. Lucifer painted as the good guy. That was certainly a new one. We sat considering everything we'd read for some time.

"That really didn't help us with the murders at all," I finally say.

Drake smirks.

"What's that for?" I ask.

"Nothing," he smiles.

"It's something," I insist.

"Nope." I hear the teasing in that one syllable word.

I slap his shoulder. "Tell me!" I can't help but smile though.

"It's just that I didn't realize you were into older men."

I slap him harder this time in the same spot. "Shut up!"

"Look, no judgment here," he teases.

My hand lingers on his arm this time when I smack him. The muscle there is so taunt and thick under the layers of his uniform. "Stop!"

We both laugh heartily. "That librarian is a pervert, but I thought the book was going to help with the murders."

"Did you specify that when you made the deal?"

"Specify what?"

"That it would help with the murders?"

I think back to it. "Well, no…"

Drake smirks again. "I admire your willingness to sacrifice for the greater good."

My face is red again. When Drake sees it, he stops teasing. "I'm serious," he says. "I really do respect you for all your efforts. You are…good."

My face flames anew, redder than ever. "I'm so embarrassed."

"You should never be embarrassed by your body."

I giggle. "I'm not, but that you saw me doing that."

Drake laughs in return. "You are dedicated."

We share a moment's gaze. Images of that vision Emilie gifted me flutter through my mind like a butterfly I can't quite catch because of its abstract flight patterns. I'm startled to find we've moved so close that our breath mingles. What is it about libraries and hot guys? "We should go," I blurt.

"Yeah, we should," Drake agrees. He stands up and we walk out together. Rowan and Barlowe catch up to us at the doors. Thoughts of my flashing session all but gone in the glow of normal conversation with Drake.

Chapter Fifty-Six
A Mischief of Imps
June – Purgatory Academy

Weeks pass. Classes, training, library, flirting with Drake. Rinse and repeat. No more murders, thankfully. Our respective trios are able to convince the majority of our classmates that it's in their best interests to travel in even larger groups. Those who don't readily agree, are dragged around by their friends. I haven't seen a group of Nephilim any smaller than four in size anywhere on the grounds of PA. It's something.

The next Tribulation arrives. There is a comforting difference about this one. Marius isn't the only one waiting for me inside the gates of Purgatory Academy when I arrive that morning. Drake is there too. A lovely warmth spreads in my chest. On top of that he gives me a small smile and a quiet "good morning."

Gressil leads us in a winding path through the hallways to Ren'el's Evocation classroom. We're seated while the faculty stand in the middle of the room. Emilie is present with an angelic smile on her face and dressed in a purple nurse costume made completely of latex. I fight off the flashbacks of our last Tribulation and work on convincing myself this can't be led by Emilie again. We're in Ren'el's room, but my fear doesn't want to listen to me.

The dean speaks up and I'm never as grateful for his annoyingly boring voice as in that moment. "This month's Tribulation will, as I'm sure at least some of you have surmised, deal with evocation. Naturally, your Evocation professor, Professor Ren'el will lead you this time."

The demon steps aside and Ren'el glides forward. A quiet grin graces her face as she speaks. "As is often the case, the instructions and objective of your Tribulation are relatively straightforward. Accomplishing it may be another thing though."

Ren'el lets that settle in before she continues, "I will evoke certain beings from another of our shared realms. Your only objective is to survive and if possible, either neutralize or evoke the beings back to their home world."

Concern creases Marius' face as he glances at me. It could be anyone or anything. Ren'el doesn't keep us in suspense long though as she begins to chant to herself quietly. The students collectively brace for whatever is coming.

Mist fills the entire room. Whatever it is, there's a lot of it judging by how dense and complete the fog is. Just as quickly as it rose, it dispels. But there's nothing there. Like many of my classmates, I scan the room. Nothing. No one. Some murmur their confusion, but others shush them as we all continue to search.

"Above," Drake says. His voice is quiet, but it carries in the silence of the room. I follow his command and look up into the darkness of the beams above. Goosebumps rise on my body as countless glowing red eyes stare back.

"Imps," Drake whispers. A few of our classmates scoff or laugh. With our collective exposure to the diminutive creatures, many of our classmates aren't taking the critters seriously.

Gabe is shifting with Eli and Trist toward us. Drake is tense and alert. I trust him about this and crouch a bit in my stance to prepare. Marius, seeing what we're doing, does the same.

It's a good thing we do because that's the moment the swarm of imps attacks en masse. "Mischief!" Drake roars.

I turn to stare at him. "Mischief?"

"It's what you call a group of imps."

"Is that bad?"

Drake stares at me. Right. It's bad. They move exactly like a swarm of bees or a group of birds, swerving in unison. But as they dive bomb the Nephilim and faculty, they're more like piranha with blood in the water.

And there's plenty of blood soon enough. The mischief targets a small group of Nephilim off to the side of the room. As they descend, the students they attack are almost blacked out of view by the sheer numbers. Their cries of pain aren't though. And only a couple of minutes later, the mischief flies back up and moves in strange patterns; we're able to see the classmates who'd been attacked. Or rather, see what's left of them. Bones. They're picked clean by the imps. Holy fuck.

The mischief takes advantage of the stunned students and dives again. This time they aim for the faculty. I don't doubt any number of the imps has a bone to pick with the professors, both metaphorically and literally. As they reach the collected angels and demons, several of the imps smash into something invisible but quite solid.

The rest of the mischief changes direction and soars back up into the dark corners of the ceiling, angry hissing coming from the imps. I chance a glance at the faculty members. Black blood and tiny, smashed body parts drip and streak down the sides of a giant protective globe. It is just like what we use to capture the imps. I never considered using it defensively, but that's exactly what the faculty have done.

I'm not the only one to notice. Drake calls out, "Protective shields!" He already has his up. Marius is standing next to him, his eyes closed in focus. I do the same and soon enough, although I've never done it before, the globe pops up around me.

Some of our classmates aren't as lucky. The mischief dive bombs over and over and wherever they strike, stripped bone and bloody bits are all that remain.

Other classmates are able to get their own defensive globes up, but when the mischief focuses on them, that collective force of imps overpowers a number of the individual globes. Together they are much more powerful than any one imp is.

I understand now why we only call up one at a time. Their numbers are part of their strength. The same could be true for the Nephilim. Pooling our strength would make it more difficult for the imps to get to us. That's exactly what the faculty has done and there is no way the imps are getting to their smug asses.

I wave to Drake and Marius. In all the commotion, I'm not as close to them as I was before. Marius sees me first and motions to Drake who looks my way. "We have to combine our globes," I shout to them thrice over the noise of diving imps and dying Nephilim.

Drake moves, concentration etched on his face as his globe shifts with him. Apparently, it's an effort because he doesn't move quickly.

However, he gets to Marius and the two of them combine their globes together. I could be mistaken, but the air around theirs might have hardened from the combination, making the doubled one stronger than individually.

The two turn toward me and begin making their way. I take the opportunity to call out to Gabe who is also under a globe next to Trist. When Gabe hears me explain, he relays the message to her. The two merge their globes and begin calling to others around them. I feel warm appreciation for the Golden Boy when they take in both Ascended and Descended.

Drake and Marius are doing the same, gathering all those closest to them. A few refuse, but the imps sense it and focus on them, breaking their mischief into smaller groups.

One of the individual bubbles they focus on is that of Eli. He's in a corner, surrounded by bloodied bodies. Gabe and Trist call him, but it's taking all of his concentration just to keep the globe up against the onslaught of imps. As other individual globes fall, the swarms combine again and more of them come at Eli. He's crouched down now, face strained with the effort, sweat beading.

Something pale streaks toward him out of nowhere. It takes me a moment to recognize Marius. He left the cover of the combined globe with Drake and is racing toward Eli to help him. I consider doing the same, but I know I would never make it in time.

Eli's globe shatters just as Marius reaches him and the imps lunge as one, teeth gnashing and gnawing. Eli and Marius' screams of pain echo as the imps begin to devour them. I lose sight of them in the utter fluttering and flying blackness of the mischief.

I cry out, tears already welling in my eyes. But just when I'm certain the two are gone, a strange light begins to glow in that flickering blackness that reminds me so much of bats in a cave. The glow is difficult to describe. It's more like an absence of light than an actual light. And yet it glows. And then suddenly, it explodes, filling the room with the unlight.

I blink several times before I can see again. Where there had been a mischief of imps, there are only little charred bodies littering the floor. Among them is a crouching Marius, holding an unconscious Eli.

The other swarms of imps combine at a speed that can only insinuate anger at the death of their kind on such a level. The mischief swells and prepares to dive at the two isolated figures. But as they do, another streak rushes passed me; it's Drake this time.

He arrives before the imps dive. As they do, he lifts a hand and a hardened globe rips into existence. The mischief moves out of the way before slamming into it, but they hover just above it for a moment, buzzing like an angry hive of bees.

Before they can build up their frenzy further, a third figure steps up. Gabe is out of his globe, Trist screaming at him. He ignores her as he lifts his own hand, focus turning his golden face a darker, more pained color.

The imps understand the same moment I do. Gabe has them in a globe, floating right there midair. They smash against it, some of them hitting it so hard their tiny bodies fall to the bottom and collect there.

Gabe is attempting to send them back to Hell, but the effort of both holding them and sending this sheer number of imps back to their home proves too much for him. It's my turn to help. I let my globe slip away and step up next to Gabe, focusing all my efforts on sending them back.

As I do so, I notice one imp in particular who has quieted at my efforts. He says something to the others and within a few moments, the frenzy calms to a standstill. The imps allow me to send them home. I don't understand why, but I'm grateful because I'm pretty sure I wasn't going to pull it off otherwise.

Chapter Fifty-Seven
Summer Solstice
June – Purgatory Academy

Every Tribulation takes another piece of me. That must be at least part of the reason the trials exist. They're there to normalize blood and death for the surviving Nephilim. All that is left of us is what both sides of this fucking divine war wanted – unquestioning and unfeeling soldiers. It's working. I'm numb. After the latest Tribulation, the Ascended numbers fell from 722 to 689; the Descended from 823 to 772.

In the face of all this horror it's strange when Gressil announces in class one day that there will be a ball for the Summer Solstice. They canceled the Spring Equinox celebration but aren't going to do that again. Despite everything, the students are excited about it. I'm no less enthusiastic than the rest. Maybe it's because we all need something normal, something fun to distract us from the terror and murders in our midst over the last six months. Faculty inform us of the two portions of the evening. First, there will be a ball held in the gymnasium. Then we'll have special ceremonies in our respective chapels.

Despite my concerns about trying to find a dress, I shouldn't have worried. In true "aunt" fashion, Carmilla sweeps me off with a girlish grin to her RV to search through her entire closet of dresses. The closet looks to be custom made. When I ask about it, the older Descended explains that she loved to dress up when she was younger. Then she surprises me by explaining many of those dresses are my mother's.

I turn to regard the vampire. "Why doesn't my dad have them?"

"No room." I almost laugh. "I told him I'd hold onto them for you. I figured you might need them."

I run my fingers over the different colors and fabrics. Some of them are extremely expensive, at least from what I know about these brand names.

"Shall we try some on?" Carmilla is grinning like a teenage girl again.

It's contagious and soon both of us are pretending to be runway models for each other. Carmilla even puts on an old song I've never heard before but it's hilarious. The artist is Right Said Fred.

Three glasses of wine and two dozen dresses later, I pick out the one I want. Carmilla and I embrace long and sweetly, the vampire telling me to hang in there and to enjoy the ball. "Having normal things in your life will help you deal with the dread of the rest."

I nod, relieved to hear it. Some of the guilt about my happiness evaporates.

The Summer Solstice falls on a Thursday and we're to be there at six in the evening my time. Barlowe refuses to talk to me as I leave, so upset he isn't invited that he is taking it out on me.

As I mistport to the mossy hill outside the gates, I consider how so many of my classmates must be coming here at all kinds of different times. The Nephilim hail from all over the world. That must have been tough for many of them and messed with their internal clocks.

I trudge up the hill, grateful I opted to bring the dress in a garment bag and my accessories in my backpack. I'll get ready in the locker room of the gymnasium.

Marius is at the gates waiting for me. "Am I ever going to get here before you?" I tease after mistporting inside the school grounds.

The vampire smiles. "I doubt it."

He hugs me. "Happy Solstice."

The whole idea of celebrating equinoxes and solstices is new to me, but my heart warms at the excitement and happiness radiating from my friend. "Happy Solstice to you," I say.

Marius slings his backpack off his shoulders, unzips it, and reaches in, bringing out a small present wrapped with a bow.

"What's this?" I ask. "Marius, you shouldn't have."

He shrugs with a smile. "It's the solstice."

"You're supposed to get people presents for it? I had no idea. I didn't get you anything." Once again, I'm embarrassed by my ignorance.

Marius isn't having it. "Just get me two for the Winter Solstice," he teases.

I can't help but smile at that. "Deal," I agree.

"Well, come on. Open it!"

"Right here?"

"Yes!" He's so excited.

I slide the bow off carefully. It's a beautiful blue that shines even in the faint light of Purgatory. Tearing off the wrapping paper, I find a small box. The lid pops off easily to reveal a necklace with four tiny elephants on it, each with an eye made from a different colored precious gem.

"It's my siblings," I whisper.

"Do you like it?"

"I love it. Marius, this is too much."

He bats me on the shoulder. "Stop. It's the solstice and I wouldn't be here without you."

I meet his gaze. "Thank you. Thank you so much. Help me put it on?"

I take it out and hand it to him. While I pull my hair up from my neck, Marius puts his hands around my front from behind and clasps the necklace for me. I look down at it. They're beautiful. "Thank you again, Marius."

He waves a hand and holds out his arm for me to take. I loop mine in his and we walk up to the school for the Summer Solstice ball.

Forty-five minutes later we're both dressed and pressed, walking into the gymnasium arm in arm again. Marius is resplendent in a black three-piece suit and a white bow tie. I tell him as much, "You look so chic."

He puts on a bashful face and proceeds to compliment me so much I tell him I won't compliment him anymore. "That was my plan." He winks as he says it.

I chose a sparkling red dress that covers only one shoulder and has a slip cut up the opposite leg. I don't love high heels because they hurt like hell and aren't great for mobility, but they are necessary for this dress...according to Carmilla who called the gown the Jessica

Rabbit dress. It was one of my mom's favorites, she told me. Then she winked and said it was one of my father's favorites too. We had a good laugh over that. My hair is up in a nest of curls, pinned into place in a manner Carmilla showed me the night before.

We come to a sudden stop in the doorway, overcome by the transformation of the gym. Usually, it smells of sweat and wrestling mats. Now there's a lovely scent of lilac in the air. I never attended prom because I was homeschooled, but this is what I imagine it looks like, if it were put on by Dracula.

Everything plays up the Goth feeling of PA from the soft lavender globes that float above us but never get close enough to touch, to the black roses adorning the round tables; the same tables create a giant circle dance floor in the middle of the room.

"It's…" Marius begins.

"Beautiful," I finish.

We share a glance and giggle before swerving to the left to find a table in a corner as is our introverted way. Seated for a few minutes, Marius asks, "Should I get you a punch?" We have a good laugh over that but do both get up to enjoy the food they have. It's much better than punch and crackers.

We've been there probably a half hour before Drake finds us. He's dressed in all black, nothing new. And yet it is. He has black slacks and a black button up with a silky black tie. If he were a portrait, and sometimes I think that is exactly what he is, the name of the painting would be "Fallen Angel." That's how I see him. He's roguishly handsome typically, but tonight for the first time he looks angelic.

"Good evening," he greets us both but stares at me.

I'm grateful the glowing lavender lights keep it dim in the gymnasium so the blood rushing to my face isn't as evident. "Hello, Drake. You look very nice," I respond.

Marius is playing his old game of eyeball ping pong, his head following back and forth between the two of us.

Drake lowers his head in acceptance of the compliment. "Thank you. You look absolutely stunning."

Now I'm really grateful for the low lights. "Thank you," I whisper back.

He opens his mouth to speak again but is interrupted by the arrival of the Triumvirate. Well, two members of it anyway. I try to hide the shock from my face as Gabe and Eli walk up to our table. I don't know what I expected, but I didn't think I would see them much tonight.

Eli is darkly handsome in an almost eerie sort of way. I wonder idly if he perhaps knew about the glowing, floating globes that basically function like black lights, but either way it works well with his suit. His pants, jacket, and shirt are all white; but because of the globes, they have this purplish glow to them. Funny enough, his tie is black. He is a sort of opposite to Marius with his dark hair and white clothing. When I look at Marius to compare more, I see the two of them staring at each other before they both look away at the same time.

Gabe is dressed in dark slacks and a white shirt with a red tie. It's nothing fancy, but he is so classically handsome already, it serves to set off his good looks. Before I can make a complete fool of myself, I blurt out the first thing that comes to mind. "Where's Trist?"

Gabe, who is staring at me the same way Drake did, stutters for a moment before motioning across the room. "She's, uh, with, other friends."

He saunters over to me. Extending his hand, he says. "May I have this dance?"

There is music playing. It's American pop music, slow at the moment. I glance at Drake whose face is a stoic mask once more, waiting for my response. Gabe is all smiles though and I can't resist it. I hold out my hand for him to take, leading me out to the dance floor.

He puts a hand on my waist and leads me around slowly in a circle, among the other dancing Nephilim. I do notice Drake sits down across the table, facing away from the dance floor. Eli is seated by Marius. They look super awkward next to each other, but happy.

"You look gorgeous," Gabe says.

"So do you," I blurt.

Gabe's smile is bright even in the low lights.

"May I ask a question?" I say.

"Of course."

"Why did you ask me to dance?"

Gabe's face screws up in surprise. He takes a moment to answer, but then the smile returns. "Because you are beautiful. And because over the last six months or so, even though you are Descended, you have become my friend."

My heart glows like the gym lights, warm with gratitude. "Thank you so much for trusting me. And for helping with our investigation. Even if we've had our ups and downs. Even if we haven't accomplished anything."

"It's the right thing to do."

"I feel like that happens here a lot less than I thought it would."

Gabe sighs. "Niger et albus, diei ac noctis, inter est grieso."

"Between black and white, day and night, there is gray," I respond. I consider for a moment. "I suppose that's life."

We dance in silence for a few more moments before the song ends. "Thank you for the dance, Lilly." There's a tinge of sadness in his voice.

"Thank you, Gabe."

He escorts me back to our table. Drake is gone, but I'm surprised to find Marius and Eli deep in conversation, both of them smiling and laughing. I try to wipe the shock off my face before they see. I catch snippets of their exchange. Eli has pulled his chair closer to Marius' and the Descended is showing him his notebook.

"Is that your secret notebook?!" I'm blurting all kinds of things this evening.

Marius looks up but his smile doesn't fade. "Yeah, I was showing Eli."

"I can see that." I'm smiling now too. "So?"

Marius sighs. "Fine. I'll tell you."

"It's poetry." Eli is the one to blurt this time. He's so excited about it. "It's wonderful."

Gabe sits down. "Poetry? Really? What kind?" He sounds genuinely interested.

Marius looks down in embarrassment at all the attention.

"Go on. Tell him," Eli urges.

I'm amazed they're talking so much. It's…adorable.

"It's a collection I'm working on. One that I want to publish."

"What's it called?" I ask.

"Vampoetry." Marius laughs a little at the title as if that would make it easier if we don't like it.

"I love it!" I exclaim. "What's in it?"

Marius shrugs. "A little of this and a little of that."

"He read a couple to me. They're really good," Eli says.

It's my turn to play eyeball ping pong, back and forth between Marius and Eli.

The rest of the evening is a blast. Drake doesn't return, but I dance several more times with Gabe and Marius, even Eli a couple of times. The four of us dance together during the more upbeat songs. Trist doesn't come over at all but does dance a couple of slow ones with both Gabe and Eli. I couldn't ask for more.

Toward the end of the evening, the four of us are seated laughing and joking when Gabe realizes what time it is. "Eli, we better get Trist. We should exchange presents before the chapel ceremony."

Eli agrees, although he looks less than pleased about leaving. I've never seen him so happy; it's even more evident by the return of his sadness. Marius' face agrees with my emotions that we hate to see it come to an end. Carmilla was right. This is nice. It feels good to be normal for a little while.

They get up and leave, but they wave goodbye before they're gone. Drake shows up almost as soon as they've left. "Where have you been all night? We missed you," I say. It's difficult to keep the hurt out of my voice.

Drake doesn't answer me. Instead, he pulls out two presents. "Happy Solstice." He hands one to me and the other to Marius.

The vampire is grinning and I have to admit, if only to myself that it's sweet he got us presents. I turn to Marius. "You really need to keep me informed about things like this so I'm not the only shmuck without a present for everyone."

He laughs as he opens his. It's a set of old-fashioned ink pens for writing in his notebook. He looks up at Drake. "They're…they're beautiful. Thank you, Drake."

The big Descended smiles.

I open mine. It's an old book. No, it's *Dracula.* I thumb it open lightly. No, it's a first edition of *Dracula.* "Oh wow. How did you find this?"

Drake shrugs in that Drake sort of way. "I know a guy."

I'm hugging him before I know what I'm doing. I pull back, book in hand still. "This is…just…thank you."

"You're welcome."

The three of us follow the other Descended from the gymnasium to our chapel. It's as beautiful as the one we visited earlier in the year, but the stained glass here showcases depictions of the Lords and Ladies of Hell. I spend the most time considering the beauty that is Lillith. Lucifer stands out as well.

Gressil calls us to order, and we all sit in the pews. Marius, Drake and I find a spot in the back. The dean of students explains, "As we honor the Summer Solstice, for angels and Ascended it is a celebration of the zenith of light. For demon and Descended, it is the turn toward the darkness."

Gressil claps his hands, and the lights go out completely. A voice rises in the darkness. It's low and masculine, but beautiful. With some surprise, I recognize it's Gressil's. Other voices join his. They must be the demonic faculty members.

They do not sing words, but their voices echo in waves and the effect is heartbreakingly beautiful as it ebbs and flows. It's like the ocean tides. Tears stream down my face as I let it roll over me in the dark.

Marius' hand takes mine and I reach over for Drake's. As the music moves toward a crescendo, light begins to return, soft at first and then brighter and brighter. And then the music comes to a sudden, echoing stop as the light returns.

I'm left blinking away my tears. Marius squeezes my hand. Drake bumps his broad shoulder lightly against my own.

As we stand to leave, The'slin opens the huge wooden doors. I watch, shocked, as Ren'el rushes in and straight over to Gressil. I can't hear what she says as the two speak in hushed tones to the side of the chapel, but I know what it means. There have been more murders.

Chapter Fifty-Eight
Leviathan
July – Purgatory Academy

There's a fucking lake underneath Purgatory Academy. It isn't a small lake either. Sure, it isn't the Great Lakes that are so big they have waves like the ocean. No, this water is calm…and dark as Hell. I can see the opposite shore across the stalactites hanging down from the roof of the cave. But it's still big.

I wonder if Barlowe would have wanted to come along to a place like this as Gressil leads us down steep wooden steps into the cavern. Docked on our side of the lake are pirate ships. Well, that's how I see them anyway. I enjoyed pirate movies as a kid, and these are exactly that. Except they're on a lake. A fucking underground lake. I'm still wondering if my eyes are lying to me.

There's a wooden dock at the bottom, but even with our reduced numbers, it can't hold all the Nephilim. The last couple of weeks have been tough for everyone. Three more Ascended have been murdered. Their bodies were found in the hallway, abandoned there sometime during the evening. They had the same bruises and scratches as the others. It definitely ruined our Summer Solstice vibes.

Suspicion between the Ascended and Descended is at an all-time high. Gabe, Eli, and Trist stay away, but communication among our Familiars continues. We're playing it safe. I have noticed that Eli's ferret visits Blackbeard quite a bit, Marius often left smiling or even laughing after the messages are relayed.

Gressil's voice echoes across the sleek walls behind us and bounces off across the cave, lost in those bleak, glassy waters. The dean of students didn't lead us here this time. Instead, he met us at the front doors of PA and our Malakim showed up, each mistporting their own student. Lenny hasn't said a word to me. In fact, we haven't spoken much at all over the last few weeks. I don't want to push him.

"For this Tribulation, you will take these ships across the lake to the opposite shore. You may not fly. If you do, you will be shot down by faculty members. You may not mistport. If you do, your Malak will decapitate you. Questions?"

Sheesh. I have to give it to him. He isn't one of those boring teachers who lectures too long. I've decided to have some fun with it though. Raising my hand, he motions to me. "What's the name of the lake?"

"It's Unnamed."

"It doesn't have a name?"

Gressil shakes his head. "It's called Unnamed. The Unnamed Lake."

"Oh." So much for my fun.

Gressil continues. "Any other questions?"

One of my classmates asks the one we're all wanting to know but are afraid to hear the answer. "What if we can't sail a ship?"

The answer is better than I could have hoped for. "They sail themselves."

There are sighs of relief everywhere. The longer I think about it though, the more I don't like it. If the ships sail themselves, where is the trial? My stomach agrees with me.

"The three ships to the left are for the Ascended. The three to the right for the Descended."

And with that we all walk down the wooden planks to the ship. Walk the plank. Hardy harr harr. For one giddy moment, I'm a pirate. I hide my stupid smile the best I can. Marius comes over to join me, looking over the side into the dark water. I have to stop myself repeatedly from saying cheesy pirate things like "Arrr, matey" or "Yo ho yo ho and a bottle of rum."

"What are you smiling at?" Marius' face is incredulous.

That wipes it off my face quickly. "Nothing. Nothing." Anxious to change the topic, I ask, "How is the ship going to steer itself without any wind?"

I needn't have asked. The sails fill as soon as the Nephilim are aboard their respective ships. There's no wind and yet they sail. I grin, pirate thoughts floating along in my mind. I'm an idiot.

Drake joins us. "I can't decide if I should warn you away from the sides or not," he says.

Marius whips his head up to stare at the larger Descended. "What do you mean?"

Drake continues to keep vigil over the Unnamed Lake. "This is a Tribulation. Something horrible will happen. My guess is something in the water."

I hate how prophetic his words are because as he says it, a disturbance ripples through the otherwise calm surface of black. "What was that?" I hate myself for sounding like the pretty teenager destined to be killed first in a slasher movie.

"That was our Tribulation," Drake says.

He calls out to the other Descended on our ship. "Prepare your magic and your shifting. There's something in the water and it's coming for us."

I've never seen him take control of a situation quite like that before. At least not with a big crowd like the squished third of the remaining Descended on a ship like this. There isn't a lot of room for them to move about with so many onboard.

That proves even truer as many of them push toward the railings to see over the edge at Drake's words. It's the wrong thing to do. A dark-skinned male not three Descended to my left is there one moment and gone the next, screams muffled inside the giant snakelike creature that exploded from the water and snatched him up. He's gone before half of us realize something horrible happened.

"That's our answer," Drake says. "Back from the edges!"

From the scream behind us, I'm pretty sure at least one of our classmates didn't heed his words in time. Most of them are pushing and shoving to the middle of the ship though. That is a problem in and of itself because there are so many of us in such a small space.

Drake stands at the edge of the massive group of Descended. And the attacks begin in earnest. More giant snakes spring up over the railing. Their colors are dark grays and dirty whites mixed with black, making them easily camouflaged in the dark underground waters.

As they have to spring for their dinner a bit farther onto the ship, my classmates and I get a better look at them. Their faces are long and pointed with razor sharp teeth on top and bottom.

"Leviathans!" Drake calls out. My brain makes a vague connection to the Bible, but that's about it.

"What do we do?" I call to him.

"Kill them!" Drake answers.

Oh good. Straightforward and easy. Classmates begin shifting at least partially so their claws are out. I follow suit and each time one of the leviathans comes snapping at me, I lash out with claws. Gore and the smell of rotten fish fill my nostrils. The leviathans screech in pain each time one of us draws blood.

While most of them are brave, lashing out with talons and magic, there are a couple of students overwhelmed with fear. Two of my classmates sprout their wings and fly off. It's only moments later I hear both scream as they fall, splashing into the lake. I catch a hint of what I'm certain were silver arrows sprouting like porcupine quills from their bodies. The roiling water where they sink demonstrates the leviathans find wounded prey pretty quickly.

A couple more of my classmates attempt to mistport. Mist rises and they're gone. It isn't a minute later mist rises again and the heads of those same classmates are dropped on the already slick deck of the ship by their now former Malakim. Fuck.

The ships sail on, but the number and ferocity of the leviathans increases. More than one slips back into the water with a screaming Descended in its jaws, even as classmates slash and rip at them with magic. Drake warned me not to use my fire, but I can't concentrate enough to unleash it even if I wanted.

As we come up on the other side of the lake, the attacks lessen. Perhaps it's because the water is too shallow for the beasts. It gives me a moment to look around at the other ships. Like our own, there's damage but they sail on to the opposite shore.

Someone touches my elbow lightly and I turn to find Marius. "We made it," he says.

I let out a sigh of relief. "We made it."

I should have known that saying something like that out loud was a terrible idea. We're coming up on the shore, but a lone leviathan rises out of the water and snaps at Marius. It would have had him too if Drake hadn't shoved him out of the way.

Time slows. It's a millennium in moments as those razor teeth crunch down on Drake's arm. I'm too shocked to consider it at the moment, but later on I will wonder how the only sound Drake made was a low grunt. Blood sprays as the leviathan bites down and drags my friend over the railing and into the dark.

Marius and I rush to the side as do several of our classmates, having seen what Drake did to save Marius. But there's no sign of him. No movement touches the surface of the water beyond the steady forward ripples of our ship.

Other Descended disembark around me but I can't convince myself to go yet. I race around the railings from one side to the other looking for a sign. Hoping for a ripple. Drake has to survive. I can't even fathom an alternative. Only when Marius gently tugs me toward the dock do I allow myself to be drawn away.

But as we come down to the shore, there's a large crowd gathered on the docks. Marius pushes his way through gently. At the center of the mob is a severed leviathan head and a dripping wet Drake, torn shirt but unharmed.

Chapter Fifty-Nine
Ghouls
August – Purgatory Academy

The Nephilim, with the help of our Familiars, keep to large groups and no more murders occur. Of course, I thought we had figured it out before and then more Ascended were killed during the Summer Solstice Ball.

It isn't long before August arrives and along with it, the next Tribulation. This time Gressil leads us to the gymnasium. The Nephilim numbers didn't fall by much during the leviathan Tribulation, thankfully. All the blood and guts went a long way. There are well over a thousand of us. That also means that the gymnasium is rather large still. However, today it's even larger than normal.

Spread out at regular intervals are nine-point stars on the wooden floor which no longer has wrestling mats covering it. Gressil explains the expectations of this Tribulation without giving away any of the horrible things that are obviously going to happen.

"Welcome to your ninth Tribulation. Up to this point, for the most part you have been allowed to work with others. This is solo work though. It is brought to you by the dedicated work of your Magic Weaving professor, Nekleth, and your dual War and Weapons professors, The'slin and Khal'ith. Now, please find a star and stand in the middle of it. Once each of you has found one, we will begin the Tribulation.”

Trepidation fills me, fraying my nerves. Marius motions for me to follow him and we head for the other side of the gym. Drake comes along too. “Any idea what this is?”

Drake thinks for a moment before answering. “I would say be ready to use your magic. Most likely, you will need it.”

I step closer and whisper, “I thought you said I shouldn’t let anyone see it.”

For weeks now I’ve faked not being able to tap into it. Drake still just flat refuses. Marius’ has finally awakened though, and it’s pretty badass to see him wielding shades of shadow as if they were weapons even if he can’t keep them solidified for very long yet.

“I don’t know that you’re going to have a choice in the matter,” he responds.

“Great,” I mutter.

We take up three stars on the back wall. Gressil’s voice, magnified, rings out. “Everyone is now situated. We will begin the Tribulation in three…two…one…”

At first nothing happens. But then I sense something nearby. I can hear it almost humming with some sort of energy. Stepping cautiously from the middle of the star, I hear it clearer. I hold out a hand to the air in front of me.

“Don’t.” Drake’s voice is muffled, but I hear him, nonetheless.

I turn to look at him, but mist rises around me. It stops at certain points and then I recognize the shape. I’m in a globe just like we use for the imps, but it’s much larger. Swirls in the mist inform me I’m not alone. The faculty mistported something into the globe with me. Shit.

I back away from the figures but feel that same humming energy at my back. There is a sort of heat to it and I stop, afraid to touch it, and sure as hell afraid of whatever is about to be revealed from the fading mist.

I’m right to be afraid. Standing in front of me are three beings I’ve only seen in my Angelology and Demonology textbook. They wear leather armor and are at least a foot taller than me. Their bulky shoulders ripple with muscles, but their faces are what really frighten me. The skin is a blotchy yellow tinged green and their heads are bald, but tusks jut out and up from their lower jaw. Ghouls. They’re creatures born of Purgatory. Cuddlebug covered them in class with us since our actual professors refuse to discuss anything from Purgatory. They’re flesh eaters, akin to zombies and living skeletons only in their appetite for meat, but with their own society.

All three growl at me. I get what Drake meant by having to use my magical abilities. Ghouls are fast as fuck and even stronger. They can be killed, but flames are best. Still, his warning about my fire clangs about in my head. I don't trust the faculty to have my best interests at heart if they find out about the eerie green fire that runs in my veins.

The ghouls don't give me time to consider it further. They obviously know how to fight together because they fan out almost immediately, one to my left and one to my right while the third remains in front of me. I back up as far as I dare without touching the humming globe. It's enough to make certain they can't flank me though.

Their growling changes pitch, moving up and down. They're communicating. Willing my claws out, I also let my fangs and horns expand out from under my skin. I even allow my tail to lash out from my tailbone. I've been practicing with it and hopefully it will be enough. If not…there won't be a need anymore.

They close in, giving me no room to maneuver. Of course, with the globe, there isn't that much space anyway. I could tap into my fire, assuming I can get it to work, but others would almost certainly see.

The ghoul on my right swipes at me. My tail strikes almost without instruction, smacking the ghoul in the face. From what I can tell, all three are male and this one stumbles back. A look of shock on his face quickly fades into anger and he surges forward again.

My tail stabs at him this time, keeping him at bay. The one to my left moves forward, but I'm just quick enough to slash out at him. He jumps back without getting cut.

The one in the middle, who is clearly in charge, bides his time. I know something has to give and more than likely it's going to be me. There's nowhere to run so I'm going to have to even up the odds somehow.

As the right ghoul lunges again, instead of keeping him at bay with claws or tail, I move toward him. The ghoul grins at this, but it soon turns to a grimace and then a bellow of pain as I jump just out of reach and my tail trips him up, sending him face first into the globe. An electrical shockwave of vibrations rips through it to join the ghoul's yell of pain. He tries to extricate himself from it, but the globe holds him in place, the lightning zapping him over and over. The light is near blinding, and I have to hold up a hand to my face. The remaining ghouls do the same.

It's my opportunity because the first ghoul finally crashes to the floor, the smell of cooked flesh filling up our joint prison. The other two are still in shock. Teehee. Shock.

I let my macabre sense of humor move me forward as fast as I can. The ghouls spot me though and close ranks. Shit. I wasn't quick enough. My offense turns to defense again just like that.

They lash out and work me back toward the globe, obviously hoping to fry me as I did their buddy. I can't let that happen and slash and smack them with my tail. The ghoul on the right reaches forward and grabs a hold of my arm, pushing me backwards toward the globe. The second ghoul rushes forward to help. Desperate to get out of the grasp of the first, I head butt him with my horns. Dazed, he isn't able to keep me from using his initial momentum against him and I throw him stumbling into the globe.

Again comes the white lightning that won't release the ghoul till he's charred meat on the floor. The final ghoul, the one who orchestrated their attacks, doesn't spare his dying comrade a second thought. He grabs me by the neck. He's so strong that he lifts me off the floor, strangling me, all the while a toothy grin on his face, watching the air vacate me.

He pulls me close and prepares to toss me into the globe to the same fate I gifted his partners. Fear, anger, and searing refusal fill me when air can't. My hands, on his forearms, light up in green flames, and the ghoul wails in agony.

He drops me and steps back, but I'm not finished yet. Yelling my rage, I bring my hands together in a thunderclap and a burning billow of flames roars toward the ghoul, engulfing him in emerald fire. His smoldering remains crash to the floor within moments.

As he dies, the globe fades. Multiple figures stand just outside of my former jail. A stoic Drake and an injured but living Marius are among them. It's Gressil who catches my attention though. "Well, well, well," he says. "How very fascinating."

Chapter Sixty
Wraiths

September – Purgatory Academy

With each Tribulation I survive, the more numbed I become. With each Tribulation I survive, the angrier Barlowe is. He's practically spitting when I return from the ghoul duel. Of course, he's a cat Familiar so spitting is perfectly natural. When I suggest that as a joke, he doesn't laugh.

He fumes over the next month. I keep waiting for the ball to drop now that the dean of students and faculty are aware of my green fire. Nothing happens though. If Gabe or Trist and Eli know about it, they don't say anything either. We continue to search the library whenever we have some extra time but come up with nothing. When I finally say something to Cuddlebug in frustration about it, he only grunts. "How do you think we feel? There have never been murders here in PA and this year we've had multiple." He stomps off without another word.

Good talk. I know the gargoyle is right and no more students have been killed in months, but the animosity between the Ascended and the Descended is so high. The one thing that gives me any kind of hope in the situation is Marius.

Ever since he survived the ghouls, he's a different person. He's more confident. He speaks up more. His fighting ability has come a long way too. He isn't at the top of our class, but he isn't at the bottom anymore either. And he's learning how to use his living shadows as weapons; that's the reason more than any other that he was able to beat three ghouls when so many of our classmates didn't.

I'm spiraling though. The Ascended numbers are down to 472 and the Descended to 593 after the last two Tribulations. The vast majority came from the single combat against the ghouls and the time for another Tribulation has arrived. There are only four left, but only a little over a thousand Nephilim live up to this point. I wonder abstractly and numbly how many usually live. When I ask Marius about it, he says, "It varies from year to year, but the faculty always state those who live are those who should." Warm, fuzzy place, Purgatory Academy.

There are so many locations on the school grounds associated with trauma now that I can barely muster the necessary cautious fear I should have when Gressil leads us again to the gymnasium. He goes through his entire spiel as per usual, stating that the War and Weapons professors are again in charge of this particular Tribulation. I don't care.

Each student is given their own nine-point star once more and I have to breathe through the anxiety that surges, an expectation of a globe enclosing me with another monster. Drake, Marius, and I take spots at the back again, but I can't muster the anger necessary to be pissed off about being subjected to life-or-death situations repeatedly.

Marius and Drake both notice and try to encourage me. Hell, even Gabe sees and tries to speak to me although things are worse than ever between the Ascended and the Descended. I barely acknowledge him.

Marius gives it one last try before we take our places in the circles, but I mumble whatever agreement I think he would prefer. Like all of Purgatory, I've grown gray on the inside. So much death and horror suck the color out of life. The worst part is I am so numb I can't even gather enough feeling to care about my lack of caring. Indifference is a bitch.

Gressil calls out to take our places in the circles as the staff come around to make certain we're ready. His magnified voice explains this Tribulation will be timed; students will only need to survive for five minutes. We don't even need to be victorious, just alive. Oh goody.

My face remains slack, devoid of emotion even if there was a tinge of fear for a moment there. I'm in no way ready for this, but I'm not certain I care anymore. I'm so dazed I don't notice immediately that Drake is standing in front of me. A small sense of surprise bounces in my chest and I'm about to ask him what he's doing, but I never get the chance because he slaps me. Hard.

I'm down on a knee before I know it and a burning rage thunders in my veins. I'm back up and in his face quick as lightning. He's faster though. He strikes me again. But this time he kisses me. I'm so shocked, I forget to be angry. The taste of cinnamon lingers on my lips and I reflexively lick it up.

My body and my mind can't agree on whether I should be pissed as hell or turned on. "There you are," Drake rumbles.

"I…Yes. Here I am."

"Good," he smirks.

Anger starts to win. "That's the second time you've done that. We're going to discuss this afterwards."

"Yes," he agrees. "We will. Because there will be an afterwards."

I want to argue more, but I understand what Drake did for me. He woke me up. Again. In a really rude fucking way. Again. He's unorthodox to put it lightly, but he is effective.

He jogs over to his own circle as a member of the faculty reaches us. I close and open my eyes. Focus returns. Whatever is coming for me, I'm going to survive it, if for no other reason than that I'm going to get Drake back…one way or another. I'll decide later which way…and for how long.

Gressil calls out and I'm enclosed in another globe. Mist rises and my senses go on high alert, ready for battle. When it dissipates, there's nothing there. And yet, I sense a presence. I shuffle as close as I dare to the globe, to the point that I can feel the crackling energy at my back. Nothing is going to sneak up on me.

At least that's what I think, because just then a whirling whisp of something vaguely humanoid rushes at me, arms out to shove me against the globe where I'll die like a bug on a zapper. On pure instinct I drop and roll toward the middle of the globe.

I face the vapor that attacked me, but there's no trace of it. I turn in a quick circle over and over but find nothing. Sense it, yes, but I don't see a damn thing. My mind shifts into overdrive, going through the catalogue of creatures we've been introduced to in our classes. There are a few that could go invisible and none of them are happy options.

I stop to listen, but as soon as I do, it attacks from behind. I shift in time to feel something hard and fast cleave through the air in front of my face. I throw back my head. I barely see the silvery thing that almost decapitates me and I'm still not certain what it is.

"Coward!" I call. "You don't even have the courage to show your face."

Apparently, my invisible stalker doesn't have a chip on their shoulder because my mocking doesn't work. Or at least it doesn't get whoever or whatever it is trying to kill me to show themselves. Fine. We'll do it my way.

I back up to the globe again, but not too close. Focusing on the embers that always burn under my skin now, I extend my arms out in front of me, my hands together and cupped. A rushing stream of green fire shoots out across the globe, and I move quickly from left to right to make certain there's nowhere for the invisible fucker to hide.

Sure enough, as I get to the end of my near complete circle of flames, there's a loud grunt of pain. I cut off the flow of fire and crouched down holding its crisped arm is my enemy. A fucking wraith. Shit. I breathe deep and remind myself that I don't have to kill it, just survive it for five minutes. Less than five minutes at this point.

Wraiths are another species from Purgatory. According to Cuddlebug they are one of the more dangerous ones. Part of the reason for that is they're born of two worlds, being both physical and mist. That's why they're able to sneak up on you; they are made of vapor when they do. But they have to be physically present to hurt you.

The other reason they are particularly dangerous is because they're so damned beautiful. I've seen depictions in our textbook, but this guy is a ghostly version of Legolas with raven hair. He smiles as if he knows what I'm thinking. The sword at his side ruins the effect though.

He's mist again. It isn't like mistporting, taking a moment. It's instantaneous. I loose my green fire, shooting forward. There's another grunt of pain, but this time closer and to my left. He appears again. I burned his other arm this time, but he still holds his sword. I did wipe his smile away though.

I light up both my hands in jade flames. The wraith allows his smile to return. "Beautiful," he whispers, his voice as soft as the mist from which he was born.

He takes a step forward and I raise my hands. Gressil's voice interrupts us, the Tribulation over. As the mist rises to send the wraith back from wherever he came, he winks at me as a parting shot. I hate the flutter in my chest…I think.

Chapter Sixty-One
Autumn Equinox
September – Purgatory Academy

Despite my semi-flirtatious moments with the wraith, there are plenty of my classmates who didn't survive five minutes against their own. The glowing numbers have fallen quite a bit. The Ascended are down to 335 and the Descended are at 481. To my knowledge no one has actually killed any of the wraiths. Marius says he barely survived, and the wraith was much scarier than the three ghouls. When I ask Drake about it, he only gives me a thumbs up. I have my suspicions, but I'm not going to push.

The month marches on and three more Ascended are killed right before the Autumn Equinox. Instead of having a celebration, Gressil lets us know we have the day off and can celebrate at home if we wish. I'm losing sleep over it, guilt eating me for not figuring out who's doing this. I redouble my efforts in the library and fend off the creepy librarian successfully without any more flash sessions.

I find nothing at all that can help with the murders and staying in larger groups isn't keeping Nephilim safe anymore. I'm angry with myself for my failure to figure this out, to stop it but it doesn't help anything.

Drake notices it though. He says something to me in the hallway on the way to lunch. "You need to get that extra energy out before you explode."

Visions of daydreams in the shower and bed flash into my mind at once. "I'm sorry, what?"

"We're going to start training together," he says. Then he keeps on walking.

Chapter Sixty-Two
Veiled Visions
October – Purgatory Academy

Usually, we have our Tribulations at the beginning of the month, but for our third to last one it's held on Halloween. As Gressil explains it to us in the gymnasium, it's a special one. He refers to it as the Veiled Visions. It's so special that the Nephilim are allowed to bring their Familiars along for once.

When I let Barlowe know, his exact words are *"It's about fucking time."* I concur.

I stand inside another nine-point star. I'm really close to being triggered permanently by these fucking things.

Gressil explains before we come in that Halloween is always the day for this particular Tribulation because it's the day that the veil, Gressil's exact word choice, is thinnest among the four interconnected worlds.

He says he isn't going to explain anymore because he knows how much we love surprises. Fucking prick. Barlowe concurs.

I close my eyes and take a deep breath. Barlowe's mind leans on mine like a cat rubbing against my legs. It's really good to have him here with me.

"Agreed," he purrs in my mind.

"Here we go!" Gressil announces.

I take one more deep breath and exhale, taking a wider stance to prepare for whatever the hell is about to come at me. It isn't mist that rises though. It's a red light, seeping out of the fucking floorboards.

I back up a little bit, so the light doesn't touch me. Barlowe follows suit. It spreads and grows brighter, forming a perfect circle. The floor is gone and I know it is because someone emerges from it.

All the fight goes straight out of me. It's a woman with burning flames of red hair exactly like mine. She wears blue jeans and a button up black shirt. I know both well, but not nearly as well as the face that smiles at me. My mom.

The tears that flood my eyes don't even have the decency to ask me to trail down my cheeks. The little shits just do it. "Mom?"

I hear my mother's smile in her words. "It's me, Little Fox."

I'm down on my knees, hands to my face.

"I know sweetie. I know. But we don't have a lot of time, so you have to listen up."

I wipe the tears away. "Right. I'm listening."

"They let me come."

"Who's they?" I ask.

My mother holds up a hand for me to wait. "I'm being held hostage in Hell."

The words burst out. "What? Why? How do I get you out?"

My mother opens her mouth to respond, but the red light grows again. My mother looks panicked. "Little Fox, listen to me. I love you. I'm so proud of you. You're almost finished, sweetheart."

The light holds my mother in place and pulls her down. I cry out, but don't step forward. "Mom. Please. Don't go."

"Ask your grandfather, sweetheart. Ask your grandfather. Goodbye, Little Fox. I love you."

I don't blink till my mother is out of sight, but the tears blur the lines of her figure as she disappears. The red glowing light doesn't though. It hums with a new life.

And another woman emerges from the red. Whereas my mother is a rose in her beauty, thorns and all, this woman is a storm encased in flesh. Even kneeling, I know she is taller than me. Her hair is red, but not that of flames like mine or my mother's. It's the color of blood.

She's muscled like a MMA fighter but has curves plenty of men, and women, would kill for. I know because the woman is completely naked. "Hello, Little Fox."

The words sound like a prayer in the woman's voice. My core warms at it. Words won't come to me.

"I've been so excited to meet you." The woman purrs even more than Barlowe.

"Yes, she does. And I fucking love it," Barlowe's mental voice sounds like he's drooling.

The woman turns her gaze on the cat Familiar. "Oh, aren't you a sweety pussy…cat."
Apparently, she's able to hear Barlowe too.

"Oh, you'd be amazed at all of the things I hear." Her voice is mischievous now.

"What did you do with my mother?" I insist.

The woman points at herself innocently. "Me? Nothing. Your mother is dead, but she's also the prisoner of someone in Hell you do *not* want to meet."

"Tell. Me. Everything."

The woman laughs. Her laughter is even sexier than Emilie's. So is her body. It's difficult to concentrate. "I'll make you a deal, Little Fox."

She steps forward until she stands directly above me. The woman's pelvis is within hand's reach. I keep my head and eyes up, staring into those black eyes that somehow glow.

"Now that is a pu-."

"Shut it," I interrupt the Familiar.

The woman laughs again and I'm able to see every single muscle and smooth curve move with the sound. "Oh, you have no idea my sweet pussy cat."

"I'd like to," Barlowe responds.

The woman hums. "We should begin with introductions. Do you know who I am, child?"

"I do." Barlowe is clearly enjoying this.

The woman winks at the cat and holds up a finger to her luscious lips in a hush motion.

The truth dawns on me. "Holy Hell."

The woman smirks. "Close enough. I'm your *Mother*, dear. I'm Lillith."

I was considering standing up given what's right in front of me, but I rethink it. This is Lillith. Lucifer's Consort. The Queen of Hell. The Succubus Queen. My queen.

"She's well worth the worship," Barlowe understands my continued genuflection.

"Yes, I am. But we'll get to that in a bit. First, we need to discuss your little investigation."

I try not to stare at the goddess' large breasts and extremely pointy nipples. It isn't easy to ignore them. "What do you mean?"

"My dear, you know exactly what I mean. You've been trying for months to figure out who is murdering Ascended. Hell would like to know what you learn."

Frustration sprouts in me. "We've been trying. But we haven't figured out anything."

"Sweetheart, don't give up. I believe in you. You'll figure it out."

"How do I know it isn't someone in Hell?"

Even her shrug is sexy. "You don't."

"Why does Hell want to know?"

For the first time, the succubus' face isn't pure sexiness. Still, even her consternation is beautiful. "We have our reasons."

"Let me get this straight. You want me to help you figure out who it is killing the Ascended here, but you aren't going to do a fucking thing to help my mother who is being tortured by someone else in Hell."

Lillith's mouth quirks. There isn't anything she does that isn't attractive. I focus on my anger to keep my hormones at bay. "Quid pro quo, my darling," she whispers seductively.

"Now you're spouting Latin at me?" I'm incredulous.

"It means-"

"I know what it fucking means," I growl.

Instead of being upset, the Succubus Queen laughs. That is way too much husk in one voice. Unfair. "My my, you are a hot-tempered fox. I like that in a woman, especially a beautiful one looking up at me so adoringly."

My mouth goes dry. My eyes want to roam that body, but I close them. "What do you have in mind?"

Lillith steps closer till her skin is within reach. Her voice grows even smokier. "If you figure out who the killer is, I will let you know who the torturer is."

I have to fight off the urge to reach out and lick that smooth skin. "Deal," I croak.

"Excellent. Now, we can move forward with our remaining business."

"There's more?"

"Oh yes, my love." There's that purr again. "It's time to show me how committed you are to being a succubus and to me as your queen."

"What do you want me to do?"

"Worship me." The queen crooks a finger, and I stand up. "Take your clothes off." It's a command.

I look around self-consciously. "They can't see us. It's just the three of us."

I glance at Barlowe. "He only gets to watch. Sorry, sweet pussy cat."

For the first time in his short life, Barlowe doesn't respond. He just watches as commanded.

I take my clothes off, one piece at a time, slowly and sensually. For some reason, I feel comfortable standing completely naked in front of the queen. Even standing, she's several inches taller. The queen leans down and kisses me. Afterwards, whenever I try to think about how to describe it, I can't. My entire body responds to it, and I know I orgasmed from that kiss alone.

When our lips part, the queen says, "One of the many perks of being me." She winks. "Now, get down on your knees. I'm going to show you another one of my many gifts."

Wordless, I kneel back down, and that mound is right there. I've never been with a woman, but I've never wanted to be so much in my life, even Emilie. I look back up at Lillith as if to request allowance and the queen nods almost imperceptibly.

I realize what the Succubus Queen meant by another one of her gifts as soon as my lips touch that soft skin for the first time. The same sensation alights on my own nether region, brilliant bursts of pleasure over and over again. Surprised, I glance up at the queen who smiles knowingly.

That is all the incentive I need. Each stroke. Every kiss. All the licks. I experience them just as I give them. It isn't long before I'm moaning into the queen's thighs, my own squeezed together, shaking. I'm not able to hold it long before I finally crash, the queen's skin catching my scream.

I fall back on my heels, breathing heavily, my eyes closed. "That was absolutely delicious." The Succubus Queen's voice brings me back to the moment, but just barely.

"Take your time, my dear. When you're ready, I have one more gift for you."

I nod and breathe deeply a couple of times more to say I'm ready. I don't know where it comes from, but Lillith is holding a weapon in her long, slender hands. It's a dagger. I've never seen one like it, not that I'm an expert in daggers even after all my months at PA. The blade is wavy.

"I will leave it to you to discover the dagger's secrets," Lillith says. "But know this. Seduction is just as powerful a weapon. If not more so."

With those words, she slides back, and the red light blooms once more, engulfing the queen in its glow. As she begins to sink below, she says one last thing. "People here know about your green fire, but you should still be careful with it."

I don't like the sound of that, but the Queen of Succubi is gone before I can ask another question.

"You should probably put your clothes back on," Barlowe suggests.

I don't bother answering verbally. Nodding will have to do. It takes longer than I would like, but my legs are still really shaky.

Chapter Sixty-Three
Revelations
November – Purgatory Academy

I learn quickly who got what weapon in the Veiled Visions because no one can help from showing them off. Trist is by far the worst. She is descended from the archangel who guarded the Garden of Eden with a flaming sword. That same ancestor has only gifted a handful of similar flaming swords to descendants. Trist's obsession with having one is fulfilled and she isn't letting anyone forget it. She pulls it out constantly to show off the flames. Her Ascended clique enjoy it, but the Descended mostly scowl at her. It's difficult to know which one Trist loves more.

Eli received a dagger. I haven't seen much of it. He doesn't feel the need to parade it around the way Trist does. I do glimpse him showing it to Marius a couple of times. The vampire lets him see his own dagger in return. It's adorable, but I make certain not to say anything. I don't want to ruin the magic of a different kind brewing between the two, even if neither of them has a clue.

Gabe doesn't brag about his either, but he has a sword even larger than Trist's. He keeps it sheathed but carries it with him. Drake, on the other hand, insists he did not receive a weapon. I have so many questions. Marius' face says the same.

I have it out with Lenny about my mother and he being my grandfather. He told me he wondered when I would figure it out. Once my anger has subsided some, I understand that it isn't Lenny's fault, and I promise him that I'm going to save my mother. He shakes his head silently.

I'm also left with a whole other level of hormones ever since my…encounter with Lillith. I'm definitely taking longer showers than I used to. Fighting helps though. I train with Drake every evening I don't train with Marius. That equals two times a week. The big Descended doesn't take it easy on me either.

Tonight we lay there on the mats, sweat glistening and temperatures high. Drake's weight shifts to keep me pinned without hurting me. He's never remained on top of me any longer than absolutely necessary for a pin before.

My body responds but my mind rebels. For one moment I'm thirteen years old again. It's a moment that lasts an eternity. My parents were in the middle of their show in the Big Top. I decided to wait where they keep the elephants instead of staying in the crowd. I had a book I wanted to read in peace and quiet without all the yelling and high emotions. Being around that too much always exhausted me.

"Well hello there darling." The peppy voice belonged to Uncle Victor. He wasn't really my uncle but like many of the circus workers that was what I called them, uncle and aunt.

I looked up briefly from my book to wave without words.

"What's you reading?" He tipped the cover up to read the title. He was so close already. He often hugged me and gave me sweets, but I never thought much of it. That night his breath smelled of tobacco and whiskey. I knew the odors well from many of the circus folk.

I was seated on a small wooden stage they erected to work with the elephants when they were practicing. My legs dangled and Uncle Victor placed a large, calloused hand on my knee, running it up and down my thigh. He'd never done that before and it felt strange.

I giggled. "Uncle Victor, that tickles."

"Oh, does it now?" He laughed. "I like making you feel good, sweet Lilly Flower."

I smiled at his silliness, but there was something underlying his words that made me feel uncomfortable. This was Uncle Victor though. He was family.

"I bet I could make you feel even better," he whispered in my ear. His hand pushed back a stray strand of red locks.

I tried for another giggle, but his voice changed. It was deeper and more serious. I didn't know what that meant, but fear welled in my stomach. I leaned back to look into his squinty eyes and his scraggly, gray beard.

"Come on, Lilly Flower. Let me show you in my RV."

"I can't," I said. "I have to stay here and wait for Dad and Mom."

"Oh, I already let them know you'll be with me. Don't worry. Come on."

Something told me that wasn't right, that Uncle Victor wasn't telling the truth. I tried to think of something else to say, but he stood up and took my hand dragging me down and off the stage.

"Uncle Victor, I really should stay here." I pulled at his arm, but he kept walking, my hand swallowed in his much larger one. "You're hurting me. Please stop." He didn't listen, but when I dug my feet into the dirt he stopped and turned back toward me. I'd never seen that look on his face. He was a different person. This wasn't silly, playful Uncle Victor. This man's face was twisted into something ugly, something dark and nasty.

Without warning, he back handed me. The rest, perhaps thankfully, was a blur. I know that I fought, clawed and bit, drew blood. They found me with skin under my nails later.

When he was finished, he told me no one would ever believe me so there was no point in telling my parents or anyone else. I'd stumbled away from his RV, alone with a torn dress and bruised face, my body irrevocably changed forever, my childhood and innocence wiped out by too large hands and sweetly rotten breath.

That night they searched for me everywhere. I don't remember who found me, but I clung to my parents afterwards. I sobbed, words completely failing me. When they finally did resurface, I didn't hold back. I told my parents what happened. My mother held me tighter, but my father pulled back and went deadly still. For the second time that night I saw a face on a trusted adult that I didn't recognize. My father was gone into the night without a word.

I never heard from Uncle Victor again. The police came around weeks later on behalf of blood family, but not a person would speak to them. I never asked what happened or what they did with the body, but I knew in my heart that was all that Victor was…a body.

It all rushes back up to grab me as Victor had. Against my will. Tears spill down my face as I lay there paralyzed under Drake, lost in my memories, those living nightmares. The Descended senses it and slides off immediately. Vaguely, I hear him call my name but not touching me.

The memories whirl and play on repeat like some demonic loop. I can't escape. I can't get away from Victor. He took me against my will. He stole something precious from me. A piece of me I'd never get back. And suddenly, that fear turns into anger. Rage. Fury.

My hands curl into fists and I don't need to look to feel those strange flames answer my unconscious call. Drake speaks my name again, but I'm trapped, the flames building in me. The fear is fuel to the flames. They crack and pop, surfacing all over my skin.

I shift but do nothing to stop the flames. I open my eyes and find myself rimmed in an eerie, green light of emerald fire. They're pushing outward. They want to burn. I want to burn. Burn the world down for all the horrors it inflicts on little girls. I want to bury those angelic and demonic powers in ash of my own making.

"Lilly." I don't know why but this time Drake's call finds me. I lock eyes with him. And I gasp. He stands there draped in flames of violet and lavender. Hell Fire. His Hell Fire.

Walking toward me, the flames move with him. They don't burn anything, and his eyes hold no fear from my jade fire. He stops inches from me and instead of reaching out with his hands, his purple flames do it for him, licking at my own. They play and dance with one another.

And just like that I crash. The memories burn away with the joyful mingling of our fire. I rush into his arms, arms I know now would never hurt me. He whispers that it's okay, all the while our flames making new and wondrous hues my eyes have never beheld before. A world of flames meant to heal. A dragon and son of Lucifer, a prince of kindness no one knows. But I know. And my flames do too.

Chapter Sixty-Four
Allegiances
November – Purgatory Academy

Drake and I don't discuss what happened in our training session. We continue to train though and to visit the library, all to no avail. Even Barlowe doesn't say anything, but he does seem to be spending more time with Drake's Familiar, Rowan. The two kittens are longer but not filled in yet.

Classes continue. Fights break out almost constantly between the Ascended and the Descended. The six of us do what we can, but mostly the gargoyles have to intervene. They can't change how the two groups feel about each other though.

Our next Tribulation doesn't help with the tension either. Gressil brings us to the gymnasium to those thrice-damned nine-point stars. The gym has grown smaller with the death of so many of our classmates.

There is a difference in the proceedings. Faculty escort the Descended to chosen stars this time. First time for that. After each Malak drops us off, the Ascended are brought to pair off in a star with a Descended. Gabe is paired with me. Drake and Marius are nearby and each of them is placed with a member of the Triumvirate as well. Eli stands across from Marius and Trist glowers at Drake. Obviously, the staff knows how to keep that divide between us. They talk big about wanting to stop the murders, but they keep us pitted against one another.

The situation gets worse. As soon as the Nephilim are all situated, the faculty bring in something I didn't expect to see here at PA again, zombies. Murmurs break out among the students almost immediately. The faculty, not the Malakim, bring them about to each star.

I have seen zombies here, both when Nekleth demonstrated his own ability over the two snakes on the first day of class and then the day I'll never forget, and perhaps will never stop having nightmares about, when he brought back Adam to interrogate him about who killed him.

This zombie is nothing like Adam. The corpse isn't fresh. I'm fairly certain there are pieces of flesh that flop off on its shuffle over here. It comes to a halt in the middle of the star, right between Gabe and me. The smell is overwhelming on my developing Descended senses. My eyes water from the putrid odor.

I try to keep the disgust off my face, but I'm not successful. Gabe doesn't even try. His words prove me correct. "This is grotesque."

I nod my agreement. But just then Gressil's magnified voice calls out. "For this Tribulation, we will be using Sway once more. And lest we forget what side we're fighting for you will be facing off against a student from the opposite side of the Divine War. Each of you will use Sway to force the zombie to attack the other. The winner is the one who has the zombie attack. The loser will have to defend themselves or force their own Sway on the zombie. We will begin in five minutes."

The faculty walk around, checking on the zombies. I can't tell what it is they are looking for. Our own zombie doesn't face either of us. She just stares off into space. From what I can tell, the woman was Asian in ethnicity, but much of her hair is gone and the flesh is definitely peeling off.

"How are we supposed to use Sway on a zombie?" I ask Gabe.

He shrugs. "I was wondering the same thing. Nekleth has made it perfectly clear only necromancers have that sort of power." He makes to twist his imaginary moustache as our greasy professor does with his actual one.

Despite the disgusting situation we find ourselves in, I burst out in giggles. However, I cut it off with a cough as the very same professor glides over to us. He obviously heard. "It's a very good question. And the answer is simple. I hold, shall we say, sway, over them."

Bad joke. Ugh. Nekleth continues though, "I have commanded them to obey the Sway. Simple, really. Even if they are living dead. Remember the eyes." He smirks as he floats away.

Gabe and I both realize at the same time what that means. These zombies aren't walking dead, animated corpses. They are living dead, souls called back up and held captive in their old bodies. Green eyes. Shit. I'm about to say something about it, but Gressil's voice rings out. "Begin in ten, nine, eight, seven, six…" I'm not going to do this. I refuse. I can kill the zombie anyway. I'm confident of that. Let Gabe win. No big deal. "Five, four, three, two, one."

Gabe has the same thought because the zombie doesn't move at all for a moment. Our pacifist ideas are wrecked because after only a few moments, the zombie turns toward Marius and Eli who are both trying to do the same thing. Their zombie, a rather large man in life, is turned toward me now.

Without any further indication, our zombie shuffles toward Eli. Their zombie lumbers toward me. That's how Nekleth keeps us honest. If we don't play, the zombies will attack our friends. Fuck.

Gabe throws out his arm as if that will help with his Sway. Apparently, it does because the woman zombie stops and turns toward me, growling. She moves slowly but she comes at me. The large male zombie has turned as well, now toward Marius.

I look at Gabe who wears a mixed look of horror and apology. I give him a curt nod of understanding but decide I will have to show him how good I really am at Sway.

Closing my eyes to keep my mind off the gnashing teeth and clawed fingers coming at me, I lock in on my Sway and push out toward the zombie. I find the woman's mind. It's so jarring I almost lose my grip on her. I experience how the poor woman feels…terrified. I can't read her mind exactly, but I feel what the woman feels. It's more like an empathetic connection. The woman doesn't understand why she's alive again and trapped in this body that used to be her but now is this gnawing thing that craves flesh; she can't help herself.

I swallow down the vomit attempting to come up and send soothing Sway to the female zombie. It washes over her, and she stops dead in her tracks, waiting for further instructions from her mistress. I hate this. I fucking hate it. I give Gabe my own apologetic look before instructing the zombie to attack.

Instead of attempting to combat my Sway, he tears the great golden two-handed sword from its leather sheath on his back. As the zombie stumbles toward him, he turns fluidly to give himself room and cuts her right in half. The pieces are on the floor in a flash, but being that she's a zombie, the upper half keeps crawling and growling toward him. Gabe doesn't use his sword this time. Holding out a hand, golden light shoots like a bolt from his hand and strikes her in the head. All that's left is a smoking smear. He catches my eye, but I can't read his face. I have to wonder if the day will come when he'll use that golden light on me.

Chapter Sixty-Five
Finals

December – Purgatory Academy

The following weeks are tense even by the standards of Purgatory Academy. There aren't many Nephilim who died in the last Tribulation, but that fact does nothing to mend rifts between the two sides. Trist was forced to burn her zombie to nothing while Drake looked on stoically. Marius struggled to fend off his zombie, but ultimately, he was able to shred it to bits. He wore the gore to prove it. Of the three pairings, Eli looked the most hurt by his victory.

The six of us haven't returned to the library together. I don't have the courage or the heart to ask Gabe to help again after that. No more students are murdered though and that's something.

School keeps us busier than ever anyhow. December arrives and with it, Finals. Beyond that, there is only our final Tribulation and the Winter Solstice Ball. Then graduation.

The nice part about Finals is that a couple of them are written exams like at a normal university or college. I know that students my age should be complaining about something like that, but perspective is everything. No one is trying to kill me during written exams and that's nothing less than a big relief.

Of course, that relief is only accounted for in two of our classes: Angelology and Demonology and Sinners and Saints. In Temptations and Fortitude, we have one final temptation and resistance session. For once, I'm paired with an Ascended I don't know well, only from a distance. The exam is nothing like the horror of our Sway Tribulation with Emilie, but it isn't comfortable. The two of us have to Sway one another into swallowing a chicken bone whole. I have no idea where they got the bones from in Purgatory, but when the Ascended submits to me and swallows it she doesn't choke, thankfully. Others aren't as lucky, but Emilie and the attending gargoyles don't let anyone die. It isn't a Tribulation, after all.

Strangely enough, Evocation and Magic Weaving aren't all that difficult. Ren'el and Nekleth both appear to think the same thing about Finals, that they won't show them anything the Tribulations haven't already proven. I'm fine with that logic and I'm not alone in that assessment. For Ren'el, we all call up one final imp and send it back. Nekleth asks us to show him one piece of magic and we're done. I laugh hysterically when Drake takes a coin out of his pocket and makes it disappear as if he were a stage magician. I'm not the only one though; I've never heard Nekleth laugh before. It's like a snake choking on something, but there are enough scoffs and laughter from the students about his audacity that most of the Nephilim don't hear it anyway. I still smile thinking about it.

The most brutal Final is definitely from War and Weapons. The'slin and Khal'ith subject us to a hand-to-hand combat tournament. The dual team of angel and demon wastes no time in getting us started. There are a lot of rounds to be had. Each fight is to submission or knock out. They're spread out all over the gymnasium and gargoyles help to officiate and make certain no one is killed.

From what I witness between my own bouts plenty of my classmates take advantage of these fights. Quite a few of them are enjoying the chance to beat the shit out of others. It comes as no surprise that the majority are facing someone from the other side, Ascended versus Descended.

The first few rounds are relatively quick. Hundreds are whittled down to dozens to only a few. I'm so proud of Marius. He makes it all the way to the round of sixteen. He smiles at me without stop. He feels the same. He has come a long way and I'm happy to see it.

The quarterfinals include all three of the Triumvirate as well as Drake and me. I've watched a couple of Drake's fights and they never last long. He waits for his opponents to make a mistake and then it's all ground and pound, tapping them all out with holds or choking them till they lose consciousness.

The'slin announces who I'm fighting. "Lilly will face Trist." I find Trist's face, pure glee written on it with her wide smile.

By this point the fights are in front of everyone. My entire class surrounds us in a huge circle as Trist and I step up to face one another. Khal'ith calls to begin. Trist sneers at me. "I've waited a long time for this."

The curly haired Ascended wastes no time, coming at me with a fury unlike any I've seen here. I'm barely able to fend out the fists and kicks. But she forces me to retreat toward the students in the circle, many of them cheering Trist on while others jeer at me.

I have to do something to get back on the offensive. It takes only one missed swing from Trist and I'm able to turn inwards back into the circle again. Trist breaks off in frustration. She wants to end me quick and fast, but it doesn't happen. I withstand the fury.

I'm not going to let Trist overwhelm me again. I step forward and throw some exploratory jabs. She blocks each one, a small smile on her face. I strike out but am not able to stop the counterstrike that smacks me below my left eye. Trist follows it up with a two-punch combo, left right. I stop the first, but the second hits me in the brow.

I kick out at Trist's leg to take away her balance. She traps my leg and uses my momentum to superman punch me in the face. The hit smacks me hard in the cheek and I hear a crack from it.

Throwing up my arms, I block the hits that Trist hammers me with, but I'm on the defensive again already. I'm never going to be able to beat her like this. But then I remember my training with Drake. He showed me how to win. I have to ground and pound as he does.

That means that I have to get closer to Trist, not retreat. Not keep a distance. So, that is exactly what I do. Trist throws a haymaker and instead of blocking it with my forearm, I step inside her guard. Locking my leg behind Trist's trailing one, I drive my shoulder into her stomach, wrapping my arms around the Ascended's thighs, and let momentum do the rest as we fall to the mats together, me on top.

Trist does her best to get out from underneath me bucking her hips, but I'm not having it. I rise up, locking my thighs around Trist's waist and begin pummeling her face with both fists. She tries to block the flailing swings, but I'm a hurricane and she can't catch them all.

My left eye is swelling shut from a hit I took from the Ascended, but my rage is enough that I close it and turn my head slightly to see Trist clearly with my other eye. I keep on swinging. Trist's face is smeared with blood, and I reach down and grab her head, slamming it repeatedly into the mat. She's out, but I only register red.

A great force grabs me from behind and pulls me off. It must have been The'slin because Khal'ith is checking on Trist. Slowly but surely, I come back down, my breathing returning to normal. My healing powers must have increased because my left eye is healing already.

It takes a while to wake Trist up, but Eli and Gabe carry her over to the wall to recover. Each of them wins in their quarterfinal bouts as does Drake. I stand by Marius as Khal'ith calls out that I will face Gabe first and Eli and Drake will fight in the other semifinal fight.

Marius whispers good luck to me as I trudge to the middle of the circle, meeting Gabe and The'slin there. The Ascended refuses to make eye contact with me. I certainly understand that, but we're going to be up in each other's business soon enough.

The'slin's voice rings out. "Bow." We do, Gabe still not making eye contact. "Fight," the demon calls.

Gabe, who is usually pretty quick to take an exploratory offensive, steps back. I suppress my surprise and circle him a bit, looking for an opening. He mirrors me but doesn't strike.

Little by little, I inch closer and throw a few punches. Gabe blocks or dodges them, dancing away. It isn't like him.

The crowd of classmates also gleans that he's acting differently. I attack a bit more, concern blooming that he's waiting with a trap. With that thought in mind, my attacks remain careful. I don't want to get drawn in.

However, the truth of the situation is revealed moments later. Trist's angry voice bellows, "Stop going easy on your girlfriend and fucking beat her!"

At first, I think it's an insult more for me than for Gabe, but when I see him grimace ever so slightly, I understand it's true. And that red rage takes me.

I move forward swiftly. My combos are fast and hard. Gabe backs up as he absorbs each one, but it isn't easy. The strain on his face gives me pleasure.

In the hopes of increasing my happiness at his struggles I aim a kick for his balls. He blocks it, but only barely. Stepping back out of my range, he looks at me with growing anger. It seems to say, "So it's like that, huh?"

I answer his unspoken question. "It's fucking like that."

He comes at me like a tornado, his movements so fast and furious I almost can't see them. They blur together. He lands several hits, but nothing that keeps me down. They have me backing up though.

Students are yelling and cheering. Most of them are for Gabe. Trist's voice is loudest and proudest, telling him to beat me to a pulp.

I refocus because I'm having a difficult time keeping up with him. A punch lands on my ribs. Another to my jaw. My ear rings from that one. I try to strike out at him, but there are storm clouds in his eyes.

Like a blonde superman he roars as he jumps into the air and slams a fist into my jaw. The next thing I know Drake and Marius are standing over me. Another voice speaks behind us. "Give her some room. Let her breathe."

Khal'ith appears above me. "Your jaw was dislocated, but we've put it back in place. It should be healed within a few hours. It's best not to talk for now though."

He motions to my Descended friends, and they help me up. They get me over to a spot in the circle. Marius stays with me, and I lean heavily on him.

I glimpse Gabe across the circle. Trist is patting him on the back and congratulating him, joy written all over her face. He's attempting to catch my attention though. I look away. I have nothing to say to him.

Drake is in the middle of the circle, facing Eli. The'slin is already calling for them to begin their fight. I concentrate on them, ignoring the other two members of the Triumvirate completely.

Eli is always tentative at the beginning of a fight. It's not indicative of his abilities though. He didn't make the semifinals for nothing. Still, he looks hesitant circling around Drake.

The Descended looks the same as always at the beginning of his fight. He waits and waits. I've never seen him attack first. No, he just wears out and frustrates his opponents. They always grow impatient before he does.

Eli is no different, but when his first strikes come, they're not weak. Eli is fast and strong, more so than Trist and nearly as much as Gabe if I were to guess. And it doesn't matter.

Drake's counterstrike happens so fast, it takes my brain a moment to comprehend what happened. But then my mind catches up with the sound of the hit. No, the slap. Drake open hand slapped Eli across the face. The Ascended goes stumbling away.

Once he gathers his balance, Eli turns with a burning anger in his eyes. His strikes are even faster and harder. There are gasps of awe, my classmates impressed.

And it still doesn't matter. There's another ringing slapping sound and Eli is stumbling away once more. This time he falls to his knees. Drake stands there as quiet and unassuming as ever. I have come to deeply care for him, but I don't understand why he would embarrass poor Eli like that. Just end it.

It's as if he hears my thoughts. Almost imperceptibly he shakes his head. It's enough for me to understand. He's pissing Eli off on purpose so he'll be foolish in his attacks.

Sure enough, Eli comes at him with more ferocity than I've yet seen in this class. His strikes are perfect, but Drake dodges and blocks each and every one. Instead of being backed into the circle of students, he weaves to the left and the right and remains in the middle of the mat while Eli's fury begins to fade.

Another slap rings out. Eli catches himself though and continues his attack, but Drake slaps him again. And suddenly, the Descended is on the offensive. His front kick catches Eli in the chest and sends him nearly flying across the mat to land on the floor near the edge of the circle. Gabe and Trist are nearby and call him to get up.

He does, but Drake is on him in a flash. I didn't even see him move. The Descended picks Eli up off the ground by the throat with both hands. He's going to choke him out like that. Holy shit.

But an anger in Eli's eyes begins to literally glow. It spreads to the rest of his body. It's that same strange color I saw from him before, but now it's so intense I see the effects of it. It's almost an anti-color. The colors around him are sucked into it, disappearing.

Drake holds on though. Eli grasps at his hands, but that glow centers in his chest. I realize a second later than Khal'ith does that Eli is going to shoot that anti-color right into Drake's face. The angel runs straight at the pair and knocks the Descended out of the way just as Eli's magic erupts, engulfing Khal'ith in it.

For a moment, there's no color in the room. It's black, but yet the absence of it. That is the best my brain can do to compute what I experience. However, color and sight soon return. What I find before me has me gasping.

Khal'ith was able to shove Drake out of the way, only to take the full brunt of the energy shot from Eli's chest, whatever it is. The'slin is cradling the angel's limp body, calling his name softly over and over again. Khal'ith isn't going to be answering any time soon. His body looks like it has been burned as well as sucked free of color. All that's left is this ashen shade and bits of bone sticking out at almost random spots in his body. Much of his hair and beard are gone too.

Drake stands up and stares at them. No one but Gabe and Trist even realize that Eli is still there. They rush over to their friend, who kneels on the mats, tears flowing freely down his cheeks. His arms are crossed over his chest as if he hopes he can hold that energy in and never let it out again.

Trist wraps him in a tight hug while Gabe stands over him watching, almost guarding. The look on the blonde's face agrees with this idea, set in stone as if daring anyone to try to hurt his friend.

Apparently, he isn't wrong. Khal'ith is still not responding and stunned silenced reigns in the gymnasium. The'slin lays the angel down gently which surprises me even more than the soft handling of his counterpart. A deep growl erupts from the demon, and he whirls about to face Eli.

Gabe steps deftly in front of his friend and Trist holds Eli tighter. I have been afraid to approach the demon while he holds the angel, but now that he's let go, I inch forward to see if there's anything to be done. Marius shadows me.

I'm surprised again when Drake steps in front of The'slin, not standing next to Gabe exactly but definitely in a defensive position. Gabe's eyes flicker to him momentarily but are almost immediately again glued to the demon.

"Get out of my way." The'slin's voice promises only one thing. Death.

"You can't." Drake's voice is matter of fact.

"You're going to defend him, when whatever the fuck that was, was meant for you."

Even the demon doesn't know what it is, that energy. Apparently, I'm not the only one hiding my power from others.

"I pushed him to it," Drake explains.

"You did," The'slin agrees. "But he is the one who killed Khal'ith."

Drake responds, "He isn't dead."

The demon shakes his head in disagreement, but a quiet voice calls the demon's name. "The'slin...it's alright. I'm...I'm alright." Khal'ith's voice is the equivalent of his wounds, raw and bleeding.

The'slin all but leaps back to the angel's side. Marius and I back up just to be safe. I'm completely baffled by the behavior of the demon. I would have thought he would be, if not outright happy about the angel's demise, at least indifferent.

But here he is clasping the angel's hand and pushing his blonde hair back from his face. It's so gentle, almost loving. Pieces of a puzzle, no matter how unlikely they might be, begin to put themselves together in my mind.

Khal'ith's body is healing. Already. I've seen how quickly the Nephilim heal, faster and faster as the year goes on. I'm fairly certain a direct hit from that strange light would have killed most, if not all of us, outright though. And yet, here is the angel, awake and patches of skin filling in once more, color returning to his ashen face.

It's a few minutes before he's able to stand, but by that time Gabe and Trist have hulled Eli away back into the circle, each slightly in front of him as if to hide him from the view of the demon. The'slin's face returns to normal, once more all snark and condescension.

"The final is between Gabe of the Ascended and Drake of the Descended." He motions for the two of them to take their places in the middle of the circle.

Khal'ith is in the circle but struggles to remain standing. When I offer my shoulder, one of the Ascended steps forward and scowls, offering his to the angel. The angel takes it, but ever so slightly nods his head in thanks to me before turning back to the bout about to begin.

The'slin is already calling for them to fight and I've never seen such rage on Gabe's face. He almost glows. It isn't the same glow that emanated from Eli. This is that golden glow that he shines, that light that kills with the Divine's justice. Fear wells up in my chest at the sight.

The Ascended takes one step toward Drake, but as he does, the Descended rises in the air and brings down one hammering fist into the blonde's face so hard that blood spatters every direction and Gabe lays on the floor unconscious only seconds later.

The stunned silence of minutes before is nothing compared to what rules the room now. It is what I imagine space sounds like, completely and utterly devoid of it. Drake knocked out Gabe with one powerful punch, so fast my brain is broken from the speed. It even takes

The'slin a moment to begin counting the knockout. Drake wins the tournament.

Chapter Sixty-Six
The Labyrinth
December – Purgatory Academy

Finals do nothing to help the relationships between the Triumvirate and our own trio. Only Marius and Eli are willing to talk to each other at all now. Gabe scowls at Drake when he thinks the large Descended isn't looking. Trist does the same with me. That makes me happier than it should.

I do want to say something to Gabe to bridge the gap, but I don't know where to start. Of course, Drake is as stoic as ever about it. When I finally ask him at lunch one day, he shrugs. "It's what they do here." I know he means the faculty and the school itself, but that doesn't mean I have to like it.

"Perhaps you could apologize?" I suggest.

Drake growls out a laugh. "To Gabe?"

I nod.

He laughs again. "Are you going to apologize to Trist?"

It's Marius' turn to laugh out loud. I scowl and give him the finger.

"Fair enough," I grumble to Drake.

The big Descended smirks and continues eating.

It isn't long before the final Tribulation arrives. I can't tell if I'm more relieved or scared. I don't even want to imagine what the last Tribulation will be; no doubt something absolutely horrible.

I'm not wrong. The day of the Tribulation, we are brought to the back of the school. We go around to the left where we get a good view of PA's cemetery, drifting off out of view in the mist.

Given the size of the school, it takes us a while to get around to the backside but when we do, I'm rendered speechless by the sight. It's a labyrinth. It's difficult to see because it's so tall but I'm pretty certain it's circular in shape.

The labyrinth is a dull white color, and it takes a moment to decipher that it's made of bone, just like the Ossa Forest. I gape at it.

"That is impressive," Barlowe says.

"It is indeed," I say aloud.

The one good thing about this Tribulation is that Gressil announced we would be allowed to have our Familiars with us. Barlowe was as happy as I was about it.

Gressil calls out to the collected Nephilim. "Welcome to your thirteenth and final Tribulation. I commend you all for surviving thus far. We have reached the end of your year here at Purgatory Academy. If you live through this final Tribulation, you will graduate and move on to serve in your respective houses in Heaven or Hell."

I shift nervously back and forth on my feet.

"Careful," Barlowe hisses in my head. *"Don't step on my tail."*

"Sorry."

"The objective of this Tribulation is to make it through the labyrinth to the center. Once you do, you have completed your final Tribulation. I shouldn't have to mention this as I'm sure you're all aware that there will be, shall we say, obstacles, along the way. You are to neutralize them in any way you can.

"You will line up single file and enter the labyrinth one at a time. Only your Familiar may accompany you. Come forward and we will begin."

With hundreds of students, there's a lot of shuffling as we get into line. Barlowe hisses at more than one Familiar as they jockey for position. The Nephilim are pushing and shoving so much because although we all enter the labyrinth without friends, that doesn't mean we can't wait for them and then march off together.

My friends and I aren't thinking about it any differently. Marius and Blackbeard are right in front of us. Drake and Rowan are directly behind us. We're pretty far up in the line too and the opening to the labyrinth is right there.

Gressil stands right next to it and signals every minute for the next student to enter. That means all our oh so clever plans to go in together aren't going to work. The first student crosses the boundary of the labyrinth, trying to get a look into what it holds, but as he steps in, the walls immediately rumble closed.

Marius looks back at me, face etched with fear. I give him a reassuring nod. "It'll be okay. We're going with our Familiars, and I will find you either way." He swallows and nods, fear not as deep in the lines of his face now, but definitely still present.

When there are only five students in front of Marius, Drake brushes past me, Rowan in tow. "Marius, let us go first. We'll find you."

Relief relaxes Marius' tension, his face lightening up and his shoulders dipping. He closes his eyes and nods, shifting to the side a bit so Drake and Rowan can take his place.

Gressil doesn't say a word to Drake when it's his turn. He only flicks a finger for him to head in. Without looking back, the maybe dragon marches in, white kitten trotting alongside him. Just as the wall begins to shift and obscure them from view, Drake turns back and nods to us.

The lump in my throat isn't easy to swallow, but I pull it off after a couple of tries. "Should I go in first?" I ask Marius' back.

He shakes his head. "We've got this." Blackbeard squawks his agreement.

"Take care of him," I say to the Dracula parrot.

His head bobs rapidly up and down as he responds. *"I won't let anything happen to him."*

Marius rolls his eyes. "It's so nice to have so many mothers."

I force the laughter out because it doesn't want to, but we need it. "Should I burp you before you go in? I hate the thought of you having indigestion in there."

My pale friend's laughter comes easier than my own. "Don't threaten me with a good time."

Gressil grunts to get our attention. Marius faces the labyrinth, heaving a big sigh as it opens up for him. To his credit, he walks straight in and only looks back once, giving me a thumbs up.

I step up and watch the wall slide closed in its magical way, now there where none had been before. Barlowe loops his tail around my ankle to reassure me. The vibrations of his purring up my leg are soothing.

"I'm surprised at you." Gressil spooks me with his closeness.

I stare the less than attractive dean of students in the eyes. "How so?"

"I told you I knew about your mother and yet you never bothered to interrogate me."

"The thought, among more violent options, occurred to me more than once," I reply.

His laughter is greasy. Not as greasy as Nekleth's but it would still do the job in clogging your arteries. "Perhaps you don't care for her then."

He's trying to get a rise out of me before I step into the maze. I understand he's trying to throw me off, make it more likely I'll get killed in there. But it works. I'm pissed. "You know, you really are a greasy little spot of a demon."

This time his laughter is oil on skin that never quite washes off. "What a pathetic come back."

The labyrinth wall shifts and opens again. I'm strangely relieved. As I walk in with Barlowe, I shift about to face Gressil who's watching me. I smile the way I imagine a serpent would and flip him off. He only grins in return as the wall takes him out of view.

I'm not going to spend another moment considering that piece of slimy shit. I face the labyrinth path but fall back with a squeak of surprise. Standing in front of me are Drake, Marius, and their Familiars.

The vampire rushes forward and hugs me. I'm so relieved, I hold tight to him in return. Pushing me back a bit, he smiles. "Hi."

Laughing, I can't help but agree with him. "Hi."

Looking around at Drake, I allow my eyebrows to do the asking.

The big Descended only shrugs as I expected. "I promised I would find you."

I quench a flaming desire to touch his hand, holding back my fingers. "Thank you," I say instead.

His eyes twinkle. "Let's go."

I'm filled with a profound sense of relief and hope. I'm with my friends. I can do this. I will do this.

"I am sure we would have done just fine on our own," Barlowe snarks.

"I'm sure we would have," I agree.

But now the six of us are together as we plunge into the labyrinth.

And are bored out of our minds for an amount of time I'm not able to count. We turn and twist our way through the labyrinth. Sometimes there's only one way. Other times we have to choose. There's nothing that suggests we're going the right way or the wrong way. So, we move on.

Marius suggests we fly up and over, but Drake throws a pebble in the air at the top of the walls. It bounces off the shield the faculty have there. We continue wandering.

The problem with nothing happening for so long is that you get used to it. You begin to consider the winding walking and the lack of direction or confrontation to be the norm. It numbs you to the fact that danger can still lurk around any corner. Of course, that's when four soldiers in full tactical gear almost light us up with their heavy-duty semiautomatics.

The rounds are still ripping through the air, snapping into the bone labyrinth and sending up dust when Marius yells at me. "I think those are human mercenaries!"

Drake is the one to answer. "They are!"

"What the fuck are humans doing in Purgatory?" I ask.

Marius shakes his head, but Drake responds. "When it's enough money…"

"For fuck's sake. We can't kill them," I say.

Marius has his fingers in his ears because the rounds continue to come. "That's suppression fire," Drake explains. "They're going to come around that corner any moment and when they do, it will be to kill us."

I've never killed anyone, not even a mercenary trying to kill me in a maze on another plane of existence. "They will kill us," Drake says again.

The gunfire stops and with our enhanced senses we hear them coming around the corner. I meet Drake's eyes and want to argue, but there's no point. He stands and turns the corner. There's more firing, but it only lasts for a moment before the screaming starts. Then there's dead silence, focus on the dead part.

Marius and I hug the wall as we inch our way to the corner. Barlowe doesn't bother with all that. He just saunters around the turn, brushing against the wall as if it were petting him.

"Clear," he calls. *"Well, that might not be strictly accurate, but the mercs are...neutralized."*

Oh shit. When I come around the corner, I see Barlowe's description is definitely an understatement of the situation. The mercenaries, what's left of them, are pieces. Drake, on the other hand, is completely clean. It's the look in his eyes that bothers me. It's as if he's waiting for our judgment.

Marius understands too. "Thank you, Drake. Next time I'll help. You're right. It's only killers in here."

Drake nods, gratitude clear on his features. He shifts to face me a bit more fully.

Marius is correct. It's necessary. "Marius is right. I'll- "

"Neither one of you needs to kill. I've got this. Keep your hands clean."

I don't understand the tone of his voice. He doesn't give me a chance either. He marches on, Rowan close by.

The rest of the way Drake is distant. Literally and emotionally. He speaks to no one as he walks out in front of us. Each time we run into the little quartets of mercenaries, he scouts ahead alone and before we can help, the soldiers are dead. They aren't torn apart again, but they are dead. Lots of broken bones, for certain.

I'm torn between being grateful for Drake and feeling awful about what he is taking on. I wonder what else he's carried for others in his life or even just this last year at PA.

Finally, we come to the center of the labyrinth. It's a wide opening in the form of a circle with a smaller circle in the middle. The tiny one is still bone white, but only about three feet tall and is open to walk through every six feet or so. We approach cautiously and step in. As we do, a light erupts around us and when I can see again, we're standing outside of the labyrinth next to Gressil, no other students have yet arrived.

"Congratulations," his bored voice monotones. "You're the first to get through the labyrinth to finish your final Tribulation."

I thought I would feel relief, but mostly I keep thinking about Drake and how he takes on all that bloody work so Marius and I don't have to.

Chapter Sixty-Seven
Betrayal
December – Purgatory Academy

It becomes evident in the next hours just how difficult the labyrinth is. My classmates don't have the luxury of a Drake, or even of having fought next to others besides their Familiars. Those who do survive come out haggard and wounded. Gunshot and knife wounds are the most prevalent. Rarely do any of them arrive with others, having braved it alone. I wonder for the millionth time how Drake found us. Even the Triumvirate comes out one at a time. Others arrive without their Familiars. These are the worst because it's like they lost a part of themselves, only a phantom limb left behind. That's what I gather from their wailing anyway. They can't be comforted, even by their friends. Finally, those who are going to come, do.

Time passes regardless of my pain and trauma. The Winter Solstice Ball arrives. I don't want to attend, but it's also the unofficial graduation for the surviving students. Marius jokes that the worst is behind us, but I can't shake the feeling that might not be true. We never caught the killer after all.

Carmilla helps me pick out another one of my mother's dresses. This time it's a black one that slits up my right leg and has spaghetti straps at the shoulders. It's satin smooth and hugs my body. In contrast with the Summer Solstice, we begin in the chapels. Drake and Marius await me at the gates as Barlowe and I mistport in. Dammit. I'll never beat them here.

Both of the gents are wearing tuxedos, and they look really good, especially Drake. His tuxedo is quite form fitting…and what a form it is. I remind myself repeatedly not to stare at him. It doesn't work.

We arrive at the chapel and the three of us sit in the back pew with our Familiars. Barlowe and Rowan are nearly grown now. They're both huge cats. I'm not certain, but I think they might be closer in size to a bobcat or lynx than a housecat. Barlowe tells me smugly that I'm correct. I tease him that he's still too skinny. His mental growl reverberates in my mind.

Again, in contrast to the Summer Solstice celebration, we begin with light instead of finishing with it. I wonder absently what the Ascendeds' celebration is like. Either way, it's strange to celebrate these things in a place that doesn't really experience any of the seasons. Still, the Nephilim are part-human at least and these temporal events are important there so they are important to us too.

Gressil led our Summer Solstice celebration, but I'm surprised to find The'slin is leading this time. He doesn't strike me as particularly religious.

The demonic faculty members are gathered near the altar, facing the students. Only Gressil and Nekleth aren't present. The'slin shares a few words about the Winter Solstice being the apex of darkness, but I don't pay a lot of attention. It's strange that Gressil isn't present. Why would the dean of students, the most powerful demon here, not be present for the Winter Solstice celebration, I wonder.

The'slin finishes and the faculty sits down in the front row of the pews. The chapel glows with candlelight both in the hanging candelabras above us and along the columns. There is no singing or chanting this time, only silence. As the candles fade so too does the light in the room. It's disproportionate but it's what happens, a graying of the light till finally there's a moment, and somehow, I understand what that moment is, the light fades completely. We're obscured in darkness. A blanket of black lays over us all. The Winter Solstice. The exact moment of it.

There's a uniqueness to the darkness. It feels alive. It's as if it were my kin. I smile into that darkness. I bask in it. I allow the connection to grow.

And for several moments, I experience a calm bliss I've never known before. It's ruined by the screams. They don't come from the chapel. Well, they don't come from our chapel. It's from the Ascended one. It has to be.

I'm up like a bolt of lightning. Barlowe crouches quickly, claws scraping on the floor. I hear it all in the dark.

Marius stirs next to me. "What is it?"

The screaming grows louder. "The Ascended," I whisper. "They're being attacked."

Drake shifts next to Marius. It's still pitch dark in the room. "We have to do something," I say.

I try to make my way past Marius, but my foot catches on something and I almost fall. I might have stepped on Rowan as I do because I hear clawed paws scatter away. A hand reaches out to catch me. Judging by its hold and size, it must be Drake.

The screaming grows louder. Others are murmuring in the chapel now. Pushing and shoving begin, but the darkness remains. Questions float in the dark, asking if they should go check on what's happening.

I'm not going to sit here and wait for them to debate it. We're in the last pew. I lean over and grab the back of it and count mentally to three before launching myself over it.

Someone slams into me. Others are up and around. There's yelling and shouting now. It's so intense, I almost lose the sounds of the screaming from the Ascended. I need light.

"You're going to have to wait on that," Barlowe says. *"The exact moment of the solstice may have passed, but we still have to wait for the darkness to fade naturally."*

"That won't do," I reply.

Focusing on my hand, I lift it slowly and that eerie green fire lights up, dancing among my fingers. It throws emerald shadows across the faces of those closest, Drake and Marius among them. The'slin is there too. He stares at me. He mumbles something about the "Eerd Fire."

Barlowe directs me to the wall, others shifting out of my way. They fade in and out of my halo of jade. I sense Drake and Marius following. When I finally see the doors in front of me, Drake is already there, using his considerable strength to open them.

Light floods back into the chapel. I extinguish my flaming hand. Drake stands in the hallway, facing us. It's almost as if there were a halo of light all around his body. The irony isn't lost on me. His baritone rings out. "We may be enemies, two opposites sides on a war between divine beings. But whatever or whoever is behind this is not playing by the rules agreed upon. This is a war of free agency, but that sound is one of butchery. It's one of coercion and death. They need our help. We must go now."

There is utter silence at his words, but I don't wait to step up. Marius does too. Everyone else mills about, but Drake doesn't wait for them to consider. He turns and runs for the other chapel. Rowan chases after him.

Blackbeard flies off Marius' shoulder as they both take off down the hall after Drake. Barlowe shoots after them. I run to catch up.

We're not able to match Drake. He moves so fast; we're all panting when we arrive at the doors. Drake is stopped in front of it, Rowan's tail twitching agitatedly next to him. Before us stands Cuddlebug, barring the doors.

Out of breath, I pant out the words. "Why aren't you in there? You should be helping. They're dying in there."

For the first time since I met the gargoyle, his face isn't etched in stone. It's carved in sadness. He looks like he wants to say something, explain, but he keeps his mouth shut.

Drake speaks up. "We're not allowed in there. It's their chapel. On top of that it's the solstice which makes it a double no."

"There is a way that you can help," he says to Cuddlebug.

The gargoyle looks at him, curiosity written on his face now.

"It's simple. You can get us in that room. You aren't spellbound against that. Fuck the rules."

Surprise and then a shark smile spread across the gargoyle's face. He pats his own shoulder and turns toward the stone wall next to the doors. Drake motions to us as he reaches out for Cuddlebug's shoulder. I realize what we're about to do. Marius grabs my hand. Our Familiars jump up onto our respective shoulders, the cats having to curl around like scarves. Drake's hand is calloused and for a split-second naughty thoughts pop up. I shake them away. Bad timing, Lilly, bad timing.

"Focus, pervert," Barlowe teases.

"Get a life, nosy," I respond.

Drake gestures to Cuddlebug that we're all ready to go. The wall begins to ripple. We go straight through. I still hold my breath.

It's a quick trip, but the shock of what awaits us on the other side is overwhelming. The chapel is a war zone. It's shaped exactly like our own, but there is destruction everywhere. The altar is completely smashed, lying in pieces on the floor. Pews are torn up. Stained glass shattered.

My sense of direction has never been great, but I understand where that giant hole in the wall behind the altar leads, straight out to the school's cemetery. Crawling in from it is what looks to be an endless army of the dead. They're chewing and clawing at the Ascended and faculty angels alike. It's utter havoc. Chaos everywhere.

Standing next to the gaping hole in the stone wall is our Magic Weaving professor, Nekleth, hands raised as more and more zombies pour into the school. Fucking Nekleth. Something nags at the back of my mind. Zombie Adam wasn't about to say "no." He was about to name "Nekleth." He killed all those Ascended.

That cemetery gives the necromancer an unending army. The only good thing about the situation is that there are so many zombies, the hole can't let them all in at once. It's serving as a bottleneck.

I look back to Cuddlebug. "Help us. Help them," I plead. "Gather the gargoyles. Call on the skeletons from the Ossa Forest."

Drake speaks before the gargoyle can. "He can't help. These are walking dead. No souls. Don't you see? This was how Nekleth pulled off all those murders. The gargoyles weren't notified because there was no violence between living beings, just animated corpses holding down Ascended and suffocating them so long even they couldn't survive."

The Descended turns to Cuddlebug. "What you can do is stand outside the doors and tell the demons and Descended what's happening. You can help them in."

The gargoyle nods, his face twisted in frustration, understanding he can't help more than that. He shifts back to the wall, rippling already, and walks through without looking back, as if it were too scary, afraid to see what's going to happen to us.

Drake and Marius approach me. The bigger Descended speaks. "We're going to do what we can to help till the others arrive." He says it with so much certainty, I almost believe we can stop this.

"I want you two to try to unbar the door. I am going to help the Ascended and angels, organize them."

I glance between the doors and the undead in the room. The doors are barred with a large plank of wood through the handles. The Ascended are tiny islands in the sea of zombies.

"Nekleth will have reinforced that wood with magic so be prepared to use yours on it. Tap into your Familiar for more energy if you need it."

It's a whirlwind of instructions, but Marius nods and moves swiftly forward. I waver for a moment, just long enough to watch Drake's hands grow into claws. They're longer, sharper, and darker than any I've seen here at PA.

He looks down at Rowan and something telepathic passes between the two. Mist rises around the feline Familiar. When the fog dissipates, Rowan is no longer the size of a bobcat. He's the size of a tiger. And his roar proves it as he and Drake wade into the waves of undead, shredding them with tooth and claw. I stare, slack jawed. There's a feline grace to Drake's movements as much as there is to Rowan's. He leaps from one zombie to the next, decapitating them one after the other.

"Fuck me. I need to figure out how to do that," Barlowe says.

"Sooner better than later," I agree.

More and more zombies pour into the chapel. The Ascended and angels fight fiercely. I glimpse Khal'ith tearing the undead to pieces with his bare hands. Gabe throws bolts of light in the shapes of daggers and other weapons, his golden sword shining as he cuts down zombies, one after the other. Trist wields her flaming sword, ripping through ranks of the animated corpses. I'm most surprised to see Eli using that dark power of his. I decide I'm going to call it a darkstar. It obliterates the zombies when it hits them, nothing but ash left over.

But it isn't enough. This is a game of sheer numbers. Nekleth wears a smug smile as he watches the destruction he's wrought. Why the fuck would he do this? Marius calls me and I turn to help, Barlowe in tow.

The zombies are ignoring us at least. Marius claps his hands together and reaches for the chains that keep the plank in place between the door handles. He screams as he grabs it. I pull him off as quickly as I can, but his skin peels off. Silver. It's fucking silver.

Marius screams and screams, layers of skin exposed to the air that shouldn't be. No fucking wonder Nekleth isn't bothering with us. We're never going to be able to touch these. I guide the vampire to a corner near the door, Blackbeard's eyes closed as he lends Marius energy to heal his hands quicker. Didn't learn that in class.

Eyes glazed, Marius mumbles through the pain. "You have to use that weird, funky green fire of yours. Burn the doors down."

My eyes get real big. "I don't know if that's going to work."

"No choice," he gasps through the pain. "I'll guard you. Go."

I have my doubts about this, but his hands are already pink, no longer bloody or blistered. Blackbeard looks like he might topple off Marius' shoulder though.

"Okay," I say.

"Can you help?" I ask Barlowe.

"Rowan explained something to me," he says.

"Oh yeah?"

"Oh yeah." He purrs the word, but it shifts into a growl as the mist rises. The growl grows deeper and when the mist dissipates there's a black cat the size of a leopard, minus the spots.

"Fucking hell," I say.

"Oh yeeeaahhh," Barlowe repeats.

"Blackbeard is pissed I didn't suggest he become a cat Familiar," Marius says.

We share a laugh, but the Dracula parrot wobbles sickly.

"Let's do this," Marius says as he stands up next to Barlowe to protect me.

I take in the chaos again. Drake understands what needs to happen. He's wading through the undead making them dead once more till he reaches others and then they move together towards another. He's already connected with the Triumvirate.

Turning back to the door, I focus on that emerald fire running in my veins. My hand lights up, flames dancing along each digit. I lay it on the door. The magic inlaid on the oak fights against my flames. Pressing hard, I focus on turning up the heat. The flow of flames increases in my body and the pressure ratchets up to burn brighter and hotter against the wood. Gritting my teeth, I light up my other hand and press it hard against the door, next to the other. I recognize Nekleth's scream, probably realizing what's about to happen. I hazard a glance back to see him staring at me, zombies suddenly stopping and turning toward us. Fuck. I yell my fury, refusing to be beaten. And the flames catch on the wood. Once they do, they spread quickly.

The zombies have just about reached Marius when I turn and yell, "Duck!" The vampire listens. The bouts of emerald flames shoot over his head, engulfing the zombies that come at us. The fire is so hot it burns them to wax almost immediately. It's messier and smellier than Eli's darkstar power, but just as effective.

Nekleth sends another wave at us. I step up next to Marius and we prepare to do what we have to, but there's a creaking and groaning of wood as a pew is hurtled at the zombies, throwing them away in large piles of bones and peeling flesh.

Drake tears another pew out of the back and runs straight at the next wave of zombies, toppling them over with a roar. Apparently, he lit the end to my Eerd Fire because it dances along the edges and then among the zombies as they scream their dying cries for a second time.

Another roar rips through the room, but this time from behind us. The oaken doors shake a couple of times. I grab Marius just in time to dive out of the way as they blow apart. Standing there is Gressil, The'slin, and the rest of the demonic faculty and the other Descended. They enter the fray with cries that promise violence and death, even for the undead.

Drake rushes over to us and we join the Triumvirate as we continue his earlier work of gathering everyone together into one cohesive fighting unit. Even with the additions of the Descended and the demons, more zombies flood into the desecrated chapel. It's brutal work and Nekleth doesn't appear to be exhausted, not even close. The number of dead on the campus grounds far outnumbers the living.

Nekleth directs more zombies at the faculty members, seeking to wear them down, to drain their magic. No one is even close to him. He might have been angered that the Descended and the demons joined the fight, but he is far from finished.

Someone has to stop the necromancer. He's the head of the snake and he has to be chopped off. I turn to Drake to suggest we do it, but he's already nodding. I might have known.

The Nephilim, demons, and angels might be more powerful, but there are so many of the undead. I knew Nekleth was powerful, but I didn't realize he was this powerful. That he is able to control so many for so long is incredible. Scary, really.

"We make for him," Drake confirms. "Three of us stay and gather with the others. Three of us head for Nekleth."

I don't bother arguing with his logic. "I'm the best with Sway. Maybe I can stop him." Drake nods.

Gabe steps up next to me. Drake doesn't argue with him.

Trist scowls, but she turns back to Eli. Marius steps over next to him as well. None of us bother with lengthy goodbyes, but wade back into the hordes of undead flesh.

I look at the Golden Boy and the Dark One. "I guess I'll ask the obvious question. How are we getting to him with all these zombies in the way?" I have to claw a couple of them in the face as I say it.

Drake smiles, "Natural abilities."

A look of confusion sprouts on my face, but it's replaced quickly by one of utter bewilderment as he crouches down low and springs high into the air, so far and fast, that he lands right next to Nekleth. Holy fuck.

The necromancer has the same feelings about the situation because he backs up almost immediately, real fear showing on his face for the first time. Sweeping his hands out in front of him, he snarls and every zombie nearby turns to attack Drake.

Gabe doesn't let the Descended fight alone. He leaps into the air the same as Drake did, landing next to him, both of them shredding through zombie flesh. His divine light is bright in the gloom and smoke, his blazing sword a scythe reaping undead harvests.

Shaking my head at the two of them and muttering to myself about showoffs, I crouch as well. I've never tried this before, but as I tense, the muscles in my thighs and calves ripple with power and I shoot into the air. Unused to basically flying small lengths, my arms windmill and I land on top of a zombie facing Gabe. There's a crunch of bones under my shoes. The formal dress is in shreds, and I've never been so grateful I wore flats instead of heels.

The blonde smiles. "Nice landing."

I return the smile and take out my dagger, the three of us wading into the gnashing teeth and clawing fingers. I catch a glimpse of Nekleth as we come closer, but he doesn't look concerned anymore and a pit of worry grows in my stomach.

This may be my only chance. I might be able to do it from here. I push my way between the two warriors, light and dark, shredding through their enemies. "Give me a moment, boys. I'm going to try something."

Gabe nods. Drake keeps destroying zombies. I meet Nekleth's gaze, that nasty sneer on his face. I lunge with my Sway, speaking low and soothing. There's chaos everywhere, but I'm certain the necromancer hears me.

"You don't want to do this. You don't want to do this," I repeat, pouring all my considerable Sway into my voice and gaze.

Nekleth laughs. Hmmm. Anticlimactic.

Fury rips through me. "We're going to have to do it the old-fashioned way," Gabe calls, panting as he continues to cut down zombies Nekleth sends at us.

The Ascended moves quicker than my eyes can register. Drake understands and shouts to Gabe. It's too late. Gabe throws a blinding wall of light that smashes the necromancer against the crumbling back wall of the chapel, next to the gaping hole where the zombies are entering.

The Ascended presses the professor against the wall with his light, burn marks beginning to show on Nekleth's clothing and then his exposed skin. He grits out a grin the entire time though which only serves to puzzle me.

A moment later I realize why Drake called out and why Nekleth is smiling. Cuddlebug emerges from the wall right next to Nekleth and moves toward Gabe. I rush toward the archim. Gabe's eyes grow wide with surprise as he sees the gargoyle coming for him. He continues to burn the necromancer, nonetheless. Cuddlebug marches right up to him and slams his face with a thundering upper cut that sends Gabe flying across the chapel, landing among the pews.

"Barlowe! You and Rowan have to help Gabe!" They move with feline swiftness among the individual fights to stand guard over him while he finds his wits. Soon, Gabe's Golden Retriever Familiar is there as well. I turn back to Drake and Cuddlebug with a sigh of relief.

With the gargoyle present, the zombies momentarily back off. They must have directions not to attack Cuddlebug or his kind. Nekleth has fallen to the floor now that Gabe's light has gone out, but he's getting back up to his robed feet.

"The rules still apply," Drake states. "No violence is allowed among the living here at Purgatory Academy."

"Shit. You have to be fucking kidding me. We won't last like this. We have to stop him. What the fuck are we supposed to do?" Frustration boils in my body.

"Do you remember you wondered how I got Cuddlebug's help?" Drake asks.

"Yes..."

Drake just smirks and then bursts into a sprint straight for Nekleth. The demon laughs as Drake approaches, dodging the zombie horde left and right. Cuddlebug stands next to me, the zombies parting around us like a river around a large stone. He doesn't speak.

When the Descended gets to the necromancer, Nekleth isn't laughing anymore but backs up against the wall, keenly aware the gargoyle isn't moving yet. I watch his eyes glance toward the hole in the wall, but he realizes he would never get there before Drake has him.

"You know the rules. You can't attack me without being attacked by the gargoyle," Nekleth sneers.

Drake cocks his head and smiles. "You wouldn't be scared right now if you thought that was going to stop me."

I stand mesmerized as the Descended stalks forward, Cuddlebug as still as stone at my side. But as Drake gets closer to the necromancer, the gargoyle shifts forward, his clawed feet grinding on the floor. I'm moving forward with him as if we were tethered together.

Drake turns back to look at us. Nekleth stands with a look of fear on his face. Before any of us can react, Drake rushes back toward us and smacks Cuddlebug in the chest, throwing him nearly as far as the gargoyle punched Gabe. I gape. Nekleth's eyes are wide.

My friend races for the necromancer as Cuddlebug struggles to pick himself up among all the zombies he just smashed to gory bits. I shake off my shock. Focusing my emerald fire ignited on my hands and moving in a slow circle I torch any zombies who get too close. Soon enough, Nekleth, Drake, and I are the last moving things within a ring of jade flames.

Cuddlebug is back up, wading through the zombies. Drake is staring at me. A small smile slips onto his face, unlike any I've seen. Raising a hand the way I did with my green fire, his lights up. I've seen those flames before, but I struggle to comprehend that he holds Hell Fire, that vivid violet. Lavender and deeper royal purple fingers of flames dance on his palm.

Turning back to Nekleth, who is too scared to move, Drake speaks. "Give me a hug, buddy." The absurdity of his words freezes both the necromancer and me.

His entire body goes up in the flames. They don't burn him; but as he embraces the necromancer, the demon opens his mouth to scream. The sound of his pain is smothered by the flames engulfing him.

Within moments, the zombies fall to the ground all around us, corpses again. When Drake backs away, all that's left of our former professor is a blackened smear on the wall. He's gone and the battle for Purgatory Academy is over and won, by both sides of the divide.

Chapter Sixty-Eight
Aftermath
December – Purgatory Academy

The last few days of our year at Purgatory Academy pass in a blur. The gargoyles do the majority of the cleaning. The graduation ceremony is held in the cafeteria, delicious food provided for all. Gressil stands by one wall, everyone facing him. The faculty are gathered around him, all of them having survived the battle, except for Nekleth of course.

Gressil welcomes us. "This marks the end of your year at Purgatory Academy, one that will live on in a unique manner never before seen and hopefully never again replicated."

It's the first time I have ever agreed with something Gressil had to say.

"Each of you has demonstrated prowess in several ways and are now prepared to receive your first assignments as you move out into the world. However, I must warn you of another unique phenomenon that has occurred this year, like never before."

The cafeteria is already quiet, but that quiet stands as if on the edge of a knife now.

Gressil continues. "The number of entering and graduating Nephilim varies somewhat from year to year. This year's number is lower than it has been in decades. It is not this that grants each of you a unique place in the history of the school. No, it is the number itself."

Drake and Marius are seated next to me at our table and I'm almost certain Gressil glances over at Drake before continuing on. "This year's class has six hundred and sixty-six graduates."

It takes a moment for the number to settle in. More than a few students stare at Drake, but not all of them. It isn't Drake who is the 666. It's our entire class.

"Rumor will flow forward. But be warned. Many will not care for these tidings and may consider it an omen. Some may even be willing to act."

There is a heaviness to the air as we all take in what Gressil is saying. There is a target on our collective backs. I try to think of it as being stupid. It's a coincidence. But I know deep down that isn't true. Things are shifting, like sand below our feet.

"So, Class of 666, you will form two lines by Ascended and Descended. Each of you will be given your first assignment."

The mumbling and whispering among the students grow louder as we line up and receive our appointments. It isn't long before I stand in front of Gressil.

With a grim smile, the dean of students leans forward and shakes my hand. His own is firm and cold. "Lilly Foxflame, I am happy to inform you that you have been accepted into the Order of the Black Rose."

I blink hard at him several times before finding words. "I'm sorry. What?"

Gressil's grim smile grows. "You will be contacted soon enough. Congratulations."

I'm being dismissed and I stumble away to sit back down and wait for Marius and Drake to receive their assignments. Neither of them appears to be shocked the way I am when they return.

When they don't say anything right away, I ask. "Well?"

Marius' face sours a bit. "I'm returning home, to take orders from my father as needed for now."

Concern wells up for my friend. "Is that normal?"

He grimaces, "A good number of us will do that. It's actually rare to receive an assignment outside of your family."

My concern for myself grows. "What about you, Drake?"

His stoic face is back in place. "The same as Marius."

I wonder again what his family is like. As much as I care for him, there is still so much I don't know about Drake. And that Hell Fire. I want to know about that. Perhaps he has answers for me and will share soon.

"What about you?" Marius interrupts my thoughts.

I hesitate. "Gressil said I would be inducted into the Order of the Black Rose."

Marius gapes.

"What is it?" I ask, worry building.

Marius answers, "Most of the Divine War is influence. However, there are a few orders among the Descended, all of them specializing and all of them prestigious and highly dangerous. The Order of the Black Rose…they're…"

"Don't hold me in suspense, vampire. What are they?" I try to tease, but even I can hear the strain in my voice.

"They're sacred assassins," Drake finishes.

I let that sink in. "I don't want to be an assassin."

"You don't get a vote," Drake says.

"There's more to it," Marius says. His face is filled with pain.

"What?" My trepidation builds. Being a hitwoman isn't bad enough? There's more?

"Most of the orders are assassins. It's their specialization that sets them apart."

"They're black widows," Drake explains. "Typically, they use sex to get close to their prey before killing them."

No one says anything else, not even some smart alec comment from Barlowe. I feel sick to my stomach.

Our goodbyes after that are brief and somewhat awkward. Marius tries a couple of times to comfort me, but what is there to be said. Drake doesn't even bother, but he does remind me that we have all agreed to meet back up again in a week. Part of me really looks forward to that, but my emotions are all jumbled now knowing I'm about to start killing others after seducing them.

Finally, the moment arrives for us to walk out and mistport home. After a year of everything we've endured it all sort of feels like a letdown, anticlimactic. Marius and I hug, long and hard, my friend showing me how much he cares. I attempt to do the same. Drake and Marius only nod to each other and the pale vampire trails off with his Familiar to mistport home, to his own new misery awaiting him there.

Drake looks like he might hug me as well, but he hesitates. Instead, he says, "Take the time you need to process this. We'll talk more in a week. I promise when we do, I'll do my best to share a bit more about myself."

My heart lightens a bit at that. We agree and go our separate ways to mistport home. Barlowe and I lounge on my bed for a while, cuddling. His purring nearly puts me to sleep, but I decide to take a shower first.

I get up off the bed. Walking toward the bathroom, I'm surprised to hear one of those deep unearthly sounds coming from Barlowe behind me, the one cats make when they're really unhappy. Exasperated at his drama and my nerves on end from the sound, I turn to chastise him. I'm met with a tremendous backhand and then darkness.

Chapter Sixty-Nine
Hell

March – Post Purgatory Academy

"You snuck up on me, you son of a bitch."

Balor growls a laugh. *"Not bad for a demon my size, no?"*

Before I realize what he's about to do, Balor rips his appendages off my brain and out my mouth; spit, snot, and cerebral fluid go flying. I gasp with a strange mix of pain and relief. I'm almost certain my jaw's dislocated, the back of my throat rubbed raw; I taste blood and bile.

My head falls forward; I'm too exhausted to hold it up. It's only a moment before Balor grasps my face in his paw, pinching my mouth open again. My head snaps back painfully as he pours something freezing cold down my throat.

I don't have a chance to spit it out, whatever it is. The cold coats my throat, my stomach lining. It burns like ice.

And then a new sensation sets in. It's like a needle of adrenaline punched into every muscle in my body. Balor releases me when I tense and scream out in shock. I'm wide fucking awake now. The pain isn't gone, but every molecule in my body is alive, each one vibrating so fast, my entire being shakes with it.

    "Hell Water," Balor purrs. *"Like Hell Fire, it's a catalyst. It won't heal anything, but it will keep you focused. And I need you focused. We have so much work to do still."*

Acknowledgments

All my gratitude goes to you, dear readers. You literally help bring my dreams true. To my "teacup," thank you for putting up with all my obsessive questions about your favorite books but more importantly the "why" behind each one.

More from Storm Dragon Publishing

If you'd like to find more to read from Draco or his publishing company, Storm Dragon Publishing, please visit our website.